In Pieces

by Alexa Land

The Firsts and Forever Series

Book Three

This book contains sexually explicit material and is only intended for adult readers.

This book is dedicated to Rianna

Reader

Listener

Giver of awesome advice

and best of all,

Friend

Contents

I live my life in pieces.

There are all these different parts of me, parts I can't bring together. There's the hooker, the student, the artist, the best friend. The lost boy.

Will the real Christopher Robin Andrews please stand up?

Nah, then again, don't.

This is my life right now. It doesn't matter which of these is the real me.

I'm a collection of fragments, bits of something broken, loosely scooped together in an open hand. And that's the best I can hope for right now. The only way I can be. Yes, I exist in pieces, but I'm holding them together.

I'm holding me together.

And I'm getting through today.

Chapter One

"It's so damn beautiful, I could cry."

"Do you really like it?"

"I love it," Mrs. Dombruso exclaimed, "and I'm leaving it like this, even after the wedding. Some day when you're a famous artist Christopher Robin, they're gonna make this place into a museum. People will pay money to see this mural!"

Doubtful. I took a hard look at the trompe l'oeil snowy forest that I'd just finished painting. The mural filled the back wall of the grand ballroom in Mrs. Dombruso's Queen Anne Victorian. She'd been busy pulling together a New Year's Eve wedding for her grandson Dante and my best friend Charlie, who'd gotten engaged at Thanksgiving. I'd been trying to help out where I could, and had been skeptical that we could pull it off in such a short time frame. But then, I'd completely underestimated the force of nature that was Stana Dombruso.

After deciding on a winter wonderland theme for the wedding, she'd had the room repainted in crisp white with blue accents before asking me to add the mural. She'd also found dozens of big, beautiful crystal snowflakes somewhere, which had been hung by a carpenter from the high ceiling. The room looked so pretty and romantic, and I was worried that my stark birch forest was hitting the wrong note.

"You sure it's not too desolate?" I asked her, scratching my cheek. I had two weeks off, from both art school and my job, and had impulsively decided to see if I could grow a beard. The answer, apparently, was no. A week into this little experiment, my mighty facial hair was about an eighth of an inch long. And it was getting shaved off before the wedding since I was the best man, so my super manly beard didn't stand a chance.

"If it was desolate, I'd tell you." That I believed. She really was the type of person to tell you exactly what was on her mind. Still though....

"Maybe if I lightened the sky, made it more of a pale blue...."

She sighed dramatically. "You're such a perfectionist! Stop fretting."

"I'm not fretting, I just want it to be right."

"Christopher, it's magical. Everyone's gonna love what you've done here, you'll see."

"Okay. I'm still going to lighten up that sky, though."

Mrs. Dombruso looked around her wistfully and changed the subject by saying, "You know, all this wedding planning has made me think that maybe I wanna tie the knot again."

"Aren't you already married?"

"Technically yes, but there are always loopholes."

"Loopholes?"

"Sure. The Catholic Church says I can't get divorced, but then, look at Henry the Eighth. He separated the Church of England from the Catholic Church just so he could divorce his wife. Which just goes to show there's always a way around these things."

I had to grin at that. "Do you have a suitor in mind?"

"Not yet. But you know, they got that internet dating now. They didn't have that when I was single. Back then, you were lucky if you had three, four guys to choose from," she said. Mrs. Dombruso had to be about eighty, but that fact rarely seemed to occur to her. "Now, it's like an all you can eat buffet. And maybe there's a tasty little appetizer waiting for me somewhere out there."

"What about Mr. Dombruso?"

"My husband has been shacked up with a slutty waitress in Florida for the past three years. And if he thinks he's the only one that can reel in a young floozy, well, maybe I'll just show him."

There was no point in trying to reason with her. When Mrs. Dombruso decided something, all you could do was brace yourself and hope for the best.

"Look at the time!" she exclaimed suddenly. "Go and change, Christopher! Charlie's gonna be picking you up for that party any minute."

"Maybe I shouldn't go. There's too much to do to get ready for the wedding, and we only have a week left."

"Nonsense! It's Christmas Eve, go have fun!" She grinned at me and added, "Maybe you'll meet a nice boy."

Not likely. "I don't want you spending Christmas Eve by yourself," I told her.

"Oh, don't you worry about me. My grandson Mikey and his children are coming over soon. The kids apparently put together a Christmas skit that they wanna perform for me. God help me," she said, rolling her eyes. The doorbell chimed downstairs, and she said, "That's probably Charlie. Hurry up and change, I'll stall him!" We'd been trying to keep the revamped ballroom a surprise before the wedding.

I went into the bathroom and traded out my painting clothes for my nicest pair of jeans. Then I put on a dark blue V-neck sweater over a white t-shirt and button-down shirt – I'd learned to layer my clothes to hide the fact that I was so skinny. After making an attempt at finger-combing my mop of curly blond hair, I glanced at my reflection. I looked pale and tired, shadows underscoring my blue eyes. None of that was new. I didn't linger in front of the mirror.

When I got downstairs, Mrs. Dombruso was handing my best friend a bunch of framed photos from the mantel. "Or maybe this one. What do you think, Charlie?"

"I don't know. Do you maybe have a photo that's more, um…current?" Charlie asked. He shot me a look of alarm as she turned her back to him and picked up a couple more photos. "Nana wants me to help pick out a picture for her internet dating profile," Charlie told me. She had, at some point, insisted that both Charlie and I call her that, to make us feel like part of her family.

She straightened her beaded baseball cap and tugged down the sleeves of her green velour track suit as she contemplated Charlie's question. "Maybe I do need a more current photo. These ones from the sixties are out of date. I have a nice one of me from the eighties, though. I just have to find it."

"Well, we'd better get going, Nana," I said, hoping to derail her momentum.

"Yeah, you're right. We can talk about this more tomorrow at Christmas dinner." As she walked us to the door, she again abruptly changed the subject by saying, "Christopher Robin, while you're out tonight, try to convince Charlie he should wear white to the wedding. That way, he'll match the color scheme."

"I'd feel like a dork in white. That's just so…*virginal*." He blushed as he said that.

"He doesn't have to wear white," I said. "It's his wedding, he can wear whatever he wants."

"We're planning to wear tuxedos," Charlie said.

"That's fine, they make some nice light blue ones that'll go with the decor."

"*Black* tuxedos, Nana."

"You and Dante can't wear black," she insisted. "It's gonna throw off my color scheme something fierce."

"Good luck getting Dante in any other color," Charlie said.

"Where is he, anyway?" I asked.

Charlie grinned at that. "He's doing some very last-minute Christmas shopping – way to procrastinate. He'll meet us at the party. See you tomorrow, Nana," he said, then kissed both her cheeks.

Out on the sidewalk, we ran into Dante's younger brother Mikey and his kids. Though just twenty-seven, he was a widower with three little boys. All of them were pulling on costumes, including Mikey. "Hi guys," he said cheerfully.

"Hey, Mike," Charlie said with a smile (he was nice enough to resist calling his future brother-in-law Mikey, like the rest of the family did). "I don't remember a giant box of corn flakes in the nativity."

Mikey was pulling on a big, rectangular cardboard cutout over his expensive suit. "I'm the manger. I don't know why I agreed to this."

"We're the three wisemens!" Mikey Junior exclaimed. He was a little seven-year-old clone of his dark-haired father, and was dressed in a red bathrobe with big, fake jewels glued to it and a giant red turban. "And this is Jesus!" He was holding a beat-up baby doll by the ankle, and hoisted it up in the air for us. I bit back a laugh.

"They did a skit at church and insisted on recreating it for Nana," Mikey Senior explained.

"Wish I could stay and see this," Charlie said with a grin, "but we're meeting your brother across town. Have fun, see you tomorrow!"

Charlie's ancient Toyota truck was parked half a block away, and as we walked down the sidewalk he scooped up my hand and gave it a friendly squeeze. My best friend was very touchy-feely. I loved that about him. "Hi Christopher. You and I match today." He too was dressed in jeans and a navy V-neck sweater, but there ended the similarities. Charlie was about six-two, a muscular former football player with dark brown hair and sparkling green eyes. He always looked like an ad for America, clean living, and apple pie.

"We do."

"So, should we be worried about Mrs. Dombruso and this whole internet dating thing?" he asked.

"Nah, she doesn't even own a computer. She'll probably forget all about it by this time tomorrow," I said. "And speaking of which, are you all set for Christmas?"

"I don't know. I'm worried that I didn't get Dante enough."

"What are you talking about? You got him plenty." He'd had the great idea to sign his fiancé and himself up for a bunch of classes they could take together, everything from gourmet cooking to conversational French to photography.

"There's nothing tangible though, nothing to unwrap."

"So, stick a bow on your head and be waiting under the Christmas tree for him tomorrow morning."

A big smile spread across his handsome face. "I know you were joking, but I'm actually going to do that. I don't think the bow will be on my head, though." He winked at me.

"Are you two spending tonight in the loft?" Even though it was still under construction, Charlie and his fiancé had been spending quite a few nights in their soon-to-be home. That was because they couldn't keep their hands off each other, and with me as their roommate they had very little privacy in our apartment.

"Yeah. Sorry, I know that means leaving you alone on Christmas morning."

We'd gotten to his truck, and he held the passenger door open for me as I said, "It's not your job to babysit me, Charlie. And you and I can do our gift exchange after dinner, so it's no big deal." I kind of wished I hadn't agreed to Christmas dinner with the Dombruso clan. That had been Charlie's idea. He was forever trying to include me in events like that, because he knew if he didn't, I'd be spending the holidays alone. It was sweet and he meant well, but I felt like such an outsider at these family gatherings.

Right now, we were on our way to another event that I really shouldn't be a part of. Charlie worked for his ex-boyfriend Jamie at an Irish pub called Nolan's, in San Francisco's Richmond district. And tonight, Jamie and his husband Dmitri were hosting a private Christmas party at the pub for friends, family and employees. Since I was none of the above I had no business attending this shindig, but Charlie insisted I come along as his guest.

The party was in full swing when we arrived, and the place was absolutely packed. Since Charlie and Jamie had dated for eight years, Jamie's half of this huge crowd all knew my best friend. Within a minute of arriving, Charlie was besieged by a flock of Jamie's sisters and female cousins, offering congratulations on his engagement and asking to hear all about the wedding.

We were soon joined by Jamie and Dmitri as well. These two were an interesting pair. They were almost total opposites in appearance and background, yet were clearly each other's soulmates. Dmitri was a gorgeous and sophisticated Russian-American former gangster with jet black hair and blue eyes, dressed in an impeccable black button-down shirt and dress pants. And Jamie was a laid-back former cop and lifelong surfer, who was growing out his sandy blond hair and had absolutely bizarre fashion sense. He was currently dressed in camo cargo shorts and a vintage Hawaiian shirt with a repeating pattern of Santas on surfboards.

When he turned to face us, I saw that Jamie had a brown and black terrier strapped to the front of his chest in one of those baby carrier things, the dog's little paws sticking straight out in front of him. Charlie burst out laughing when he saw Jamie, and gave him a hug around the little animal. "Dude, why are you wearing Tippy?"

"Maureen's on her honeymoon, so Dmitri and I are babysitting," Jamie explained. "The dog's completely freaked out because my sister's gone. He wants to be carried constantly, and every time I try to put him down, he starts peeing on everything. So I figured this way, at least I'd have my hands free."

"The baby carrier is completely crazy. You know that, right?" Charlie was still grinning.

"It's good practice," Jamie said cryptically, with a big smile.

"Hi Christopher," Dmitri said, extending his hand. "Merry Christmas."

I shook hands as I said, "Same to you," and started to apologize for crashing their party. But before I could get that out, a tall blonde who looked like a Barbie snuck up behind him and covered Dmitri's eyes.

"Guess who!" she exclaimed.

"Oh my God, Cat!" Dmitri said, whirling on her and grabbing her in a hug, sweeping her off her feet. "What are you doing here?"

"Celebrating Christmas with you, of course."

"When'd you arrive?"

"My plane landed an hour ago, I came straight from the airport. Hi Jamie." She leaned over and kissed his cheek as he said hello, and then she gave Charlie a smile and a flirty wink.

"You flew in that outfit?" Dmitri asked. She was wearing a tight, silver mini dress and five-inch heels. The dress was covered in sequins and would have made anyone else look like a disco ball, but on her it was hot.

"Like I'd want to get molested by every TSA agent at the airport! I changed in the cab on the way over here."

"I thought you were spending Christmas with Joe's family."

"Joe Rudin and I are kaput. I'm having the marriage annulled," she said, brushing her long hair back from her face. "I don't know what I was thinking, marrying that man. Why didn't you talk me out of it?"

Dmitri rolled his eyes at that. "Like you ever listen to me."

Cat noticed me awkwardly trying to slip away and grabbed my hand. "Hi, sorry to interrupt. I'm Catherine, Dmitri's cousin." She blinded me with a dazzling smile.

"Christopher."

"You single, Christopher?" she asked.

"Very."

"You gay?"

"Again, very."

Her smile increased a few hundred watts, and she linked arms with me. "Let's team up. I'm on the prowl tonight and need a wing man. You take the gay ones, I'll

take the straight ones, and we'll flip for the bi boys. The
men at this party won't know what hit 'em." That I could
believe. The woman was sex on stilettos.

I knew the moment Dante Dombruso entered the party,
just from my friend's expression. Charlie's face lit up
beautifully, his jade green eyes sparkling, a smile on his
full lips. It didn't matter that there were a couple hundred
people in this room. Every single one of them disappeared
as far as my friend was concerned, except for one person.
"Excuse me," Charlie murmured, and pushed into the
crowd. He and Dante reached each other in the center of the
dance floor, and Dante gathered him in his arms and kissed
him, passionately, deeply. The kiss was so hot that
everyone in a fifty yard radius should have been fanning
themselves.

"Which of them do you have a crush on?" Catherine
whispered, her arm still linked with mine.

Apparently I'd been staring, and looked away quickly.
"Neither." That was kind of a lie. I did have a bit of a crush
on Charlie, I'd had it from the moment I met him. But that
was so completely pointless, and I was working on getting
over it. "I guess I just envy that thing between them," I
said. "I can't even imagine someone looking at me with
such blind adoration."

"You don't need blind adoration. You need to get laid," she informed me.

"Why do you say that?"

"Because it's what we *all* need. Come on, let's go check out the boys at the bar." To her cousin she said, "I'm in town for two weeks, D, and I'm staying with your sister Ani, only she doesn't know it yet. And while I'm dying to catch up with you, right now I need to find a big, buff boy toy to make me forget all about Joe Rudin. Merry Christmas, cuz!" She kissed his cheek and towed me toward the bar.

"So how do you know my cousin?" Catherine asked as she plunked herself down on a barstool and crossed her mile-long legs.

"I don't really. I'm friends with his husband's ex."

"His name's Charlie, right? I've heard about him."

"You actually just winked at him back there."

"That big, sexy brunette? Damn. I was hoping he played for my team."

That was as far as we got in our conversation before a tall, buff frat boy type swooped in and asked Catherine to dance. She winked at me and led him to the dance floor as I slid onto her barstool.

That had been incredibly short-lived, but at least she'd rescued me from having to make awkward small talk with

Jamie. Not that there was anything wrong with Charlie's ex-boyfriend, he was a perfectly nice guy. But I was always a bit uncomfortable around him. Maybe it was simple jealousy of the long, complex history he shared with my best friend. Or maybe it was the fact that he used to be a police officer. I wasn't fond of people in law enforcement, and even though Jamie was nothing like a typical cop, I still found myself tensing up around him.

I turned around and asked for a bottle of water when the bartender came by, then studied the other men at the bar from beneath my lashes. Unlike Catherine, I really wasn't looking to get laid tonight. My only goal was to make a break for it as soon as I could do so without hurting Charlie's feelings. He meant well by bringing me along to this party, but this was his world, not mine. I really didn't belong here.

An incredibly beautiful blond at the far side of the bar caught my attention. He looked familiar, and I soon realized why. He noticed me looking at him and gave me a friendly smile, then came around to my side of the bar and squeezed in beside me. "Hi," he said. "How's it going?"

"Good. You?"

"Doing well, thanks." He wasn't hitting on me, he was just being friendly. I knew the difference. "I'm Hunter."

"I know," I said with a little smile. Hunter Storm was the most famous gay porn star in San Francisco, and one of the most famous in the U.S. For any gay man to pretend not to recognize him would be like trying to say you never watched porn. Yeah right. "I'm Christopher."

"Nice to meet you, Christopher. Do you work here at the bar?"

"No, my friend Charlie does. I just kind of got dragged along tonight."

"Do you know a guy named Cole that works here?"

Suddenly I realized what this guy was doing here. Cole and Charlie worked together, and I'd once heard Cole tell the story of his now famous ex-boyfriend. "I do, but I haven't seen him tonight." Hunter looked disappointed. "Were you hoping to run into him?"

"Yeah. I figured he'd be here."

"Not that it's any of my business, but didn't you two have some sort of falling out?"

Hunter grinned at me and tucked a strand of shoulder-length blond hair behind his ear. "You could say that. He's talked about it?"

"Just once. He said you two broke up."

He lowered his gaze and said, "You're being nice. He probably said I tore his heart out."

That was exactly right, actually. "Why are you looking for him?"

Hunter shrugged beneath his expensive black leather jacket. "I know he hates me. But, well, it's Christmas and all. I don't want us to get back together, we were terrible as a couple, but I just…I miss him, I miss his friendship. So I thought I'd come by and try burying the hatchet. See if maybe the whole peace on Earth, good will toward men thing even extends to ex-boyfriends."

"If you want to, you can hang out with me until he shows up," I said.

"I'd like that." A little table opened up nearby, and we moved over to it. Hunter shot me a flawless smile and said, "So, you obviously know what I do for a living, since you knew my name. What do you do, Christopher?"

"I'm a full-time art student at Sutherlin," I said. That was only part of the story – the part I actually told people.

"Oh wow, that's cool. I really admire people in the arts. What's your area of interest?"

"I'm a painter. Or, you know, I will be when I finish school."

"That's awesome. You ever show your work?"

"I actually have some pieces in a show in late January, at the Tremont Gallery." It still blew me away that I was going to be included in an upcoming new artists show at the most prestigious gallery in the city. That was due to Charlie's fiancé. Dante was an acquaintance of Ian Tremont, the gallery owner, and had arranged for Ian and me to meet. It was the first time I'd be showing anywhere outside of school, and pretty much a total dream come true.

"Oh my God! You must be amazing. That place only shows the best of the best."

"I just got lucky."

"You're way too modest. For you to be showing at the Tremont Gallery, you're obviously a big deal." He fidgeted with the drink in his hand, not meeting my eyes. "Now I'm actually kind of embarrassed."

"What do you mean?"

"Well, you know. Given what you do, and given what I do for a living…."

"Oh come on."

"I'm serious."

I paused for a moment, then admitted, "I pay for art school by working as a prostitute. You and I both make a living by taking our clothes off, so there's no judging here."

His big blue eyes went wide with surprise. "Really?"

"Like I'd make that up."

He actually visibly relaxed, leaning back in his seat and grinning at me. "Thanks for telling me that."

"I don't usually bring it up. But you didn't have the option of keeping quiet about working in the porn industry, so it was only fair to be honest with you."

"It's always so awkward meeting new people," he said, playing with his glass. "It seems like every gay guy has seen my films, and they all have these preconceived notions of what I'm supposed to be like. They expect perfect little twink Hunter Storm from Man-on-Man Productions, there to fulfill all their fantasies. Not Hunter Jacobs from Idaho, who maybe has a few fantasies of his own. You probably can relate, in your line of work."

"Definitely." After a moment I added, "I feel stupid telling you this, but I actually get a lot of work from men calling up my escort service asking for a Hunter Storm type. So, I feel like I should thank you for boosting my income."

He smiled at me. "God, I'm sorry. It's bad enough that *I* have to be Hunter Storm. But now it turns out you do, too. I hope they don't ask you to recreate any of the super classy scenes from my movies."

"Sometimes," I said with a grin, then added, "You know, now that I've met you in person I have to say, my clients must be so disappointed."

"What are you talking about?"

"They're expecting you and get me, which has to be one hell of a letdown."

He rolled his eyes at me. "Come on! You're adorable, Christopher. And you and I could be brothers."

While it was true that he and I were the same physical type, both in our early twenties and around 5'9 with a slim build, blond hair and blue eyes, we were like the before and after in some grand makeover. He really was incredibly beautiful, it was no wonder he was so famous. At best, I was kind of cute.

*****

We ended up talking for a couple hours, and after a while he decided Cole was a no-show. "Maybe that's for the best," he said. "It's not like he would have wanted to see me anyway."

Hunter finished his latest drink – he'd put quite a few whiskey sours away over the course of the evening – and turned to me with a sexy smile and a mischievous look in his eye. "So, Christopher, do you want to get out of here? Maybe go back to my place?" I hadn't seen that coming. We'd had a pretty strong buddy vibe going to this point, and I hadn't expected him to hit on me.

I had to think about my answer for a moment. I couldn't even remember the last time I'd had sex for fun, since I never dated. How could I in my line of work? Who'd be willing to share their boyfriend with countless strangers? I didn't normally bother with casual sex, either. I was enjoying Hunter's company, though. And despite my complaints about being dragged to this party, I wasn't really relishing the thought of spending Christmas Eve alone, so I found myself agreeing to go home with him.

"Let me just find my friend and tell him I'm leaving," I said as we got up. I craned my neck, looking for Charlie, and Catherine caught my eye and waved at me. She was at a table with the frat boy and a few of his buddies. I also noticed that Jamie and Dmitri were slow-dancing in the middle of the dance floor, kissing tenderly and all wrapped up in each other. Jamie had apparently handed the dog off to someone so he and his husband could cozy up. Charlie, though, was nowhere to be seen. He'd been keeping an eye on me over the course of the evening, flashing me a big smile and a thumbs up when he saw me chatting with Hunter. But then he'd left us alone, probably assuming Hunter and I didn't want to be interrupted. I hadn't caught a glimpse of him in over half an hour.

Maybe he and his fiancé were making out in the back. I turned to Hunter and said, "I'll meet you out front in five minutes, okay?"

"Sure. I'll try to get us a cab," he said, shooting me a dazzling smile before pushing into the crowd.

I waded through the mass of bodies and finally arrived at the door marked *employees only*. I ignored that and went right on through, looking left and right for Charlie. He wasn't in the employee dressing room, so I stuck my head in Jamie's office. Also empty.

"Hey."

I spun in the direction of the voice. A gorgeous guy with short light brown hair and sky blue eyes was coming toward me. He was at least six-two and totally built, the type of guy that probably spent six days a week at the gym. I usually wrote men like that off as a bit vain for my taste. But the fact that this one was wearing the world's most ridiculous Christmas sweater managed to offset the Wally Workout thing. I mean, how could you think badly of a guy in a Rudolph sweater with the red plastic nose blinking on and off?

"Hey yourself."

He stopped about a foot away from me. "I'm looking for my cousin. Have you seen him?" Christmas Sweater was clearly drunk off his ass, and grinned at me happily.

"Well, that all depends on who your cousin is."

"Jamie. It's his bar, lucky bastard. I wish I owned a bar," he slurred.

That seemed like the worst idea ever. "You're extremely drunk," I pointed out helpfully. "Tell me you aren't planning to drive home in this condition."

"No. Drunk driving is *bad*. Really, really bad." He leaned a little closer to me, and his grin erupted into a full-blown smile. "Wow, you're incredibly beautiful."

"And you're completely shit-faced."

"That's such a gross expression," he said. He was still smiling down at me.

"True."

"You know what's awesome?"

"Beer? Cousins who own bars? Reindeer sweaters?" I guessed.

He laughed at that, swaying a little on his feet. "Well, yes. All of the above. But most of all, the fact that you're standing right here. Under that." He pointed toward the ceiling, and I glanced up and saw that Jamie had stapled an absolutely enormous hunk of mistletoe above his office door.

His smile lit up his whole face, his blue eyes sparkling even through the beer buzz. And then in a move showing a lot of finesse for a drunk guy, he scooped me into his arms and tilted me back a little, like a couple in some old movie.

I kind of expected a slobbery peck, but what I got instead was deep and passionate and downright toe-curling. I wrapped my arms around his broad shoulders and held on for dear life as this guy, this drunk cousin in a reindeer sweater, delivered the single best kiss of my entire life.

When he finally pulled back, he murmured, "Whoa." Exactly. And then he said, "Oh man, I feel dizzy." He swung me upright and let go of me, then took two steps into Jamie's office and face-planted right over the arm of the long sofa against the wall.

I chuckled at that, leaning into the doorway to take a look at this guy. He was out cold, face down, feet up in the air and snoring. I left him there to sleep it off.

Chapter Two

Hunter's apartment was beautiful, in a too-perfect sort of way. He'd probably paid a high-end designer the big bucks to come up with this sleek, modern interior, though the end result was a little sterile. The views of San Francisco from the floor-to-ceiling windows were breathtaking, though.

He led me to his bedroom and pulled me down on top of the thick grey duvet with him, his mouth finding mine. After a minute he pulled off his jacket and shirt, revealing a smooth, lean body, and went back to kissing me.

But something occurred to me after a while. Hunter was just going through the motions, performing for me just like he did when the cameras were rolling. I knew better than anyone when someone was faking it, since I faked it for a living.

I kissed him softly before saying, "We don't have to do this if you don't want to, Hunter. I get that it's miserable to be alone on Christmas. And if the real reason you brought me home is just for the company, we don't have to have sex. We can just hang out."

"You came here expecting to fuck me. I wouldn't go back on that."

I brushed his hair from his face and asked gently, "What do you really want tonight, Hunter?"

"I don't want to be alone," he admitted quietly.

"Do you really want to have sex with me?"

"I...."

"It's fine to say no."

"I mean, if you want to, that's fine with me."

"But would you prefer to just hang out?"

His blue eyes were full of emotion as he said, "I'm sorry."

"Don't be." I kissed the tip of his nose and stood up, pulling him to his feet with me. "We can just shift gears, and make this into a sleepover."

"Is that really okay with you?"

"Honestly, I didn't come here for sex," I admitted. "I just came here to be with you."

His face lit up with a genuine, unguarded smile that made him seem far younger than twenty-two. "All anyone ever wants is to take me to bed. Sometimes, I feel like that's all I'm good for. You don't even know how nice it is to be with someone who just wants me for me."

We stayed up all night playing football video games, laughing and joking, our legs tangled together on the couch (and I want it known for the record that I kicked his ass at Madden). Finally, around dawn, we went hand-in-hand to his bedroom and curled up under the covers, holding each other securely.

He snuggled against my shoulder and said, "Merry Christmas, Christopher."

"Merry Christmas, Hunter."

"I had so much fun tonight. Can we do this again soon?"

"Absolutely."

He lightly ran his fingertip across the inch of skin that was exposed on my belly where my t-shirt was riding up, and told me, "You're a really beautiful boy, you know."

"But I'm not your type at all, am I?"

He grinned and said, "I have a really bad habit of falling for big, beefy, muscle-bound jocks."

I grinned too. "In that case, you would have loved the drunk guy that kissed me under the mistletoe while you were out hailing a cab."

"Oh yeah? Did you get his number?"

"Nope. He passed out right after he kissed me."

Hunter chuckled at that. "Must have been some kiss."

"Oh it was. But he was so drunk that he probably won't even remember it in the morning."

"What did this guy look like? I'm wondering if I spotted him at the party."

"Tall, broad shoulders, gorgeous blue eyes, and most ridiculous Christmas sweater I've ever seen."

Hunter looked up at me with a huge smile. "Rudolph?"

"Yes!"

"Oh man, that guy was smoking hot, even with the train wreck of a sweater. Think how much fun it'd be to get him out of it." We both smiled at that, and he added, "You should ask around. You could track him down, get his number."

"Nah. It was thirty seconds under the mistletoe, brought on by enough beer to take down a team of Clydesdales. No point in making it into anything more than that."

"If you say so," he murmured, settling in, his head again on my shoulder.

Okay, sure, I would have loved to see that guy again. He was gorgeous, and that kiss was amazing. But like I said before, I didn't date, so nothing could have come of it anyway.

Besides, when he sobered up in the morning, assuming he even remembered what happened, he'd probably be freaked that he'd locked lips with a man. I mean, he *had* to be straight. No self-respecting gay guy would ever be caught dead in that sweater.

When I awoke, it was early afternoon. I raised my
eyelids a fraction of an inch, then sat straight up in bed and
stared wide-eyed at Hunter. He'd just stepped out of the
bathroom, buck naked and towel-drying his wet hair. He
had the most flawless body I'd ever seen, lean yet toned,
his skin all-over tan without a single blemish. He was also
completely smooth, waxed absolutely everywhere, which
seriously must hurt like hell.

"Wow," I murmured, "Like I said, my clients must be
sorely disappointed. I am in no way a Hunter Storm type."

"What're you talking about?"

"You're perfect."

"Hardly."

"No, you really are." I knew I was completely staring
at him, but I just couldn't help myself. Then I said, "This is
going to sound super pervy, but would you let me paint you
some time?"

"For real?" He tossed the towel over a chair and came
and stood beside the bed, untangling his long hair with his
fingers.

It was ridiculous that I was still staring at him, and I
finally looked away. "Maybe you want to put on some
boxers or something."

"Why? It's not like you haven't seen me naked before."

Well, who hadn't? Seeing a couple of his films was a far cry from the live-and-in-person version, though.

Hunter climbed up on the bed and kissed my shoulder, then said, "If you're serious about wanting to paint me, then sure. I'll pose for you on one condition."

"What's that?"

He laid back onto the pillow and grinned at me. "After every session, you and I go head-to-head in Madden."

His damp hair was strewn around his face, big blue eyes sparkling, full lips curled into a cocky smile. It made me wish I had a sketchbook handy. I grinned at him as I swung out of bed. "Think you can handle defeat after demoralizing defeat?"

He laughed at that and threw a pillow at me. "I know I can beat you."

As I headed for the bathroom I said, "Is it okay if I hop in the shower? I'm expected for Christmas dinner with my best friend's fiancé's family in about an hour."

"Sure. Help yourself to whatever you need."

When I returned to the bedroom ten minutes later wrapped in a towel, Hunter was still sprawled naked across the bed. "What is this you're doing here?" I asked, grinning and drawing a circle around him in the air with my finger.

"Trying to entice you to blow off dinner with your friend's fiancé's family and stay with me instead." He smiled at me cheerfully.

"I thought we already determined that we're not each other's type."

He shrugged and put his hands behind his head, a wicked gleam in his eye. "How much of your type do I really have to be for you to flip me over and bury your cock in my ass?"

"I don't fuck my friends, Hunter. I do occasionally kiss them, however," I said, and leaned over and pecked him on the lips. "Did we learn nothing from last night? You don't need to entice me with sex. Instead, how about remembering that you own some clothes and coming with me to dinner?"

Hunter sat up and looked at me with a hopeful expression. "Really?"

"Yup."

"Would that be okay with everyone?"

"Sure. If anyone asks, we'll just tell them you're my evil twin."

He laughed at that. "Why would I be the evil one?"

"Because you're the one that's naked on the bed," I said with a grin.

"Yeah, good point."

"Hey, would it be weird if I asked to borrow a shirt? I don't think I have time to run home and change."

"No problem," he said, swinging out of bed and leading the way to a walk-in closet (despite myself, I checked out his perfect little butt on the way). Hunter asked, "So, is there anything I should know about your friend's fiancé's family before we get there?"

"Let's see…they're all a bunch of lushes, they're Sicilian, and they're pretty gay-friendly. Oh, and a reasonably large percentage of them are in the mafia."

He thought about that for a beat, then said, "Cool. I've never been to a mafia Christmas dinner."

*****

Dinner was being held in a restaurant owned by one of Dante's cousins, since Nana's ballroom (the usual site for family gatherings) was currently being renovated for the wedding. And even though we arrived right at the designated start time, the party was already in full swing, in typical Dombruso fashion.

Charlie spotted me right away. He jogged across the restaurant and grabbed me in a hug as soon as I stepped in the door. "Merry Christmas, Christopher. So how pissed off are you at me?"

I grinned at that. "You mean for ditching me at the party while you and your fiancé snuck off for a little holiday merriment?"

"Exactly."

"I'm not mad. It gave me the opportunity to get to know Hunter." My new friend was standing off to the side, and I grabbed his hand and tugged him closer. I'd texted Charlie last night from the cab on the way to Hunter's place, letting him know I was leaving the party. I hadn't mentioned I was going home with anyone, though. "Hunter Storm, Charlie Connolly."

"It's just Hunter Jacobs today," he told me with a grin. "There are no cameras rolling."

"Oh," said Charlie, his eyes wide with surprise. "You're Cole's ex."

That obviously wasn't what people usually said when they met Hunter, and this response caught him off guard. "Um, yeah. I am."

Charlie smiled at him and said, "Sometimes this city feels like such a small town. It seems like everyone knows everyone. Come on in guys, and make yourselves comfortable. By the way Christopher, Cousin Rachael's been asking about you." He gave me a big wink and I rolled my eyes. At Thanksgiving, Cousin Rachael had tried to have me for dessert.

"Hunter, you may have to make out with me at some point. Just so you know," I said as we followed Charlie into the restaurant.

He grinned at that. "Not a problem. Should I ask why?"

"It might finally give Cousin Rachael the message that I'm gay, because somehow this—" I swept my hand down the length of me "—hasn't gotten the point across." Hunter chuckled at that.

A few minutes later when Charlie excused himself and crossed the restaurant to speak to Dante's brother Mikey, Hunter turned to me and whispered, "Oh my God, your best friend is *gorgeous.*"

"I know."

"God I love the hunky jock type. Why is he engaged?"

I pointed out the big, muscular figure that had just come out of the kitchen. "That's Dante, his fiancé."

"Mercy," Hunter murmured, running his eyes up and down all six feet, four inches of Dante Dombruso. "I see why he's engaged, and it's so wrong that I'm picturing myself as the cream filling in a Dante-Charlie sandwich right now." I laughed at that and he grinned at me. "Sorry, I know that's inappropriate. I'll try to keep my dirty sex fantasies to myself with regard to your friends." Dante had come up behind Charlie and taken him in his arms, kissing his shoulder. Charlie turned, laced his fingers in Dante's thick black hair and kissed him deeply, as Hunter said, "Aw man, and now I'm jealous. They're so sweet together."

"I know. They're perfect for each other."

"Christopher Robin!" a familiar voice called from across the room. Mrs. Dombruso had also come out of the kitchen. She was in her electric wheel chair, cutting a swath through her family members to get to me, who dove out of the way to keep from getting run over.

Hunter turned to me with a huge smile. "Is that really your name?"

"Yup."

"It's so cute." He was still beaming at me and I rolled my eyes, poking his ribs playfully. I actually liked my name, even if it was a bit on the cutesy side. My mother had named me that despite my father's protests, a whimsical tribute to a character in a children's book. Knowing my father, that had to have been a major triumph.

Hunter laughed, squirming ticklishly, and grabbed my hands just as Mrs. Dombruso came to a stop before us. She was wearing a red velvet ball gown and enough pearls to single-handedly wipe out the world's entire oyster population, and her white hair was coiled up in two Princess Leia buns on either side of her head.

"Christopher Robin, there you are! And who's this, your brother?"

"No ma'am, this is my friend Hunter. I hope it's okay that I brought him."

"Of course it is! What, you think I'd turn a friend of yours away at Christmas? Screw that! Make yourselves comfortable, boys. And after we eat, I'll show you my new laptop computer! It's a real hum dinger. I've been working on my online dating profile, but it still needs some of that, you know. Creative embellishment. You two can help me. My family refuses to help, they think I'm too old to date. Bunch of ageists!" She yelled that last part to make sure they all heard her. Soon she returned to the kitchen, not trusting the professional chefs to prepare dinner without supervision, and we went and joined my roommates.

After I introduced Hunter and Dante and we settled in at the table, I told Charlie, "Mrs. Dombruso got a computer. That doesn't bode well. How did she even buy one today? Aren't all the stores closed?"

"I gave it to her for Christmas," Dante admitted with an abashed expression. "She asked for it a week ago, I didn't know she intended to try online dating. She told me she wanted it to type up her recipes. I'm so gullible when it comes to that woman."

Charlie grinned at him. "You really are."

"Once, when I was a kid," Dante said, "my grandmother adopted a dog with three legs, one ear, and the worst case of mange you've ever seen. His name was Stewie. I hate to imagine the strays she's going to drag home once she hits the dating sites. I just know she's going to end up with Stewie's human counterpart."

"Oh man," Charlie said, "I'm picturing that, a guy with mange, one ear—"

"And three legs," I added with a grin.

"Here she comes," said Dante as his grandmother rolled back out of the kitchen. "I'm willing to offer a major cash incentive to whoever manages to 'accidentally' fry her new laptop with a conveniently spilled cocktail."

Over dinner the conversation turned to the subject of Gregory Cogburn, the city's new chief of police. I wasn't sure which of Dante's relatives were involved in organized crime, but the new chief had the whole family slightly on edge.

"I don't think there's reason for concern," Dante's brother Vincent said. "Cogburn's setting his sights on making sure the city has a pretty face for the tourists. Apparently he's going to be pouring all sorts of resources into wiping out prostitution, that's his first big campaign. He wants the working girls off the streets. I hear he's going to be gunning for the escort services too, he wants 'em all shut down. None of that concerns this family." Exactly three people besides myself in this group knew who that *did* concern, and Charlie, Dante and Hunter all snuck glances at me.

I had two main goals when it came to my current occupation: make it out of the business without catching any life-threatening diseases, and make it out without an arrest record. My life was seriously fucked up right now, but I held on to a lot of hope for a future so much better than my past and present. I wanted to make sure nothing I did now jeopardized that.

Hunter took my hand. "Well, you can always come and make movies with me if you need a change of career," he whispered. I smiled at him and gave his hand a squeeze. But that was something I'd never consider. I didn't want evidence of how I'd chosen to spend my early twenties following me into my later life, working against me when trying to build a career and get taken seriously as an artist. Porno movies, like public arrest records, were forever.

After dinner several couples headed to the little dance floor in one corner of the restaurant, Charlie and Dante among them. Hunter and I hung back at the table, leaning against one another and watching the couples, and he said, "I love that this family is so accepting of your friends' relationship. If I'd ever tried to dance with a guy at a family function, my relatives would have completely freaked. They probably would have tried to perform some kind of gay exorcism or something."

I grinned at that. "What would a gay exorcism involve exactly?"

"Oh, you know: the whole lot of them donning mullet wigs, which for a large percentage of them would be redundant, and then playing sport fishing videos while reading from the Sears catalog. That'd drive the gay right out of ya."

I burst out laughing. "I think that'd drive the good taste out of you, more than the gay."

"Same difference."

After a while I asked, "Do you ever talk to your family?"

"No, not anymore," he said. "When I announced I was moving to California with Cole two years ago, my parents told me 'if you walk out that door, don't ever bother coming back.' Needless to say, I went anyway." He was quiet for a moment, toying with his dessert fork. And then he said, "I tried to reach out to them a couple times after that, but they wanted nothing more to do with me. I've mostly accepted that, I made my choice and knew what the consequences would be. It only bothers me on days like Christmas, when I miss being part of a family."

"I understand. I was on my own for a long time before I met Charlie. Now he's become my family, he's all I have."

"You have these people too," Hunter said, gesturing at the room.

"The Dombrusos have taken Charlie into the fold because he's marrying Dante, and by extension, they've been nice to me because I'm his friend. But I'm an outsider. I know it, and they know it."

I wasn't expecting the slap upside my head. "Ow!" I exclaimed, and spun around to see who'd whacked me.

Mrs. Dombruso was standing behind me with her hands on her hips. She was out of the electric wheel chair, so I hadn't heard her come up behind me (she was perfectly capable of walking – she just sometimes chose not to). "Bullshit!" she exclaimed.

"I'm sorry?"

"Bullshit! No one here sees you as an outsider but yourself, Christopher Robin," she informed me. "What do I have to do, legally adopt you to make you realize you're part of my family? Because I will, you know!"

I grinned a little. "I don't think you can legally adopt twenty-year-olds."

"Details! Now come on and dance with your Nana, Christopher Robin. And cut the crap about not being a part of this family. If I hear any more talk like that, there's going to be hell to pay!"

"Yes ma'am," I said as I let her drag me to the dance floor, shooting an apologetic look at Hunter over my shoulder. He was chuckling delightedly.

By the time I made it back to the table, dessert had been served. Hunter scooped up some cheesecake and held his fork out to me as he said, "You have to try this, it's amazing."

I pulled back reflexively. "No thanks."

He put the fork down and watched me for a moment before saying gently, "I couldn't help but notice you didn't eat anything at dinner. I'm forever on a diet too, so I get it. But it's Christmas, Christopher. Why not treat yourself a little?"

"I'm not dieting," I admitted. "I just have some issues when it comes to food."

"What kind of issues?"

"I don't want to go into it right now," I said, fidgeting with my napkin.

Hunter squeezed my shoulder. "I'm sorry. I didn't know."

"I know. Look, it's no big deal. I'm not even hungry."
I shot him a smile, which he returned even though he still
looked a little worried.

That had been a total lie. I was fucking starving. I
hadn't planned on spending last night at Hunter's, so I
hadn't eaten since sometime yesterday. I was used to
always being hungry, but I was pushing it today, and soon
I'd start to get really light-headed. There was nothing I
could do about it now though, literally nothing here I could
make myself eat.

Sixteen months ago, I'd been drugged and brutalized
by one of my customers. I'd ingested the drugs by being
stupid enough to eat a sandwich the man offered me. As a
result of that incident, I'd developed an aversion to almost
all food. The back of my throat closed up when I tried to
swallow anything, and my gag reflex kicked in ferociously.

The one exception, for reasons I couldn't begin to
understand, were these gross little bright orange snack
crackers with peanut butter filling that came six to a pack at
the convenience store. I had absolutely no idea why I
tolerated them and nothing else. But I was grateful that
there was at least one thing I could make myself eat.

I'd learned to live with my food issues, adapting to
them like I did with a lot of things in my life. It wasn't
going to be like this forever. But for now, I was getting

through it day by day. And sometimes, like now, hour by hour.

Chapter Three

"So, hooking up with a porn star. That's pretty hot," Charlie grinned. It was the day after Christmas and we were on the couch in our apartment, enjoying the Christmas present I'd gotten him – and he'd gotten me. We'd both bought each other Xboxes and the same football video game. Yeah, I'd splurged. But it had been a really long time since I had anyone to buy a Christmas present for, so I let myself go overboard.

It was pretty funny that he'd gotten me the same thing, and it showed how in sync we were with each other. For now the gifts were redundant, but they wouldn't be for long. He and Dante would soon be moving into their big loft apartment in the Marina District, which was almost fully renovated.

"We didn't hook up. We just hung out."

"Uh huh."

"We intended to hook up, but ended up as friends instead. We spent all night doing this," I said, gesturing at the TV with the video game controller in my hand.

Charlie's eyes were glued to the screen, his brow knit in concentration as he worked his controller. "You spent the night with a porn star, and played video games," he said incredulously.

"He's more than a porn star. Just like I'm more than a hooker. Hunter's actually a really nice guy."

He looked at my profile. "I'm sorry. I didn't mean—"

"I know." I tapped the controller and turned to smile at him. "And I just won again. I'm the king of football." I'd always loved the game. But with my build, this was the closest I'd ever come to playing it. As I stood up and stretched I asked, "Hey, how did Dante like his Christmas presents? I forgot to ask."

"He's excited about the classes. And I did what you suggested, I waited for him naked under the Christmas tree with a big red bow…um, on my lower back. Well, not *under* the tree, you saw how small the tree was that we got for the loft. But he got the idea."

Just then, Dante breezed into the apartment and announced, "We're all set." He'd bought Charlie a Land Rover for Christmas and they were heading up the coast to Mendocino, a little inaugural road trip with the new car.

Charlie beamed at him, then got up and grabbed me in a hug. "See you in a couple days, Christopher. Please don't let Nana run you ragged with the wedding prep. I mean it. If there are any last-minute details, I can take care of them when I get back."

"There's not much left to do. Besides, you know Mrs. Dombruso wants to keep everything a surprise, so she wouldn't let you help anyway."

"Oh man," Charlie exclaimed, "I forgot to tell her I invited eight more people to the wedding. Is that going to create problems with seating?"

"It's fine, I'll let her know. Out of curiosity, who'd you invite?"

"I reconnected with several of Jamie's family members at his Christmas party. I practically grew up at their house from the age of fifteen on, so his sisters and a few other relatives apparently consider me family and want to attend the wedding. I assumed they all thought I was a jerk after the way I broke up with Jamie. But they were so sweet when they saw me, and I wanted to include them."

Dante had ducked into the bedroom, and now emerged with an overnight bag. He was trying to be subtle about the fact that he was also carrying a metal briefcase, which I happened to know was full of sex toys. I grinned at that. They were so going to get kicked out of whatever bed and breakfast they landed in, since neither of them could be quiet to save his life when they were messing around.

"Have fun, you two," I said as I walked them to the door.

"Thanks. Take care Christopher, see you soon." Charlie kissed my cheek before stepping out into the hallway.

"Bye, Christopher. We'll be home late Wednesday," Dante said with a smile, before following his fiancé out of the apartment.

It was so quiet once they left. It was going to be weird living here by myself when they moved into the loft – even though they were already gone half the time. But then, I wouldn't be living here for long. Charlie was subletting this apartment from Jamie, and the lease was up at the end of March. Then I was going to have to find a more affordable place to live.

Dante had been trying to convince me to move into a unit one floor down from his and Charlie's new place. He wanted to give me the apartment rent-free, in exchange for painting a mural in the restaurant he was renovating on the main floor of that building. But that was so obviously charity. No way was one mural equivalent to a whole apartment.

I hated the idea of people trying to take care of me. I'd learned to be independent at a young age, out of necessity. Okay, maybe I didn't always do the best job taking care of myself. But still, it was important to me to know I could survive on my own. You really couldn't depend on other people, they always let you down. I'd known that since I was five.

I glanced at the time on my phone, then went to change my clothes. I had an appointment today at the Tremont Gallery, and was equal parts nervous and excited. I changed my outfit three times before finally heading to the bus stop.

The Tremont Gallery was housed in an imposing art deco structure in Pacific Heights. Ian Tremont was old money, using his trust fund to buy this place and his influence among the city's elite to turn it into a powerhouse in the art community. He wasn't just a rich kid with a hobby, though. Ian had a great eye and a keen understanding of his subject, and was highly respected coast to coast. People at school called him a star maker, since he'd discovered several painters and sculptors that had gone on to become international icons.

I stood outside the building for a couple minutes, killing time because I was a little early. I was also trying to calm my nerves. Ian intimidated me. Actually, this whole place did. I'd met him twice, once at a dinner arranged by Dante, who was a poker buddy of Ian's, and again a couple weeks ago when I brought several of my paintings to the gallery at his request. He'd selected eight of them to be included in his annual new artists show, which still absolutely floored me.

At the designated time, I gathered my courage and pushed open the door to the gallery. The place was huge, an open central hub connecting several rooms, every wall dotted with artwork. Ian was in the center of it all talking to a couple of people, one of which held a camera. I thought I shouldn't interrupt them, and waited my turn off to the side. But as soon as he spotted me, Ian gestured at me to join them.

"Ah, here he is," Ian said, beaming at me. He gathered me in a hug when I came up to him, which I returned awkwardly. I had gotten the impression that Ian had a bit of a crush on me. He'd been so attentive both times we'd met, and seemed to find excuses to touch me. I almost didn't know how to respond to that. I mean, on one hand I was flattered. Ian was a handsome man of around thirty, articulate and well-educated. On the other hand though, it was really important that we kept this relationship on a professional level. He had to know that. I took my fledgling career seriously, and messing around with gallery owners was inappropriate to say the least.

The two people with Ian turned out to be a reporter and photographer from the San Francisco Chronicle, here to do a story on the new artists show. The reporter asked me several questions about my work, which were sort of tough to answer. All my paintings were photo-realistic, small moments in time captured on canvas. And they were almost all autobiographical, though I never actually painted my likeness in any of them. Since I wasn't about to discuss my childhood, or any of my past, really, with a reporter, and certainly wasn't going to tell him I was a rent boy, I could only answer his questions in the vaguest terms.

It was odd being interviewed, I'd never done anything like that. I could tell the reporter was a bit frustrated by my clipped answers. He did seem genuinely impressed with my paintings though, which helped put me at ease…slightly. As we talked, the photographer snapped a few pictures of me standing self-consciously beside a couple of my paintings. I wished I'd dressed better than jeans and a sweater.

Finally, when the interview was over and the reporter and photographer left, Ian led me with a hand on my lower back to his office. The gallery was empty except for the two of us, since it had been closed for the holidays and wouldn't reopen until after New Year's.

I settled into a chair in front of his big desk, and he took the chair beside me as he asked, "Was that your first interview?"

"Yeah. I didn't know that was happening today."

"I told you there would be some press prior to the event. There will also be several reporters at the show itself. Giving interviews is an important skill, any artist has to be able to sell himself." I almost grinned. I knew all about that, actually. "You did fine today, don't get me wrong. And with practice, you'll get even better."

"I was nervous," I admitted.

"You have no reason to be. Your work is exceptional." Ian leaned forward and rested his hand on my knee. Was he hitting on me? He changed the subject by saying, "So, how are you, Christopher? Did you have a nice Christmas?"

"Yes sir. Did you?"

He smiled at me. "You don't have to call me sir. You know you can just call me Ian." His hand slid up my thigh.

"Ian...." I began, and his hand slid a little higher. Oh yeah, definitely hitting on me.

"You're such a beautiful boy, Christopher," he said, his voice low and seductive. "I felt drawn to you right from the start. Did you feel it too?"

When I first met Ian, I'd been star struck. Here was a legend in the art world, paying attention to me, actually listening to me, talking to me like I mattered. It had been a rush. And yeah, okay, I'd also found him attractive. But no way would I to do something as stupid as sleeping with a gallery owner. Something like that could destroy my reputation in the art community in two seconds flat. It was basically the equivalent of a starlet sleeping with a director in order to get a part, and no one would take me seriously as an artist if that reputation preceded me. "I think we just need to keep this professional, Ian," I said, getting up from the chair.

To my surprise, that wasn't the end of it. "No one has to know," he said. "I don't kiss and tell." He got up and stood too close to me, and ran his hands down my arms. I was really thrown off. He had to know how inappropriate this was, especially given the power he held over me, my entire future resting in the palm of his hand.

"I'm sorry," I said, taking a step back as he moved toward me. "We can't do this."

"Sure we can," he persisted, his hands on my body.

I tensed up and said firmly, "Please stop, Ian."

He quit advancing and watched me for a long moment, his expression unreadable. Then he smiled, but it didn't reach his grey eyes. "Okay," he said pleasantly, taking his seat again. He turned the discussion to the upcoming show, and I sat down warily.

That entire encounter had left me shaken, but I was careful not to let it show. I was good at pretending everything was okay, given my line of work. I'd told Charlie once that I lied for a living. In a way, that was true.

I could lie with every part of me, my face, my voice, my body. I used that skill on a daily basis when I was working, pretending I was enjoying whatever my clients chose to do to me. It was surprising that I would have to use that skill now, in this environment.

We made small talk for maybe five minutes before he told me he had to prepare for another appointment. He was obviously dismissing me, and I was relieved. I hoped that the next time I saw Ian, we'd be able to put this behind us.

Chapter Four

"You should feel so proud, Christopher Robin."

"So should you," I told Mrs. Dombruso, whose arm was linked with mine.

"We did good, no doubt about it."

The first guests for Dante and Charlie's wedding were going to arrive at any moment. Valets stood at the ready outside to park the cars in a nearby rented lot. Downstairs, a small army of caterers were putting the finishing touches on the food. And here, in the completely transformed ballroom of Mrs. Dombruso's Queen Anne Victorian, the scene was pure magic.

The space was lit by the soft glow of hundreds of white candles, the big crystal snowflakes hanging from the ceiling sparkling and reflecting the candlelight. Clusters of pine trees filled in the corners of the space, decorated with white lights and smaller crystal snowflakes, adding to the forest effect along with the mural. It really was beautiful.

"Oh my God." We hadn't heard Dante come up behind us, but now we both turned toward him. He looked absolutely astonished as he took in the space, and grabbed first Mrs. Dombruso and then me in a hug. "Thank you, both of you. I can't believe you did all of this. I love it, and Charlie will too."

"Yeah, wow, it looks like Disneyland!" A little old man with a garish red toupee had come up behind us, dressed in a light blue leisure suit.

"Boys, this is Rodney," Mrs. Dombruso said with a huge smile. "He's my date. I met him on the internet!"

Dante and I both tried to cover our surprise as we shook hands with Rodney. And Mrs. Dombruso leaned in and whispered, "Told you my husband wasn't the only one who could reel in a young babe. Rodney's only seventy-two!"

After a few minutes of conversation, I excused myself and went and found my best friend in one of the guestrooms. He was already dressed in his tux, as was I, and he looked absolutely gorgeous. When I pulled him into a hug, I could feel his entire body shaking with excited energy. "I can't believe I'm getting married today," he said happily.

There was something in his green eyes though, some sort of shadow, and I asked, "Are you okay, Charlie?"

He nodded and smiled at me. "Yeah, fine."

"Did something happen between you and Dante?"

"No! God no."

"So what's wrong?"

Charlie sat on the edge of the big bed in the center of the room and said, "You can really read me, Christopher. How are you so good at that?"

"It's easy when you love someone," I told him gently, sitting beside him and gathering his hands in mine.

"So," Charlie said quietly, "my dad called me a few minutes ago. He said he's coming down with a cold, and can't make it to the wedding."

Anger welled in me. His father was a homophobic asshole who'd kicked Charlie out of the house when his son came out to him. Later on, probably when he realized he needed Charlie more than his son needed him, his father had tried to make amends. The two of them had been slowly working on building back their relationship, getting together about once a week for a couple beers or to watch a game. Charlie had been optimistic when his father had agreed to come to the wedding. It would have been a big step toward truly accepting that his son was gay, instead of just tolerating it because he had no choice.

I grabbed him in a hug and held him tightly, and he sank into it. After a while he said quietly, "I knew that asking him to come to the wedding was maybe more than he could handle. But I wish he'd told me sooner that he wasn't coming. I'd kind of gotten my hopes up. He was going to be the only family I had here, besides you."

Charlie was an only child and his mother had also declined the invitation, saying she couldn't afford a ticket to San Francisco. When Charlie had told her he'd pay for it, she'd made another excuse. It just broke my heart, and at the same time it enraged me. Charlie was such a good person. He didn't deserve to be treated like this, especially by people who were supposed to love him unconditionally.

"Your dad's not worth it," I said quietly. "Please don't let him cast a dark cloud over your wedding day. You're about to go out there and marry Dante, a man who loves you with all his heart and soul. That's what you need to focus on."

"You're right." Charlie still held on to me, and I stroked his back reassuringly. "I'm incredibly lucky. I have Dante, and I have you. What more do I need?"

"Well, you don't necessarily need 'em," I said with a little grin, "but you know you're getting a package deal with your fiancé. Along with him come about four dozen Sicilians that all love and accept you, chief among them, Nana."

"Yeah, that's true. Is that a good thing or a bad thing?" Charlie let go of me and sat up, giving me a smile.

"It's a good thing. Mostly." I smiled too.

He reached out and picked up my hand. "Thank you Christopher, for always being there for me. You know when I call you my family, I mean it with all my heart, and in the best possible sense of that word."

I looked down at our joined hands. I'd been a loner before I met Charlie, afraid of letting anyone get close to me. Initially, he'd kind of been forced on me. Thank God. I couldn't imagine my life without him now. I said softly, "You're my family too, Charlie."

Why did I feel like I was saying goodbye to him? It wasn't like he was moving to the Moon. He and Dante already spent almost every waking moment together, it's not like things would change that much once they were married.

But still, some irrational part of me felt like I was losing him. I pushed down the sadness that had no place at a wedding, and pulled up a smile. "It's about that time," I said. Charlie flashed me a brilliant smile and nodded, and we headed for the door.

Charlie and Dante had decided to walk down the aisle together, and when they met in the hallway in front of the closed double doors to the ballroom, they smiled at each other with pure adoration. "I love you so much," Charlie told his fiancé.

"I love you too, angel. More than anything," Dante replied.

They started to lean in for a kiss, but Mrs. Dombruso smacked her grandson's arm. "Save it for after the ceremony! It's about to begin, so look sharp. Come on, Christopher, walk me to my seat. And you two: no smooching before the I-dos!"

We slipped through the double doors (the room still hadn't been revealed to Charlie, and I was looking forward to the big *ta da* moment), and I walked down the aisle with Mrs. Dombruso on my arm. She wore a sparkly white velvet gown, her hair piled in an elegant up do, and I told her, "You look beautiful, Nana."

She patted my hand. "You're such a good boy, Christopher Robin. And you look very handsome in your tux, even if it isn't blue."

The string quartet played, and the assembled crowd smiled at us as I led Nana to her seat in the front row, beside Rodney. I then took my place up on the little stage beside Dante's brother Mikey. Dante's brothers Vincent and Johnnie stood on the opposite side of the stage, and the wedding official, a little round man with a ruddy face, took his place in the center.

The music swelled, and the crowd rose to its feet. Two of Dante's cousins pulled open the big double doors, and the couple walked down the aisle hand in hand. All the hard work to pull this wedding together was worth it when I saw

Charlie's expression of delighted amazement as he took in his surroundings.

They stepped onto the stage and turned to face each other, joining both hands. The love and trust in his eyes as Charlie looked up at Dante was breathtaking. That was what I needed to focus on, not my own misplaced sense of loss. I loved my best friend and wanted him to be happy, and here he was, claiming his happiness.

The official began the ceremony, welcoming the guests. And then he just kept talking. In a way that was good, it gave me a chance to calm my turbulent emotions. It would have been kind of inappropriate for the best man to burst into tears during the wedding.

I had plenty of time to get a grip, because it turned out that the man was incredibly long-winded and actually launched into a huge speech about the entire history of marriage. This guy should have been an actor, he clearly loved being up on stage with everyone listening to him. I would have been annoyed that he was throwing off the ceremony, but Dante and Charlie were so wrapped up in each other that they clearly didn't mind the soliloquy.

As the official went on and on, I began idly scanning the crowd. There were at least eighty people here, the majority of which were related to Dante. Nana had obviously told them all what to wear, because most of the crowd was dressed in white and shades of blue. She'd gotten them to match her color scheme, even if she'd failed with the wedding party, all of whom were wearing basic black.

Suddenly, my breath caught.

In the fourth row on the right was the gorgeous guy from Christmas Eve, the one that had kissed me under the mistletoe. Now there was something positive to focus on. He'd exchanged Rudolph for a tasteful pale grey suit and tie, and God he looked good. Though really, he'd been handsome even in that slightly insane sweater.

I realized after a moment that I was completely staring at him. And surprisingly, he seemed to be staring right back. I was tempted to glance behind me and check if maybe someone else was in his line of sight. But that couldn't be the case, given where I was standing. I grinned just a little, and was rewarded with a dazzling smile. *Wow.* I almost said it out loud, but thankfully stopped myself in time.

I forced myself to drag my attention away from the total hottie, and tried to focus on the wedding official instead. He was still on a roll with his speech, and was now up to the middle ages in the history of marriage. Apparently, in parts of Europe at the time it was customary for the wedding guests to rush the bride at the end of the ceremony and tear off pieces of her dress, which were considered good luck. Awesome. I was so glad I knew that now. I almost rolled my eyes, and glanced at Dante and Charlie. I didn't think they were listening. They were still staring into each other's eyes with such amazing love and devotion, as if the whole room had fallen away and it was just the two of them.

I snuck another look at Reindeer Sweater, who, it turned out, was staring at me with a lopsided grin. *Damn.* That was some mouth. His lips were full and sensuously curved, and a deeply defined sexy cleft ran vertically from just beneath his nose to the v-shaped indentation in the center of his top lip. Despite myself I licked my lips, remembering exactly what that mouth of his was capable of. That drew what looked like a sigh of longing from him in return. Or maybe that was just total wishful thinking on my part.

The wedding official's drawn out speech was finally winding to a close, and I focused my attention back on the ceremony. The vows were next, and I watched with rapt attention as Charlie and Dante pledged themselves to each other, now and always. It was so incredibly beautiful, the love between them practically a tangible thing. When they were pronounced husbands, Dante took Charlie in his arms tenderly and kissed him like it was the very first time. The kiss was so pure, so true, so full of promise.

The string quartet began to play, right on cue, and Charlie and Dante stepped down from the little stage into a chorus of applause and cheers, all the onlookers rising to their feet and descending on the couple. Mrs. Dombruso strong-armed her way through the crowd, using her date as a battering ram, and kissed and hugged both Dante and Charlie before barreling toward me.

"It's ten minutes to midnight!" she exclaimed. "There goes all our careful timing. I thought that official would never shut the fuck up! We gotta get ready for phase two!"

We leapt into action, clearing away the chairs that the guests had been using and rolling back the little stage with the help of Rodney and Dante's brothers. When the guests saw what we were doing, several of them joined in, grabbing chairs and clearing the big dance floor beneath their feet. Meanwhile the caterers brought in tray after tray of champagne, and the DJ rolled in his equipment and quickly started setting up while the newlyweds were inundated with hugs and handshakes and congratulations.

We got the last of the chairs cleared from the dance floor just as the crowd started chanting, "Ten! Nine! Eight!"

I ran for the little utility closet in the far corner of the ballroom. "Seven! Six!" Mrs. Dombruso and I had one more surprise for Charlie and Dante. It had been my idea, and I hoped to God it worked. I flipped a series of switches. "Five! Four! Three, two, one!" the crowd yelled, and I flipped the last switch on the twin machines concealed in the false ceiling, sending a gentle cascade of real snow over the crowd. I listened carefully, then smiled with satisfaction as everyone gasped, then cheered and applauded. Now *that* was a winter wonderland. It was so over the top, but completely worth it.

"Hi."

I turned toward the voice behind me, and my smile widened. Without another word, Reindeer Sweater stepped forward and scooped me into his arms, and delivered a New Year's kiss to end all New Year's kisses. I wrapped my arms around him, my eyes sliding shut, my lips parting for him. My God, this man could kiss! It was passionate, electric, and it made my heart race.

He pulled back long enough to ask, "What's your name?" before kissing me again.

"Christopher," I whispered against his lips. "What's yours?"

"Kieran." He pushed me against the wall and ran a series of kisses along my jaw, and licked my earlobe before saying, "I was worried that I'd only dreamt meeting you under the mistletoe, that you weren't real." His hands slid under my tuxedo jacket and he untucked my shirt, his big hands finding bare skin as he clutched me to him.

"You were really drunk."

"I know."

I slid my tongue into his mouth, and he sucked it gently before whispering, "Just in case you weren't a dream and I ran into you again, I made sure I was ready."

"What do you mean?"

He grinned at me, his beautiful blue eyes sparkling, and fished in his jacket pocket. Then he held up a little brown sprig of something. "I've been carrying this around every day since Christmas Eve."

I laughed and asked, "Is that mistletoe?"

He dropped the crispy leaves back into his pocket and ran his fingers into my hair. "Yup." He kissed me once more, then rested his forehead against mine.

"I think mistletoe's magical properties expire after Christmas."

"I was hoping if I saw you again, you'd grant the mistletoe an extension. But as it turns out, I found you right in time for the biggest kissing excuse of the holiday season. Happy New Year, by the way." He smiled brightly, bringing out a lone dimple in his left cheek.

"To you, too. Why do you need an excuse to kiss me?"

"Because most people aren't okay with a total stranger doing this to them." His mouth found mine yet again, and it was a couple minutes before we said anything else.

"I guess it all depends on the stranger." I ran my hands up his broad back and held him to me, kissing him for another long, wonderful moment. But eventually, I made myself let go of him and murmured, "I really need to get back out there," inclining my head toward the celebration going on outside the door.

He took a step back from me, then ran his fingers through his short, light brown hair as he said with an embarrassed grin, "I know. Sorry that I'm making you neglect your duties as best man." I tucked my shirt back in and straightened my jacket, then leaned against the wall behind me. After a few moments he asked, "So, aren't you going back out there?"

I grinned at him. "In a minute. What about you?" All that kissing had been more than a little stimulating.

"I need a minute, too." He smiled and leaned against the opposite wall, tilting his head slightly and watching me. Then he said impulsively, "Go home with me tonight Christopher, after the reception."

"Absolutely." There was no debate. I wanted this man, plain and simple. Finally, I pushed off the wall and said, "Okay, I'm going back out there. You coming?"

He winked at me. "Not quite yet. Another minute or two and I should be ready for polite company."

Once I rejoined the reception I focused on Charlie and Dante, and was of course at Nana's constant beck and call. But several times, Kieran and I caught each other's eye in the crowd, exchanging smiles of happy anticipation. I asked Charlie at one point, "Do you know that guy?" indicating Kieran across the room, talking to Jamie.

"Sure, that's Kieran Nolan, Jamie's cousin," Charlie replied. "He's a great guy, I've known him since high school. I was so glad that we reconnected at the Christmas party." One of the guests came up to Charlie then, and as he turned to speak with her I watched Kieran closely.

He was now getting dragged out onto the dance floor by twin girls of around ten or eleven in matching powder blue dresses, a couple of Dante's second cousins. As the girls yelled something to the DJ, Kieran caught my eye and grinned, looking a little embarrassed. He then proceeded to dance the hokey pokey with the girls as they giggled and squealed with delight, his moves comically exaggerated, and I burst out laughing. The 'shake it all about' in particular almost brought me to my knees, wiping tears of laughter from my eyes as the crowd that had formed around the trio cheered and applauded. When the music ended, he bowed formally to each girl, and then smiled and tipped an imaginary hat to me, blushing a lovely shade of pink. Oh yeah, I liked this guy.

Later on when he brushed past me, he whispered in my ear, "Admit it. You can't wait to take me home after witnessing my mad hokey pokey skills." I beamed at him as he smiled and winked, continuing on to the buffet.

*****

The reception flew by and before I knew it, Dante and Charlie were headed to the limo, off to spend their wedding night in a posh hotel before heading to the airport to begin their three week honeymoon in the South Pacific. Out on the sidewalk, Charlie pulled me into a hug and said, "I can never thank you enough for all you did. Everything was so beautiful. I still can't believe you even made it snow!"

"You're welcome. I'm glad Mrs. Dombruso let me help."

"You did more than help, you made it magical. I love you, Christopher." He kissed my cheek.

"I love you too." And I was *not* going to start crying.

When he let go of me, Jamie came up to us and grabbed my friend in a hug. "I wish you all the happiness in the world, Charlie."

"Thanks, Jamie. Same to you, by the way. I wasn't at a place where I could say that when you got married, but I really wish you and Dmitri all the best." Jamie had gotten married just a few months before, shortly after he and Charlie broke up. It had taken Charlie a while to get over Jamie, but ultimately things had worked out perfectly for both of them.

"Thank you, Charlie." They held on to each other a moment longer, and then Jamie kissed Charlie lightly on the lips before stepping back from him. He kept his tone upbeat when he said, "See you in a few weeks. Have a great time on your honeymoon."

There was something in each man's eyes, an unspoken goodbye to the past they'd shared. Charlie and Jamie's story was one of love and loss, heartbreak and healing. Ultimately, it was a story with a happy ending for both of them, each finding the love of their lives. But their happy endings had come at the price of the destruction of something beautiful between the two of them. Even knowing everything had worked out just as it should, I couldn't help but feel a little melancholy as I witnessed their very last act of letting go.

Dante came up behind his new husband and rested his hands on his waist, and Charlie turned and took Dante in his arms and kissed him deeply. They finally waved to the assembled crowd and got in the limo, to a chorus of goodbyes and congratulations. After they drove off and most of the crowd dispersed, I stood alone on the sidewalk for a few moments. The night was damp and cold, and I tilted my face up to the fine mist hanging in the air and shut my eyes. *It's not goodbye*, I told myself. I'd been so lonely before I met Charlie, but it wouldn't go back to being like that. In addition to becoming my best friend, he'd also brought a lot of people into my life.

Mrs. Dombruso was one of those people. I went back inside to see if she needed help with clean-up, and found her doing the tango with her date on the empty dance floor. I grinned at that, and then my grin widened at a gentle touch on my shoulder. "I can't wait to have you all to myself," Kieran whispered in my ear. He was so warm and solid when I leaned back against him, and I closed my eyes again and just enjoyed the feeling of him for a few moments as he slid an arm around my waist.

When the music ended and the DJ began to pack up his stuff, Mrs. Dombruso and her companion came up to us. "Christopher Robin, you were an angel throughout all of this," she said. "And I'm glad to see you're rewarding yourself for a job well done." She gave me an exaggerated wink, then leaned in and slapped Kieran's ass. He let out a surprised bark of laughter as the color rose in his cheeks.

"Do you need help with anything before I go, Nana?"

"Nope. Your hottie just helped me by bringing all the chairs downstairs so they can go back to the rental company," she said, beaming at Kieran. "I also got my grandson Vincent around here somewhere, and a whole crew coming in tomorrow to clean up. Ah, there he is now." Vincent had just come into the room, his jacket off and his sleeves rolled back, and began gathering up glasses. He looked a lot like his big brother Dante, with the same thick, dark hair and muscular build. There was a solemnness to him though that set him apart, his brown eyes behind their wire-framed glasses lacking that spark that his older brother had. He was a man that seemed to carry a burden, and I often wondered what that was whenever I saw him at family functions.

I turned my focus away from Vincent and said, "Well, okay, if you're sure."

"You go have fun, boys," Nana said.

"It was a wonderful wedding, ma'am," Kieran said politely, shaking her hand. "Thank you for your hospitality."

She beamed at him and said, "A boy with manners. Now isn't that sweet?" And then she added, "You treat my Christopher Robin right now, you hear? Because if you don't, I'm gonna track you down and kick your ass."

Kieran fought back a smile and said, "I will ma'am, I promise."

"Bye Nana, I'll talk to you soon." After I hugged her, Kieran and I left, hand in hand.

"You okay to drive?" I asked when we got to the valet.

"I only had one glass of champagne. I want to remember every moment of tonight," he told me. That should have sounded like a line, but he said it sincerely.

The valet brought around a rusty light blue Ford Mustang from probably the late 1960s, and as Kieran held the door open for me, he said, "Christopher, meet Sally."

"Mustang Sally? Cute," I said as I slipped into the passenger seat.

When he got behind the wheel he told me, "My Sally girl's a work in progress, I just bought her a few months ago. She belonged to the grandfather of a friend of mine and was rusting away in a backyard in Burlingame. He didn't see her potential, he just thought she was a broken down piece of junk. I've managed to get her purring like a kitten, but outside she still needs some TLC." The engine had sounded more like a tiger than a kitten when the valet brought it around. Kieran obviously knew what he was doing.

He ran his thumb along the steering wheel, looking a bit nervous, and ventured, "So, I have an indecent proposal for you."

"More indecent than asking me to come home with you tonight?" I said with a grin.

He nodded. "Do you have plans this weekend?"

"No."

He met my gaze. "Me neither. So how about a little road trip? My house is far from romantic. But my family has a great little cabin up at Lake Tahoe, and the thought of being naked in front of a big fireplace with you for the next forty-eight hours is the best thing I could possibly imagine."

"But you don't know me at all. What if you decide you can't stand me after a couple hours? Then what?"

Kieran smiled at me. "First of all, that's not going to happen. But even if it did," he joked, "then we could just stop talking to each other and make out for two solid days. I already know we're wildly compatible in that area."

"It's kind of a crazy idea, going away with a stranger."

"I don't have a problem with crazy."

I watched him closely as I chewed my lower lip. He seemed so safe, so inherently kind and decent. But the idea of going away for a whole weekend with a virtual stranger was at the edge of my comfort zone, my past experiences and my trust issues looming large. "I'm not sure if I can do this," I said quietly.

"It's your call. No pressure. We can always stick with Plan A if you don't want to go away with me, and get a hotel room or go to your place or something. Well, unless it's me you're having second thoughts about." He looked so uncertain, an unexpected vulnerability creeping in and making him seem very young all of a sudden.

I stared into his eyes for a long moment. And somehow I knew, just absolutely knew for a fact, that this man would never hurt me. I felt it right down to my core. From everything I'd seen of him, and the way Charlie had vouched for him, and my gut reaction right now, I knew this would be okay.

I leaned in and kissed him gently, then said, "I'll need to run by my apartment and grab a few things."

"Is that a yes?"

"Yes."

He looked so happy, his smile lighting up his whole face. "Awesome. This is going to be great."

Kieran dropped me off at my apartment with a promise to return in twenty minutes with his own packed bag. I watched him pull away, then hurried upstairs, full of nervous excitement.

Once inside, I grabbed my backpack. It was light blue and fairly beat up, and at some point I'd sketched an elaborate, stylized sunburst onto the front of it with a Sharpie. It looked like a sixth grader's school bag, but it would have to do.

Into the bottom of the bag went every pack I had of the only thing I ate (I wasn't looking forward to explaining that one to Kieran) and a few bottles of water. Some clothes and toiletries were next, and I stuffed the front pocket of the pack with lube and an obscene quantity of condoms. Well hell, judging by how hot it was to kiss this guy, I had a feeling we were going to need them.

*****

Nineteen minutes after he left, Kieran pulled up in front of my building. I'd already been out on the curb waiting for him for a few minutes, fidgeting nervously with the hem of the sweatshirt I'd changed into. He jumped out of the car and opened my door for me, but I hesitated and said, "Are you sure about this? You really don't know anything about me." I'd been thinking about that while I packed – there was *a lot* he didn't know.

"You don't know anything about me either. Which is kind of great, when you think about it. We have no expectations to live up to, we both get a clean slate. In fact," he said with a grin, "I think we should keep it that way and make this weekend all about living in the moment. Let's skip the painful backstories and leave our baggage here in San Francisco. Let's just concentrate on relaxing and enjoying each other."

I nodded, then looked down at the asphalt. Kieran reached out and took hold of my chin, gently tilting my head up until I met his gaze. "You okay?"

I should have just blurted it out, I should have told him I was a prostitute. It felt wrong to keep that from him. But God, I so desperately wanted the chance to get to be someone else for a whole weekend, and to spend time with a sweet, beautiful man that didn't think of me as a whore.

"Having second thoughts again?" he said softly, misinterpreting my hesitation. "If you don't want to do this, I understand. To be honest, I'm nervous about it, too."

I tilted my head back to look up at him and gave him a little grin. "What would you have to be nervous about?"

His answer absolutely floored me. "I've never been with a man before, Christopher," he confessed. "But I want to take the leap. I'm so attracted to you that I'm just letting it propel me past the out-and-out terror of finally doing the thing I've been thinking about forever." He smiled a little. "That's what I have to be nervous about."

My shock must have been spelled out all over my face. "So, you're actually willing to lose your virginity with me?"

"I'm not a virgin. I've been with women," he said embarrassedly.

"But never a man."

"No, never a man."

"Do you want to top or bottom?"

He broke eye contact as he mumbled shyly, "Bottom." Then he looked up at me and asked worriedly, "Is that what you were expecting from me? Because I'll do whatever you want."

It was ideal, actually. I preferred to top, but usually bottomed for my job. "That's perfect," I said reassuringly, and he looked relieved. "I just have to ask though, why are you doing this now?"

"Because you feel like the right guy, and it feels like the right time. Plus," he said with a little grin, "this might sound stupid, but I made a New Year's resolution to finally come out, and embrace the fact that I'm gay. This is a pretty huge step toward that goal."

"Kieran, are you sure you're ready for this? And are you sure I'm the one you want to be with for your first time? Don't you want to wait until you're in a relationship?"

He shook his head. "I'm not at a place in my life where I want a relationship. I guess I should tell you that up front, too. I'm not looking for anything long-term. Is that okay?"

"Yeah. I'm actually on the same page."

"That's good."

After a moment, I said, "We should probably get in the car. It's a long drive to Tahoe."

He looked surprised. "Really? I was sure you were going to back out, that you'd changed your mind about me."

"Oh no, definitely not." I leaned in and kissed him tenderly.

I had this odd urge to protect him all of a sudden, to keep him safe now that I realized what was on the line. My own first time had been terrible, both of us completely inexperienced, and I didn't want that for Kieran. The fact that he was so willing to give himself to a stranger was frightening, he could have easily ended up with the wrong person, and this could have been miserable for him.

So to come back around to my earlier dilemma, maybe it ultimately didn't matter much who or what I was. Maybe the important part was that I would take excellent care of Kieran and make sure his first time with a man was pleasurable. This was just one weekend, he didn't want anything long-term anyway, so what difference did it make if he knew I was a prostitute? Maybe my job was even a positive. He'd put himself in the hands of a seasoned professional, after all, and I could make sure he loved every minute of this.

"Come on," I said, touching his face gently. "Let's get going."

Chapter Five

I awoke in Kieran's arms, warm and comfortable. It was a more than three hour drive from San Francisco to Lake Tahoe, and we had been so exhausted when we got to the cabin sometime early that morning that we'd tumbled into bed and fallen asleep immediately.

A fire burned in a big river rock fireplace to our left, clusters of rustic tchotchkes dotting the mantel – salmon carved out of wood, and that sort of thing. The walls and floors of the cabin were cedar, and cheerful plaid curtains framed picture windows that provided a great view of lovely sapphire blue Lake Tahoe some distance below us.

I sat up and pushed my unruly hair out of my eyes, and gave him a smile as I said good morning. Sunlight spilled across his face, and I noticed for the first time the tiny freckles scattered across his nose and cheekbones, subtle and oh so very cute.

Kieran looked like he'd been awake for a while. He'd changed into a white t-shirt and pajama bottoms, his hair was combed, and he smelled like toothpaste. He tucked an arm behind his head and smiled up at me. "Good morning to you, too."

"No fair," I said. "You got up and groomed, and I'm all gross and disheveled."

"You look beautiful," he told me.

I grinned at that. "Liar. There's nothing pretty about bedhead and morning breath. I'm going to use the restroom and do something about all of this. Don't go anywhere." I found my backpack and carried it into the restroom with me.

When I emerged a couple minutes later, Kieran was right where I left him. I didn't look much better. My hair was still out of control, and my clothes – which I'd slept in – were a wrinkled mess. But at least I too now smelled like toothpaste. I bent over the bed and kissed him, and he pulled me down on top of him and deepened the kiss.

I could feel his cock hardening beneath me, and I parted his legs by climbing between them as my tongue caressed his. I sat up a bit, pulled his white t-shirt over his head and murmured, "God you look good." As much as I disdained the gym hound lifestyle, the end results were undeniably impressive. He had big biceps and strong, broad shoulders, a sculpted chest and perfectly defined abs. I kissed my way down his body, then tugged at the drawstring on his red flannel pajama pants and pulled them down a few inches. He was already fairly hard, and I took his thick cock between my lips as he drew in his breath and ran his fingers into my hair.

It was difficult not to switch over into automatic pilot as I sucked him. Sex for me was usually totally impersonal – my body went through the motions while my mind stayed safely detached, distant. I'd been a prostitute for the last five years, it was all I knew anymore. Sure, I had a little casual sex from time to time. But I'd checked out during most of those encounters too, and just let whatever random guy I was with use me to get off. That was basically what sex was to me.

But I didn't want to do that now, not with Kieran. He – and I – deserved better. I looked up at him as I slid my lips up and down his thick shaft. He had propped himself up on his elbows, watching me, his breath fast and shallow. As we made eye contact, he moaned, "Oh God Christopher, yes." That helped root me in the moment. I wasn't Christopher when I was working, I was Austin, the fake name helping to distance me from the job.

I stayed locked on those gorgeous blue eyes as I took my time sucking him, massaging his balls gently as he moaned with pleasure. Eventually I picked up my pace, sucking him harder and faster, building his climax. Soon his cock twitched, and I knew he was going to cum a moment before he told me.

I slid him out of my mouth and started to pump his shaft with one hand, still caressing his balls with the other, and Kieran arched up off the bed, crying out, thrusting into my hand as he emptied himself across his stomach and chest. I loved seeing him like that, lost in the pleasure, as he braced himself against the mattress, his hands grasping the sheets. I milked him right to the end of his orgasm, then brought him down slowly with a few more gentle strokes until he was completely sated.

He couldn't speak for a few moments, trying to catch his breath, his body shaking. I took the opportunity to grab some tissues from the nightstand and clean him up, then laid down beside him. Kieran rolled toward me and pulled me into his arms, and kissed me before saying softly, "Thank you, Christopher." He grinned at me and added, "That was intense. I thought I knew what a great blow job felt like, but I had no idea until today."

His lips found mine again, and after just a few minutes he'd revved right back up. My cock throbbed as Kieran's hands fumbled with my belt. When he got my zipper down he slid his hand into my jeans, caressing my hard-on through my briefs. His other hand ran up my back, under my shirt.

We were chest-to-chest, and I could feel his heart racing. Only some of that was arousal. He was in unfamiliar territory, he'd never even touched a man before. When he pulled back to look at me, still gently rubbing my cock through my underwear, there was such raw vulnerability in his eyes. "Is this alright?" he asked, his voice a rough whisper.

"Perfect."

After I pulled my t-shirt and sweatshirt off over my head, he bent down and sucked one of my nipples. I rolled onto my back for him, and he sat up and tugged my jeans and underwear off, then my socks. His fingertips explored my naked body, gently, carefully, while he dotted kisses on my chest, my neck, my stomach. At one point, he ran his tongue up my shaft slowly, almost experimentally, before kissing his way back up my stomach and chest, kind of easing his way into all of this.

I was embarrassed by how thin I was, my ribs and hip bones clearly defined under my pale skin, and worried that Kieran would find it unappealing. But his expression as he circled his fingertip over my little pink nipple was blissful. I couldn't imagine why he'd denied his sexuality for so long, but now that he'd decided to take this huge step, I was so glad to see he was clearly enjoying this, and enjoying me.

Unbidden, memories of my own first time so many years ago crowded my consciousness. It had been horribly painful, hurried, my boyfriend Jason as inexperienced as I was. He took me with only a little spit for lube and no preparation, because neither of us knew any better. I cried all the way through it. I'd been so young, so stupid. I'd thought I loved him, and would have done anything for him.

Jason devastated me, tore my heart out in ways I hadn't even imagined possible, just a few months after taking my virginity. I tried never to think about it...or him.

To distract myself from thinking of it now, I rolled over so I was on top of Kieran and kissed him deeply, straddling his body. His hands slid up my back, holding me to him. He'd relaxed over the last few minutes, but now his heart was again beating wildly – he was nervous about what was going to happen.

"You sure about this? Absolutely sure?" I asked, cupping his face in my hands and looking into his eyes.

He nodded. "I'm ready to do this, I've been ready for a while."

"I'm going to make this so good for you, Kieran," I promised before my lips found his again.

I stroked his hard cock as I kissed him, then got the lube out of my backpack and put a little on my fingertip before massaging his opening. As he spread his legs for me I asked, "Have you ever had anything in you?"

He shook his head and grinned embarrassedly. "I've been tempted to put toys in me, but I was pretty sure it'd hurt."

I carefully slid my finger into him, working him open slowly. "That feels good," he murmured. He scooped up my free hand with both of his and held it against his chest as I went a little deeper, as if comforting himself with it. That gesture struck me as really touching somehow.

It took a long time, but eventually I worked a second finger into him, getting him ready to take me, sliding my fingers in and out of his tight little opening. I ran my other hand down his body and wrapped it around his hard cock, stroking him as I prepared him. He looked so sexy splayed out on the bed, eyes closed and lips parted as he gently rocked his hips, thrusting into my palm and riding my fingers.

Finally when I knew he was ready, I eased out of him and rolled on a condom, then worked more lube into him. Kieran propped himself up on his elbows and watched as I lined up my cock with his little hole, then pushed gently. He drew in his breath when the tip entered him and he looked up at me, maintaining eye contact as I held still, letting him get used to it. When I felt him relax a little, I slowly slid into him. "You doing okay, Kieran?" I asked when I had a couple inches in him. He nodded, but even through his arousal I could see fear in his eyes. "You sure you want me to keep going?" I asked gently.

"Yes. Oh God, please don't stop," he whispered. I dropped down on top of him and kissed him as he held on to me, returning the kiss, parting his lips for me.

I pushed into him a little deeper, then began sliding in and out of him, and he gasped against my mouth before murmuring, "God yes Christopher, fuck me." I took him a little harder, and he moaned and started rocking up off the bed in sync with my thrusts. I could feel the shift in his body, fear and tension finally falling away, pleasure taking over.

It felt so incredibly good to be inside him. I raised myself up just a little to look into his eyes, the connection between us electric. He smiled at me, and he was so gorgeous, so sweet and sexy and trusting. I took him deeper still, working myself into him until he'd taken all of my length.

I raised up off of him just enough to reach his cock, and began stroking him as I fucked him. After a few minutes he cried out and came across his stomach and chest, and seeing that triggered my own orgasm. I yelled as I came and he grabbed my ass, pulling me even deeper into him as I thrust again and again. When I was spent, I laid down on his chest and his hands slid up my back, holding me to him as we both caught our breath.

Kieran tilted my chin up and kissed me before saying, his eyes sparkling, "That was absolutely amazing."

I smiled self-consciously and eased out of him, holding the condom in place, then discarded it in the trash before collapsing beside him. He pulled me into his arms and kissed me again. God he could kiss. We stayed like that for quite a while, kissing and caressing, all wrapped up in one another.

It was hard to end it, but we were both a sticky mess. Eventually I sat up and said, "I'm going to get a shower. Want to join me?"

"Absolutely." He grinned and swung out of bed, and I took a moment to admire the view as he headed into the bathroom. He had a dimple above each smooth, perfectly sculpted butt cheek, which was sexy as hell. I smiled and hurried after him.

Showering together was sweet and sensual at the same time. Kieran washed me gently, then held still and let me wash him. He seemed to take great pleasure in being washed, giving in to a passive side of him that I guessed didn't show up in his day-to-day life very often. When we got out of the shower, I wrapped a towel around my waist and sat on the counter beside the sink, drying him carefully.

I ran the towel down first one arm, then the other, and turned his big left hand over in both of mine. A healing cut ran the length of his thumb.

"That looks like it must have been painful."

"It was. I took some time off right after Christmas to reroof my house, and did that when I was peeling off the old shingles with a metal scraper. I have a really bad habit of daydreaming when I'm right in the middle of something. I'm lucky that all I did was cut my thumb, I could have tumbled off the roof."

"What were you daydreaming about?"

"You."

I smiled at that. "Bullshit."

He grinned too. "I know that sounds like a total line, but it's actually true. I kept replaying that kiss under the mistletoe over and over in my head. I almost convinced myself it had to be a dream, because no kiss was ever that good." Kieran stepped closer and took me in his arms. "But then my dream boy turned out to be real." His kiss was just as smoking hot as that first one.

When we finally broke apart, Kieran said, "I want you to take me right back to bed, but if we do that, we'll starve. Let's get dressed, and I'll take you to a great local diner. After that I'll show you my favorite spot on the lake, and on the way back here we can pick up some groceries. That way we won't have to leave the cabin for the rest of the weekend."

*****

I didn't eat anything when we got to the diner, claiming not to be hungry. Kieran obviously thought that was odd, but was polite enough not to say anything. After lunch, he drove part way around the lake and pulled into an empty parking lot. It was really cold with plenty of snow on the ground, but the sun was shining. Kieran handed me a thick, cream-colored fisherman sweater from the back seat of his car. I pulled it on over my sweatshirt, rolling back the sleeves, and he took my hand and led me into a stunningly beautiful little cove.

"This is Sand Harbor," he said. "It's been my favorite place in the world since I was little."

The cove was scattered with big round boulders and punctuated with snowy pine trees. The sky today was a vivid blue, but it paled in comparison to the lake. The water was a deep, sparkling sapphire and incredibly clear, the rocky bottom perfectly visible. I'd never seen anyplace so beautiful.

Kieran walked up to the water's edge and crouched down, trailing his fingertips across the surface of the lake.

After a while he said quietly, "My great grandfather built the cabin in the 1920s, and my mother inherited it about fifteen years ago. Mom passed away when I was eleven, and when my dad died a few months ago, both the cabin and our house went to my brother and me. It still seems weird that it's mine now."

"I'm sorry about your parents."

"Thanks. And sorry that I accidentally just violated the no-painful-backstories rule we established for this weekend." He grinned a bit, picked up a smooth little stone and stood up, then threw it side-armed across the surface of the water. The pebble skipped five times before disappearing below the lake's tranquil surface. It was such a cute, boyish thing to do that it made me smile.

He spent several minutes skipping stones, lost in thought, and I wandered along the shoreline a short distance before finally perching on a big, round boulder. I tilted my face up to the sunlight, breathing in the fresh air. It was easy to see why this was Kieran's favorite place. I felt so good here, like I was a million miles from my real life and all my problems.

We had the cove to ourselves, and after a while Kieran came up to me and gathered me in his arms. He kissed me gently before saying with a shy smile, "Not to be presumptuous, but I brought along your lube and some condoms. I was kind of hoping you'd fuck me here."

"In broad daylight? What if someone comes by?"

His eyes sparkled mischievously. "I'm willing to take that chance. But we should probably make this quick."

We ducked into a half-circle of high rocks, which blocked the view from the street and the hillside behind us. I pushed him back against one of the big, round boulders and kissed him again, and he rubbed my cock through my clothes. As soon as he felt me get hard, he unzipped his jeans and tugged them and his underwear down to mid-thigh. He then turned around and bent over, his arms resting on a boulder, raising his ass for me and widening his stance as far as his clothes would allow.

I unzipped my jeans and rolled on a condom, then massaged some lube into him as I worked him open. He was soon ready for me, and moaned with pleasure as I slid into his body. We fucked hard and fast, and I reached under him and jerked him off as I thrust into his tight little hole again and again. In just a few minutes, we were both cumming violently. He bit back a yell and shot all over the side of the rock he was leaning on as I bucked into him.

When we finished, he dressed quickly. I pulled off the condom and did the same, then wrapped the prophylactic in a tissue and tucked it discreetly in my pocket for later disposal.

"Thank you," he said softly. I kissed him gently and we stepped out of the shelter of the rocks. We took one more walk hand-in-hand along the shore before heading back to the parking lot. An elderly couple passed us, heading into the cove as we were leaving, and Kieran and I both grinned at our close call.

After a quick stop at the grocery store (I bought bottled water, and Kieran bought enough food for five normal men), we returned to the cabin. As soon as the groceries were put away, I gathered Kieran in my arms and kissed him, then stripped both of us naked, leaving a trail of clothes to the bedroom. "New rule," I said with a grin. "No clothes the remainder of the weekend."

"Awesome rule," he said with a smile, falling onto the bed and pulling me down on top of him.

We ended up kissing and cuddling for a long time, our arms wrapped around each other. It took a while for me to notice it had clouded up and started snowing, and when I pointed this out to Kieran he whispered, "*Please* let us get snowed in for a month." He kissed me deeply, his tongue in my mouth, the full length of my body pressed against his.

"I feel like I can never get enough of you," he said after a while. "Like no matter how much I hold you and kiss you, I'll always need more." I felt exactly the same way, which worried me.

Eventually he met my gaze and said softly, "Will you please fuck me again?"

"You're not too sore?"

He shook his head no, so I grabbed a condom and took him on his back, his arms and legs wrapped around me, my face inches above his. I watched his every expression as I thrust into him, slowly, deeply. "Oh God, Christopher," he whispered, begging me with his eyes, though for what I didn't know.

I'd never felt so good, so connected to anyone. I said his name, and that made him smile and reach up to caress my cheek. "I'm yours," he whispered. God, if only that were true.

We both came within moments of each other, but I remained inside him for a while afterward. He held me as we caught our breath, and when I started to sit up he gently pulled me back down to him and said, "Not yet. Please?"

I grinned at him. "We're a sticky mess."

"Don't care. I love having you inside me."

Kieran looked so perfectly happy, relaxed against the pillows with a tranquil smile on his face. He was the most beautiful thing I'd ever seen, and I was filled with such intense longing that I almost didn't know what to do with it all. I put my head on his chest and held on to him as his strong arms encircled me.

Don't ruin it, I chastised myself. *You know this is just a weekend fling. Just enjoy this moment.*

When I finally eased out of him, I asked, "Are you sore after all of that?"

"Doesn't matter," he murmured. "I want you to keep fucking me, all weekend."

I discarded the condom in a nearby trash can and went and filled the big claw foot tub. When the bath was ready I got Kieran, leading him by the hand. We got in the tub together and relaxed for a while before I picked up a wash cloth and the soap and began cleaning him gently.

He let his eyes slide shut as he leaned back against the tub and murmured, "It feels amazing when you take care of me." I loved seeing him let go, letting me lead.

After the bath, Kieran built up the fire in the master bedroom and asked, "Want to watch a movie?" When I agreed, he opened the doors to the armoire on the far side of the room, revealing a television, then padded naked into the living room.

He was back a minute later with a stack of boxes. "Yes, we're sporting the finest VHS technology up here at Casa Nolan. And we have nothing but family movies from the eighties and nineties. Are you going to think I'm a total idiot if I suggest we watch The Goonies?" he asked with a grin, holding up one of the boxes.

I smiled at him. "I've never seen it, and am up for it if you are."

He beamed at me and cued up the tape, then took a flying leap onto the bed, making me bounce. I laughed delightedly, and he took me in his arms and leaned against the pillows, pulling the thick chambray comforter over us. "I love movies," he said quietly as we settled in. "Always have. I think I started using them as a way to escape reality after my mom died." My head was on his bare chest, and I kissed the spot over his heart as I laced my fingers with his.

Kieran kept glancing at me throughout the movie to make sure I was enjoying myself. During a few key scenes, he grinned and quietly quoted the dialogue along with the characters. It was absolutely endearing.

When it was over he turned to me with a hopeful expression. "Did you like it?"

"Of course. It was great."

That made him happy, and he snuggled against me. "I loved this movie as a kid, I watched it over and over. I was forever trying to convince my older brother to hunt for pirate treasure with me. I even put a sign on the door of my bedroom that said 'the goondocks.' Deep down, I will forever be a goonie," he said with a big, goofy grin that made me smile.

"I think that technically, you might be too hot to be a goonie," I teased.

"Oh no, I'm a goonie through and through. And I can prove it," he said, his blue eyes sparkling.

I raised an eyebrow at him. "Oh yeah? How?"

He leapt out of bed and said, "Wait here," then dashed from the room. I smiled happily and settled back against the pillows. I could hear him rattling around in another part of the cabin, maybe digging through one of the closets.

Not five minutes later, he leapt through the open bedroom door, put his hands on his hips and threw his head back, striking a triumphant pose. He was wearing grey sweat pants beneath blue shorts with white piping, a sleeveless muscle shirt, and a headband. In other words, he was dressed exactly like one of the characters in the movie we'd just watched. As a finishing touch, he displayed a 1980s workout contraption, a series of springs with handles at both ends, and started doing a comical series of reps with it – again, exactly like the character in the movie.

I doubled over laughing. "Oh my God," I managed after a while, gasping for breath. "That's dead-on. Was that a Halloween costume?"

"Nope," Kieran said happily. "It's all just stuff that ended up here at the cabin over the decades." He came and stood beside the bed, a huge smile on his face. "Still think I'm too hot to be a goonie?"

"No," I said, and we both burst out laughing.

"Admit it." He wiggled his eyebrows at me. "This outfit's a total turn-on. You're thinking, damn, I want to do this guy, but only if he leaves the headband on."

I laughed again, grabbed him around the waist and pulled him down on top of me. He caught his weight on his elbows and kissed me, his blue eyes still sparkling with happiness. "I do want to do this guy. Despite the headband," I told him with a big smile.

"Mmmm," he murmured, then rolled us over so I was on top of him and kissed me again.

I chuckled against his lips. "The outfit really has to go."

"So take it off me." His broad smile brought out that one cute dimple.

I stripped him naked and kissed him deeply, then slid my index finger between his lips. He sucked my finger for a few moments, and then I pulled it out of his mouth and reached between his legs. His big cock twitched against his belly when he saw what I was doing, and he spread his legs wide for me. I gently fingered his tight little hole as he murmured, "Yes," and began rocking on my hand. I loved penetrating him, I couldn't get enough of it. I pushed my finger into him up to its base as he looked up at me with such total trust in his eyes, such beautiful surrender.

I brought him to orgasm using only my hands, one finger inside him as I stroked his cock. He was completely spent after that, but as I washed the cum from his body with a damp cloth he murmured, "What about you? I want to make you cum too."

"That time was just for you," I said as I dried him off. "A reward for some of the best laughs I've had in ages. Between your goonie outfit and the hokey pokey at the wedding, I don't know when I've ever laughed so hard." I smiled at him as he gave me a groggy grin.

"I like making you happy. Gonna nap." He was already half asleep. "You're so beautiful," he murmured randomly right before he dozed off.

I sat on the edge of the bed and watched him for a while, then wandered naked into the living room. The fire in here had gone out, so I rekindled it before taking a look at the photos on the mantel. One showed two little boys of around four and six, proudly holding up two ends of a rope strung with half a dozen fish. The younger boy had to be Kieran, cute and grubby in a striped t-shirt riding up over his round belly.

Another photo must have been taken at the same time, because Kieran was wearing the same shirt. It was a family portrait, mom and dad and the two boys. His mother had been willowy and dark-haired, her warm brown eyes alight as she smiled at the camera. Kieran and his brother both looked a lot like their dad in this photo, who'd been a big, muscular guy with a handsome face and blue eyes that crinkled at the corners. They all looked so happy.

For some reason, I felt a bit like I was violating Kieran's privacy and turned away from the mantel. I took a soft, worn quilt from the back of the brown leather couch and wrapped myself up in it, then went out onto the deck that was right off the living room.

The view from out here was beautiful. I crunched barefoot across the newly fallen snow, which of course was so cold that it stung, but I didn't really care. I pulled an Adirondack chair out from under a little covered seating area against the house, dragging it to the center of the deck, and curled up on it to enjoy the scenery. The snow was still falling very lightly, so I stuck my hand out of the blanket and watched the little flakes melt as they touched my palm.

It was remarkably peaceful, the snow somehow creating a hush over the landscape. It was also incredibly cold, but I stayed out here anyway even as my nose started to run, dabbing it with the back of my hand. It was just such a rarity to find myself in a place like this, I almost never left the city. I wanted to enjoy and appreciate every moment of it before I had to return to reality.

When Kieran found me about half an hour later, he kissed me and exclaimed, "You're half frozen!"

"It was worth it. It's so gorgeous out here."

"I know what you need. Come on, let's get in the hot tub." He held out his hand to me.

"There's a hot tub?"

"Yup. That was my dad's one addition to the cabin after my mom inherited it. I checked the water and turned it on this morning while you were sleeping, so it should be perfect by now." He led me by the hand down a little staircase at the side of the house.

The hot tub was nestled in a little grove of pines. The location was very private, which was good, because Kieran was buck naked and I wore only a blanket. I shivered as he folded the big brown cover in half and set it aside. He then turned a knob that brought the tub to life with bubbles and jets.

He hopped right in, but I sat on the edge and stuck just my feet in at first, after hanging the blanket over a tree branch. I was so cold that it felt almost unbearably warm. "You were very productive this morning," I told him.

"I had a lot of motivation," he said, holding his arms out to me with a smile.

I slid over to him, then slowly lowered myself into the hot water until I was sitting on Kieran's lap, straddling him, my arms around his neck. I let myself relax, my head on his shoulder, his arms around me. It felt so good to be held like this. Eventually I noticed it had started snowing heavily, and I leaned back and tilted my face up to the sky, closing my eyes. Impulsively, I opened my mouth and stuck my tongue out, catching a few flakes.

After a few moments I realized I must look pretty stupid like that, so I closed my mouth and sat up self-consciously. Kieran was watching me, and smiled as he said softly, "You're enchanting, Christopher." He pulled me to him and kissed me with an intensity that sent a tremor through me. I was the first to break the kiss, hugging him tightly, tucking my face into his shoulder as my heart raced.

God I wanted this man. I wanted him so damn much. And that realization actually really frightened me. I didn't know how to cope with being this attracted to someone, with this much longing. Even if I *could* get involved with someone, despite my job, a relationship was so far out of the question. I just really didn't think I had it in me to let someone get that close to me. Not that he even *wanted* a relationship, he'd told me flat-out that he didn't. Ugh, I seriously needed to get a grip.

We stayed in each other's arms while I got my turbulent emotions in check, and finally Kieran said, "Much as I hate to say it, we should probably get out. I don't want you to get dizzy."

I nodded in agreement and swung off his lap. He climbed out, shut off the jets, and grabbed the blanket, which he held open for me. When my feet hit the redwood decking around the tub I almost fell over, my head spinning. He caught me easily, wrapped the blanket around me and started to pick me up, but I said, "Just give me a minute." He did as I asked, and I murmured, "Go on ahead, you must be freezing."

He grinned at me. "I'm not going anywhere. I really don't want you passing out and tumbling down the hill." He leaned against the handrail to the stairs and waited, his skin pink from the hot water. "Sure you don't want me to carry you?" he asked after a bit, and I shook my head no.

I stuck a hand out and steadied myself on the edge of the hot tub, doubled over while I waited for the dizziness to subside, and he said, "You're probably hungry, in addition to not being used to the water temperature. I'll cook us a good meal when we get inside."

I glanced at him and said, "I, um…I wouldn't be able to eat it. I'm on a special diet." After a moment, I admitted, "Well, that's not exactly true. I just have a lot of food issues. I brought some crackers along, they're the only thing I can make myself eat."

He mulled that over for a while, then said gently, "Okay," and let it drop, even though his brow was creased with concern. He could see how uncomfortable this subject was making me, and I loved the fact that he didn't push.

Finally the world stopped spinning, and I climbed the stairs ahead of Kieran and went inside. We took turns in the shower to rinse off the chlorine. Then as he busied himself in the kitchen, I got a pack of crackers and a bottle of water, sat in front of the fireplace in the living room, and ate my dinner.

After making and eating his dinner, Kieran joined me, stretching out on his side on the rug before the fireplace. He was laying directly behind me, and I felt his gentle touch trace my shoulder, my arm, my hip. "What happens if you try to eat anything else?" he asked quietly.

"My throat closes up and I start gagging."

"Are you getting help?" His voice was so soft.

"I tried. I went to a few therapists. Now…now I'm just dealing with it on my own." That was kind of a lie. I wasn't dealing with it at all. I was just living with it, surviving day by day.

Instead of saying anything else, Kieran slid closer, his warm body pressing up against my back, and curled himself around me, slipping an arm around my waist and holding me securely.

"Please don't try to fix me," I whispered. "I hate it when people do that."

"Okay." His voice was still so gentle.

After a while, I stood up and held my hand out to him. "Come on, let's go to bed."

"You tired?" he asked as he took my hand.

I grinned at him. "No." He got my meaning right away and jumped to his feet, leading the way back to the bedroom.

*****

Sometime in the quiet middle of the night, I was awakened by a series of kisses across my bare shoulders. I was face down in bed, Kieran's touch warm on my skin. "You awake?" he whispered.

"I am now," I mumbled groggily. "What's up?"

"I want to show you something. Unfortunately, it involves putting on clothes. Are you game?"

I watched his hopeful expression in the light from the fireplace as I tried to wake up, and finally murmured, "Yeah, okay."

We layered up. I put on all my clothes, and he provided me with a knit cap, scarf, and mittens, along with an enormous ski jacket. "This is an awesome look," I said, glancing down at myself when I was fully outfitted.

"You're adorable," he told me, grinning happily. He too was dressed in a full winter ensemble, but on him, it looked rugged and outdoorsy. I just looked like a fifth grader in Minnesota going out for recess.

Kieran took my gloved hand in his and led me out of the cabin, a blanket draped over his arm. It had stopped snowing, the night sky clear, but it was stunningly cold and very dark. He led me up a little path through the pine trees, climbing the hillside behind the cabin, the snow crunching under our feet. "Can you actually see where you're going? Because I can't see a thing," I said.

"More or less. But I don't really need to see, because I know this path like the back of my hand." He stumbled on something then, and quickly righted himself. "Except for that branch. That's not usually there." He chuckled and continued to lead the way.

Finally we emerged into a little clearing. "Well, that's certainly a nice picnic table," I deadpanned. "Can we go back to bed now?"

"You're going to like this, I promise." Kieran brushed the snow off the tabletop, then wrapped the blanket around himself and sat on the table. He held his arms out to me and I sat between his legs, leaning back against him. He encircled me in a warm, comfortable embrace, wrapping the blanket snugly around both of us.

The sky was a riot of constellations. "Are we here to see the stars?" I asked.

"Kind of," he said, his voice hushed. "Give it a minute."

A little streak of white darted across the sky just then, and I sat up and spun around to look at Kieran. "I just saw a shooting star!"

He smiled at me. "Keep watching."

Not two minutes later, I saw another one and gasped, clapping my hands together like a five-year-old. "That's kind of miraculous," I exclaimed. "How could I see two shooting stars in one night?"

"You're watching the Quadrantids," Kieran said. "There'll be more."

"What is that?"

"A meteor shower that happens every January."

I drew in my breath as two more faint streaks raced each other across the night sky. "It's amazing," I said softly, settling back into his arms. "Thank you for showing me this."

He cuddled me securely, a smile in his voice as he said, "I hoped you'd like it. I've always kind of been an astronomy geek. Not everyone appreciates something like this, though."

"How could anyone not appreciate this? It's magical," I said softly. An especially bright streak of light slashed across the inky blackness, burning up brilliantly, and I accidentally let out a little cheer before realizing there were probably neighbors within earshot. Kieran smiled at that and kissed my shoulder.

We watched the sky for maybe an hour, before the cold drove us back inside. Kieran stoked the fire, then joined me under the blankets. His cheeks were rosy from the cold, his blue eyes alight with happiness. He was absolutely radiant. I smiled at him as I gathered him in my arms and said, "Thank you again for showing me that. I'll never forget it."

"I'm so glad you enjoyed it."

I caressed his hair, and after a while I said, "There's a lot more to you than meets the eye, Kieran. You're really different than I expected, based on my first impression of you."

"Oh God, my first impression. You mean the one where I was drunk off my ass and dressed like a crazy person?"

I laughed and said, "Yeah, that one. What was up with that sweater, anyway?"

"My cousin Erin gave it to me last Christmas as a gag gift, and I kept threatening to wear it in public. She was at the party, and *mortified* to see me actually dressed in that thing." He chuckled delightedly. And then he added, "Little did I know that the most beautiful boy I'd ever seen would be waiting for me under a clump of mistletoe. Had I known that, I would have dressed better."

"It was kind of cute."

He smiled at me. "It was kind of insane. Also, for the record, I don't make a habit of public drunkenness. But then again, maybe it was good I was drunk. Otherwise, I would never in a million years have gotten up the courage to follow you back there and kiss you."

"Follow me? I thought you were looking for your cousin."

"That was just my drunken attempt at drawing you into conversation."

I grinned at that. "Smooth."

He grinned too. "Thanks. The mistletoe was just dumb luck, though."

"So, anything else I should know about that night? Seems our meeting was far less coincidental than I was led to believe."

"Well, as long as I'm confessing things, I'll also admit that you were the reason I was so drunk. I'd spotted you across the bar earlier in the evening, and kept telling myself, *just one more beer, and then I'll go up and introduce myself.* I kept stalling over the course of eight or nine beers. I'd never approached a guy before and was so nervous, especially because I'd set my sights so high. It would have made sense to start with someone easier, not the most beautiful boy in that bar. You completely intimidated me."

"Oh come on! Did you see who I was sitting with? *That* was the most beautiful boy at the party, not me."

"Your companion didn't interest me in the slightest. All I saw was you." His smile was soft and dreamy.

"I don't know how you manage to make even the most blatant line sound so sincere," I teased.

He settled against my chest, "Oh, it isn't a line. I have no game whatsoever. If I tried to use a line on you, it would be something like, *are those space pants? Because they make your butt look out of this world.* Which, in addition to being horrifying, isn't even original."

I chuckled at that. "Well, I guess a guy that looks like you do wouldn't need lines anyway. You'd just have to flex a huge bicep, and panties would drop all around the room."

He looked up at me with a big smile. "You're completely making fun of me."

"No I'm not. I will admit that I judged you by the bod when I first saw you. I've never known what to make of people that hang out at the gym forty hours a week, or whatever."

He rolled his eyes, but he did it good-naturedly. "Just FYI, the 'gym' in this case is a set of free weights and a machine in the empty bedroom next to mine. I spend a lot of time confined to the top floor of my house, because my roommate is…difficult. About the only thing to do up there is work out. It's also the main way I burn off stress." He grinned broadly and added, "You hated everything about me when we met. It's a miracle you didn't kick me in the nads when I went in for that kiss."

"On the contrary. I thought you were stunningly handsome. Still do," I admitted. "Also, you know your way around a pair of lips. So once that kiss was deployed, I was firmly on Team Drunk Guy."

"Awesome. I kept thinking of you as Dream Boy after that night, and you were thinking of me as Drunk Guy. Which is my own fault, I suppose." He was still smiling.

"No," I said, shaking my head in mock seriousness. "I didn't think of you as Drunk Guy. I thought of you as Rudolph."

He laughed delightedly at that. "I should have had the sense to jettison that sweater before I went after you. But I wasn't entirely rational by that point."

"Well, eighteen beers have a tendency to do that to a person."

"Not eighteen! Eight! Maybe nine. Ten, tops."

"Ten!" I exclaimed.

"Kind of explains the whole super flattering passing out portion of the evening."

Chapter Six

Time passed far too quickly. Kieran and I must have broken some kind of record for the number of times two people could have sex in a forty-eight hour time period. He was completely insatiable, but then, so was I. There was so much more to the weekend besides just great sex, though. We had such an easy rapport, and I thoroughly enjoyed his company. He was sweet and charming and considerate, and I'd gotten really attached to him, despite myself.

We were both quiet on the long drive back to San Francisco. He kept reaching over and taking my hand, holding it until he needed to shift gears, then picking it up again. When we were almost home, he blurted nervously, "Would you go out with me?" Then he added, "I know this was just supposed to be a weekend fling, and neither of us is looking for a relationship right now. But I really want to see you again."

"I don't date, Kieran."

"Ever?"

"It's just not something I do," I said quietly.

"Why not?"

"It's complicated." God, was it complicated.

I really wanted to give him a different answer. I wanted Kieran so damn much that it scared me, and I felt terrible about turning him down. But how could we date? Given my job, my life, my personal issues, it just seemed so impossible.

"Fair enough," he said, trying to keep his tone light. After a couple minutes, he ventured, "So, in that case, would you maybe be willing to try some kind of friends with benefits arrangement? We're *so good* together that I don't want it to end, and maybe that's a no-pressure solution."

I wanted so much more than just sex with Kieran. But it was all I could really offer him, so I agreed to his proposition. At least this was something, a way to keep him in my life. He recited his number, which I typed into my phone, and then I sent him a quick text so he'd have my number as well. When he pulled up in front of my apartment, he turned to me with a hopeful expression and said, "How about one more for the road?" I didn't have to ask what he meant.

We rushed upstairs and started kissing urgently, tearing each other's clothes off the moment the front door closed behind us. I ended up bending him over the back of the couch and taking him hard and fast. He pulled off his t-shirt and threw it over the sofa, so when he came he hit that and not the upholstery. I had to grin at how considerate that was.

Afterwards, he got dressed as I carried the soiled condom to the bathroom trash and washed up a bit. When I came back into the living room, he was dressed only in his jeans and sneakers, the soiled t-shirt wrapped up in a little bundle in his hand. He was standing by the back wall of the living room, staring at the series of paintings I'd hung there, and said, "These are astonishing. Who's the artist?"

"Me," I admitted self-consciously.

Kieran turned to me, eyes wide with amazement. Then his face erupted into a huge smile. "I know you said you were an art student, but this is so far above and beyond. You're incredibly talented."

I murmured, "Those are all kind of rough, I'm still learning."

"They look perfect to me."

"They're not."

He watched me for a moment, then leaned in and kissed my cheek. "Well, I'd better get going. Thank you for an amazing weekend, Christopher."

"Thank you too, for everything."

"Let's get together sometime this week. You say the word, and I'll be here with bells on. And nothing else." He smiled at me, and headed for the door. I wanted to stop him, ask him to stay the night. But instead, I just wrapped my arms around myself and watched him go.

The next day was Monday, which meant the end of my two week winter break. When I opened the front door to leave for school, a thick nine-by-twelve envelope that had been leaning against the door dropped into my apartment. I picked it up and tore it open, then slid out the thick sheaf of papers. On the top of the first page, in small, tidy printing, was written:

This isn't me trying to fix you. It's me caring about you. –K.

Kieran must have been up half the night doing research. The packet contained information on every clinic and specialist in the bay area addressing eating disorders and phobias, which he'd printed from the internet.

Briefly, I glanced through the packet. I'd actually already done all this research, I knew about these supposed experts. And the reason I hadn't gone to see any of them was that I was afraid. I was scared to death that if someone tried to tinker with my problems and got it wrong, then I'd start to reject the one and only thing I could eat. If my issues got worse instead of better, if I stopped being able to eat anything at all, I'd end up institutionalized and hooked to an IV, because that would become the only way I could survive. That idea was nothing short of terrifying.

I thought it was sweet that Kieran cared enough to do this for me, though. I put the packet on an end table in the living room and went to school. It was the first day of the new quarter, and I was excited. For three hours today, I would get to immerse myself in nothing but art. I never felt more upbeat and optimistic than when I was in school.

Unfortunately, it was also my first day back on the job, so after class I went into the restroom and hid in one of the stalls as I changed out of my baggy t-shirt and jeans. I took a little drawstring pouch from my backpack, and dumped a few pieces of silver jewelry into my palm. I positioned a C-shaped piece of metal with a little silver ball at the top inside my navel and pushed it through my skin. It emerged about a quarter inch below my belly button, where I twisted a little silver ball onto the end of it. My nipples were also pierced. I tugged on one to get it hard, then slid a little silver ring through it before doing the same with my other nipple.

There were several more places that I was pierced, some far more intimate than this. But today's particular client only liked these three pieces of jewelry. I personally hated my piercings. I'd only gotten them because in this line of work, it paid (literally) to add a bit of spice, to

122

occasionally present myself as more than just a generic little blue-eyed blond. The majority of my client base found my piercings exotic, a turn-on. As soon as I was able to retire from prostitution, the body jewelry was going in the trash.

I was already wearing skimpy little bright blue briefs under my clothes, and I pulled on a pair of skin-tight low-rise black jeans and a tight, cropped t-shirt. A lot of escort agencies let their boys wear whatever they wanted when they went to meet their clients, but the one I worked for thought whores should dress like whores. I pulled a huge sweatshirt over my work clothes so I could leave campus without completely embarrassing myself, but still felt self-conscious.

I hopped on a bus and headed across town to meet my client. He was one of my regulars, fucking me once a week like clockwork, always on his lunch break. Like so many of the men that used the escort service, he was a wealthy middle-aged guy that went home to his wife and kids at the end of each day. In other words, he was a total douchebag. This one worked at a law firm in the financial district, and kept a little efficiency apartment close to his office solely for this purpose. I arrived before he did and let myself in with my key, then shucked my sweatshirt and shoes and socks. I double-checked the nightstand for lube and condoms before getting on my knees near the door and waiting for him.

The client's name was Ned. At least, that's what he told me. He expected me to be submissive, and always had me wait just like this for him. He booked me for two hours at a time and often kept me waiting for well over an hour, just because he liked the thought of me uncomfortable and on my knees. He always had me wait dressed too, because he enjoyed making me strip myself while he watched.

I knew as soon as he let himself into the apartment that this was going to be a rough session. Even without looking at him, I could feel the tension in him, could hear it in the way he slammed the door and threw his keys on the coffee table. I kept my eyes on the carpet like I was supposed to, and watched his polished loafers as they came into view.

He stood there for a long minute, just daring me to look up at him, daring me to ask a question. I knew better. Suddenly, he grabbed my hair and jerked me upward, then backhanded me across the face. He hit me so hard that my vision blurred for just a moment, and I cried out despite myself. He'd never hit me like this, not once in the eight months he'd been fucking me. It threw me off, but only for a moment. I regained my composure and cast my gaze downward, even though he was still pulling my head back.

"Did you enjoy your two weeks off, bitch?" His voice was low, menacing. I didn't answer. I wasn't allowed to speak to him, it was part of his particular brand of control freak. "You know I expect to fuck your worthless little cunt once a week. Did you stop to consider that when you decided you deserved a vacation?" He shook me by my hair and backhanded me again. I was expecting it this time, and I didn't react at all.

That really annoyed him, and he dragged me by my hair across the room and threw me on the floor next to the bed. "Strip, you fucking whore," he growled. I took my clothes off without hesitation.

Treating me like shit was a real turn-on for him, and he unzipped the fly of his beige suit and pulled his dick out, stroking himself as I undressed. As soon as I was naked, he grabbed my hair again and pulled me up to his crotch. I steeled myself and opened my mouth. Not surprisingly, he fucked my throat violently. He didn't have a lot of stamina (thank God) so after just a few minutes of this he threw me on the bed and put on a condom. That was solely for his benefit, of course. He obviously didn't give a shit what happened to me.

He lubed his shaft quickly (again for his benefit) and mounted me with one hard thrust. *Almost over*, I told myself as I lay motionless, face-down on the ugly floral bedspread. *He never lasts longer than five minutes. Soon it'll be over, and I can go home.* He fucked me hard, grabbing my hair, yanking my head back. It hurt, but it didn't matter. None of it mattered. It was just my body, I reminded myself. And it had survived so much worse than this.

He came in record time, probably because he was so turned on by abusing me. He pulled the condom off and threw it on the bed next to me, then zipped up and left without a word. God I fucking hated that jerk.

I reached under the nightstand, mad at myself because my hands were trembling, and found the pair of long-handled salad tongs I'd hidden there months ago. I used them to pick up the soiled condom and throw it in the toilet (that was a regular habit of his). Then I glanced at my face in the mirror. Well, at least it didn't look like I was going to have a bruise from where he'd backhanded me. I put the tongs back in their hiding place and got dressed in my school clothes, still angry about the fact that I was shaking. This man didn't matter. What he did to me didn't matter. I shouldn't be upset over a couple slaps, I was tougher than that.

I was grateful that I only had the one job today. On the long bus ride home, I curled up into myself a little and closed my eyes, trying to shut out the world for a few minutes and calm and steady myself. This was the bad thing about taking time off from my job: the transition back was always really difficult.

Since I no longer had roommates, I didn't have to pull up a cheerful façade when I got home. I had a terrible headache. How did anyone actually get off on having their hair pulled? It just sucked. I wished I could take some Advil, but pills were impossible, of course – I'd never be able to swallow them. I stripped as the tub filled, then climbed in and slid down so all of me was underwater except for my mouth and nose.

I stayed in the water until it got cold, then toweled off and put on a big pair of sweat pants and a thick sweatshirt, and went to the kitchen with my backpack. I pulled out a packet of crackers and set them on the kitchen table, retrieved a plate and napkin and a bottle of water, and sat down to a late lunch. There's no point in saying I was hungry. I was *always* hungry.

I unwrapped the crackers and arranged them neatly on the plate in a little grid. No one was around to watch me do this so I could go ahead and play it up, pretend this was a real meal. Six square cracker sandwiches were in each cellophane-wrapped pack. They were the most unnatural shade of neon orange, each set of two crackers held together with a thin smear of peanut butter. I didn't know why these were the only things I could eat, why my messed up little brain didn't see them as a threat. Though if I had to guess, maybe it was because they were almost entirely unlike food, completely artificial and processed.

I picked up the first cracker sandwich and took a small bite. And immediately the back of my throat closed up, my gag reflex engaging. Oh God, no. *No!* Panic welled up in me, my breathing coming in short, fast gasps. I spit the bit of cracker into a napkin and grasped the edge of the little glass-topped table. *Please no.* I just *couldn't* develop a phobia to these, too.

I pushed back from the table, whispering to myself, "Just give it a few minutes, then try again." I went and curled up in a little ball at one end of the couch and pressed my eyes shut. Oh God, this was bad. I pulled my blanket off the arm of the couch and covered myself with it. Why was this happening now? I'd lived on nothing but these exact same crackers for the last sixteen months. I'd been able to tolerate them. I didn't understand why today was different.

I knew it was stupid that I hadn't been dealing with this, that I hadn't been actively working on trying to get better. Right after my food phobia began, I went to three different therapists, but each one kept focusing on trying to get me to quit prostitution. As if I needed them to tell me the job was bad for my self-esteem, duh. None of them seemed equipped to deal with the more pressing issue, the fact that I couldn't make myself swallow ninety-nine-point-nine percent of all the food on the planet.

So I'd just done what I always did: I figured out how to survive without anyone's help. Through lots of trial and error, I found the one thing I could actually tolerate eating. And I decided that for the time being, that was good enough.

After a long, stressful hour, I returned to the kitchen and threw the crackers in the trash. I got a fresh, sealed pack, and unwrapped it carefully. I drew a deep breath, then took one tiny bite. And I was able to swallow it. Relief flooded me. I was still okay. I was still surviving. For today at least, I was holding it together.

Chapter Seven

I hated the fact that I thought about Kieran so often.

I had decided to give it a full week before arranging to see him again. I needed time to get over him. Today was only Thursday, it had only been four days since our amazing weekend together, and I wasn't going to give in to temptation yet. Never mind that I missed him with every part of me – the sound of his voice, his pleasant, masculine scent, the way his arms felt around me, the trust in his eyes when I was inside him…God, I needed to stop thinking about him.

Around ten p.m. I was dressed in bulky sweats, the top and sides of my hair pulled back in a messy ponytail. I was curled up on the couch with a blanket over my legs, a sketch pad on my lap. I was supposed to be doing an assignment for school, but what I was doing instead was staring at a blank page and thinking about sky blue eyes, and little freckles, and a sensual upper lip with a perfect V in the center of it. I was a million miles away when a knock on the front door startled me out of my daydream.

I took a look through the little round security viewer embedded in the door, and was surprised to see Kieran standing out in the hallway. "Hey," he said when I swung the door open. "I'm sorry to drop by without calling first. I left my phone at home, and was just out driving around...."

He was obviously upset about something, though he was trying to act like everything was fine. I didn't know what had gone wrong in his life today, what had caused the pain he was trying to conceal beneath his dark lashes. But I knew why he was here, I knew exactly what he needed from me. It was the same thing I needed.

Without a word, I pulled him to me and kissed him. He sank into it, grabbing hold of me as he returned the kiss passionately. Then he kicked the front door shut and peeled off his t-shirt and my sweatshirt, and dropped to his knees in front of me, splaying out his big hands on my back as he held me and peppered my stomach with kisses. He pulled down my sweats and took my cock in his mouth, which surprised me. He'd only licked me hesitantly during our weekend together. Having never given a blowjob before, he'd been reluctant to try.

But now he wrapped his lips around my cock and looked up at me as he began sucking me almost urgently, the need clearly spelled out in his eyes. He didn't stop until I was rock hard and leaking precum onto his tongue. With shaking hands, he unzipped and pivoted around, pushing his jeans and boxers to mid-thigh, then getting on his hands and knees for me. I hurried across the room and grabbed lube and a condom from my backpack, then went to him and prepped him with two fingers and lots of lube as I rolled on the condom with my other hand. When he was opened up for me, I pushed my cock into him as he whispered, "Yes." Holding on to his hips for leverage, I sank into him with a sigh that was almost a sound of relief. God I needed this. It felt so good to be inside him, his little hole tight and warm around my cock, his body strong and solid beneath my hands.

He completely gave himself over to it, rocking back onto me, impaling himself, his yells and moans raw. I reached underneath him and took hold of his achingly hard cock and jerked him off as we fucked. He still hadn't finished by the time I came, so I stroked him to orgasm as my cock filled him. Finally he shot across the hardwood floor, bucking into my hand and crying out. It was as much a cry of anguish as pleasure.

Kieran got up a bit shakily after that and pulled up his pants, then went into the kitchen and returned a moment later with a fistful of paper towels. He wiped up the mess he'd made on the floor and went back to the kitchen to throw the towels away. I heard the water running as he washed his hands and face, the edges of his light brown hair damp when he returned.

By the time he'd done all of that, I'd disposed of the condom and gotten dressed, and was leaning against the back of the couch, watching him closely. He scooped up his t-shirt and held it in his hands as he stood rooted in place for a long moment, not looking at me. He probably felt guilty about coming here like this, maybe even embarrassed. I almost expected him to leave without saying anything.

But instead, he crossed the few feet between us, dropped to his knees in front of me and hugged me around my waist, burying his face in my sweatshirt. I stroked his silky short hair, and we stayed like this for a long time before I ventured, "Do you want to talk about whatever's bothering you?"

"I really don't." His voice was subdued, his head still resting against my belly.

I went on stroking his hair for a while, and finally said, "Come on, let's go to bed."

He got up and went into the bedroom without discussion. While he stripped off his sneakers and jeans and got under the covers, I brushed my teeth and tugged the elastic band out of my hair, then shut off the lights and got in bed with him.

This was actually the first time I was letting myself sleep in this bed, instead of on the couch like usual. Dante and Charlie had officially moved out and left me with all their furniture (which I was going to return to them when the lease was up and I moved out of here). I'd replaced their silk sheets with a new set of simple light blue cotton ones. Even so, it hadn't felt like *my* bed and I'd avoided sleeping in it, but it was time to get over it.

Kieran was over on the far side of the mattress, laying on his side facing me, his eyelids lowered. "Come here," I said quietly. He slid across the space between us and I took him in my arms.

"Thank you for this," he said. "I promise not to make a habit of showing up unannounced and then being a pathetic mess."

I kissed the top of his head. "I'm glad you're here."

He looked up at me. "Really?" I nodded, and he settled back against my chest. He was quiet for a couple minutes before asking, "Will you please fuck me again on Saturday night?"

It seemed a little odd to word it so bluntly, but maybe he was trying to make it clear he was only talking about sex and not a date. That had been what I'd agreed to, after all. "What time?"

"I get off work at eight, so I should be able to get here by eight-thirty," he said. "Is that okay?" I nodded and drew him into my arms a bit more securely.

*****

It wasn't that surprising to find myself alone the next morning. Kieran had left a note on the nightstand before slipping out quietly. All it said was: *Thanks again, Christopher. See you Saturday.*

I showered and dressed just in time to open the door to a sleek, pulled together Hunter. He was dressed all in black, from his sunglasses to his leather jacket to his jeans and cowboy boots. "Good news," he said by way of greeting, smiling cheerfully, "your muse has arrived." He breezed into the apartment and kissed my cheek, then gestured with the huge to-go coffee cup he was holding. "I'm yours for the morning, so just tell me how you want me."

We'd exchanged several texts since Christmas, and Hunter had agreed to be the model for my junior project. I was going to owe him big-time after this. The project was an intensive subject study, which involved not only a whole series of sketches, but no less than three paintings and one sculpture. Hunter had agreed to sit for me without reservation, even when I explained to him how much time would be involved.

"Make yourself comfortable on the couch," I said as I crossed the room and picked up a drawing pad and pencil.

"I just want to do a few preliminary sketches today, this is going to be really informal."

He took off his jacket, then tugged off his boots and socks and sat cross-legged at one end of the couch. I sat at the opposite end, tucking my feet under me, and began to draw. "Can we talk while you work?" he asked. "Or is that too distracting?"

"It's fine. So how've you been, Hunter? What's going on in your world?"

"Oh, you know," he said with a little frown. "My life is nonstop glamour and excitement. I kind of have a stalker. Lucky me."

"Oh my God! Who is he? What's he done?" My pencil froze in mid-air above the sketch pad.

He held up his hand, palm facing me. "It's not a big deal. Once in a while in my line of work, fans get a little obsessed. But most of them are perfectly harmless."

"Has he threatened you?"

"Yeah. But it's probably nothing. I'm trying not to let it get to me."

"Have you contacted the police?"

"There's no reason to. It's just a few emails. I'm being stupid to even give it this much thought."

"Promise me you'll get help if it gets worse," I said.

"I will, I'll go to the police if the threats escalate. Don't worry, Christopher, it'll be fine. I shouldn't even have brought it up."

"I'm glad you did. I want to know what's going on with you."

"Like I said, nonstop glamour and excitement." He gave me a little grin and settled back against the arm of the couch. "Let's change the subject, that one's kind of depressing. I seriously don't even know why I mentioned it. And you'd better start drawing, Christopher, because I'm aging rapidly over here and will be far less cute the older I get." I watched him for a long moment, and he held my gaze steadily.

"If you need to talk about it, please come to me, Hunter."

"I will. I swear. Now get busy, Michelangelo." After watching him for another moment and realizing he really wasn't going to say anything else about this, I tilted up the drawing pad and got to work, worry still eating away at me.

When I finished sketching him, Hunter slid over so that he was sitting right beside me on the sofa. He wrapped his arms around me as he watched what I was doing, and I put my free arm around his shoulders while I continued to shade one of the drawings. Hunter craved physical contact, more so than anyone I'd ever met. Through our conversations over the past few days, I'd learned he was really promiscuous, spending almost every night in someone else's bed. I suspected it was for the physical contact far more than the actual sex. To me it was obvious that underneath the flawless exterior, there was just a lonely, vulnerable boy that desperately wanted someone to love him. Not that he'd ever admit it. He laughed off his promiscuity and tried to pretend he didn't need anyone.

"You made me look so handsome," he said, studying the drawing on my lap.

"You're absolutely gorgeous, Hunter."

"Thank you for saying that." Just like he needed physical contact, he also needed a lot of reassurance. He frequently hid his insecurity behind a lot of cockiness, but at times, he'd let me see behind the façade.

"It's the simple truth, darlin'. You're a work of art," I told him as I used the tip of my pinkie finger to soften a shadow on the sketch.

He pulled back a few inches and beamed at me. "What was that?"

"What was what?"

"You just turned southern on me. Oh my God, it was so cute! Say something else."

I grinned at him and said in my usual tone of voice, "I make a conscious effort not to talk that way. But sometimes it leaks out when I'm not paying attention."

"Where are you from?"

"Georgia."

His expression got all dreamy. "I always wanted to go to Savannah. I've never been to the south, I imagine it's all horribly romantic."

"Uh, no. There was nothing romantic about *my* south. To me, it's all just something to forget, and leaving the accent behind is part of that."

Hunter put his head on my shoulder as I turned my attention back to the sketch pad. "Fine. But I still love the way it sounds. Someday, I want to find a man with a deep drawl."

I grinned a little. "You told me once that you like big, dumb jocks. Now you've added a southern accent to the mix. Aim a little higher, Hunter."

He smiled at that. "You mock me. But my southern stud is out there somewhere."

"He's in a convenience store in Alabama. Hell, he's in *all* the convenience stores in Alabama. Take your pick. You'll find big, dumb jocks with a drawl by the dozen."

"Wanna go on a road trip, Christopher?"

I laughed at that. "Sorry Hunter, you're on your own. When I left the south, it was for good. I'm never going back there."

He sighed dramatically. "Killjoy."

Someone knocked on the door then, and I opened it to find Mrs. Dombruso dressed in a camouflage track suit, a rhinestone-studded camo baseball cap on her head. I stepped back to let her in, and as she came into the apartment she said, "Hi Christopher Robin. Oh, and hello there, Hunter." He gave her a friendly wave. "I'm on my way to the shooting range, I figure that's probably a good place to meet men. I was going to invite you along, but it looks like you're busy."

"Hunter and I are doing a project for school. We were just finishing up."

"Oh good. So do you want to come and blow away some targets with me? It's a lot of fun. And like I said, there's no shortage of men at these places."

"No thanks. Guns make me nervous."

"What? Why?"

"They just do," I said.

"Maybe you just need to spend more time around 'em, maybe that's your problem," she said.

"Actually, I grew up around them and they still really make me uneasy."

She stared at me for a beat, then shrugged her skinny shoulders and said, "Suit yourself. If I find any cute gay homosexual boys at the gun range, do you want me to give 'em your number?"

"No thanks, Nana. I'm good."

"You still seeing that big, buff hottie from the wedding?"

In some sense of the word. "Yeah."

Mrs. Dombruso beamed at me. "I'm glad to hear it, you two are cute together." She turned and headed out the door, and called over her shoulder, "But if it doesn't work out with the two of you, call me! I got all kinds of ideas for meeting hunks, and I could use a wing man."

Chapter Eight

I had four back-to-back jobs on Saturday, one of them a two hour BDSM session, and was tired and shaky by the time I got home. It always took me a little while to pull myself together after something like that. I stood under a hot shower for a long time and looked myself over. The good thing about that client was that he was a highly experienced Dom, and knew how to inflict pain without leaving lingering marks on my body. It was the mental aspect far more than the physical that took a bit of recovery time.

Four clients in one day was really too much, but I had to make up for the time I'd taken off at Christmas. That was why I had four appointments again tomorrow. I'd recently wiped out most of my savings to pay this quarter's tuition, and payment for next quarter was due in just a couple months.

When I'd worked the street, it wasn't unusual to get fucked by as many as a dozen men a night. But each of those encounters would last only a matter of minutes. Clients who used escort services paid a lot of money for an hour of my time, and they most often made a point of using all of that hour (or even two or three hours, like that Dom). It was tough to endure such long sessions.

I went to bed and burrowed under the covers. It was only seven, I still had a little time to recuperate before Kieran came over. After a while, my phone buzzed on the nightstand, and I tilted it to face me. Kieran had texted, telling me he was running late because he'd gotten wrapped up with something at work. That was a good thing, actually. I didn't want to be so out of sorts when he got here, and this would give me more time to rest and to get a grip.

It was almost nine thirty by the time he arrived, and when I opened the door, my jaw dropped. Kieran was dressed in full police uniform with a dark blue shirt and pants, badge, and a little engraved name tag that said K. Nolan, his hat in his hands. All that was missing was the holster and gun. I mumbled, "Please tell me you're a stripper."

He grinned at that. "God no. I would suck as a stripper, I have no moves whatsoever. I'd be up on stage doing the chicken dance from my cousin Maureen's wedding." But when he saw how stunned I was, he grew serious. "I know a lot of people hate cops, but please tell me you're not one of them."

"Oh. Um, no. This was just really unexpected. Come in," I stammered, stepping back and trying to pull up a veneer of practiced calm. I didn't *hate* the police exactly, but they did make me really uncomfortable. I'd had a bad experience with them a while back. And the fact that I did something illegal for a living only added to my unease around them.

Kieran came and stood right in front of me as I shut the door. "This makes you nervous, though," he said, resting a fingertip on his badge. "I should have told you I was a cop, I didn't know it would be a big deal. Actually, I thought you'd probably already have guessed it, since you know I'm Jamie's cousin and most of our family is in law enforcement."

I didn't say anything for a long moment, trying to calm my nerves and put this in perspective. That was a little challenging, since I was already barely holding it together after the day I'd had. Normally, this might not have made me feel so rattled and vulnerable.

He continued, "I didn't say anything about it during our weekend together because my job's pretty stressful, and I was trying to go with that living-in-the-moment thing, instead of venting about work." I nodded, but still remained silent.

Unexpectedly, Kieran got down on his knees and looked up at me, putting his hat on the floor beside him. "It's still me, I'm the same person. Please try to look past the uniform, Christopher," he said softly. Hesitantly, he put his hands on my waist and rested his cheek against my stomach.

Just as hesitantly, I reached up and stroked his silky hair. I took a deep breath, then another. And I realized this was my problem, not his. It wasn't Kieran's fault that I'd developed a criminal mentality, that I saw the police as a threat. And he had nothing to do with the incident that had turned me against the police in the first place. He was the same sweet guy he'd always been.

I bent down and tilted his chin up, my lips finding his. And as soon as I kissed him, my nervousness fell away. The electricity between us was as strong as ever, and I deepened the kiss as he parted his lips for me, tasting his mouth. His big hands slid up my thighs, and he unbuttoned and unzipped my jeans, then pulled down my briefs and wrapped his hand around my hardening cock, stroking me as we kissed.

His cerulean eyes locked with mine as I straightened up, and he took my cock in his mouth. And, okay, maybe it was a little perverse, but there was something so incredibly hot about the fact that he was in full uniform while he sucked me. I had never found anything even remotely sexy about a man in uniform, until this moment. Now the juxtaposition of an authority figure on his knees made my cock throb.

I ran a hand around to the back of his head and thrust carefully, and Kieran moaned with pleasure, his eyes sliding shut. So I thrust just a little more, sliding a couple inches in and out of his warm, wet mouth. He pulled off me for just a moment and looked up at me as he whispered, "Harder. Please," before taking my cock in his mouth again.

I knew he was really inexperienced, and I also knew it was all too easy for this to turn from pleasurable to miserable. So I kept my thrusts short, contained, the hand on the back of his head there to guide, not restrain. He grabbed my butt with one hand while he fumbled with his zipper, freeing his straining cock from his uniform, and stroked himself while he sucked me. After a couple minutes he pulled off me and begged, his voice rough, "Please Christopher, harder. Fuck my mouth." He engulfed my cock again, sucking me with all he had, and I increased my thrusts incrementally, watching him closely for the first sign of distress.

Kieran looked up at me again as my cock slid between his wet lips. I loved it when he did that, locking eyes with me at the most intimate moments. And his eyes told me everything I needed to know – how much he wanted this, how much he trusted me, how connected we were to each other. I thrust just a little harder and he moaned around my cock.

My orgasm was building, and I said, "Do you want me to cum in your mouth, Kieran?" I knew I was STD-free, that wasn't my concern. I just wasn't sure if he was ready for something like this.

But he nodded as much as he could and murmured, "Mmhmm," around my cock. I increased the tempo of my thrusts, still being careful not to take him too roughly, and in the next moment I was crying out and unloading down his throat as he sucked me, his sweet, wet, warm mouth drawing every drop of cum from my balls. He swallowed me down without hesitation, lost in the moment, and then cried out as his own orgasm sprayed across the floor, sucking me throughout it.

He eased off me carefully when we were both spent. I stepped out of my jeans and briefs and held my hand out to him, helping him to his feet. We were still right beside the front door to my apartment. I led him to the bedroom and pulled him onto the mattress with me, wrapping my arms around him, and Kieran held on to me tightly, his head on my chest as we caught our breath.

After a while he said quietly, "I think I've always known I was gay. But the fact that I'm so submissive is news to me. I never saw myself like that, it's not who I am at work or in any other aspect of my life. I don't really know what to make of it."

I mulled that over before saying, "I'm curious why you never slept with any men before me."

He shrugged and said, "Lots of reasons, I guess. For one thing, I grew up being told it was wrong to be gay. To say my father was homophobic is putting it mildly. I knew he was wrong and bigoted, but even so, his prejudice affected me. It made me think I had to hide what I was, or risk being rejected by everyone I cared about."

He was quiet for a while before saying, "I told you my dad passed away a few months ago. Of course when he died, it's not like my first thought was 'hey, now I can come out of the closet!' I had a lot to deal with. I still do. But then you came along, and I was just so attracted to you...." After a moment he added quietly, "You've been really good for me, Christopher. You're patient and understanding, and I like how uncomplicated this is."

Uncomplicated, little did he know. As if there was anything uncomplicated about a cop going to bed with a prostitute.

He kissed me gently. We made out for a long time, soft and tender slowly evolving into hot and heavy. "Please fuck me," he whispered after a while.

"God yes," I murmured as I cupped his ass with both hands, pushing my erection against his.

"Uniform on or off?" he asked.

"On."

He got on his knees and grinned at me over his shoulder. "It's growing on you." He slid his dark blue pants and his boxers down to just below his butt and fell forward onto his hands.

"You've single-handedly made the uniform hot," I told him with a smile as I prepped his little hole with lube and first one, then two fingers. "I'd never have thought it possible."

He chuckled at that. "Yeah, I've never seen the appeal, myself. But I'm glad you've gotten past your initial disgust and somehow turned it into a positive."

"Not disgust, just surprise. I thought you were probably a college student, it never occurred to me that you're a cop."

"I graduated from U.C. Davis two years ago. I'm twenty-three, how old are you?"

"Twenty. I'll be twenty-one at the end of this month."

Kieran smiled and said, "I love that we're comfortable enough with each other to have a normal conversation while your fingers are inside me."

I smiled too. "It's probably a little weird that we're carrying on a conversation right now. I should make you stop talking."

"Oh yeah? How are you going to do that?"

"Like this." I crooked my fingers and began massaging his prostate.

He cried out and dropped from his hands to his elbows, thrusting his gorgeous ass up in the air. All he could manage was, "Mmmmm," as I kept up the stimulation for another minute.

Finally I couldn't wait any longer and rolled on a condom with one hand, my other still inside him. I withdrew my fingers and immediately replaced them with my cock, and began taking him hard and fast, grabbing his hips and pulling him back onto me.

"I love having you inside me," he ground out, his voice gravelly as he bounced on my cock, meeting each thrust into him with a hard thrust back. I picked up my pace, the sound of my body slapping against his filling the room, and he begged, "Please Christopher, don't hold back. Make me ache, make it so I feel you in me for the next few days, so no matter where I am, what I'm doing, I'm reminded of this."

I got up into a crouch and gave him exactly what he asked for, driving myself into him almost brutally, and the harder I fucked him the louder his chant of, "Yes, yes, yes!" Kieran writhed under me and threw his head back, pure sex, wild and primal. His words degenerated into grunts and yells as he completely gave himself over to me. I came so hard that the room spun, but even after I came, I kept thrusting into him. I needed more. I needed this to not end yet. I needed…oh God, I knew what I needed.

I pulled out of him and asked, my voice rough, "Will you fuck me, Kieran?" He looked surprised but he nodded, and when I asked him to lay on his back he complied immediately. I yanked off my rubber and threw it on the floor, then rolled a new condom onto his cock and slicked it quickly. Straddling his body, I guided him into me as we both moaned with pleasure. I fell forward and held his gaze as I rode him, and when he said my name, it came out as a gasp.

I unbuttoned his uniform and ran my hands up his smooth, bare chest as I fucked myself onto him. When he came he arched up off the bed, holding onto my waist, crying out as wave after wave of his orgasm tore from his body. It was so intense that aftershocks rocked him for a long time afterward as he continued to thrust into me.

Finally when he was spent, I collapsed onto his chest and he held me securely and kissed my hair. When he caught his breath he whispered, "I assumed you didn't like that. You avoided it during our weekend together."

"I don't always like it. But it's different with you." What an understatement.

"How so?"

I tucked my head into the space between his neck and shoulder and said softly, "Normally, when I bottom I feel helpless and out of control. But you don't make me feel like that. You make me feel—" I almost said *safe*, but then realized how waifish that sounded. So instead I said, "You make me feel like I can trust you."

He tightened his arms around me. "Same here."

We were quiet for a while until I asked idly, still curled against his chest and running a finger along the edge of the badge pinned to his open shirt, "Do you like being a police officer?"

"Yeah. It's the only thing I've ever wanted to do. Granted, some days the job sucks, because I deal with people at their absolute worst. But I like making a difference."

I mulled that over, and he asked softly, "Is it alright if I spend the night here?"

"God yes. I want you to stay with me," I murmured as I snuggled against him, his cock still inside me.

Chapter Nine

The next morning, I was awakened by gentle fingers brushing my hair from my face. I was on my stomach near the edge of the mattress, and raised my lids to find Kieran at eye level with me, a sweet smile on his lips.

"Hi baby," he said softly. "I'm sorry to wake you, but I have to get going. I'm working a double today, it's a big day down at the station. I didn't want to leave without saying goodbye."

I sat up a little and pushed my hair back. He was kneeling beside the bed, fully dressed in his uniform, his hat again in his hand. I ran my fingertips over his cheek and traced the sexy curve of his lips, which made him smile, bringing out his lone dimple. "You're even beautiful in the morning," he told me.

I rolled my eyes at that as I fell back against the mattress. "You're delusional," I told him. "But very cute. You know, for a cop." I gave him a big smile.

He grinned at me and leaned in and kissed me so incredibly tenderly. Then he told me, "I'm going to come over after work tonight, around ten p.m. if that's okay. And not just so you can fuck me." He brushed the hair from my eyes again and said, "Tonight, I want us to renegotiate."

"Renegotiate what?"

"The terms of our agreement."

"Kieran—"

"I know you said you don't date, and you don't want a relationship. I thought I was on the same page, and that this friends with benefits thing would be a good solution. We'd still get to be together, but without strings or complications." He scooped up my hand and said, "But Christopher, I want more. I want *you*. Screw the complications! I want us to date. I want to introduce you to my friends. I want you to be a part of my life, and I want to be a part of yours." He kissed the hand he was holding, and then he let go of me and got up. "Just think about it. I'll see you in thirteen hours, at which point, let the negotiations begin." He winked at me, and turned and left the bedroom. A moment later, I heard the front door open and close.

I stared at the ceiling for a while, mulling all of that over. The phone on my nightstand buzzed after a few minutes, and I glanced at the text. It was from Hunter, asking if we were still meeting at the studio on campus later that day.

Instead of answering his question, I texted: *Kieran wants us to start dating.*

He wrote back: *Is that what you want?*

It's impossible with my job, was my reply.

The phone rang in my hand, and when I pushed the on button, Hunter said, "*You can date.* You're not the first hooker in the history of the world to try to have a relationship. If he really wants to be with you, he'll deal with it."

"How do you envision that scenario? Every day, I'd gave him a cheerful wave and say, 'bye honey, see you after work!' and then I'd go out and get screwed by a bunch of guys? He'd have to have zero self-esteem to agree to that shit."

Hunter said, "Well admittedly, it's not ideal."

"Also, guess what he does for a living?"

"With that bod, I'm going with male stripper."

"I wish. No, I found out last night he's a cop."

"Oh *shit.*"

"Uh huh."

"Does he know what you do for a living?"

"No. I've managed to avoid bringing it up, he just thinks I'm an art student. I'm sure he'll be thrilled when he finds out the truth."

"Well," Hunter said, "if you really want to date him, I guess you're just going to have to quit your job."

"Oh yeah, because it's so easy to make the money I need doing anything else."

Hunter paused for a moment, then said gently, "Maybe the job's not the issue. Maybe you're afraid of having a relationship, and are looking for excuses to avoid dating so you won't get too close to anyone."

"I know that's part of it, actually," I admitted.

Have you ever actually been in a relationship?"

"Just once, a long time ago. It…didn't end well."

"Let me ask you something," he said. "Do you like Kieran? Do you want to be with him?"

"Yeah. God, I really do."

"So you'll figure out how to make this work. You'll find another way to make a living if it comes to that."

"I have to finish school," I persisted. "I promised myself I'd see it through, no matter what. And that means I have to keep turning tricks, which in turn means I can't date anyone."

"Is there some reason you're not just taking out student loans like everyone else?"

I sighed and said, "Yeah. There's a reason."

"Because everyone's eligible, you know. You don't even need good credit, or proof of income, or whatever."

"I know."

"The only reason you'd possibly be turned down is if, like, you were worth a million dollars or something. Every other person on the planet is eligible for financial aid. I think they'd probably even give student loans to murderers on death row, as long as they weren't sentenced to be executed before they could repay the loan."

"I know you mean well, Hunter, but I have actually looked into financial aid. I'm not an idiot. If I thought there was some alternative to selling my body, don't you think I'd be doing it?"

"I don't know," he said, shifting the phone. "I mean, you've been turning tricks a long time, right?"

"Five years."

"Christ, you started when you were fifteen?"

"Yeah."

"Damn," he muttered. Then he said, "Well, after all that time, maybe prostitution doesn't seem like a big deal to you anymore. Maybe it seems normal. So maybe you've stopped looking for alternatives."

"Believe me," I said, "it hardly seems normal." On some level though, it was true that I *had* gotten used to being a prostitute. I'd learned to accept the negative aspects of my job, I'd adapted to them. When I was first on my own, I'd tried so hard to figure out other ways to support myself, but I didn't look for alternatives anymore. What I did instead was work hard in school, trying to build a future that didn't include selling myself.

Hunter sighed and said, "Babe, I don't know what to tell you. Apparently you're not going to stop turning tricks, and yet you *want* this guy. I don't have a solution for you."

"I know. I don't have a solution either." I sighed and rolled out of bed, heading toward the shower. "So, to go back to your original subject, can you meet me on the Sutherlin campus in an hour? We should be able to get in a couple solid hours of studio time before this afternoon."

"Sure. What's this afternoon?"

"I have several jobs, including two with new clients. That's not my favorite thing. My regulars may be a bunch of douchebags, but at least they're a known commodity."

"See, that's the nice thing about porn. There's not that unknown factor. I know exactly who's going to be fucking me, and I know it's safe, supervised. I said it before and I'll say it again: you should come and work with me."

"It's not really a solution, Hunter." I hadn't bothered to explain my goal of not having my current mistakes follow me into the future, because I didn't want to insult him.

"Yeah okay, maybe not."

*****

At least my afternoon started with a regular, a nice guy who bought me for an hour a week and always spent half

158

our time together holding me and kissing me before we had sex. We always met in his apartment (this one was actually single), and he never did anything to hurt me. It wasn't true that *all* my clients were douchebags, I just tended to lump them all together.

But after that session, I had to steel myself for something I absolutely hated. I was meeting with Larry and Doc, the two men that ran my escort service. I needed to collect my pay from before my vacation (always cash in an envelope) and was also picking up a key to a hotel room. One of today's new clients had reserved a room ahead of time in an upscale hotel, and wanted me waiting naked in bed for him.

The problem with going and seeing Larry and Doc was the terms of my employment agreement. I'd taken this job right after I'd been drugged and brutalized, fresh out of the hospital. I'd been desperate to get off the streets, so I probably would have agreed to anything they asked. What I'd agreed to was letting each of them fuck me twice a month.

This shouldn't have been a big deal. I was fucked day in and day out by all kinds of men. And Larry was okay, it didn't bother me that I had to sleep with him. He was just an average guy in his late fifties with fairly straightforward needs. Doc, though, was another story. There was something really creepy about him, in addition to the fact that he was a straight-up pervert. The rumor among the working boys was that Doc had at one time been a real M.D., but that he'd gotten kicked out of the medical profession for sexually molesting his patients. I found that really easy to believe.

Their office was in a nondescript building housing accountants and other mundane businesses. The sign on the door said SJC Enterprises, and the front room was a bland reception area with two desks that Larry and Doc used, a sitting area, and a couple potted plants. But there was a second room to their offices as well. Behind the perfectly ordinary front office, Doc had set up a combination doctor's office/torture chamber, the centerpiece of which was a big examination chair with stirrups, like those used for gynecological exams. Only this one included leather straps to hold you in place.

When I got to their office, I locked the door behind me as usual, and Larry said, "Hello there, Austin! How are you, son?"

"Fine thank you, sir. How are you?" I was already stripping myself, folding my clothes and putting them in a neat pile on the couch by the door.

"I'm well, thanks. We missed you over winter vacation. Did you have a nice Christmas?"

"Yes sir, thank you for asking."

Doc came in from the back room then and said, "Ah there's my favorite employee." He sat on the edge of his partner's desk and watched me undress, rubbing himself through his pants. "I got everything all set up in back for your health checkup, Austin. Your next client isn't expecting you for a couple hours, so we'll be able to have a nice, long exam." I fought back a shudder as I crossed the room to them and got on my knees.

*****

I was shaking as I left the office. Doc had made sure to keep me as long as possible, even giving me money for a cab so he could keep me an extra few minutes before sending me off to meet my next client. I desperately wanted to go home and shower, then get in bed and stay there for two or three days. But I still had two more clients to get through before this day was over.

I pulled on my big sweatshirt before entering the lobby of the upscale hotel near the Embarcadero. I hated places like this, they made me feel so self-conscious. I was forever worried about being identified as a hooker and kicked out by security. That had, of course, happened to me more than once, and it was always incredibly humiliating. I kept my head down and moved as quickly as I could without attracting attention, the key card already in my hand.

The card gave me access to the elevator, and I rode to the twelfth floor. When I let myself into the hotel room, I checked the time on the clock by the bed. I had only minutes to spare before the client was due to arrive. Doc really had kept me as long as he possibly could.

After undressing quickly, I grabbed a small bottle of lube and a couple condoms from my pack and hurried to the bed. I tucked the supplies under a pillow and got on my hands and knees facing away from the door, as instructed. *Please let this client be vanilla.* I fought to control a tremor in my right leg. My body was already so depleted, and I was emotionally raw. If this next client was rough with me, I didn't know how I'd handle it.

After just a couple minutes, the hotel room door clicked open behind me. I didn't turn around, I'd been told not to. Fear coursed through me. I hated this unknown factor. The man's footsteps were muffled on the carpeting as he crossed the room to me. I held back a flinch as his hand caressed my butt, and then slid between my legs and fondled my genitals. He was wasting no time.

"This is such a beautiful sight," the man said, his hand closing around my balls. "Even better than I'd imagined."

The voice was familiar.

Chapter Ten

I disobeyed orders by looking over my shoulder. Ian Tremont smiled down at me as panic shot through me.

"Hi Christopher. Or is it Austin, since you're on the clock? You know, it was very frustrating to find out that the boy that shot me down in my gallery was actually a whore. Why didn't you just put out like a good boy and save me the distastefulness of actually having to pay to fuck you?"

"How did you find out I was a prostitute?" My voice sounded so small.

"Oh, it wasn't hard. My family keeps a private investigator on the payroll, we like to know who we're working with." I swung off the bed, putting the mattress between us. His voice was low, dangerous, when he said, "Now, did I say you could get up? Get back on your knees, Christopher."

"No."

"I'm sorry?"

"No," I repeated. "I'm not going to do this. I said no at the gallery and I meant it. I'm not sleeping with you."

"You're bought and paid for, boy," Ian hissed. "Now get back on your fucking knees." His eyes were so cold, so cruel, his posture menacing.

I rushed across the room and grabbed my clothes and backpack, hugging them to my chest. "I'll make sure the agency gives you a full refund. But I *am not* doing this." Even though I was naked, I started to head for the door.

Ian stalked toward me and yelled, "If you go out that door, your career as a painter is *over!* Do you hear me, you fucking whore? Not only are you out of the new artists show, but I will see to it that you're blackballed in the art community!" I grabbed the door handle, and he yelled, "If you leave before I'm through with you, you will be *so fucking sorry!*"

I didn't even think about it, I just bolted from the room. A middle-aged couple stared at me as I ran naked down the hallway, anger and shame burning in me. Finally I got to the fire exit and burst through the door. I was afraid Ian might follow me, so instead of running down as he would expect me to, I ran up two flights of stairs. Only then did I dress myself, my hands shaking so violently I could barely get my clothes on.

I needed a few minutes to pull myself together, and curled up in a little ball on the cold concrete landing, hugging my knees to my chest tightly. I'd been stupid to run, and knew it was going to cost me – maybe my entire career. But I had felt so betrayed by Ian. I'd liked him and trusted him, and thought he respected me as a person and an artist. For him to then turn around and have me investigated, to buy me and bring me to a hotel, after I told him I wouldn't sleep with him? That hurt me and infuriated me in equal measure.

I stayed in the stairwell for a while, wanting to make sure Ian was long gone by the time I emerged. Finally, I pushed myself to my feet and took a few deep breaths to steady myself. I had one more appointment today. Just one. Then I could go home.

After riding the bus across town, I tried to put Ian out of my mind as I knocked on the door to the cheap motel room. The guy who opened the door was big and burly with buzzed off hair, a tight black t-shirt and an ugly smirk. He stepped aside, and when I came into the room I saw there were two more beefy alpha types waiting inside. Oh God, it was going to be a gang bang, probably a brutal one by the look of these guys. A little tremor went through me, but I fought to conceal it.

"Hi there, sweetheart," the man said. "So tell me, what do I get to do to you for the money I paid?"

My voice sounded thin to me as I said quietly, "Anything you want, as long as you wear a condom. Gang bangs cost extra, though."

"What's your name, sweetheart?"

"Austin." The lie was effortless. I studied the filthy, worn out carpeting, clutching the strap of my backpack tightly.

"Well Austin, the good news is, this isn't a gang bang," the man said as he pulled a pair of cuffs from the back of his waistband. "The bad news is, you're under arrest." He chuckled a little and added, "Or maybe it's bad news either way. Maybe you were looking forward to taking a bunch of dicks up your ass. Hmm?"

Panic flooded me, and without even thinking about it I whirled around and flailed for the door knob. The man's big hand shot out and grabbed me by the collar of my t-shirt, which tore right down to the hem as he whipped me around and slammed me against the motel room wall. I cried out as my cheekbone and mouth impacted, tasting blood and feeling it run down my chin as my lower lip split open.

He wrenched my arm painfully behind my back and said, "Really? You thought you could run? How fucking stupid are you?" A cold metal cuff was snapped onto my wrist, and he began to recite my Miranda rights. The amusement in his voice was unmistakable.

This can't be happening.

It felt like my entire life was unraveling. I was put into the back of a police van, and then I sat there at least a couple hours. Every twenty minutes or so, the doors opened and another boy was loaded into the van with me, his cuffs fastened to the metal bench like mine had been. I was miserable and shivering, my thin, torn t-shirt useless against the cold, and I was scared out of my mind.

I tried to calm down, tried to think. Who could I call to bail me out? I wished to God Charlie was in the country. He would have helped me, but no way was I going to bring this shit into his honeymoon. There was Hunter, but this was a hell of a lot to ask of a very new friend. Mrs. Dombruso? She'd bail me out, but I'd be so ashamed to have her find out I was a prostitute. Kieran also might have bailed me out, but he was the very last person I wanted to see me like this, and I hoped to God he didn't work wherever I was being taken.

Finally we were driven across town, then led from the van and brought into the police station single file, hands cuffed behind our backs. We were deposited on wooden benches along one side of a big room full of desks, and as I fought back my panic, I looked around me. Eight other boys had been brought in with me, and there were already about a dozen young men and women on the benches when we arrived. Some of the younger ones were in tears, while others were trying to appear indifferent. I didn't recognize any of them, but our clothes made it pretty clear we were all in the same line of work.

Suddenly, a commotion across the room caught everyone's attention. Larry and Doc were being led in, both handcuffed, and Doc was absolutely furious, his face red, his voice raised. He was yelling about his constitutional rights and about suing the entire police force. An older woman was being led in with them. I knew she ran one of the other big escort services in town, though her name escaped me. This had obviously been a major sting operation, and I wondered if more agencies had been targeted besides those two.

A few police officers were watching this spectacle, and obviously all of this was highly entertaining to them. They joked and laughed, leaning against a couple of the desks. Callous bunch of assholes. What could they possibly find funny about any of this?

I pressed my eyes shut for a few moments and took a deep breath. I felt like throwing up, and desperately wanted to wake up from this nightmare. More than anything, I just wanted to go home.

And then this entire terrible situation got so much worse. I glanced up, and locked eyes with a police officer that had just come into the room. *Oh God, no. Please, no.*

Kieran stood rooted in place, eyes wide, lips parted in surprise. We just stared at each other for one very long moment across the sea of desks. It felt like time stopped moving, both of us suspended there.

In the next instant, Doc went completely ballistic. He kicked over a chair, yelling at the top of his lungs, and all the officers that had been watching the proceedings like it was their favorite TV show snapped into action, rushing to restrain him. Doc managed to kick one of them in the balls before three more officers took him down, face-planting him onto the linoleum.

I'd been so distracted by the pandemonium that the hand grabbing my arm startled me. I looked up at Kieran as he pulled me to my feet without a word and marched me to the back of the station. Along the way, we passed a big pile of bags and purses that had been heaped on one of the desks, and he snatched up my backpack, the one with the big sunburst drawn on it, without breaking his stride. He led me down a long hallway, pushed open a door marked 'emergency exit' and dragged me out into a little alley.

"Kieran, what are you doing?" He unlocked the cuffs around my wrists, and when my hands were free I turned to stare at him. "But you could lose your job." My voice was a hoarse whisper.

"Go," he said, his expression unreadable. "Get out of here." He thrust my backpack at me and ducked back into the station, the heavy door swinging shut behind him.

I stared at the closed door for a long moment, completely stunned. Then I dropped to my knees and unzipped my backpack as my hands shook violently and my heart raced. I took out my big, hooded sweatshirt, put it on over the torn t-shirt and pulled the hood up over my hair, then quickly checked for my ID. It was still in the pack. I zipped the backpack and slung it over my shoulder, and walked out of the alley at a steady, unhurried pace. I waited until I was a full two blocks from the police station before I started sprinting.

Chapter Eleven

I'd never been so happy to be home in all my life. I shucked my clothes on the way to the bathroom, and stood in the shower until every drop of hot water was used up. Then I got dressed in layer after layer of clothes, capping it all off with Kieran's big fisherman sweater. His pleasant scent enveloped me, providing as much comfort as the sweater itself.

God, Kieran. Why had he helped me? I was so grateful, but it also made me sad that he'd risked his job for me. He'd done something that I was sure must be completely out of character. And he'd done it right after discovering that I was a whore. I hoped to God that his temporary lapse in judgment wouldn't end up costing him his career.

I climbed in bed, wrapping myself up tightly and pulling the blankets over my head, leaving only a tiny opening to breathe through. My body trembled as all of the adrenaline from this evening drained away.

After a while, I started mulling over some practical issues, like what I was going to do to support myself. The escort service was obviously out of business, probably some of the others in town had been shut down tonight as well. If I couldn't find a job with another agency I'd have to go back to working the street, a proposition that filled me with dread. I knew all too well how dangerous that was. Plus, with the current crackdown on prostitution, there was a very good chance I'd wind up right back in jail if I did that. I couldn't really see any alternatives, though.

And God, then there was the thing with Ian. I wondered if he'd make good on his threat to blackball me in the art community. If he was serious about that, then my career as an artist was over before it had even begun. If I couldn't get a gallery to represent me, what was left? Selling my paintings at coffee houses for a few bucks? Okay, sure, that would still allow me paint, but I'd had much higher aspirations, such big dreams about making art that mattered and being respected for it. That dream was all I'd had to hold on to.

I remembered suddenly that eight of my best paintings were at Tremont's gallery. I'd have to go tomorrow and get them back, because Ian was probably enough of an asshole to throw them out now that I was no longer in the new artists show. Man, was that going to suck.

I lay there for a long time, cocooned in blankets, trying to think through my problems. And every time I heard a siren, which was often in this city, I flinched, my heart rate speeding up, my body going into high alert. I felt like a fugitive, with this irrational fear that the police were going to track me down and drag me back to the station.

So when a loud knock rattled my front door, I leapt out of bed like a shot. I knew I was being stupid. The police had no way of tracking me down, unless Kieran had second thoughts and turned me in. But that would get him in all sorts of trouble, so it wasn't likely.

I opened the door to Kieran, and we both just watched each other for a long moment. Finally, I stepped back and he came into the apartment. He was in full uniform right down to the gun, which made me more than a little uncomfortable. A radio receiver on his shoulder made it clear he was still on duty.

He was obviously angry, which instantly put me on the defensive. I already felt so ashamed at how he'd found me, my emotions on edge after the day I'd had. I was sure he was going to tell me off, as if I needed someone to lecture me about how wrong it was to work as a hooker.

"Tell me they made a mistake," he said. "Tell me you're not a prostitute."

"There was no mistake," I said quietly.

He absorbed that for a beat, then took hold of my chin, turning my injured cheek toward him. His voice was low when he asked, "Who hurt you?"

"It doesn't matter," I mumbled.

"Did one of the arresting officers do this to you?"

"What difference does it make?"

"Was it Jorgensen? Big white guy with a crew cut?"

I stepped back from him, pulling out of his grasp and wrapping my arms around myself. "I have no idea what his name was."

"So this *was* done to you by a police officer."

"I tried to run," I said. "It was stupid. That got me thrown against a wall, which is when my face got banged up. The cop didn't smack me around or anything, if that's your concern." Kieran swore under his breath, and I mumbled, "I really don't know what difference it makes. What am I going to do, press charges? Like anything would happen to him. The police don't care when boys like me get hurt. No one does."

"*I* care." When I didn't respond to that, he asked, "Have you had run-ins with the police before? Is that why you were so uncomfortable when you found out what I did for a living?"

I looked up at him and frowned. "I'd never been taken into custody before, and it probably wouldn't have happened tonight either if my head had been in the game. I *have* had to deal with the police before, though."

"That can't be uncommon in your line of work."

I stared at him for a long moment, then said, "It wasn't while I was working. A little over a year ago I was drugged, raped, and almost beaten to death while on the job. The officer that came to take my statement when I was in the hospital was sweet as could be. Right up until the moment I told him I was a prostitute."

His eyes went wide, his lips parting slightly. I ground my teeth together before continuing, "It was really special to watch the way his eyes glazed over, to notice how he stopped taking notes as soon as he found out what I was. His entire attitude changed, the way he talked to me, the way he looked at me. It was like I stopped being a person to him. What had been done to me didn't really seem to matter anymore."

"I'm so sorry that happened to you," he said, his tone softening.

"What part?"

"All of it. Did they ever find the person that hurt you?"

"Hell no. They probably barely investigated."

"You don't know that."

"I know no one ever followed up with me. And no one was caught. Because like I said, cops don't give a shit about what happens to boys like me."

Kieran stared at me for a long moment, a little muscle working in his jaw. He crossed his arms over his chest, and finally said in a low voice, "I want you to explain it to me."

"Explain what?"

"Explain how a boy as smart and beautiful and talented as you could sell yourself for sex. Explain to me how you could treat yourself like that."

"I don't have to explain anything to you." I was definitely on the defensive, bracing myself, waiting for him to start yelling at me.

Even though he was angry, he kept his voice level as he said, "I need to understand this. I need to understand how the most amazing guy I've ever met lets himself get fucked for money. Because honestly? That's the most baffling thing I've ever come across in my entire life."

I muttered, "It's not like I had a lot of career options as a fifteen-year-old runaway."

"Oh God," he said softly. I hadn't been looking for pity, and I really didn't want to offer him excuses. But that was the truth of it.

I said, "It was a question of survival back then. And yeah, I kept doing it, because really, what difference did it make if I sold myself a little or a lot? I was already a whore, so I kept turning tricks. It pays for school and it keeps a roof over my head, and I really don't need you judging me for it. I already judge myself plenty."

"I'm not judging you, I'm just trying to understand."

"I don't need you to understand this, Kieran. Just like I don't need to understand how the fuck you're a cop. I don't need to understand how you can be a part of a group of people that can come and take a statement from a boy in the hospital, a boy that was almost beaten to death, who's so fucking scared and severely injured, and treat him like garbage because of what he's had to do to survive!" I really didn't want to lash out at Kieran, but it was so hard to separate him from every other cop I'd ever had to deal with as he stood there in that uniform.

"That was one individual! We're not all like that. I would never treat a victim that way, not in a million years!"

"I know that." We stood there awkwardly for a long moment, and eventually I blurted, "Why did you help me tonight, Kieran? Why did you risk your job like that?"

"I had to. When I saw you there, I didn't think, I just reacted." He looked away. "I've never done anything like that. You're right that I risked my job. But I *had to*. I didn't have it in me to leave you there, not when you looked so fragile, with your shirt torn and your face bruised and bloody—"

"I'm not fragile. There's nothing fragile about me," I insisted, instantly back on the defensive. "And I didn't need you to swoop in and save me."

Kieran sighed in frustration. "Come on, Christopher. Is it really so hard to admit you needed me tonight?"

"I don't need anyone," I mumbled, wrapping my arms around myself.

"Keep telling yourself that."

"It's the truth. I've taken care of myself since I was a kid."

"You call *this* taking care of yourself?"

"I've done the best I could." I tried to sound strong, but my voice shook a little. Kieran's expression softened and he started to reach for me, but I pulled back and said emphatically, "It may not look like it to you, but I'm doing okay. I'm surviving. I *don't* need anyone, and that's just the way I want it."

He said quietly, "If you don't need anyone, then I don't know what I'm doing here." He started to leave, swinging the front door open. But then he paused and turned back to me. "But did you ever stop to consider the fact that maybe *I* need *you*? I need you so fucking much that it scares the shit out of me, and if you think that's easy for me to admit, you're dead wrong. And, I don't know,

maybe I helped you tonight as much for myself as for you."
He left the apartment, the door clicking shut behind him.

I stared after him for a long moment. He needed me?

Kieran needed me.

Those words had a huge impact on me. I felt protective
of him all of a sudden, and completely remorseful for
acting so defensive. I'd been so caught up in my own
drama that I hadn't even stopped to consider his feelings in
any of this. I flung the door open and stepped into the hall.
"Kieran, wait!"

He stopped walking, even as he asked, "Why?"

I said softly, "Come back. Please?"

"My dinner break was over ten minutes ago. I have to
go back to work." He remained rooted in place, though.

"Thank you for getting me out of there."

He looked over his shoulder and watched me for a long
moment, then said, "You're welcome."

"I don't know how to repay you for what you did."

"Who says you need to repay me?"

"I do. I was so scared tonight. And what you did for
me…it was huge, Kieran. My whole life, I've tried so hard
to be self-reliant, to make sure I never depended on anyone.
But now I feel indebted to you, and I don't know what to
do with that."

"I really don't expect anything in return."

"I know, but still."

"I have to go back to work," he said again, his expression unreadable. I wanted to go to him and take him in my arms. But I didn't know if he'd pull away from me, and I would hate it so much if he did. So I stayed where I was.

I nodded, wrapping my arms around myself, and he slid a little switch on the receiver on his shoulder and spoke into it, reporting that he was back on duty. He took a long look at me before turning and heading down the hall.

*****

I was laying in the dark, staring at the ceiling when my phone rang sometime in the middle of the night. I glanced at Kieran's name on the screen and answered with a quiet, "Hi."

"Hi. Did I wake you?"

"No. I couldn't sleep."

"Me neither."

"I'm sorry about earlier, Kieran. I shouldn't have lashed out at you."

"I'm sorry too. I shouldn't have come over like that and confronted you, not when I was so upset and angry."

"I should have told you sooner how I made a living," I said. "You had a right to know."

He was quiet for a few moments before saying, "What are we going to do about this, Christopher?"

"What do you mean?"

"A cop dating a prostitute. How do we make that work?" he asked.

I sat up in bed. "You still want to date me? Are you kidding?"

"You're all I think about, and that's been the case since the moment I met you. Your career choice might piss me off, but it doesn't change how I feel about you."

I grinned a little and swung out of bed, wandering into the living room. "Right back at ya."

He chuckled and said, "My career choice pisses you off?"

"A little bit, yeah. Even though I know that's just me being prejudiced. It's wrong to judge the whole lot of you by a few assholes."

"Given the way you were treated, both today and after your assault, I get it. I think I'd hate cops too, if I was in your shoes."

"I don't hate cops. I merely dislike and distrust them. But that's never applied to you," I said as I paced slowly around the living room.

"Good to know." After a pause, he said, "I want to reopen your case, Christopher. If the investigating officer didn't give it due diligence, it needs to be reexamined. The man that hurt you needs to be behind bars."

"Do you have the authority to do that?"

"No, but my Uncle Ray does. He's a senior detective, he could easily reopen the case if I asked him."

I perched on the windowsill in the living room and rested my head against the glass, a little shiver going through me. "Maybe you shouldn't do that."

"Why not?"

"Because," I said softly, "Even if you find him, your only evidence is the testimony of a hooker. Think that's going to stand up in court?"

"We have to try. There might be other victims, he could still be hurting people."

"Oh God, what if that's true?"

"I'm going to reopen the case."

After a pause, I said quietly, "Okay. I'll do whatever I can to help you catch this guy."

"Did you ever meet with a police sketch artist?"

"No, but there's really no reason to do that."

"Why not?"

"Because I can draw him for you more accurately than any sketch artist. I know exactly what he looks like."

"Really? You remember him clearly, even months later?" he asked.

"I have recurring nightmares about what he did to me, so I constantly recall what he looks like. I wasn't...I wasn't unconscious yet when he...." The lump in my throat cut me off.

"Jesus," Kieran whispered.

I was still perched on the windowsill, and noticed a rusty Mustang parked across the street. When I shifted my position, I saw a familiar shape silhouetted on the front steps of my building, holding a phone to his ear. I wondered why Kieran hadn't come up and knocked on my door.

I said, "Am I going to have to come down to the station if you reopen the case? Because after my abrupt departure earlier tonight, maybe that's not the best idea. The douchebag that arrested me might recognize me."

"That's another thing. Jorgensen shouldn't get away with injuring you. He's always teetered right on the line when it comes to excessive force."

"We can't do anything about that, Kieran," I said. "Not without calling attention to the fact that you broke the rules and turned your boyfriend loose after he was arrested."

"Boyfriend?" he repeated. I could hear the smile in his voice.

The color rose in my cheeks. "I didn't even realize I'd said that."

"That's what I want, though. We're already so much more than friends with benefits. Aren't we?"

"Yes. Although I don't have an answer to your earlier question. I have no idea how a cop and a rent boy date. Actually, I've never had any idea how a prostitute could date *anyone* without the job being a major issue."

"You'll just have to quit."

"It's not that simple."

"Of course it is."

I sighed and rested my forehead against the glass again. "If I quit, then I have to drop out of school. Sutherlin costs a small fortune. And I made a promise to myself that I was going to finish my education, no matter what. I'm not going back on that, not even for you."

"What about student loans?"

"Not eligible."

"So, borrow what you need to pay your tuition from me. I inherited some money when my dad died. It's probably more than enough to see you through."

"Thanks, but no. I don't do that."

"Borrow money? Why not?" After a beat he added, "Wait, don't tell me. It's part of that 'I don't need anyone' thing you've got going on, right?"

"I don't."

"*Everyone* needs other people. The expression is *no man is an island*. It's not *no man is an island except Christopher Andrews*. And needing other people doesn't make you weak, or vulnerable, or whatever it is you're worried about. It just makes you human."

"I've been let down in the past. Whenever I depended on others, they failed me drastically. I never want to be in the position of relying on anyone ever again."

"I can swear that I'll never let you down, but I don't expect you to believe me."

I said softly, "Come upstairs, Kieran."

He glanced over his shoulder and saw me at the window. For a long moment neither of us moved, just staring at each other across the distance. Finally he got up and disappeared from sight.

I was waiting for him in the open doorway to my apartment. When he reached me, Kieran stopped right in front of me, watching me for a long moment. And then he tilted my chin up gently and kissed me.

I took his hand and led him to the bedroom, and he kicked his shoes off before getting under the covers fully clothed. Immediately, we gravitated into each other's arms. We were both quiet for a while, his fingertips idly tracing my spine through the three layers of clothing I was wearing. Eventually I whispered, "I have absolutely no idea how you and I are going to make this work."

"Me neither. But we'll figure it out."

"I hope so."

He looked up at me. "You do?"

"I want you, Kieran. Even though I don't think I'm capable of being in a relationship, of truly trusting someone and letting them get close to me."

"But you want this. You want me," he said softly.

"Yes. God, so much."

"So that's our starting point." He kissed my cheek and settled comfortably into my arms.

Chapter Twelve

I awoke before Kieran and watched him sleep for a while, before leaning in and kissing him gently. He grinned, eyes still closed, and returned the kiss. We spent a long time like this, wrapped up in each other's arms, our kisses sweet and unhurried. Finally he opened his eyes just a little, his expression blissful and content, and said, "Hi baby."

"Hi." I smiled at him and leaned in and kissed him again, hugging his body to mine. I felt so good right in that moment, so calm and relaxed, the nightmare of yesterday pushed so far back that it almost felt like it had happened to someone else. It would have been wonderful to spend the whole day right here, just like this.

But we were soon interrupted by enthusiastic, rhythmic knocking. I rolled out of bed and opened the front door to find Hunter beaming at me. "Never fear, your muse is here," he announced, sweeping past me into the apartment. He was again dressed all in black, a sleek leather messenger bag resting against his narrow hips.

"What time is it?"

"Ten a.m., sunshine. You know, you have the most out of control bedhead ever," he said with a big smile, reaching out and rumpling my curls. "It's awesome."

"I hate morning people," I said with a grin.

"But you love me." He was still flashing his perfect smile.

"Yes, but I'll have to rethink that if you persist with this alarming level of perkiness. Why are you so happy today, anyway?"

"I had a good night."

"What was his name?"

He thought about that for a minute, then said, "I have no idea, actually. But damn, was he sexy. I think he was Brazilian. Neither of us understood a word the other was saying. It was the perfect twelve hour relationship." He winked at me before taking a drink from the fifty-five gallon drum of a coffee cup in his hand, and flipped his sunglasses up onto the top of his head.

All of a sudden, his expression became grave. "Sweetie, what happened to your face?"

"It's nothing," I said. He still looked concerned, so I added, "Seriously, I'm fine. No cause for alarm."

"Did it happen on the job?"

"Yes. Now could we please stop talking about it?" I said.

"Do you swear you're alright?"

"I swear. Please, let's talk about something else."

Hunter knit his brows and finally nodded, his blue eyes troubled. Kieran came into the living room a moment later, and Hunter hit him with a smile, letting the subject drop for my benefit. "Well hi there, you must be Kieran. I'm Hunter."

My friend stuck out a slender, graceful hand, and Kieran shook it as he said, "Hi Hunter. Why do you look familiar?"

"Because you watch gay porn." Hunter grinned at him as I fought back a laugh, and Kieran turned an interesting shade of pink.

"Oh. Um…right."

I said, "Hunter is helping me with my term project. I forgot that he was coming over this morning."

"Christopher is drawing, painting and sculpting me. Don't worry, it's all very tasteful. Disappointingly so," Hunter said with a wink. Then he exclaimed, "Oh!" and set his coffee cup down on an end table. He flung open his messenger bag and pulled out a copy of the Chronicle with a flourish. "I almost forgot! Guess who's featured in today's paper?" A big color photo of one of my paintings was on the front page of the arts section.

"Shit," I murmured, sinking onto the back of the sofa.

Hunter raised an eyebrow at me. "Hmm. I was expecting rejoicing and group hugs, not terse statements involving excrement."

"I, um…I'm not in the new artists show at the Tremont Gallery anymore," I said quietly.

"Why not?" Hunter wanted to know.

I explained what had happened with Ian as concisely as possible. When I concluded, Kieran was livid, and Hunter growled, "I fucking hate rich people. They think they can have anything they want. What a total douchebag."

"I'm so glad you didn't sleep with him," Kieran muttered.

"Me too," I said. "I knew I sunk my career as an artist when I left that hotel room. But there was no way I could go through with it when I felt so betrayed by him."

Hunter looked from Kieran to me, then said, "So, um…looks like everything's out in the open with you two now, huh?"

"Yeah. Kieran knows I'm a prostitute."

"I'm glad you guys finally talked about it," Hunter said. Kieran and I both shifted uncomfortably, and seeing this, Hunter blurted, "Well, anyway, it's Tremont's loss that you won't be in his art show. You should read this article." He was still clutching the newspaper, and held it up and gave it a little shake. "The reporter raves about your paintings, and people are going to flock to the gallery expecting to see them. Tremont's going to look like an idiot when he has to explain that you're not in the show any more because he was too much of an asshole to take no for an answer."

"I'm guessing that's not exactly the explanation he'll offer. And shit, that reminds me that I need to go get my paintings back from the gallery this morning, before Ian throws them out or something. That's going to be awkward as hell."

"I'll go with you," Kieran said. "I'll even go in uniform if you want, in case he gives you trouble about returning the paintings."

"Oh yum, that's right, you have a uniform," Hunter purred. "Damn, I need to find me one of you. Do you have a brother, by chance?"

"I do," Kieran said with a little frown. "He's an asshole."

"I don't have a problem with that."

"And he's straight."

"Says you." Hunter was still smiling. But then he remembered the conversation in progress and said, "Wear the uniform, it'll shake Tremont up. I'll go with you guys, too." He tossed the newspaper on the couch, then snatched up his coffee cup. "So come on. Let's go rescue

Christopher's masterpieces from the big bad billionaire before the douche disposes of them."

"This isn't a group effort, Hunter," I said. "I'm going to go get my paintings back by myself. I appreciate the offer, though."

"Why would you do this by yourself?" Hunter exclaimed. "That Tremont asshole might give you a hard time, you need backup."

Kieran sighed and said, "Christopher has a thing about accepting help from others. I assume that's what this is."

"Well, tough shit. I'm going along. Just try and stop me," Hunter said, tilting his head back and looking at me with narrowed eyes, as if challenging me to disagree with him.

I sighed and said, "I'm going to get a shower. Then I'm sneaking out the bathroom window so neither of you tries to come along."

"How about if we go with you, but wait in the car?" Kieran asked. "Does that violate your independence policy? We promise not to do anything that could be construed as helpful." He was teasing me a little, a half-smile on his full lips.

I sighed and said, "Fine, you can wait in the car. But no macho jump-in-and-save-poor-little-Christopher maneuvers. I mean it. I've got this."

"Well," Hunter said with a grin, popping up the collar of his leather jacket. "I can *try* to reel in all this macho. But it's not going to be easy." I smiled at that and kissed his cheek on the way to the bathroom.

When I returned to the living room fifteen minutes later, Hunter and Kieran were glued to the TV playing my football video game. "Hey look," I said with a smile, coming up to the back of the couch and absently gathering Hunter's silky hair into a ponytail. "You found someone else to kick your ass at Madden." I was dressed in my best outfit (a black button-down shirt and black pants, which made me look like a Hunter wanna-be), concealer cream hiding the bruise on my cheek and the already-healing split lip.

"I'll have you know I'm winning," Hunter said.

"But only because I've never played this before," Kieran pointed out, his brows knit as he jerked the controller in a half circle.

I dropped Hunter's hair back onto his shoulders and said, "You two have fun. I'll be back in a bit," then turned and tried to flee the apartment.

Both men dropped the game controllers and scampered around the couch after me. "Nice try," Kieran said. "But you said we could come along, remember?"

"I only said you could wait in the car," I said, and swung the front door open. I gasped at the sight of Stana Dombruso on my doorstep, skinny arm raised as if she'd been about to knock. She was dressed like an escapee from a 1980's jazzercise video in a purple leotard, hot pink tights, purple legwarmers, and a thick, hot pink headband. The ensemble was topped off with a demure white cardigan and a giant black handbag.

"Oh good, I caught you at home, Christopher Robin," she said. "I was just on my way to the gym to check out all the hunks. Seems like a good place to meet men, don't you think? I wanted to see if you could come with me, maybe give me a few pointers on how to use all that exercise equipment. I don't wanna look like a poser."

I smiled at that. "I've never been to a gym in my life. But you know who has? Both of these guys. Kieran and Hunter would be more than happy to show you the ropes. I actually have something I need to do."

"And we're going with you," Hunter chimed in.

"Oh," said Mrs. Dombruso. "Where are you boys off to?"

Before I could get a word out, Hunter blurted, "We're on our way to get Christopher's paintings back from a despicable gallery owner that wronged him."

Mrs. Dombruso's watery brown eyes lit up. "Screw the gym! That sounds like way more fun. Count me in!"

"Oh dear God," I mumbled under my breath. Then I said, "I'm going alone. Thank you, all of you, but no."

It was as if I hadn't even spoken. Mrs. Dombruso rubbed her bony hands together and said, "Oh boy, I haven't gotten to threaten a scumbag in ages! Hang on a second…." She fished around in her handbag, then shoved a huge pair of glasses on her face. She kept digging in the bag for another minute before pulling out an enormous silver handgun. "There we go. Good thing I brought along Dirty Harry. I almost went with a puny little Saturday Night Special today. But it's as if I somehow knew I'd be seeing some action."

Kieran immediately went into cop mode. "Ma'am," he said, his body becoming tense, "I'm going to have to ask you to hand over the weapon."

"Fuck that! Get your own gun," she said, dropping it back into her handbag.

"Are you aware that it's illegal to carry a concealed weapon in the state of California?" Kieran asked her. I had to grin.

She fished in her purse again and pulled out a wrinkled rectangle of paper. "Don't get your shorts in a bunch, sexy. I got my permit to carry concealed right here. Damn, if I didn't know better, I'd swear you sounded just like a cop. And that would suck, because I saw the way you made my Christopher Robin's eyes light up at my grandson's wedding. So I'd sure hate to find out he'd gotten himself mixed up with one of *that kind*."

Kieran shot me a look, and I gave him an apologetic smile and a pat on the arm. Mrs. Dombruso whirled on the heel of her white Keds and said, "Come on, let's go bust some heads!" She hurried out of the apartment.

"You both want to help?" I asked Hunter and Kieran. "Keep Mrs. Dombruso from wrecking the gallery, and/or shooting Ian Tremont." I rushed after her.

I was surprised to find a white stretch limo double-parked in front of the apartment. "I feel like I'm going to prom," Hunter said with a giggle as he and I climbed in after Mrs. Dombruso.

"Nana, why didn't you return the limo after the wedding?" I asked her.

"I figure, life is short. Especially when you're eighty. Why not live it up a little?" she said. I couldn't argue with that logic.

Kieran pulled the door shut and slid onto the seat beside me, and we were off. He picked up my hand and held it firmly on the drive across town. Even though I was acting tough, he knew I was nervous. I couldn't let myself be intimidated by Ian Tremont though, because my paintings were too important to me. I'd given him the very best I had for the art show, and they were coming home with me.

When we pulled up in front of the pristine white gallery, I hopped out at the curb before the limo had fully stopped moving and gaped at the front of the building. Two vertical fabric banners, each about five by twelve feet, hung on either side of the front door. *New Artists Show* was spelled out at the top. And on both banners was a huge full-color reproduction of one of my paintings. It was actually an intensely personal piece depicting a five-year-old boy standing alone at the side of a road. I'd struggled with the decision to include it in the show, but it was the single best thing I had ever done, and I'd wanted it to be my way of introducing myself to the art world. Seeing it used as advertisement and hanging outside that asshole's gallery filled me with rage.

Kieran went ahead of me and held the door to the gallery open. Impulsively, I grabbed both banners, one in each hand, and pulled. They fluttered from their moorings, and I dragged them through the door.

A camera flash caught me off guard, but I didn't break my stride. Several people were in the center of the gallery,

Tremont among them, and they all turned to me wide-eyed as I swept in, the banners billowing behind me.

"Who the hell are you?" a stuck-up sales associate with a pinched face wanted to know.

I ignored him and marched up to Tremont, letting my indignation carry me along in place of actual confidence. I decided as long as I was making a spectacle of myself to take it all the way, and said in a loud voice as I dropped the banners on the floor, "I've come for mah paintings, Tremont. Y'all obviously won't be needing 'em anymore. Not after kickin' me out of the new artists show and threatenin' to blackball me in the arts community because I refused to sleep with you." Damn, my accent dial was set to Maximum Scarlett O'Hara. But other than that, I was proud of myself for holding it together as well as I was.

Tremont went full-on deer-in-headlights and stammered, "Now Christopher, let's just calm down, okay? Some things were said yesterday, you and I had a bit of a misunderstanding. Of course I still want you in the show, you're our featured artist."

An elegant-looking woman of about sixty exclaimed, "Featured artist? Is this C.R. Andrews?"

"Yes, ma'am," I said, extending my hand, which she shook. "You can call me Christopher."

"I'm Mary Malloy, Fine Arts editor of Stylemaker Weekly. Mr. Tremont didn't mention the fact that you were out of the show. In fact, he told me he's representing you, and was just singing your praises."

"Forgive me for sayin' so ma'am, but Ian Tremont is a lyin' sack a shit. I'm not under contract with this gallery, and in fact, I've just come to collect mah paintings." God I wished I could reel in my accent, but it was off and running like a – if you'll excuse my total southern breakdown – thirty pound catfish on a twenty pound line.

"Oh," Mary said, raising a well-shaped eyebrow. "Then who represents you, Christopher?"

"No one."

"Yet," Hunter chimed in from somewhere close beside me.

Mary grinned at me. "I'm guessing you'll be getting plenty of offers after the article in today's paper. That reporter was highly impressed with you, and after seeing your work and meeting you in person, I can see why." She gestured to the left, and I noticed my paintings neatly displayed on a white wall in an adjoining room.

"It was a pleasure meetin' you, Ms. Malloy. Now if you'll please excuse me, I'm going to collect my paintings and be on my way."

The photographer ran ahead of me and began snapping photos. I assumed he was with Ms. Malloy, but I didn't really know or care. I reached my first painting and gingerly removed it from the wall, then popped it carefully from the frame Ian had put it in. I set the frame down and handed the painting to Kieran, who was right beside me. He gave me a big smile as the flash went off again. Hunter and Mrs. Dombruso saw what I was doing and also began removing and unframing my paintings.

The photographer said, "Damn, this is some good stuff," as he kept clicking away. "And here I thought this was going to be a dry puff piece about an upcoming gallery show. Instead, we're witnessing the birth of art's new bad boy." That was so ridiculous that I had to grin.

It took only a minute to remove the paintings with all of us working together, and then we headed for the door, each of us carrying two canvases. The photographer hadn't stopped taking pictures, and he asked me, "Who are these people with you, Christopher?"

"We're his entourage," Mrs. Dombruso chimed in. "All the best artists have one, you know." She flashed him a big smile as he snapped her picture. "Is my photo gonna be in Stylemaker Weekly?" she asked him. "I was just on my way to work out when I got called in to help

Christopher," she said. "Normally my personal style is a lot more, you know. Edgy."

I held the door open for her and my friends, and they filtered out in a row. The photographer followed us onto the sidewalk and snapped a few photos of Hunter before suddenly lowering the camera and stammering, "Oh my God, you're Hunter Storm! I'm a huge fan. Huge!"

My friend grinned at him. "Dude, that's like walking up to someone and saying, 'Hi. I watch a ton of porn.' I appreciate the sentiment, though," Hunter said with a wink before climbing into the limo.

I handed one of the canvases I was holding to Kieran after he climbed in the vehicle, and the photographer said, "Could you hold that one up, Christopher?" I did as he asked, and he fired off a dozen shots. I happened to be holding my favorite painting, the one of the young boy, which had been printed onto the banners. Okay, the one representing me as a kid right before my mother's funeral. Like I said, this one was intensely personal.

Ian, who had frantically been trying to explain himself to Mary Malloy during all of that, caught up to me and said, "Christopher, can I have a moment? Maybe we can work something out here."

I leaned in and whispered, "Can you even begin to comprehend what a total lowlife someone has to be to get turned down by a prostitute?" And then I got in the limo and pulled the door shut.

As we rolled down the street, my friends erupted into cheers and applause. "I stand corrected," Kieran said with a big smile. "You really didn't need any help with that. You were amazing."

I leaned in and kissed him, then collapsed against the seat. "I'm grateful for the moral support. That was scary as hell."

Hunter said, "You seemed cool as ice. Well, except for your accent going full-on Jimmy-Jeb-Joe-Bob. But oh my God, the way you dragged those banners in behind you! Way to make an entrance, you diva!" He looked absolutely delighted.

"I was just really angry. I wasn't actually trying to make a scene."

"Since when are you southern, by the way?" Kieran asked with a grin.

"He's from Georgia, but pretends he's not," Hunter supplied helpfully.

"That was more fun than I've had in ages," Mrs. Dombruso said, her dark eyes sparkling. "Beats the hell out of the gym, I'll tell you that right now. Though it would have been even more fun if I'd gotten to brandish my piece."

"Christ," Kieran muttered.

She dropped us back at my apartment, and Hunter and Kieran helped me carry my paintings upstairs. Hunter kissed my cheek and said, "You're my hero, Christopher Robin. Way to stand up for yourself. Now I'd better run, I'm going to try to make it to yoga class since I'm not posing for you today."

"You haven't been working much lately," I observed as I walked him to the door.

"Nope. I made a film a week for each of the last twenty-two weeks. You know what that is? That's too damn much Hunter Storm. I'm taking a little break." He called goodbye to Kieran, and waved over his shoulder before disappearing down the hall.

I closed the door behind him and turned to Kieran, who was watching me with a wicked grin. "You know what you need?" he asked, his voice low and sexy.

"Victory sex?"

"Exactly." He grabbed me in a fireman's carry and jogged into the bedroom as I let out a startled laugh, and deposited me on the edge of the bed. We both stripped quickly, and then he fell to his knees and dove onto my cock.

"Damn. Triumphing over evil gallery owners really makes you horny," I joked as he took me down his throat.

He sucked me for a few moments before pulling off me and saying, "*You* make me horny. You were amazing. I've never seen confidence like that." He licked and kissed his way down my shaft.

"I was mad, not confident."

"Either way, you were fucking awesome. When you pulled down those banners and trailed them in behind you, you looked like a rock star. I wanted to fall down on my knees and worship you." He looked up at me with a grin and a gleam in his eyes. "And now I can." He took my cock in his mouth again and sucked me until I was hard and throbbing between his lips.

Kieran was shaking with anticipation when he finally slid his mouth off of me, his cock pressed up against his flat belly and leaking precum. He got on his knees on the edge of the mattress and spread his legs wide, his gorgeous ass completely exposed for me, and said, "Make me yours, Christopher."

"With pleasure," I murmured as I quickly deployed a condom and worked lube into Kieran's little opening.

I stood behind him and grabbed his hips as I pushed my cock into his body. We fucked hard and fast, and I reached under him and jerked him off as I pounded him. His tight hole milked me perfectly, his big, powerful body glistening with sweat as he drove himself back onto me again and again. We both came within seconds of each other, yelling so loudly they probably heard us a block over.

After I cleaned us both up a little I climbed on top of Kieran, who was now flat on his back on the mattress. I straddled him with my knees on either side of him, supporting my weight, my arms around his shoulders, and he wrapped his arms around me and held me for a while before saying quietly, "I hate to bring down our good mood, but we really should go see my uncle today. I want your case reopened as soon as possible."

"Okay, we can do that." I didn't move though, and neither did he. "Or we could just stay like this all day."

"We can come back to bed after we go to the station. I have the day off. We can go right back to this position."

"Just five more minutes. Please?"

"Sure baby," he said, nuzzling my hair.

After a while I said quietly, "You realize that asking your uncle to reopen this case means he's going to find out you're dating a prostitute."

"I know."

"That doesn't concern you?"

"I can deal with it."

After another minute I said, "I'm going to have to go back to work, either today or tomorrow. I guess I'm going to have to start working the street again, since my escort service must be out of business now."

"Over my dead body."

I raised myself up on my elbows and looked at him. "Excuse me?"

"You heard me. Over my dead body are you going back to prostitution." He said it calmly and levelly, holding my gaze.

"It's not really your call, Kieran."

"I'm making it my call. You're no longer a sex worker. It's that simple." There was no challenge in his voice or his expression, he was merely stating a fact.

I raised an eyebrow at him. "I don't actually respond well to being told what to do."

"I know."

"So what do you think you're going to do, exactly? Are you going to tie me to the bed and prevent me from leaving the apartment?"

He grinned a little at that. "If anyone was getting tied to the bed, it'd probably be me. Don't you agree?"

I sat up, still straddling his naked body, and crossed my arms over my chest. "I'm serious. You can't decide this for me."

"Stop being so stubborn, Christopher."

"I'm not being stubborn, I'm being realistic. If I stop working, I'm homeless within a month. Again. Because yeah, been there, done that, and let me tell you, it sucked. And then in two months when my tuition comes due, I'm out of school. And there goes my future, every dream I ever had, all my plans and every promise I made myself."

"Or," Kieran said, relaxing under me and tucking a hand behind his head, "you and I draw up a formal document outlining the terms of the interest-free loan I'm going to give you, you keep paying your rent and tuition, and you stop working a job that's endangering your life."

"We talked about that."

"We didn't really. You just told me you didn't want to be dependent on anyone. But taking out a loan doesn't make you dependent. It doesn't give me control over you. It doesn't even mean you have to stay with me. It's just a loan."

"I'm not comfortable with borrowing money from you."

He shrugged and said, "Do it anyway."

"Or what?"

Kieran grinned at me. "What do you want, an ultimatum? Borrow money from me, or else I'm going to put on my police uniform and follow you everywhere and scare away all your potential customers so you *can't* work? Would you respond to that?"

"No."

"Let me be your solution."

I sighed and swung off him, and followed my trail of clothes across the bedroom, putting on my good outfit again. He was still naked on the bed, and when I was dressed I went and stood beside him. "I thought you were in a hurry to get to the police station."

"This is more pressing."

I looked down at him and traced the perfect V in the center of his upper lip as I said, "I'll consider it."

"You're lying to appease me, aren't you?"

"Yes."

"Just give it some thought. This offer isn't going to expire." He got out of bed and kissed me, then began gathering up his clothes. It was the same outfit from the night before, and he said, "We should probably swing by my house before going to see my uncle, so I can shower and change. I want to look decent when I out myself to my family."

"When you – oh God, that's right."

Kieran pulled on his boxers and jeans as he said, "Once I tell my uncle I'm dating you, every one of my

relatives is going to find out I'm gay within the hour –
that's how news travels in my family."

"How do you think he'll take it?"

"Uncle Ray didn't flip out when his own son, my
cousin Jamie, came out. The only person who really reacted
badly to Jamie's announcement was my brother, Brian." A
little crease of concern appeared between his eyebrows. "I
guess I'll actually be outing myself to him first, since you'll
meet my brother when we go to the house."

Kieran lived in Noe Valley, and he drove us there after
we'd both gotten dressed. We'd let the subject of my job
drop for now, so we could go take care of this. "You're
going to have a lot of questions when you see my house,
and when you meet Brian," he said. He seemed a bit
uneasy. "Here's the Cliff's Notes version of what you need
to know. The house looks like shit because when my mom
died twelve years ago, my dad let the place go to hell. I've
managed to do some work on it in the few months my
brother and I have owned it, but I still have a long way to
go. Sometimes I wonder if I'll ever get it all done.

"And then there's my brother." Kieran shifted gears as
the Ford climbed a hill, then said, "Brian's a war veteran.
He was in Afghanistan, and got injured over there. The war
changed him, far more than just his injury. He's…well, just
don't take anything he says personally, okay?"

I saw what he meant about the house as soon as we pulled into the driveway. But if you looked past the boarded over front window, the dead tree in the raised planter that comprised the front yard, and the faded, peeling paint, the place was a cute, compact two story Victorian with great details. The roof was new, and recently built stairs led up to the front door, sharing space with a wide wheelchair ramp.

"I finally got the porch and stairs done a couple days ago. I need to prime and paint them next weekend," Kieran said as we reached the little landing before the front door. I glanced to our left, where the big bay window was boarded over with a new-looking sheet of plywood. Shards of glass sparkled in the raised planter bed below it. Kieran saw me looking at that and sighed. "Next time, I'm putting in Plexiglas. It's the second time Brian's done that." He offered no further explanation as he turned the key in the lock.

The interior of the house was dark, all the curtains drawn. The living room was musty and cluttered, everything shoved against the walls, a big TV broadcasting a sports channel the most prominent thing in the room.

I didn't see Brian until he suddenly rolled forward into the entryway in a manual wheelchair. He was a double amputee, both legs of his sweat pants tacked up, one at the knee, one above the ankle. Brian looked a lot like Kieran…if Kieran ever decided to completely let himself go. His brown hair was long and disheveled, he had a full, scraggly beard, and his clothes were stained and worn.

"Where the fuck you been, Kier?" Brian asked by way of greeting. "And who the fuck is this?"

Kieran took a deep breath and said, "This is Christopher. We've been going out since New Year's."

Brian's eyes narrowed, and he stared at me for a moment. Then he turned back to Kieran and said menacingly, "You want to explain that shit?"

"There's nothing to explain. I'm dating Christopher. End of story."

Brian growled, "Are you seriously standing there telling me you're a fucking faggot?" My mouth fell open. I couldn't believe he'd just called his own brother that.

"Yeah. I'm gay. Deal with it," Kieran said. He was trying to act tough, but I could sense real apprehension in him. Brian started to roll forward in his wheelchair, and Kieran got between me and his brother, squaring his shoulders.

Brian looked startled, as if he'd expected Kieran to back down, and hissed, "My own brother, a goddamn homo. If Dad wasn't already dead, this would have *fucking killed him!*" he yelled, then spun in his chair and disappeared into the dark interior.

Kieran exhaled slowly, then took my hand. "Sorry about that," he said quietly as he led me upstairs.

The top floor was vastly different from the downstairs. Kieran led me past a little home gym to a bedroom at the end of the hall, which was bright, cheerful and tidy. The walls were freshly painted in a nice shade of light blue, and crisp white curtains hung at the row of big windows overlooking an overgrown backyard. A little twin bed was pushed up against one wall, a writing desk beside it. A mini fridge, shelves and a microwave made up a little makeshift kitchen.

"I'm going to take a quick shower. Make yourself comfortable," Kieran said. There was sadness in his eyes, but he was trying not to let it show. He kissed my forehead and ducked through a doorway to our right.

I wandered over to the one solid wall in the room, the only one without doors and windows. It was covered nearly floor to ceiling in framed art prints and unframed postcards, many from the Art Institute in Chicago. The collection was heavy on modernists with a dash of impressionism thrown in, Wyeth and Hopper side by side with Seurat, Duchamp, Chagall, Matisse, Caillebotte and a few others.

I was still studying the art wall when Kieran came out of the bathroom several minutes later, a towel around his hips. He crossed the room to me and slipped his hands around my waist. When I glanced up at him, I saw that his blue eyes were tranquil again, the incident with this brother compartmentalized away somewhere.

"Most of those were my mom's, she had them hung up all over the house," he said, indicating the collection. "She loved art. In fact, she was an art history major in college, but dropped out when she married my dad."

I leaned back against him. "Did you go with her to the Art Institute?"

He nodded. "That trip to Chicago was the highlight of my childhood. I was ten, and just the two of us went. My dad and brother certainly had no interest in going to a museum, but she'd instilled her love of art in me and I was thrilled to go with her." Kieran continued softly, "My mom had all these plans to save up and take me to the world's great art museums. New York was next on our wish list. Only, she died of cancer a few months after our trip to Chicago."

"I'm so sorry, Kieran."

"She was already sick while we were there, but she'd been putting off going to a doctor. My mom always put everyone's needs ahead of her own, she never made herself a priority."

After a pause he said, "She would have loved you, Christopher. And she would have been in awe of your talent, just like I am."

"I actually inherited my ability from my mom," I said quietly. "She was a wonderful artist. I wish I had some of her paintings. I remember a couple of them that used to hang in my nursery."

"What happened to them?"

"I don't know, actually. She killed herself when I was five, and my father purged the house of all of her things right after that. The paintings disappeared, along with every photo of her, all her clothes, everything. When I asked him about them later, he refused to talk about it."

"Oh God, Christopher." Kieran tightened his grip on me and I leaned my head back against his shoulder.

"I managed to keep a couple photos of her. Even at that age, I somehow had the foresight to hide them from my father. I took them with me when I ran away from home ten years later. But then, I was mugged within six hours of arriving in San Francisco. The person that stole my suitcase...he had no idea just how much he was taking from me, how precious those photos were. Not that it would have made a difference to him."

I cleared my throat and carefully extracted myself from Kieran's arms as I said, "God, way to make everything about me. I'm sorry. You were telling me about your mom, and then I just had to launch into my own story. I—"

Kieran cut me off with a gentle kiss, then said, "Thank you for telling me about your mom. I'm willing to bet that's not something you talk about a lot, and I'm grateful that you opened up to me."

"We should probably get going," I told him, looking at the floor. "I want to get to the police station and get this over with."

He of course saw right through my clumsy attempt to close the subject, and touched my cheek as he said, "Okay, baby. It'll just take me a minute to get dressed." He left me with the art wall while he crossed the room to his closet and put on khakis and a button-down shirt.

Thankfully, Brian wasn't around as we went back downstairs and out the front door. We drove across town and parked in the visitor lot at a police station that Kieran referred to as Central. I pulled up all the false bravado I could muster, feeling incredibly self-conscious as we wound our way through the busy station. I so clearly didn't belong here…at least, not on this side of the holding cells.

Kieran, on the other hand, was of course perfectly at home in this atmosphere, relaxed and confident, greeting half the people by name. It really drove home the fact that he and I lived in vastly different worlds.

Ray Nolan was a heavyset man of around fifty with thick salt and pepper hair and sharp sky blue eyes. He had company. His son Jamie sat in one of the chairs before his desk, chatting with his father, ankle crossed over his knee. Jamie stopped talking abruptly when he spotted us, looking from Kieran to me with a raised eyebrow. He paid particular attention to Kieran's hand on my lower back. "Hi guys. I didn't realize you two knew each other," Jamie said. He smiled at us, but his expression was guarded. He knew what I did for a living and I could only imagine what he thought of me, though he always made an effort to treat me cordially.

"We've been going out since New Year's," Kieran said levelly.

"Oh!" Jamie's eyes went wide, while his father looked like he'd just been hit in the face with a frying pan. "So, you're—"

"Gay," Kieran finished for him. "You're the first family members I've told, apart from Brian, who found out less than an hour ago."

"How did Brian take it?" Jamie asked.

"Better than I expected him to," Kieran said. "But that's probably just because I caught him off guard. I'm sure he'll go ballistic next time he sees me."

"That wasn't him going ballistic?" I asked.

"No, not even close. Brian has a violent temper. He didn't even break anything, so I'm expecting him to make up for it later."

"Oh." I wondered how on Earth Kieran lived with such a volatile person.

He turned to the man behind the desk and said, "Uncle Ray, this is Christopher Andrews. Christopher, Raymond Nolan." I leaned over the desk and shook hands awkwardly. His uncle still looked stunned. "I actually brought Christopher here to discuss a cold case with you," Kieran added.

Jamie took that as his cue, and got up as he told his cousin, "Come by the bar sometime this week Kier, let's have lunch and catch up." To me he said, "Nice to see you again, Christopher." *Yeah, I'll bet.* He studied me carefully as he said that.

"Same here."

Once he departed, Kieran and I sat in the two wooden chairs positioned in front of the desk, and Ray said, "I didn't see it coming when my own son came out to me. And I sure as hell didn't expect this from you, Kieran. My brother, God rest his soul, woulda fuckin' lost it if you'd ever told him you were gay." There were a lot of photos on the credenza behind him. In one of them, he and Kieran's father, both in police uniform, grinned at the camera with their arms around each other's shoulders. I recognized him from the pictures at the cabin.

"I know, Uncle Ray. That's why I kept quiet about it while Dad was alive. But you accepted Jamie, and I was hoping maybe you'd accept me, too," Kieran said.

"Of course I accept you, Kieran, no matter what. I love ya like a son, I always have and always will. Though I gotta be honest, I'm kinda stunned that all of a sudden everyone's comin' outta the closet. I mean, who's next? Brian?" They both chuckled at that.

"Yeah, not likely."

Ray shifted in his squeaky office chair and asked, "So, what's this about a case?" Apparently he was ready to move on from the whole gay revelation. It seemed kind of anticlimactic.

"Christopher was assaulted almost a year and a half ago," Kieran said. "No arrests were made. I want the case reopened."

"So why'd you come to me? Why didn't you take it to your captain?"

"Orevitz isn't the most gay-friendly cop on the force. Sure, he's careful to appear politically correct now that he's captain. But I remember him when he was still moving up the ranks, he and my dad were really close. I remember the way they used to talk about gay people and the offensive jokes they'd tell, and I just don't want him anywhere near this case."

Ray exhaled slowly. "Kinda puts me in an awkward position. Let's hope this case originated out of Central, that'd give some justification as to why I'd be the one reopening it."

"I actually have no idea where it originated," Kieran said.

"Lemme take a look at it. Might be there's no more investigating to be done, maybe they hit a bunch of dead ends. But it doesn't hurt to pull the file and give it a look-see." He put on a pair of glasses and grabbed a pad of paper from his cluttered desktop. "So, Christopher, do you remember your case number?"

"No sir."

"Okay. Then give me your full name and the date and location of the assault. I can look it up that way." He handed the pad and a pen to me and I wrote down the information. When I gave it back to him, he looked at it, and then he looked at me. Finally, he turned to the big computer on his desktop and typed with one index finger.

When he found what he was looking for, he said, "Good news. It did originate out of this department, so it wouldn't be inappropriate for me to originate the request to reopen the case." He scrolled through the report for a few moments. Abruptly, Ray's back stiffened, and he ground his teeth together. I could guess what he'd just read. He turned his attention to his nephew and said, "Kieran, are you aware of what this young man did for a living at the time of this incident?"

"Yes sir," Kieran said. "I'm working on getting him out of the business."

I didn't say anything to that, studying my hands in my lap. Ray stared at us for a long moment and finally said to Kieran, "So you're dating a prostitute. That's what you're telling me?"

"I'm dating *Christopher*, sir. Please try to look past his job, and see that for the first time ever, I've found someone that makes me happy. Someone that means the world to me."

His uncle mulled this over for a while before asking, "Did you two meet on the job?" I wondered how I was supposed to interpret that question. Was he asking if Kieran had paid for sex, or if he'd arrested me?

Kieran raised an eyebrow at that. "No sir. We met at Jamie's Christmas party, and again at Charlie Connolly's wedding."

After another pause, Ray said, "You gotta know this relationship is gonna wreak havoc on your career. Probably in this day and age, many of your colleagues will accept the fact that you're a homosexual. But the fact that you're dating a gay prostitute, that ain't gonna sit well with nobody."

"I know," Kieran said quietly. "But it doesn't matter. All that matters is Christopher."

I looked over at him and studied his handsome profile. And then wordlessly, I picked up one of Kieran's hands and held it between both of mine.

Kieran gave me a little smile, then turned back to his uncle. "I'm willing to deal with the fallout from this relationship. I know that it's going to cause a lot of rifts with members of our family, and with my coworkers. It's a price I'm willing to pay."

"I'm not sure you fully understand the level of harassment we're talking about here. I've seen many a cop forced to leave the department when his fellow officers turned on him, often for perceived offenses way less than this. You love this job, Kier, it's all ya ever talked about since you were little. If you're forced out, then what?"

"Nobody's forcing me out. I don't care how bad it gets."

Ray lowered his voice. "It's more than just the looks and comments you're gonna get. What's gonna happen if your coworkers are slow to respond when you need backup? You could get killed or hurt on the job if you don't have the support of your fellow officers."

My eyes went wide. "They wouldn't really do that, would they?"

Ray shrugged. "I'd like to say no. And of course, the official policy is that any cop that did something like that would be suspended immediately. But does it happen? Think about it. Your coworkers are pissed at you and you put in a call for backup. You think they're gonna bust their ass getting to you? They'll respond to the call, they wouldn't blatantly ignore it, but an extra minute or two as they take their time getting there could mean the difference between life and death." Ray shifted in his seat and added, "Now I wanna be clear. Is this every cop I'm talkin' about? Hell no. Is it even the majority of 'em? Of course not. But the fact is, there will always be a few individuals that'll let their personal opinions affect the way they do their job."

"That's terrible," I murmured.

"That's reality. I'd like to say that police officers are somehow a cut above, that we're not prone to cruelty and pettiness and all that bullshit. But I been on the force a long time, and I've seen plenty I ain't proud of. And here's what I know: we're no worse than the general population, but we're no better either, no matter what we tell ourselves."

"I can handle it," Kieran said, his brows knit.

"If it gets bad, I want you to come to me. Promise me, Kier. I don't want you dealing with that shit on your own," his uncle said.

"Yeah, okay," Kieran muttered.

Ray watched his nephew for a long moment, then turned his attention back to the computer screen. He scrolled down a little farther, and then murmured, "Shit." He read for a few moments, then looked at me. "I'm sorry about what was done to you, Christopher. That's a hell of a thing to live through."

"Thank you, sir," I said quietly.

"From what I see at a glance," Ray continued, "there wasn't sufficient follow-up done on this case. The lead officer was Rupert, he ain't on the force anymore, got let go for alleged misconduct. Maybe he slacked off on this case, maybe he didn't. I don't know at this point, but we can find out. I'm gonna requisition the original file and put in an official request to get this reopened."

"I want to be assigned to the case," Kieran said. "I know it's unusual to pull in someone from a different station, but I want to make sure this gets all the attention it deserves."

"You know I'm not gonna bring you in, Kier. There's a huge conflict of interest. And there's no need for you to be involved anyway. You put the case in my hands, so trust me with it. I promise you I won't let it fall through the cracks again."

After a few moments, Kieran begrudgingly agreed. Then he said, "Christopher can provide a sketch of the perpetrator. I want that included in the file."

"Good, that'll be helpful. I'm also gonna want to re-interview you, Christopher, as soon as the case is officially assigned to me. Is that gonna be a problem? Would you feel more comfortable with another officer that isn't related to your boyfriend?" Ray asked. I studied him for a moment. He obviously wasn't thrilled that his nephew was involved with me. But he was already treating the case with professionalism, despite his personal feelings.

"I'd prefer it to be you, sir." My voice sounded so small to me.

"Alright," Ray said. "I'm gonna file all the necessary paperwork soon as we're done here. Should just take a day or two to get this all up and running. Leave your contact information, and I'll set up an interview time with you when it's officially reopened." He pushed the legal pad toward me, and I jotted down my address and phone number. He looked surprised when he saw the address I'd written, and said, "Oh. You're living in Jamie's old apartment."

"Yes sir. I was Charlie Connolly's roommate before he got married."

"It's a one bedroom apartment."

"I slept on the couch."

I wasn't sure what Ray made of all that. But after a moment, he muttered, "Yeah, okay."

Kieran stood up and extended his hand to his uncle, who shook it as Kieran said, "Thank you, sir. I appreciate you taking the time to hear us out."

Ray held his hand out to me next. "I'll be in touch soon," he said as we shook hands. "You may want to take some time and write down all you remember about your assault. I know that's gonna be difficult, but the more details I have, the better. If you could have that sketch ready by the time we meet, that'd be helpful, too."

"I will. Thank you, sir."

"And Christopher," he added, "you really ought to reconsider your career choices. You seem like a decent kid. Probably you could figure out a way to make a living that ain't illegal."

Chapter Thirteen

I was quiet as Kieran drove us back to my apartment.
Finally when he pulled up to the curb, I said softly, "I
didn't think about it. I didn't think about how being with
me would affect your life."

"It doesn't matter. There are always people that will
question my choices. But they're *my* choices, and I don't
care what anyone else thinks."

"Sure you do. You didn't even come out before now
because you were worried about how others would react.
And now your family knows you're dating a prostitute. I'm
so sorry about bringing all these complications into your
life."

"I *used to* worry about what others might think, but
I'm growing up now. I'm just not going to let people's
opinions dictate how I live my life anymore." He kissed me
gently, then rested his forehead against mine.

"I don't get it," I admitted. "I don't get why you'd put
yourself through so much to be with me."

"No?" The corners of Kieran's lips turned up in a little
smile. "Someday I'll explain it to you." He kissed me
again.

I sighed and said, "I want to get that sketch and summary over with for your uncle, and I'm not going to be very good company after that. Can I call you tomorrow?"

"Sure baby." He wound a lock of my hair around his index finger. "But if you change your mind and decide you don't want to be alone, just text me and I'll be right over."

I wasn't willing to let go of him just yet, so I laced my fingers together at the back of his neck and bought myself some more time with him by asking, "What're you going to do this afternoon?"

"A homeowner's work is never done. I need to sand the stairs and landing, get them ready for painting. I need to replace that front window, too, but I guess that's kind of pointless right now. Brian's pretty pissed at me, so he'd probably just break it again."

"How did he break it last time?"

"He threw a dinner plate through it."

"Why?"

"Because he didn't like what I made him for dinner," he said with a frown. "I don't really cook for him anymore, there's no pleasing him. He prefers frozen dinners to what I was making for him anyway."

I studied him for a moment, then said, "Brian needs help. You know that, right?"

"Oh, I definitely know that. He needs counseling as well as physical therapy. You can't actually force someone to get help, though. Whenever I try to bring it up, he just explodes," Kieran said. He was quiet for a few moments before he added, "He was going to go into law enforcement after the Marines, and feels like his entire future was taken from him along with his limbs. I get why he's so angry. I just wish I knew how to help him." There was so much pain in his eyes when he said that.

I hugged him for a long time, and had to force myself to let go of him. "I'll talk to you soon, Kieran."

He kissed me again. "Okay, baby." I ran my fingertips over his cheek before getting out of the car.

Once in my apartment, I changed out of my good outfit and went for full-on comfort, sweats and lots of layers of clothing, topped with Kieran's sweater. Then I curled into a ball on the couch and thought about what Ray Nolan had said.

Finding out what Kieran could face on the job because of me was horrifying. Our relationship could literally endanger him, if it meant losing the support of fellow officers petty enough to let their personal opinions affect how they did their job. I felt sick to my stomach at the thought of Kieran in danger and not getting the help he needed fast enough, because of me.

I was bad for him, that was the bottom line. I'd cause problems for him on the job, and I'd drive a wedge between him and his family. And the closer we got, the more problematic my job would become. I had known right from the start that he and I couldn't date. But I'd let myself get attached to him anyway, and let him get attached to me. I'd selfishly spent more time with him, because it felt so amazing to be with him.

The thought of breaking up with him tore my heart out. But it just felt so inevitable. Even if I quit working, all that really did was elevate me from hooker to ex-hooker. Was that going to change anyone's opinion of me? Was it going to make Kieran's life any easier? I doubted it. Kieran deserved so much better than me, and all the grief and complications I brought into his life.

Before I could even begin to figure out what I was going to say to him, though, there was an awful task that I had to tackle. I sighed and uncoiled myself from the couch, then went and found a pencil and sketch pad. I returned to the sofa and tucked my feet underneath me, and took a deep breath as I folded back the cover. I had to get this sketch done for his uncle, it was important. Ever since Kieran brought up the fact that this person could still be out there hurting other boys, I'd been determined to do my part to catch him.

Drawing the man that had assaulted me was upsetting, to say the least. The first sketch wasn't quite accurate, so I tried again, and again. Finally, with the fourth sketch, I got it right, and took a long look at the face on my drawing pad. He was maybe his late thirties, his appearance remarkable only in its utter lack of remarkability. He was Caucasian with thinning brown hair and regular features. The only thing that stood out was a half-inch long scar on his upper lip in the shape of a backwards question mark. Other than that he was almost generic, the kind of guy you passed on the street without a glance or a thought.

I took the three initial drawings to the kitchen, folded them up into tight little squares, and threw them in the trash, then leaned against the counter and wrapped my arms around myself. I thought back to that summer afternoon sixteen months ago and shivered, despite the layers of warm clothing.

I'd been out on the street for hours, and had planned on working late into the night since tuition for fall quarter was due in just a few days. It had been unseasonably cold, a strong wind blowing off the bay. When the man approached me and bought me for an hour, I remembered being glad that I'd get to be out of the wind for a while. We walked to a nearby seedy motel, one I'd been taken to by other customers a million times before. He already had a room, and he made conversation with me as I sat on the edge of the bed.

"I'm kind of nervous," he'd said with a shy smile. "I don't do this a lot. Mind if we just talk for a while before we get started?" I'd assured him that was fine. None of that was uncommon. "I'm going to have some dinner while we talk, I skipped lunch," he told me as he opened a red and white cooler that was on the little table. He picked up a sandwich, peeled back the plastic wrap and took a bite, then indicated the cooler with a casual gesture. "There's plenty more. Help yourself to some food if you want." He took another big bite.

I remembered considering that for a long moment. There were no warning bells going off. This guy just seemed so normal, so nonthreatening. And besides, he was eating the food he'd brought, which also helped put me at ease. It was dinnertime, and I was hungry. So I thought, why not? Why pass up a free meal? I'd save money on dinner, plus I wouldn't have to miss out on potential customers by taking a dinner break later.

I had thanked him as I took a sandwich from the cooler. And then I made the biggest mistake of my life.

Whatever the sandwich was laced with went to work quickly. Before I'd even finished eating, the room started to go in and out of focus. My arms and legs felt so heavy. I dropped the sandwich and started to fall, but the man caught me and put me on the bed, and began stripping me. I tried to talk, tried to ask him what was happening, but I couldn't make my mouth form words.

And then he'd started hitting me. I'd been beaten many times, but this was something else entirely, beyond brutal and out of control. Fear and panic welled up in me. I'd never felt more helpless, more frightened. He was talking to me as he beat me...I wanted to remember what he was saying, but the more I tried to concentrate on it now, the more it slipped from my grasp.

I had tried to fight against the drug at first, tried to stay awake, because I knew that once I passed out, it was all over. He was going to kill me, I was sure of it. But when he began to rape me, I stopped struggling to remain conscious. As I blacked out, I felt myself letting go, welcoming the end.

Four days later I woke up in a hospital, hooked to all kinds of machines. By chance, I'd been found in a dumpster by a homeless woman that had been looking for cans and bottles to turn in for the five cent deposit. I'd been left to die, naked and bleeding, thrown out like trash. I don't know how or why I survived, and it was a miracle that the woman found me when she did. I always wanted to find her and thank her, but she'd given the police a fake name when they arrived on the scene following her 911 call (I knew that because the officer that came to talk to me at the hospital said she gave her name as Mariah Carey, and described her as an Asian woman in her late sixties).

I grabbed a lined notebook and pen out of my backpack and sat at the kitchen table, then wrote all of that down for Detective Nolan, trying to include every detail that I could think of. And when I finished writing, I closed my eyes and replayed all of it yet again, trying to pull up more details. What the man had been saying as he beat me might have been important to the case, but I just couldn't remember.

I reached up and brushed tears off my cheek with a hand that was trembling. I wasn't sure when I'd started crying, and I made myself stop. Yes, a horrible thing had been done to me. Yes, it left me with some issues that still were unresolved. But crying about it wasn't going to get me anywhere.

A knock on the door startled me, and I pushed back from the table and went to answer it. I was surprised to find Jamie standing out in the hall, his brows knit and his arms crossed over his chest. "We need to talk," he said. I repressed a sigh and stepped back to let him in.

"So, here's what it looks like from my perspective," he began when I'd shut the door behind him. "First, you latch on to my ex-boyfriend Charlie. All of a sudden, you two are BFFs and he's letting you live in his apartment. And then as soon as he gets married, you somehow latch onto my cousin. Kieran and Charlie are a lot alike. They're two of the sweetest, most trusting guys on the planet, and it would be so easy for someone to take advantage of them."

"Someone like me, a lowlife hooker," I finished for him. I stared up at Jamie and noted distractedly that his eyes were the same cerulean blue as his cousin's. "I wish I had the energy to tell you to go fuck yourself, Jamie. I really do. But if you want to think I'm some parasite that's somehow using your ex and your cousin, knock yourself out."

"Tell me I'm wrong," he persisted. "I *want* to be wrong about this, for both Charlie's and Kieran's sake."

"What exactly do you think I'm using them for?"

"Money, I assume. And this apartment. Charlie and Dante paid off the remainder of the sublet through the end of March when my lease is up, so you're living here rent-free. That makes me your landlord, by the way, since Charlie was subletting this place from me."

I had no idea that my former roommates had paid off the sublet, and knew how that looked. I also knew how it would have looked if I'd ever actually borrowed money from Kieran. It really wasn't a mystery why Jamie was confronting me like this. All he saw when he looked at me was a whore. And sure, a typical hooker might exploit kind, trusting men like Kieran and Charlie. Jamie had no way of knowing I wasn't that kind of person, and I doubted anything I had to say would make a difference to him.

Normally though, I still would have tried to defend myself. I would have told Jamie where he could shove his accusations. But right now, when I was already so raw, I just couldn't muster the will to fight. I turned from him and crossed the living room, and started to pack up my backpack. "What are you doing?" Jamie asked.

"I'm moving out of your apartment. You can watch me if you want, to make sure I don't steal any of Charlie's furnishings." I packed my sketch pad and pencil, then went and got the notebook from the kitchen table and packed it as well, along with my crackers from the cupboard. I could go and find a cheap motel, the kind of place I'd lived in before Charlie asked me to be his roommate. I didn't need Jamie to do me any favors by 'allowing' me to stay here.

"Wait," Jamie said. "I didn't come here to kick you out. I just came to talk."

"No you didn't. You came here to warn the whore away from your ex and your cousin. Well sorry, you can't do anything about the fact that Charlie and I are friends.

And I've already decided to break up with Kieran. So you could have saved yourself the trip over here."

That seemed to derail Jamie's momentum. He trailed after me as I continued to gather my few possessions and asked, "Why are you breaking up with Kier?"

"What difference does it make? You should be thrilled. Your cousin will be safe from the evil hustler who's obviously just looking to cheat him out of his inheritance." I had gone into the bedroom and pulled an old duffle bag from the bottom of the closet. I shucked off my sweat pants and put them in the duffle, and pulled on a pair of jeans.

"I'd just like to know what brought this on all of a sudden."

"Your father made me realize how detrimental a relationship with me would be to Kieran," I said. It was more complicated than that, of course, but that would suffice as an explanation for Jamie. I pulled off the layers of clothing I was wearing and exchanged them for a t-shirt and hoodie, then picked up the fisherman's sweater and thrust it at Jamie. "This is your cousin's. Could you please see that he gets it back?"

He took it from me as he said, "Would you please stop packing for a minute and talk to me?"

I sat on the floor in front of the open closet and pulled on my beat-up sneakers as I said, "There's nothing to talk about. I'm getting out of your apartment, and I'm getting out of Kieran's life. Yay, you win! Big day for Jamie Nolan."

"Does Kieran know you plan to break up with him?"

And that was the sentence that finally triggered my breakdown. There'd been so much pain, so much hurt over these last two days, so much building up in me. And all of a sudden the dam just gave way, at the thought of how much being blindsided by me would hurt Kieran. I managed to say, "No, but I have to do it. It's for his own good." And then I burst into tears. I was furious at myself for crying in front of Jamie, of all people. But there was just no holding it back.

When I started sobbing, Jamie crouched down beside me and pulled me into his arms, holding me securely. "Hey," he said gently, stroking my back, "it's alright, Christopher. It's going to be okay."

"Stop being nice to me," I managed after a while, when I'd calmed down enough to form sentences again. "You fucking hate me. Go away so I can act like a wuss in private."

He grinned a little at that. "You're not acting like a wuss, and I don't hate you. Though if you break Kieran's heart, I might have to kick your ass."

I sniffed and said, "Anyone who hurts Kieran deserves to have their ass kicked."

"He's crazy about you, you know. I called him on the way over here. You should hear the way he talks about you."

I dragged the back of my hand over my eyes, taking a couple ragged breaths and trying to calm myself. Embarrassingly enough, Jamie was still cradling me in his arms. And even more embarrassingly, I was letting him. "He deserves so much better than me," I murmured.

"Do you care about him? Really, truly care?"

"God yes."

"Then you're exactly what he deserves."

"A hooker with a boatload of personal issues? I don't think so." I sat up and took a few deep breaths, and Jamie rested his hand on my shoulder.

"You really need to find another line of work, Christopher."

"As if I don't know that."

"You know, when Charlie returns from his honeymoon, he's going to be helping Dante run their new restaurant, so he won't be coming back to work for me. That means I'm one waiter short at the bar and grill. Maybe you could come to work for me," Jamie said.

I raised my eyebrows at him. "Do you remember why you came over here in the first place? You don't trust me. Why would you offer me a job?"

"I think I worked in law enforcement just long enough to learn to question people's motives. But just from talking to you for a few minutes, I can see I was wrong about you. You obviously care about my cousin, and breaking up with him would be devastating for both of you. You two should be together."

"I don't know about that." I leaned against the wall and repeated what Ray Nolan had said about possible backlash from Kieran's fellow officers.

Jamie asked, "Did you talk about that with Kieran?"

"Yeah."

"And what did he say?"

"He said he was willing to accept the consequences. But—"

"But nothing. Kieran's a grown man, he can decide what's best for him. If he thinks he can deal with it, then let him deal with it. And my dad only said that *could* happen, not that it was guaranteed. My cousin has a lot of friends on the force, they're not all going to turn their backs on him."

"Well, his family's also going to be thrilled he's dating a prostitute."

"It sounds like you're making excuses not to be with my cousin. But you just told me you care about Kieran, so what gives?" I looked away, and he said gently, "I don't know anything about you Christopher, but I'm guessing maybe you had it rough in the past, maybe that's what brought you to prostitution. Maybe it's not so easy for you to trust people. Is that it?" I shrugged noncommittally, even though he was right on the money. Jamie continued, "Whatever you've been through before, whatever it is that's making you shy away from the idea of a relationship...let me just say that, if ever there was a person deserving of trust, it's my cousin. Kieran is *such* a good guy, through and through."

"Well, you've certainly done a one-eighty," I said, glancing at Jamie from beneath my lashes. "You went all the way from wanting to warn me away from your loved ones to advocating for a relationship."

Jamie grinned at me. "I can admit when I'm wrong. And I'm so glad I was wrong about you."

"I still don't know what you're basing that on."

"It's just a feeling I get about you. And I'm usually right about people. You know – the second time."

"My first impression of you was wrong, too. You're not actually a douchebag."

Jamie laughed at that. "You thought I was a douchebag?"

"I thought there was a distinct possibility that you possessed certain douche-like characteristics."

Jamie was still smiling as he pushed himself to his feet. "Well, I'm sorry for whatever I did to give you that impression. But now that you've absolved me of my doucheyness, how about that job offer? I really could use a waiter, and you really do need a different job."

"Thanks, but no freaking way could I afford Sutherlin on a waiter's salary."

"Have you looked into financial aid?"

"Ugh," I muttered. "Why does everyone assume I'm too stupid to have thought of that one myself? *Yes*, I've looked into financial aid. It's not happening."

"Are you sure? You know, if you wanted me to, I could help you with your student loan applications. I was awesome at finding money when I was in college – grants, loans, scholarships, you name it. I even helped some of my family members by showing them how to get financial aid, too. I know you think you're ineligible for some reason, but I'm telling you, there's money available for all who need it."

But I shook my head and said, "No, I'm telling you, I'm not eligible."

"Sure you are."

"Jamie, I'm not."

"Why not?"

"Because," I admitted, "I'm worth about thirty-two million dollars."

Chapter Fourteen

"You're…wait, what?"

"You heard me."

"Yeah, but I don't get it. If you're worth that kind of money, why on Earth would you work as a prostitute?"

"Because I refuse to take a cent of my father's money. I would rather do *anything* besides that. And given what I do to make a living, you can see how literally I mean that."

"So…I take it you and your father don't get along,"

"Uh, yeah. You could say that."

"And the thirty two million dollars…that's where, exactly?"

"In a trust fund under my name, which became accessible when I turned eighteen. Under my *real* name, I should say. Andrews was my mother's maiden name."

"What's your real name?"

"Christopher Robin Longotti. My father calls me Chris, which is why I hate that nickname."

"You can't possibly mean…."

"Yeah, *the* Longottis. Reggie Longotti is my father."

Jamie sank onto the edge of the mattress and stared at me for a long moment. "Reggie Longotti? Head of one of the most powerful crime families in the eastern U.S.?"

"Semi-retired. He's lived on a horse ranch in Georgia for a while now. But he still keeps his hand in the business, even from the boondocks."

He absorbed that for a beat before asking, "Does your father know where you are right now?"

"More or less. He probably knows I'm still in San Francisco. When I was younger, he used to send his lackey to drag me back to Georgia on a regular basis, and he never seemed to have any trouble finding me. But once I turned eighteen, I started threatening to have my father arrested for kidnapping, so he finally backed off."

"Does he know you're a prostitute?"

"I really doubt it. Jimmy, the lackey he always sent to bring me back home, said he wasn't going to tell my father he'd found me working the street. Which was smart, since it would have infuriated my father and I wouldn't put it past him to kill the messenger."

"Does Kieran know any of this?"

"No. So far, I've sort of avoided unloading all my baggage on him."

He exhaled slowly. "How do you think your father would feel about you dating a police officer?"

"He'd hate it. But then, he hates everything I do. He hates the fact that I'm gay, and an artist, and that I refuse to take a cent of his dirty money. Dating a cop would go on the long list of stuff about me that pisses him off."

"Do you think it'd be dangerous for Kieran if your father knew about him?"

I said, "I think my father may have finally given up on me, I haven't heard from him in months. So no, I don't think he'd pose a threat to Kieran."

"What's a semi-retired gangster doing on a horse ranch in Georgia, of all places?"

"My mother was from Georgia. She met my father on a trip to New York. He wanted her to stay with him, but she hated the city, so he followed her down south and bought her the ranch as a wedding present. He ended up liking the rural lifestyle and stayed on, even after her death. He's breeding race horses now, which kind of figures. He always loved the track."

"This is all really surprising. I had no idea about your family."

"It's not something I talk about a lot. And," I added with a grin, "it's such a TMI answer to your original question."

"Well, I can now see why student loans are probably out of the question."

"Yup. It might be a different story if I had a fake social security number. But as it is, on paper, Christopher

Andrews doesn't exist, and Christopher Longotti is loaded. And neither of them is getting a cent in financial aid."

"If it's not something you talk about, why did you just tell me all of that?"

"I don't know," I shrugged. "Maybe it was just one too many people asking me why I hadn't gotten student loans. And it's not actually a secret or anything. I just tend not to bring it up."

"When I was still on the force, I'd hear your father's name mentioned periodically. He may not be as retired as you think. And the stuff he's rumored to be involved in is pretty hardcore."

"Not surprising. I never directly witnessed him breaking the law, but I wouldn't put anything past my father, up to and including murder."

"You know who the Longottis' biggest rival is, don't you?"

"No. Who?"

"The Dombruso crime family," he said. "Your best friend's new in-laws. Neither family has been content with just dominating the east or west coast. Both have always had bigger aspirations."

"You're kidding."

"I wonder if that's why your father always sent someone to retrieve you, rather than coming for you himself. If he set foot in San Francisco, it would probably trigger a major turf war with the Dombruso clan."

"This is all news to me. I left home at fifteen, and even before that, I steered clear of my father's business. So I never heard him mention the Dombrusos."

"You're going to tell Kieran all of this, right?" Jamie asked.

"Yeah. Like I said, it's not a secret or anything."

"You know that my husband used to be involved in organized crime, don't you?" Jamie said, and I nodded. "I think he and I are proof that you and Kieran can still make a go of it, despite your vastly different backgrounds."

"It's not so much our backgrounds that worry me. It's all the day-to-day issues, my job, his job...."

"Yeah, you guys do have some things to work out."

"This is true."

Jamie got up off the mattress and said, "I need to get back to the bar, I'm supposed to cover the front of the house because one of my employees is taking the afternoon off. But look, if you ever want to talk, I really hope you'll come find me. And the job offer still stands." I walked him to the front door, and he turned to me and said, "I'm sorry for the way I came over here."

Impulsively, I gave Jamie a hug and said, "Just keep looking out for Charlie and Kieran. It's great that they have you in their corner."

Once he left, I went and located my phone and dialed Kieran's number. When he answered, I said, "We did this all backwards, you know. We skipped the whole dating thing and went straight to sex. I think we should rectify that situation."

"Okay. How do we do that?"

"I want to take you out, Kieran. On a real date, one where we don't just make a beeline to the bedroom. Are you free this evening?"

"Most definitely. What did you have in mind?"

"Dinner and a movie, something nice and normal. Well, okay, I won't actually be eating anything, so it won't be *that* normal. But I want to do this right, Kieran." I shifted the phone and perched on the edge of my bed. "It kind of freaked me out when you said you wanted to renegotiate our friends with benefits thing. Getting involved with anyone is a really frightening proposition. But I want this, and I'm willing to do what it takes to make it happen."

"So am I."

"Okay. So, I'll see you at seven p.m. Um, could you pick me up? I don't actually have a car."

"Sounds good. It'll be our first date, you know."

"It will."

"Oh, and there's something you should know, Christopher," he said.

"What's that?"

"I'm kind of easy, I actually put out on the first date," he said lightly. "See you soon, baby." I had a huge smile on my face as we ended the call.

*****

We did just what I'd suggested for our first date. I took him to a cute little Italian place for a meal, and afterwards we went and saw the latest action blockbuster at the theater. It wasn't until we got back to my place that the date veered away from the conventional.

"Is it weird that my cock's hard because you tied me up?" Kieran asked. I'd used strips of an old t-shirt to fashion makeshift bindings, and he was currently naked and spread-eagled on my bed, held securely to the metal bedframe.

I shook my head. "Not weird at all."

"I had a girl I was dating do this to me once, just my hands. And I freaked out on her. I made her take the bindings off after like ten seconds, even though it had been my idea. I guess I didn't really trust her. But with you, I feel incredibly secure."

I leaned down and kissed him, then cuddled against his chest. "I'm glad you do."

"I want us to slowly test my limits. I want to give myself to you completely, and I want to find out how deep my submissive side runs. Would you be willing to do that?"

"Yes. But you're right about the slow part, we shouldn't rush it."

"No. Especially since we just started dating today." He smiled at me cheerfully.

I sat up and reached behind me, massaging his balls before sliding lower and stroking the soft skin beneath them. He practically purred, then asked, "Since you have me completely at your mercy, what are you going to do to me?"

"This, for starters," I said, rolling a condom on his hard cock and slicking him. I positioned him at my opening and sat all the way down on his thick shaft as he moaned with pleasure. I began riding him with languid, rolling movements, up and down.

"I love this, with you on top. It makes me feel like I belong to you."

I smiled at that and said, "Do you want to add another element to the mix?"

"You can do anything you want to me, Christopher."

I shivered with pleasure at that. After riding him for another minute, I pulled off of him. I grabbed a small suitcase from the bottom of the closet and put it beside him on the bed, then mounted his cock again, picking up right where I left off.

He glanced at the suitcase and grinned. "We going on a trip?"

"Oh yes," I murmured, unzipping the case as I kept up the rhythm on his cock. When I flipped back the lid to reveal a big selection of sex toys, his breath caught.

"Oh wow," he whispered.

I pulled out a medium-sized dildo and lubed it up, then reached behind me and spread some lube into his little hole before slowly working the toy into him. His expression was pure bliss, and he held my gaze as I began to fuck him with it, deep, long thrusts in and out. I matched it to my pace on his cock, and as I increased the force of the thrusts into him, I rode him harder. "This is amazing," he whispered, his breath fast and shallow. "I've never felt anything like it." It reminded me just how innocent he was, and yet how trusting and willing to follow me wherever I led.

I took him just a little harder with the toy, bouncing on his cock with more force, and he threw his head back and moaned, reflexively thrusting up into me as I rode his cock and fucked his ass. After a few minutes he cried out, his entire body convulsing as he came violently, bucking up off the bed, pulling on his restraints. I rode out his orgasm, and when he was spent I carefully eased off his cock, holding the condom in place.

I still hadn't finished, which barely occurred to me. The hooker in me was used to not finding release. But Kieran begged, "Please baby, finish in my mouth. Fuck me."

"I don't know if we should do that while you're tied down. It could be too intense," I told him as I gently brushed his damp hair off his forehead.

"Please, Christopher. Use me. I need it so bad." His voice was a rough whisper.

I shook with desire and climbed up so I was straddling his face, and bent my hard cock downward, sliding it into his open mouth. I was careful with him, but gave him what he asked for, fucking his mouth. He was learning to control his gag reflex, relaxing his throat, figuring out how to position his tongue, tilting his head back a bit.

"You're doing great, Kieran," I whispered encouragingly, pleasure arcing through me. Soon I was cumming down his throat, and he swallowed me eagerly. As my orgasm ebbed, I pulled out a few inches and he sucked my cock before I finally slid it from his lips.

"Thank you," he whispered.

I removed his condom and eased the toy from him. Then I untied his hands and feet, before cleaning him up with a wash cloth and snuggling with him under the warm blanket. He was asleep in a matter of minutes, and I propped myself up and watched him for a while.

It felt like Kieran was the one taking most of risks with this relationship, not me. He was putting so much trust in me, letting himself be vulnerable, letting me lead him through a whole world he'd never experienced. It made it easier somehow to let myself begin a relationship with him, my own insecurities put into perspective by his faith in me. I curled against him and draped an arm over his chest, and held him securely as he slept.

Chapter Fifteen

It seemed weird that Charlie knocked on the door to the apartment. I still considered it his place, even if he had officially moved into his new loft right before the wedding.

It was late January. Kieran and I had been "officially" dating for a couple weeks. Despite my intentions to take it slow, we couldn't get enough of each other, so we wound up spending almost every night together here in my apartment. It wasn't all sex, though. We spent as much time talking and getting to know each other as was spent between the sheets.

Charlie had just returned from his honeymoon, and as soon as I opened the door, he grabbed me in a huge hug and swung me around. "I missed you," I exclaimed.

"I missed you too, Christopher."

"Bullshit. You were too busy having fun to miss anyone," I said with a grin as he set me on my feet. Charlie looked amazing, tan and healthy and radiating happiness. Married life was most definitely agreeing with him. "So, how was the South Pacific?"

"Heavenly. Dante chartered a sailboat, it was incredibly romantic. And everyplace we went was so beautiful. It was just absolutely perfect." He beamed at me as he took my hand and led me to the couch. "It was hard to come back to the cold and rain." The last week in San Francisco had been flat-out gloomy.

"You should have stayed another month."

"Oh, it was tempting, believe me. But Dante had to get back to the restaurant remodel, and of course I wanted to be back for your debut art show. Not to mention the fact that Dante and I have a couple classes starting next week that I signed us up for at Christmas."

"I'm not showing at the Tremont Gallery anymore." The new artists show was actually tomorrow. I hadn't heard a word from Ian Tremont since I'd gone to take back my paintings. Mary Malloy had called to follow up with me, though. But she was clearly just trying to build up some kind of salacious sex scandal involving Ian and myself, and I refused to play into that. We did discuss my work a bit, but apparently nothing had come of it, because that was the last I heard from her.

Also, despite the article in the local paper, agents hadn't exactly been beating down my door trying to sign me. Maybe that was because the article made it sound like Tremont was representing me. Or maybe no one was interested.

I was back to being just another art student, and an unemployed one at that. I'd stopped turning tricks after my escort service got shut down, and had put in applications at shops and restaurants all over town in the last couple weeks, but hadn't gotten any interviews. Why would I? I had absolutely no work history to include on the applications, since I wasn't about to write: Hooker, age 15 to present. My chances of finding a legitimate job were pretty grim. Even still, I didn't consider taking Jamie up on his job offer, because it felt too much like charity.

"I already knew that about the show," Charlie said with a big smile. He pulled a rolled up magazine out of his back pocket and said, "I found out as soon as our plane landed. Have you seen this?"

"Seen what?"

"Oh good, I get to be the first to show you." Charlie unfurled the glossy current issue of Stylemaker Weekly. Staring back at me from the cover of the magazine was – me!

"Oh my God!" I exclaimed, as he handed me the magazine.

It was a photo taken in front of the gallery. Mrs. Dombruso was peeking out the open door of the limo behind me, and Hunter was off to the side. I was holding my favorite painting, the one of myself as a young boy, which was clearly visible in the shot. I looked brave, defiant. The caption splashed across the photo was: The Art

World's Bold, Bright Future. "They retouched my dark circles," I said with a little grin.

Charlie burst out laughing. "*That's* your response? You're on the cover of a national magazine! I got off a plane at SFO and there was my best friend, at every newsstand! Do you get how freaking *huge* this is?"

"Why on Earth would they put me on their cover? I'm nobody."

"They think you're going to be the next big thing, obviously, and they want to be able to say they discovered you."

Just then, someone knocked on the door, and I let in an excited Kieran. He was waving a copy of the magazine, and yelled, "Christopher, guess what!" He held at least a dozen copies in the crook of his arm. When he spotted the magazine in my hand and my friend on the couch, he exclaimed, "Damn it, Charlie! I wanted to be the one to tell him!" He crossed the room and piled the magazines on the coffee table.

Charlie got up and hugged Kieran as he said cheerfully, "You need to be quicker, Kier."

"I see that! When did you get back from your honeymoon?"

"About an hour ago. I had Dante drop me off here, he needed to go and deal with some kind of mini crisis with the restaurant remodel."

"So, by the way Charlie, Kieran and I are dating now," I said.

"Did you meet at my wedding?"

"We'd kind of met at Jamie's Christmas party, but hooked up at your wedding. And have been hooking up ever since," Kieran said with a slightly embarrassed smile.

Charlie took the magazine from my hands and flipped a few pages, then said, "I actually already figured out you two were together, based on this." The picture he turned to showed Kieran and me side by side. I was handing him a painting that I'd just removed from the gallery wall, and he was giving me the sweetest smile. "They have you listed as *unidentified man*," Charlie said with a grin.

"Sorry about that. The reporter never asked me who any of you were," I said. "She didn't seem all that interested in facts, to be honest with you."

"It's really more of a photo essay than an article, though she does manage to hint at a juicy sex scandal," Kieran said. "That photographer got some great shots, though. And there's a whole sidebar on Hunter. He'll be thrilled."

"Oh he will," I said with a smile. I flipped through a few pages of the magazine. There was a huge photo of me dragging the banners into the gallery, covering two pages. The photographer had been quite talented. It was a great, dynamic shot, and I was surprised at how confident I looked. I turned another page and grinned at the photos of Nana in her exercise gear, liberating my paintings along with Kieran and Hunter.

"I'm sorry I missed it," Charlie said. "I would have gladly helped. I could have been *unidentified man number two.*"

"It wasn't planned. I was going to go by myself, and then it all just snowballed into this group outing."

"What happened between you and Ian, anyway?"

I explained it to Charlie as concisely as I could, and he looked stunned. He said, "Dante's going to be livid. I'm sure he had no idea Ian was such a snake, or he never would have introduced the two of you."

"Dante had no way of knowing this would happen," I said. "Ian was perfectly charming when I first met him. He only got ugly after I turned him down."

"I'm still so pissed at him," Kieran muttered. I gave him a hug and kiss to soothe him a bit, and he perched on the arm of the sofa behind me and rested his hand on my shoulder.

"Watching you two together is kind of surreal. I was absolutely sure you were straight, Kier," Charlie said.

"Yeah, I was kind of going for that inaccurate impression for a long time."

"How long have you known you were gay?"

"Probably about as long as you have," Kieran told him with a grin. To me he said, "Charlie and I have been friends since high school, we even played on the football team together. It's kind of a shame that we both waited so long to come out, because it would have been really nice knowing I had an ally back then."

"You played football too?" I asked Kieran. When he nodded, I said, "Then how come you suck so bad at Madden?" I grinned innocently.

Charlie burst out laughing, and Kieran said, "Because that's not football! It's a video game! It has no basis in reality. You want me to tackle someone in real life, I'll tackle the hell out of 'em. There's no correlation between working a controller and the real thing!"

My phone rang, and I was still chuckling as I answered it to an excited Mrs. Dombruso, asking me if I'd seen the magazine. I assured her I had, and she gushed, "I'm so proud of you, Christopher Robin. And that's a great picture on the cover, you look so handsome." Then she added, "I look pretty hot, too, in that photo. This is gonna give me a real advantage in meeting some stud muffins."

We spoke for a couple minutes, and after we disconnected, Charlie got up and flashed me a huge smile. "I'm thrilled for you, Christopher. Both because of the magazine, and because you and Kieran found each other."

"Thanks," I murmured as Kieran and I exchanged grins.

Charlie said, "I'm seriously tired, I need to go home and crash. I'll call you tomorrow, okay?"

I walked him to the door and kissed his cheek. "Sure. I'm glad you're back."

"Me too. I'm gone a few weeks and miss all kinds of drama and excitement!" Then he called, "Bye, Kier. You two take care of each other, you hear?"

"Count on it. Good to see you, Charlie," Kieran said.

Once he left, I gathered Kieran in my arms. "I didn't realize you and Charlie were so close. That makes me happy."

"We were friends for a long time, but when he and my cousin broke up, things got a little awkward. He distanced himself from Jamie's family, me included. It wasn't until I saw him at the Christmas party that we really reconnected, and he ended up inviting me and Jamie's sisters to his wedding."

"Good thing, too. Otherwise, we never would have found each other." I snuggled against his chest.

"Sure we would, one way or another. I had been trying to get up the courage to ask Jamie about the beautiful, curly-haired boy at his party. But of course I wasn't out yet at that point, so I didn't really know how to approach the subject."

I kissed him deeply, then grinned and asked, "Do you want to move this into the bedroom?"

"God I want to, but I can't." He tilted my chin up and kissed me again. "I actually have to be at work soon. I just stopped by to surprise you with the magazine. Or, you know, fail to surprise you, thanks to Charlie."

Once he left, I pulled my shoes and hoodie on, grabbed my backpack, and boarded a bus bound for the Tenderloin. It felt like a different world when I stepped off the bus – a world that, until quite recently, I'd inhabited. Litter and graffiti marred the landscape, homeless people sharing the sidewalk with hookers and dealers and everyday folk passing through on their way to someplace better than this.

I glanced at the rent boys as I made my way down the street. I should be among them, but as I'd said, I hadn't worked since the escort service went under two weeks ago. Partly, it was because of Kieran. Prostitution in general and working the street in particular was a huge point of contention with him, and I obviously understood why.

The other part of it was that I just couldn't quite make myself go back to street hustling. I was scared to return to that life, the emotional scars of my assault still so fresh, even after all this time.

So, I'd more or less retired from prostitution, but I didn't feel any different. Maybe it was something that never really let you go...maybe it lived under your skin forever.

Besides, part of me really didn't believe it was over. I kept thinking something would happen, my life would somehow go askew as it had so many times before, and I'd be forced to sell myself again. If things got bad enough, if I got desperate enough, it wouldn't matter that I was afraid. I'd end up out here regardless of that.

Until that did or didn't happen though, I really didn't know what I was going to do for income. I'd already accepted the fact that I would have to take a leave of absence from school until I saved up enough to pay tuition. Maybe I'd only have to take a couple quarters off if I managed to find a full-time job soon and was able to save aggressively. I probably wouldn't be able to afford more than one quarter a year, so the remainder of my undergraduate studies could end up spread over several years. But I'd made my peace with that. I would still get it done, no matter how long it took.

Finally, I arrived at my destination, and pushed open the heavy glass door at Havilland House, which wasn't a house at all. This building, a former department store, had been converted back in the 1970s to a combination community center, shelter during winter, teen runaway outreach and soup kitchen. Back when I'd first arrived in San Francisco, I'd spent many a cold winter night on a mat on the floor in the big main room. It probably literally saved my life. I would have gotten so ill out in the rain and cold of more than one San Francisco winter if this place hadn't given me shelter.

I hadn't been back here in almost two years, which was when I'd finally managed to afford a room in a residence hotel. And the place hadn't changed at all. The linoleum floor looked as yellowed and stained as ever, and the dingy white walls still held a patchwork quilt of random flyers for drug counselors, and therapists, and local churches, and a million other outreach programs. I wondered if anyone ever actually switched them out, or if they just added new flyers as they came in. Maybe there were decades worth of now-defunct services up on that wall. Not that it mattered. I'd never once seen anyone reading them.

It was fairly chaotic. Lunch would be served in about an hour, and already a large cross-section of the city's poorest residents were milling around the "lobby" at the front of the big main room while volunteers worked quickly and efficiently to prepare enough food for a crowd. I wound my way through the throng, and eventually emerged at a little office.

I stuck my head through the door, and saw a familiar face behind the desk. Oliver Avers was a lean African American man of about sixty, who as far as I knew ran this place as a volunteer. He was soft-spoken, and radiated calmness more than anyone I'd ever met. He was concentrating on a pile of forms on his beat-up metal desk, and when I said, "Excuse me, Mr. Avers?" he looked up at me and smiled.

"Well, hello Christopher. It's been a long time. How've you been?"

In addition to his Zen-like calm, the other magical thing about Mr. Avers was his memory. He could recall the names of everyone that came in here, which was hundreds of people. I had no idea how he did that, or how he possibly remembered me years later.

"I'm good thank you, sir. May I have a moment of your time?"

"Of course. Pull up a chair."

I did as I was told, then unzipped my backpack and pulled a sheet of paper out of a thick cardstock folder. "I just wanted to ask if you happen to recognize this man," I said, and handed over the flyer.

Ray Nolan had succeeded in reopening my case, but there had been very little to go on. After he reinterviewed me and distributed the sketch of the man who'd assaulted me through all the law enforcement channels, there wasn't a lot left to do. No forensic evidence had been collected, and there were no witnesses besides me, so the investigation quickly ground to a halt.

But I couldn't get Kieran's words out of my head: this man might still be out there hurting other people. When it became clear that the police couldn't do much for me, I felt a responsibility to try to do something myself. So for the past few days, I'd been taking flyers with the sketch I'd made and the man's physical description around town. I began with places that rent boys frequented, including every by-the-hour fleabag hotel in this part of town. Now I was expanding my canvassing to include places like this that worked with runaways and sex workers, just on the off chance that someone would recognize him.

Honestly, I didn't know what would happen if a suspect was actually identified, since without corroborating evidence, I didn't really think my testimony alone would be enough to put this man in jail. But still, I felt I had to do something.

Mr. Avers took the sheet of paper from me and studied the sketch carefully, then read the information at the bottom. Finally he said, "I'm sorry, I don't."

He started to hand it back to me, but I said, "Would you mind posting that? Maybe someone else will recognize him."

"Sure thing, Christopher," he said, and set the flyer on his desk. "This crime he's wanted for, were you the victim?"

"Yes sir. I almost died in that assault, and I'm worried that more boys like me might be hurt by that man."

"I'm proud of you for taking an active role in seeking justice," he said. "Few people would do that."

"I didn't do anything about it for over a year. I guess I just expected the police to handle it, only they never did. I'm ashamed that it took me so long to get involved."

"Don't look at it that way. You're right that the police should have handled it. Most victims of violent crime really don't get involved like this, and you should be commended for being so brave."

"Oh, I'm not brave. I'm just trying to do the right thing," I said, and got up from my chair. "Good to see you again, sir. Take care."

The main part of Havilland House had become even
more crowded as lunch grew near. I left Mr. Avers' office
and began to weave my way through the crowd, headed for
the exit. When a hand grabbed my upper arm, I
immediately went into the defensive, whirling on whoever
was holding on to me, my adrenaline pumping.

The young brunette with glasses gasped, and grabbed
me in a hug. "Christopher! It *is* you!"

"Hey Jeffrey," I said, returning the hug as soon as I
realized who it was.

"You're okay," he said, still holding me tightly. "I
thought you were dead."

"Why did you think that?"

He pulled back a little bit, but kept holding on to my
upper arms. His big brown eyes were shining with unshed
tears under his long bangs. "Well, because you disappeared
right at the same time as Angel and Jody Lyton. There were
rumors of a serial killer stalking young, blond rent boys. I
thought maybe he got you, too."

I was shocked at that. "I didn't know about that
rumor."

"Yeah. You know, it was just among our population.
The cops didn't believe us, they said you all probably just
moved on to another city. But I knew that wasn't the case.
Angel had left his backpack with me, it had everything he

owned in it and he would have come for it before taking off."

"Jeffrey, can we go talk somewhere quiet?"

"Yeah, sure. I gotta be back before they start serving lunch though, I'm working the coffee station. But I have a few minutes."

We headed toward the back of the building, Jeffrey hanging on to the sleeve of my hoodie like he thought I might disappear. He'd changed a bit in the last couple years. He was as tall as me now, and his lean body had filled out just a little. Back when I knew him, he was a scared sixteen-year-old runaway from Modesto, newly arrived in the city. I was a couple years older and a lot more street-smart. So I'd tried to help him out a bit, offer him some pointers on how to survive.

What I mostly remembered about Jeffrey was one cold winter night when we'd slept side-by-side on the floor of this building. I'd awakened and realized he was sobbing silently, trying not to attract attention in the crowded shelter. When I reached out and touched his shoulder, he'd crawled into my arms and went right on crying. I held him all night. He'd seemed really embarrassed the next morning, and avoided me after that.

Soon after, I'd moved into a residence motel in a different neighborhood. I would still see Jeffrey occasionally, because I worked the street in front of the Havilland. He always seemed to be holding it together, often better than I was. Once I was assaulted and went to work for the escort service, I no longer had a reason to come to this part of town and didn't see him at all anymore.

Looking back now, I felt guilty that I hadn't done more to help this kid. But I was homeless and selling my body on the street, getting beaten up and robbed regularly because I was small and an easy mark, and just trying to live through each day. When you're that focused on your own survival, you don't have a whole lot to offer other people.

We had reached a little dormitory at the back of the building, and Jeffrey unlocked a door with a key he kept around his neck on a string. He pushed the door open and went and sat on a little twin bed with a red wool blanket. "This is my room," he said proudly. "I work here now in exchange for room and board. Nice, huh?"

His narrow little bed was in a corner, the wall above it covered with pictures cut from magazines. Some of the pictures were tropical beaches and flowers. The rest, well, those broke my heart. They were pictures of houses, of families, of smiling, happy people. Jeffrey lived about a million miles from the world in those images. I wondered how he could bear to look at the false promises and fiction that those photos advertised.

I pulled up a smile as I sat beside him and said, "It's really nice, Jeffrey. I'm happy for you."

"It's all because of you, Christopher," he said. "You helped me so much when I first came to the city. I wouldn't have survived without you."

"What? No, I didn't do much," I said.

"Sure you did. You were my only friend, at a time when I needed that so bad. You gave me lots of advice, you taught me how to survive. You even brought me here to Havilland House for the first time. Do you remember?" I did now that he'd mentioned it, I had almost forgotten.

"It's because of you that I didn't turn to prostitution," he continued. "You convinced me to find another way to get by. And you're the reason that I have this home and this job now, because you brought me to this place. I owe you so much."

I felt the color rise in my cheeks. "I didn't really do anything. I was too wrapped up in my own drama to really be of much help."

"You did more than you realize, and I'm so happy to find out you're alive. I was devastated when I thought you'd been killed."

"God, I'm sorry. I didn't realize you'd thought that, or I would have come to see you."

"It's not your fault. We weren't really friends at that point, so why would you have come here? I only knew you went missing because I would always watch for you. You always worked the same spot right down the street, every single day. Until one day in August over a year ago, when you were just gone."

"I got attacked," I said as I pulled a flyer from my backpack. "By this man." I handed him the sheet of paper and said, "If you ever see him, stay far away from him. He's really dangerous."

He took the flyer and said, "See? You're still looking out for me. I'll watch out for him, and I'm so sorry you got attacked."

"Does he look familiar?"

He studied the drawing closely, his brow knit. But then he said, "Naw. I've never seen him."

"You said two other boys disappeared at the same time. What do you remember about that?"

"It was that same August. I met both Jody and Angel here at the community center, they'd both come in for lunch. They were around my age, maybe a little older. Jody was really funny, he knew like a million dumb blond jokes, even though he was blond. Angel, he was real sweet, real quiet. It was obvious how he earned his nickname."

Jeffrey bent over and fished under his bed, then pulled out a red backpack. It was a child's pack with a cartoon race car on it. "This is Angel's. He would ask me to watch it for him when he went out to work."

"Was he a prostitute?"

"Yeah. He and Jody both were. They disappeared a week apart, Jody first. You disappeared the week after Angel. It was weird, the disappearances were always on a Thursday, I remember that."

"That *is* weird. Why would it always be a Thursday?"

"No idea." He unzipped the front pocket of the backpack and took out a Velcro wallet, then slid a photo from it and handed it to me. "That's Angel. I actually don't know what his real name is. I've looked through his bag, but nothing has his name on it." The photo was of a beautiful boy of about fifteen with long, tousled blond hair and big blue eyes, cuddling a scrawny brown dog.

"Did Jody and Angel know each other?"

"No, not really. I mean, you know how it is here. Everyone kinda knows everyone. But they weren't friends or anything." I didn't have the same perspective as Jeffrey, I'd never gotten to know anyone when I'd come here, apart from him and Mr. Avers. But then, Jeffrey was far more social than I was. I'd always just kept to myself, just like a lot of people that lived on the streets.

"Did any boys disappear after me?"

"No. I mean, not that I noticed. It's not like I know every single boy that's out there, though. I only know the few that come to the Havilland."

Could the police really overlook something as big as a serial killer? I mean, I didn't have a lot of faith in law enforcement apart from Kieran. But still, that seemed like a *huge* thing to miss.

"You know, I kept his stuff all this time," Jeffrey said, "because I kept hoping Angel would come back for it someday. I didn't want to believe he was dead, just like I didn't want to believe you and Jody were. And look, now here you are, alive and well! Do you think maybe they're alive, too? That maybe they really did just move on to another city like the police said?"

My gut told me that both of those boys had met the same fate by the man that had hurt me. They'd probably been killed, their bodies never recovered, the way mine was supposed to have been. I wasn't about to say that to Jeffrey though, as he sat there looking at me with so much hope. So I stuck a smile on my face and said, "Maybe," even as sadness washed through me.

He looked so happy as he took the photo from me and returned it to the wallet, then put everything back together and slid the backpack under his bed. "I'm gonna keep hanging on to his stuff. Maybe Angel will show up one day, just like you did." God, if only.

I took a pen from my pack and wrote my cell number on the back of the flyer I'd given him. "Jeffrey, it was great seeing you. It's almost lunch time and I know you have to get to work, so I won't keep you. But here's my number. Would you please think back to when Jody and Angel and I vanished, and try to remember if there was anything unusual about those days? Call me if you think of anything. Or you know, if you just want to talk."

"Yeah? Would that be okay?"

"Of course."

He lowered his gaze as he said, "I'm sorry I got weird on you after that night in the shelter. Later on, I really regretted pulling away from you like that. But I was just so embarrassed."

"You shouldn't be. We all break down in tears at some point or another. Sometimes you just need to let it out."

Jeffrey looked up at me and said, "Oh no, not about that. I was embarrassed about the other thing."

"What other thing?"

"Really? Do you honestly not know?"

I shook my head no, and he colored slightly and said, "I woke up with a huge boner that morning when you were hugging me. I was mortified. I'm not even gay, I don't know what the hell happened there."

I smiled at him and said, "Not only did I have no idea, but it wouldn't have been a big deal if I had known. You're not the first guy to ever sprout some morning wood, you know."

"Yeah, but come on, not when a *dude* is holding me."

I chuckled at that and said, "Well, next time something embarrassing happens, just talk to me about it. Don't slink away in shame."

"Yeah, okay. But for the record, I'm not planning to get any more boners around you."

We walked together to the front of the Havilland. A huge line had formed. It was a brisk January day, and people were here for a chance to get out of the cold for an hour, as much as for a hot meal. The shelter wouldn't open until tonight at eight p.m., per local regulations. "Seems like there are more homeless people than ever," I mused out loud.

"Yeah. So many people rely on this place. I really don't know what's going to happen next month."

"What's next month?"

"We're being shut down because the building's not earthquake safe. Mr. Avers had been fighting the city for years, but we lost."

"This place has been here for decades! How could the city shut you down now?"

Jeffrey shrugged. "I dunno."

"What are you going to do? Where will you go?"

"Mr. Avers is trying to pin down a temporary location. You know he's not just going to let this place fade away, there's too much need. He's done a lot of fund raising and gotten a few grants, we should be able to rent a place. It'll probably be a lot smaller than this, but it'll be something anyway."

"How much money is needed to fix up the Havilland?"

"About fifty-five million dollars, all told. It's kind of insane. I mean, think about it. The city wants to shut this place down because they think it's unsafe. But how safe is it for all these people to go hungry, and to sleep on the streets in the rain and cold? How many of our population aren't going to make it through the winter without our help?"

After we said goodbye out on the sidewalk and Jeffrey went inside to work the lunch shift, I pulled out my cell phone and read a text from Kieran, asking where I was. I texted him my location, and he wrote: *I'm close, I'll meet you there in a couple minutes.*

True to his word, a black and white police car pulled up to the curb almost exactly two minutes later. Kieran was in full uniform, and in total cop mode. He scanned the crowd, his body language alert, one hand resting on top of his holster. I soon saw why. He was the outsider here, vastly outnumbered by the prostitutes, pimps and drug dealers who saw him as a threat. Nobody said anything to him or approached him, but the tension in the air was palpable.

"Hi baby," he said when he came up to me. He was on duty, so he didn't touch me. It wasn't very professional to cuddle your boyfriend on a crowded sidewalk, after all. "How's it going?"

"Good. I think I may have had a major breakthrough."

"Really? Did someone recognize the sketch?"

"No, something else happened." I repeated Jeffrey's story about the other missing boys. And then I asked, "Do you think it's possible that the police department could miss something as major as a serial killer?"

"Sure. If the victims didn't have families and no one reported them missing, a serial killer could absolutely go unnoticed."

"Do you think that's really what happened?"

"I think there's too much of a pattern there to ignore the possibility. And maybe this new information will prompt the department to put more resources on your case."

"It's odd. Why would they always disappear on a Thursday?" I asked.

Kieran shrugged, then pointed over my shoulder. "Maybe that's why."

I looked behind me at a big, beat-up garbage truck working its way noisily down the alley beside Havilland House. Thick metal arms slid into the pockets on either side of a blue dumpster, then hoisted it up and shook the contents into the top of the truck. A loud whirring sound indicated a built-in trash compacter going to work. Today was Friday, garbage day in this neighborhood.

"Oh God," I murmured, a trickle of horror running through me. That could have been my fate. The man that hurt me threw me away like trash in a dumpster. If the garbage truck had gotten to me before that homeless woman, I would have been crushed with tons of garbage and hauled off to the dump. My body would never have been recovered. No one would have even been looking for it.

"Hey," Kieran said gently, his hand on my arm. "You alright, baby?"

I nodded, then cleared my throat and turned back to him. "So what do we do now?" I asked.

"Let's meet when I get off work and brainstorm. And of course you should call Uncle Ray and tell him what you found out," he said. "By the way, the reason I wanted to meet you here was because I need some more flyers, I ran out. Do you have some?"

"Sure," I said, and pulled a stack of papers out of my backpack. Even though he wasn't assigned to the case, Kieran had been helping in an "unofficial" capacity, asking questions and putting up flyers around town. Ray wasn't thrilled about Kieran's involvement, unofficial or otherwise, but he was a realist. He knew the department's budget was too tight to assign a lot of personnel to a cold case with so little evidence. So he'd begrudgingly decided to look the other way while Kieran helped me.

He took the stack of papers and rolled them into a tube, tapping them on his palm. He wanted to say something to me, and was working up to it. I knew the signs. Finally he said, "So...if I asked you to stop distributing flyers and asking questions, would you?"

"Why?"

He grinned at that. "It's never just a yes with you." Then he said, "If you're right about the serial killer angle, then this case is far more dangerous than I realized. I was already nervous about you going into the roughest parts of the city and asking questions. But now, if there really is a serial killer out here and you're distributing his photo and stirring things up, what's to stop him from coming after you? You're the only real evidence in this case, and eliminating you would mean he gets to remain a free man."

That thought was nothing short of horrifying. But I took a deep breath and said, "This man may have killed two boys, and almost killed me. Maybe there were more victims too, other boys that we don't even know about. You have to know I'm not going to stop looking for him."

"Please, Christopher. This is a matter for the police. It's not your job to bring him to justice, it's ours."

"The police don't have the time or resources to canvas like this."

"They'll allocate resources now that you found this new information. You can step back, you've done your part."

"There's more I could be doing."

Kieran sighed and dragged a hand over his mouth. And then he tried a different approach. "You've been out here every day this week. You're missing classes, and I know how important school is to you."

"I talked to my teachers, it's fine. The main thing I'm supposed to be doing right now is my junior project, and Hunter and I have been meeting regularly to work on that."

"*Please* go back to your regular life, Christopher. I'm begging you. I'll take over the canvassing."

"You can't. You're not even supposed to be helping me, this isn't your case."

"Then I'll take a leave of absence. I'll do it as a civilian, just like you're doing."

I grinned at him and said gently, "Why do you think I'd want you out here in harm's way? I'm no less worried about you attracting the attention of a killer than you're worried about me."

"But I've been trained for this! If he comes after me, I'm equipped to handle it."

"Go back to work, Kieran. We can talk about this tonight."

"Will you be done for today at least? Please? Go back home for the time being."

"Actually, I'm meeting Hunter on campus in about an hour, so I was ready to wrap it up today anyway."

"Thank God," he murmured.

"I'll see you tonight, Kieran," I said, reaching out and giving his arm a little squeeze. "Be careful out here, okay?"

"Always am. Be careful too."

Chapter Sixteen

I'd called Ray Nolan right after speaking with Kieran and told him what I found out. He'd made arrangements to meet with Jeffrey and hear his story, but that wasn't happening until Monday. Today was only Saturday, and I was in a funk.

I didn't know what to do about my case, where else to distribute flyers or who else to speak to. Knowing that a potential serial killer could be out there, and knowing I might be the only one who could put him in jail, had added a whole new sense of urgency to the case. I had decided to cancel my meeting with Hunter yesterday, despite what I told Kieran, and had gone up to every single rent boy I could find, showing each one the sketch of my attacker. And today, I'd turned around and done it all over again, just in case there were a few more boys on the street that I'd missed on Friday. That got me nothing but exhausted, and I was rapidly running out of ideas.

On an unrelated note, this was also the day of the New Artists Show. The incident with Ian still stung. And knowing the show was happening today was just really depressing somehow.

Everything was feeling just a little out of control at the moment. I needed a job. I needed to focus on my schoolwork. I needed leads on the case. Hell, while I was listing stuff that needed fixing, how about the food issues that threatened my health on a daily basis? There was so much in my life that I needed to address. But instead, here I was, lying in bed feeling sorry for myself and staring at the ceiling. It just all seemed so overwhelming that I didn't know how to approach any of it.

Well, even if I didn't know how to help myself, I did know how to help other people, and I'd done something yesterday afternoon that I felt good about. I'd placed a call to the accountant in Macon, Georgia that administered my trust fund. My father employed him to pay the annual taxes on the account and 'manage my portfolio.' I had instructed him to liquidate the entire account, and have all of the money deposited anonymously into the account for the Havilland House Fund. It wasn't enough, it wouldn't save the Havilland. But it would make a difference. The accountant had freaked out, of course. But it was my money and my decision, a fact that I reminded him of repeatedly before he finally agreed to do as I asked.

When I had told my father I'd never touch a cent of his dirty money, I'd meant it. But I decided to add an addendum to the end of that sentence: I'd never touch a cent of my father's money for personal use. Giving it to a community center was something else entirely. I wasn't going to be stubborn enough to let that money go to waste, not when it could be doing some good.

Knowing the trust fund was gone was a relief somehow. I had always felt I should do something about it, but had never figured out what until now.

There was a knock at the door, and I rolled off the mattress and went to answer it. Kieran was dressed up in the grey suit he'd worn to Charlie's wedding, his blue eyes sparkling. He looked incredibly gorgeous, and I told him that as I stepped back and let him in. "Why aren't you dressed yet?" he asked, taking in my sweats and bare feet. "I told you I was taking you out."

"I know, but I'm really tired. Can we just stay here and curl up on the couch and watch movies instead?"

A little crease of concern appeared between his eyebrows. "Were you out canvassing again today?"

"Yeah, all day. I just got home a little while ago."

"I thought we talked about this." We actually had, for quite a while last night.

"We did. And I told you that while I appreciated your concern, I had to keep going on this."

He crossed his arms over his chest. "Your stubbornness could get you killed. You know that, right?"

"I'm not stubborn, I'm tenacious. And please don't be mad at me. I'm too tired to argue with you."

He sighed and relaxed his posture, pulling me into his arms. "Well, as long as you're too tired to argue with me, I might as well make a confession. I did something yesterday afternoon that's going to piss you off."

I kept my arms around him, but tilted my head back to look up at him. "I don't know if I want to hear this."

"I went to Sutherlin and paid your tuition for next quarter."

"Damn it, Kieran!" I let go of him and took a step back.

"I know you didn't want to borrow money from me. So, now you haven't. Consider that just…a random act of kindness or something."

"An eighteen thousand dollar random act of kindness? Are you kidding?"

"I knew you'd be pissed, but it's worth having you mad at me. I believe in you, Christopher. I believe in your talent, and I want you to be able to continue your education." He grinned at me and added, "And if you feel the need to punish me for going behind your back, I'd like to suggest that wooden paddle you keep with your sex toys."

"I would never actually use that on you when I was pissed off, just FYI."

"Come on, get dressed. We're expected somewhere, and you can be mad at me on the way."

"I really don't feel like going out. And by the way, I'm paying you back, every cent. I have some money in savings that I was going to put toward my tuition, I'll start with that. And as soon as I find a job, I'll begin making weekly payments." I sighed and added, "I really wish you hadn't done that."

"I don't want you to pay me back, and I know you didn't want me to do that. But I'm doing it again next quarter, and the one after that, and the one after that, right up until you graduate."

"And you call me stubborn!"

"You *are*!"

"I'm going back to bed."

"No you're not," he said gently.

I glared at him, and he smiled at me sweetly. "I hate it when you tell me what to do in such a nice way that I feel like an asshole for arguing with you," I said.

"Come on, baby. There's a big surprise waiting for you. Get dressed, and let's go."

"A surprise? Because spending a huge chunk of your inheritance on my tuition wasn't enough? Now you're doing something else for me?"

"The surprise isn't from me, it's from Dante and Charlie. I'm just supposed to get you there. In retrospect, telling you about the tuition payment probably shouldn't have happened until after I'd delivered you where you need to be."

I sighed and crossed my arms over my chest, and Kieran added, "Charlie's so excited. This surprise means a lot to him."

"Really?" I asked, grinning a little despite myself. "Playing the best friend card? You know I wouldn't want to disappoint him."

"No, you wouldn't. So come on, get dressed and let's go. For Charlie." He was grinning, too.

I felt my resolve weakening, and reached out and ran his blue silk tie over the palm of my hand. "What am I going to do with you, Kieran?"

"You can let me take you out, and then bring me back here afterwards and spend all night punishing me," he said, his voice low, a sexy half-smile bringing out his dimple as he held my gaze steadily. "Actually," he added, "we still have a little time, I'm early. You could begin punishing me right now if you wanted to."

A shiver of desire skittered through me, but I said, "I'm serious about not playing at punishment when I'm actually upset with you."

He sank to his knees and rubbed his cheek against the bulge in my sweats. "Yeah, but we both know it wouldn't really feel like punishment to me anyway."

"Stop being so sexy when I'm trying to be mad at you." I ran my palm over his short hair as he kissed my cock through my clothes and grinned at me. "Damn it," I murmured, before bending down and kissing him deeply. Then I said, "This is just sex. Not a punishment, not anything else. And I'm still upset that you went off and paid my tuition when you knew that I didn't want you to do that. Just because we're about to fuck doesn't change anything."

"Yes sir," he murmured, and then he smiled at me innocently and asked, "How do you want me?"

Lust rocketed down my spine, straight to my cock. "Oh sure, *now* you're submissive. But then you go off and defy my wishes."

He was fully embracing his inner sub now, though. "I'm sorry, baby. I don't mean to be defiant. I just want to make things better." He rubbed his cheek against my cock again, his hands sliding up my thighs.

The full truth of that last statement really resonated with me all of a sudden. That was exactly what he'd been doing, just trying to make things better. And that was a huge part of who he was, a giver through and through. I sighed and said, "Promise me you'll talk to me next time, before running off and doing something that drastic."

"I promise."

I bent down and kissed him again, and said softly, "Thank you, Kieran."

"What are you thanking me for?"

"Paying my tuition so I can stay in school."

His eyes went wide, his face lighting up with a big smile. "You're thanking me?"

I nodded. "It still makes me uncomfortable, you know I hate feeling indebted to people. And I'm going to pay you back, every single cent of that money. We can draw up that loan agreement we talked about a while back and set up a payment schedule." I ran my hand over his cheek as I said, "But the part of me that isn't freaked out by this is grateful. You're a very sweet, if occasionally stubborn person, Kieran."

He chuckled and said, "That's a pretty fair assessment."

"How much time do we have before this surprise that you're taking me to?"

"Well, the surprise really doesn't get started until you get there," he said with a shrug. "So I suppose you could take your time. You know…with whatever it is you need time for." He grinned at me innocently.

I took his hand, led him to the bedroom, and stripped us both naked, then guided him onto his back on the bed. After prepping him gently, I rolled on a condom and sheathed myself in his body. I held his gaze as I moved in him slowly, deeply, our connection so intense that a tremor went through him. He parted his lips, his breath coming in short gasps, and I slid my arms behind his shoulders, holding him as I took him. It was the exact opposite of the kind of sex he'd probably been expecting, but it was so right in that moment.

"I belong to you, Christopher," he said, his voice a rough whisper. "Every part of me, for as long as you want me."

"Oh God, Kieran." I kissed him as passionately as that very first time.

Later, when we'd both finished, I held him in my arms and murmured, "And now I *really* don't want to get up."

That prompted him to roll out of bed, pulling me to my feet with him. "I'm so excited for you to see this surprise," he said. "I really hope you're going to love it."

He picked up his shirt, which was draped over the corner of the headboard, and hesitated before saying, "This is going to sound really lame, but thank you. You know, for that," he said, tilting his head toward the bed. "The way you take care of me absolutely amazes me. And I just want you to know I'm grateful for it." He grinned embarrassedly and quickly changed the subject by saying, "Okay, enough awkward speeches. We've got places to go and people to see!"

I pulled him to me with a hand on the back of his head, and kissed him deeply. Then I said, "Do I get any hints about this surprise?"

"Nope."

"And it's a get-dressed-up kind of thing, obviously," I said, indicating the shirt he was pulling back on over his broad shoulders. "I don't actually own a suit, though."

"I only own two kinds of clothes: jeans, and this suit. I'm probably over-dressed. You should feel free to wear whatever you want."

"Well, that's not entirely true," I said, pulling on a pair of briefs from the dresser. "You also own a really nice reindeer sweater."

He beamed at me and said, "Oh, don't start teasing me about Rudolph, because I *will* retaliate. I'm not above wearing him in public to humiliate those around me, as you well know."

I laughed at that and said, "I'm actually quite fond of Rudolph. Don't ever get rid of him."

"Wouldn't dream of it, baby," he said. "Someday we can hang that sweater above our mantel as a reminder of where it all began. Think that red nose will still be blinking fifty years from now?"

That was actually a hell of a statement, but I decided not to read too much in. Instead I said lightly, "I think you just suggested that we have your sweater taxidermied and mounted over the fireplace. Poor Rudolph!"

He laughed at that. "I was picturing it framed, but you have something with that idea. I bet a skilled taxidermist could get ol' Rudolph looking awesomely lifelike."

When we finally made it downstairs, I was shocked to find a black town car waiting for us. The driver put down his Kindle and came around and opened the door for us, and I glanced at Kieran with a raised eyebrow. He said, "Don't look at me. This was Dante's idea, he thinks parking is going to be problematic where we're going. That guy really doesn't do anything halfway."

To the driver I said, "Sorry about keeping you waiting, I didn't realize you were down here."

"It's all good," he said with a grin. "I get paid regardless, whether I'm driving or reading."

When we were settled comfortably in the big back seat, I asked Kieran, "Do you know what Dante used to do for a living?"

"Of course. Every cop in the city knows his name. Not that anyone ever pinned anything on him, but still, he's pretty infamous in this town. Why do you ask?"

"I was just wondering how something like that sat with you, knowing that a friend of yours married a former mobster. And your cousin Jamie did, too, for that matter."

"From what I hear, both Dmitri and Dante have completely turned their lives around. I'm really not going to condemn them for their past."

"That's a pretty open-minded attitude," I said.

He added with a grin, "For a cop."

"I didn't say that."

"It was implied."

I rolled my eyes at him, then idly twisted one of the buttons on my black dress shirt. After a moment I ventured, "Did your cousin Jamie ever tell you about the conversation he and I had when he came over to my apartment?"

"He only told me a little. He said that he acted like an asshole and went over there to make sure you weren't, like, taking advantage of me or some shit. I threatened to punch him if he ever did anything like that again."

"I told him some things about my family when we were talking. And I just never got around to telling you, I guess," I said. "My father is retired mob, too, kind of like

Dante. Well, except that I like Dante, and my father is an asshole. My real last name's Longotti. I'm going to have it legally changed to Andrews, my mother's maiden name. That's actually the present I'm giving myself for my twenty-first birthday at the end of this month."

All he said to that was, "That's a good present."

I raised an eyebrow at him. "Really? You're not shocked to find out I'm the son of Reggie the Roach Longotti?"

"That's kind of a gross nickname."

"It's because he can't be killed, like a cockroach. He's been shot, stabbed, and blown up, but he was perfectly fine after each of those incidents." I stared at Kieran for a moment, and he smiled at me placidly. And then I exclaimed, "Jamie told you! That's why you're not shocked about this!"

"Of course he did, but he made me promise not to tell you. He knew he was speaking out of turn, but he just couldn't help himself."

"So, you've known about this for a couple weeks, and never said anything."

"Yup. I knew you'd get around to telling me eventually."

"I guess ever since my case got reopened, I've been pretty distracted. I always had every intention of telling you."

"I know, baby." Then he added, "Just FYI, I don't think you should mention any of that to Charlie."

"Why not?"

"Because he'll tell Dante, and Dante might tell one of his relatives. And…well, that could be bad."

"Because there's some kind of feud between their family and mine? That really doesn't have anything to do with me."

"You and I know that, but I'm not sure his family would see it that way. There's a lot of bad blood there."

I frowned and said, "Well, now I feel like I'm keeping a secret from my best friend."

He tried to distract me from my impending guilt by smiling at me and saying, "You know, you're very blond for an Italian boy."

"I take after my mother, although my father's family is northern Italian, and they tend to be fair. And you are so bad at subtly changing the subject."

"Yeah, I really am."

I happened to glance out the window, and realized where we were. "Oh God," I said. "Please tell me we aren't crashing the new artists show at the Tremont Gallery."

"Hell no."

"Then where are we going?" The driver turned onto the street where the gallery was located. It was total pandemonium, cars circling and looking for parking, a news van double-parked and adding to the congestion, people running through traffic, big searchlights giving the whole thing the feel of a movie premier. "Wow," I murmured. "I knew the show at the Tremont Gallery was big, but I didn't know it was *this* big."

"It's not," Kieran said. He had a huge smile on his face.

"Okay, I'm lost," I told him.

"I know." Kieran leaned forward and called, "We can just hop out here, Ed, there's no way you're making it down that street. I'll call you when we're ready to be picked up, and you can meet us a couple blocks over."

"Sure thing, Mr. Nolan," the driver said.

Kieran hopped out of the car and held his hand out to me, and I took hold of it as I stepped out into the street. We wove our way through stopped traffic over to the crowded sidewalk, and Kieran put his arm around my shoulders. The Tremont Gallery was a half-block ahead, we were headed right for it. "I'm serious, Kieran, I don't want to see Ian. There's no point in confronting him. I just want to put that whole ugly incident behind me."

"You will, baby. You're about to get so much closure."
We stopped on the sidewalk right in front of Ian's place. I
was about to dig my heels in and refuse to go inside. But
then he took hold of my shoulders and spun me away from
the gallery.

The big brick building directly across the street was
ablaze in color and light, the spotlights actually picking out
the front of *that* building and not the gallery, techno music
pumping from the open doors. That was where the crowd
was headed, an endless stream of people pouring inside.
The front of the dark red building had been painted in a
huge white signature, the letters six feet high. It read *C.R.
Andrews.* "Welcome to your opening night, Christopher."

"I don't understand."

"Dante was really upset about what happened between
you and Tremont, since he'd been the one to introduce the
two of you. To make amends, he decided to host a pop-up
art show in your honor."

I grinned a little. "Directly across the street from Ian's
place?" I glanced over my shoulder. There were a few
people inside the gallery, but it was sedate compared to the
gala going on across the street. "I feel bad for the other new
artists in Ian's show."

"So did Dante. That's why he's offered each of them a show of their own. Just not tonight, because this is your night."

"When did he do all of this? He just got back from his honeymoon a day ago."

"Apparently former gangsters really know how to get stuff done. He mobilized the whole Dombruso clan. I guess that old building belongs to a friend of one of his cousins. They've all been scrambling for the last twenty-four hours. Charlie and I helped, too."

My grin got a little wider. "It looks more like a rave than an art opening."

"Which is perfect for art's new bad boy," Kieran said with a big smile.

"Oh God."

"The media seems to have caught wind of all of this," he said, tilting his head toward the news van.

"Probably because Dante called them."

"Probably. Do you want to sneak in the back? I know the way. This all seems to have gotten a little…huge."

I considered that and said, "Nah. All of this…it's kind of great. I think I'm just going to go right in the front door and drink it all in."

"That's my baby," Kieran said with a proud smile. "And we are so having victory sex tonight when we get home." He gave me a playful wink and grabbed my hand, and we stepped out into the street.

I very nearly made it unnoticed into the front door of the brick building. But suddenly someone yelled, "There he is!"

The throng erupted in cheers and applause as the color rose in my cheeks. I recognized some familiar faces in the crowd, a few Dombrusos mixed in with some of my fellow students from Sutherlin. It was all absolutely surreal. A girl from my life painting class yelled, "Way to go, C.R.!" Kieran hugged my shoulders securely as we moved forward, and the crowd parted for us, just a little.

Inside the door were huge stacks of Stylemaker Weekly, the one with my picture on the cover. Okay, that was embarrassing. We stepped through the little foyer and into a huge main room. The space was wall-to-wall people. And it was punctuated every few yards by tall cylindrical columns about eight feet high and three feet across. At first, I thought the columns were holding go-go boys. Each handsome young guy at the top of each column was dressed in black and picked out by a spotlight. But when the guy closest to us turned in our direction, I saw that he was holding one of my paintings in gloved hands, displaying it to the crowd. So were each of the other boys on each of the columns. Man, was that over the top. I smiled at Dante's flair for the dramatic.

And speaking of Dante, he and Charlie suddenly appeared beside me. Dante looked concerned as he leaned in and yelled over the music, "Is it too much? It is, isn't it? Did I completely freak you out?"

I stretched up and kissed his cheek. "It's amazing. Thank you."

He looked relieved. Charlie grabbed me in a hug, then yelled, "We have a private balcony. Come on, let's go up there before you get trampled."

We went through a doorway guarded by a huge bouncer and climbed a staircase, and emerged in a loft with a big seating area overlooking the main floor. The music was slightly muffled from here, so we could talk without yelling. A little buffet had been set up. In addition to all kinds of snacks and appetizers, a silver serving tray was artfully arranged with several packets of the crackers I ate. I grinned at that, then went to the railing at the edge of the loft and looked down at the crowd.

"Dozens of people have been asking whether your paintings are for sale," Dante said as he came up and leaned on the railing beside me. "I wanted to talk to you about that. I know you were planning to sell the eight pieces that were going to be in Tremont's show, and they're all here.

We also went to your school and talked to some of your classmates and teachers, and they helped us pick out another ten paintings of yours that were in your studio on campus. Do you want to sell them? It's your call."

I thought about it for a few moments, and then I said, "Sell them all." I took out my cellphone and pulled up a picture of my favorite painting, the one of the five-year-old boy at the side of the road. "Except this one. I regretted putting it in Ian's show. I think I want to hold on to it."

"I'll be sure that one doesn't get sold. Do you want to discuss pricing for the others?"

"Nah. Just ask whatever you think is fair. I owe Kieran some money, maybe I'll earn enough to make a few payments." I glanced at him over my shoulder. He and Charlie were chatting happily at the buffet, each holding a beer in one hand and a snack in the other. He caught my eye and winked at me, then flashed me a huge smile before saying something to Charlie. I turned back to my companion and said, "Thank you again for doing this, Dante."

"I am so fucking sorry that I introduced you to Tremont. I thought he was a decent guy, that's how he acts in public. I had no idea that he would treat you like that."

"It's okay, you didn't know. Anyway, it's not like he's the first guy ever to treat a whore like a whore," I said, lowering my gaze.

Dante gently took my chin and tilted my face up so I was looking him in the eye. "You're not a whore. You've done what you had to in order to survive, and that has nothing to do with who you are as a person. You deserve respect. And any man that doesn't give you that deserves to be dropped nuts first into a tank of piranhas."

I grinned at him and said, "That's the most mafia-like thing I've ever heard you say."

He grinned too and let go of my chin. "I have about a hundred and fifty threats on standby involving testicles. It probably won't surprise you that I learned each and every one of them from my Nana."

I laughed at that and said, "Definitely not surprising. Is she here, by the way?"

"Of course. She wouldn't miss something like this. Last I saw her, she was out on the dance floor at the back of the building with her date, Seymour." Dante rolled his eyes. "This one is wearing about forty pounds of gold chains and keeps taking out his dentures and pretending to do ventriloquism with them."

I laughed again and said, "Awesome." My phone buzzed in my pocket, and I pulled it out to read a text. I said to Dante, "Hey, my friend Hunter, who you met at Christmas, is downstairs. Can you tell that big bouncer to let him up here?"

"Absolutely." Dante pulled an earpiece on a wire out from under the lapel of his black suit jacket and spoke into it.

A minute later, Hunter swept into the loft, gorgeous as ever and towing a big blond guy in a Stetson behind him by the hand. "Oh my God, Christopher!" he squealed, and grabbed me in a hug. "This is incredible! Best art show *ever*! I think half of San Francisco is downstairs."

When he let go of me, he greeted Dante, then waved at Charlie and Kieran and yelled, "Thanks for the invite, Kier! You're a saint among men!" He turned back to me and said, "Oh, by the way, this if Olaf. Olaf, go have some snacks while the grownups talk," Hunter said, and the big cowboy grinned happily and went off to the buffet. My friend watched him go, then turned to me and said, "He's dumber than a rabbit trying to knock up a squirrel, but you should see his shlong. Lord almighty!"

I grinned at that and Dante asked, "Is he from Texas?"

"No, he's from Oakland. I just stuck the hat on him for fun," Hunter said with a wink.

"Where'd you find this guy?"

"I was at the Man-on-Man Productions offices to sign off on a new product line, and he wandered in off the street, looking for an audition," Hunter said, turning and watching his date hork down a tray of appetizers. "My agent tried to kick him out, but then Olaf dropped trou right in the middle of the office, and he got signed on the spot. You're looking at the next big thing in gay porn. Literally," Hunter said, turning to me with a huge grin and a wink.

"How long have you known him?" I asked, and Hunter glanced at his wristwatch.

"Four hours. Four long, *long* hours." He looked immensely pleased.

"What's the product line?" Dante asked, obviously highly entertained by all of this.

Hunter looked a little embarrassed as he said, "Flavored lubes. Specifically, flavored lubes that guys will like. You know: beer, barbeque, bacon…."

I burst out laughing and covered my mouth with my hand. "Oh, ew. Please tell me you didn't taste them all."

"You know, laugh all you want, but that bacon-flavored lube is genius. You could squirt that shit on a burger, I'm telling ya."

"Bacon lube is either the best idea I've ever heard, or the worst," Dante said. "I don't know which."

"What's the best or worst idea?" Charlie asked. He and Kieran had joined us, and Kieran came up behind me and slipped his arms around my waist.

"Bacon-flavored lube," Dante told him.

"The best," Charlie said with a smile. "What guy wouldn't buy that?"

"Me," I said.

"You haven't even heard the best part," Hunter said with a huge smile. "It's organic, Kosher, and cruelty-free."

"Kosher, cruelty-free bacon lube," Kieran repeated. "I'm trying to get my head around that one."

"No actual pigs were lubricated in the making of this product," Hunter quipped, and we all burst out laughing.

"Please tell me your face isn't on the packaging," I said.

"Uh, no. But wouldn't that be awesome? I could be wearing a yarmulke and riding a pig, bucking bronco-style. Come get yer kosher cruelty-free bacon lube, ya'all!" Hunter grinned, then added, "Um, I might be featured in a series of print ads, however. Without the pig and the yarmulke, although I suppose they could always be Photoshopped in later."

I started laughing again, dabbing tears from my eyes. I was having the time of my life. Absolutely nothing could ruin this night for me.

"Chris, we need to talk," a voice behind me said.

Nothing but that.

Chapter Seventeen

Kieran and I both turned to face my father. Reggie Longotti had met my mother when he was in his fifties, and was now seventy-six, but he really didn't look it. He wore a finely tailored dark suit and tie, his thick white hair impeccably styled. It had been almost three years since I'd seen him. That was the last time he'd paid his employee to fly out to San Francisco and drag me kicking and screaming back to Georgia. It had been shortly after my eighteenth birthday, and I'd threatened to have him arrested for kidnapping. That had put an end to the forced homecomings.

"Is there someplace we could go to talk?" my father asked.

"What part of I never want to see you again was unclear?" I said, my voice low. Kieran was right beside me and must have felt the tension in my body. He shifted subtly, fully alert, ready to defend me if necessary.

"Yeah, you know what? You said a lot of things, Chris. Like, 'I'm never gonna touch my trust fund.' And then what do you do? You cash it out and send it to a fucking homeless shelter!"

"You damn well better not have stopped that payment."

"If only I could! But the fucking thing was in your name, and I couldn't stop it. I mean, who the fuck sends thirty-two million dollars to the fucking *homeless*? That's insane!"

"Holy shit," Hunter whispered.

"It was my money and my decision."

"Well it was a fucking piss poor decision! That money was your future, and now you have nothing!"

"I have nothing?" I asked incredulously. "Look around you! What do you think is happening here? That's my name on the front of this building, and those are my paintings downstairs! These people are my friends, and this man is my boyfriend! I have *nothing*? Bullshit, Reggie. I have more than you ever will."

"What, this dog and pony show? You proud of this? I seen better at Ringling Brothers. And great, you got a queer boyfriend, good for you." My father crossed his arms over his chest.

"You know, if I even *sort of* gave a shit about your opinion, that might have hurt. But nothing you say matters to me."

"You don't give a shit about what I think? Yeah, right. Come on, the only reason you gutted your trust fund and sent it to the fucking homeless was so you could deliver a nice, big fuck you to your old man," my father growled.

"That had nothing to do with you! I sent that money to Havilland House because they needed it, and I was never, ever in a million years going to use it for myself."

"Like hell you weren't! It was just a matter of time. You thought you were being tough, you thought you were sending me a message by letting the money sit there. But there would have come a time when you needed it, and you would have dipped into that fund. As soon as times got desperate, you would have realized you weren't too good for your old man's 'dirty money' after all. I *know* you would have caved." He looked so smug.

"As soon as times got desperate? Where do you think I've been living all this time, Disneyland? I sent that money to the shelter where I used to sleep on the floor each winter, down the street from where I used to sell my body as a prostitute. You don't think I got to desperate *years ago*?"

My father looked absolutely stunned, all the color draining from his face. When he finally spoke, he said, "That's how much you fucking hate me? That you'd rather...rather do *that* than take my money?" I just stared at him.

He shook off his shock and glared at me as he said, "I didn't kill your mother, Chris. I know you think I drove her to suicide, but I didn't. She was unstable, she—"

"Don't you *ever* fucking talk about my mother."

He stared at me for a long moment, then growled, "You know, I've had about enough of this bullshit. We're getting out of here, and you're coming home with me."

"No chance."

"What else you been doing besides whoring yourself out? Drugs? You're skinny as a heroin addict. You're coming home, and we're getting you help. End of discussion."

"I'm not going anywhere with you."

"Oh, I think you are." My father pulled a compact black handgun out of a shoulder holster and pointed it at me. Fear slid down my spine as he said, "You need help, Chris, you need to come back to the family. This is for your own good, you're obviously not making rational decisions."

That instantly flipped Kieran's cop switch, and he said, "Why don't you put the gun down, and let's all talk about this."

I swallowed the sudden dryness in my throat and said, "Even you aren't enough of an asshole to shoot your own son, Reggie."

"No, you're right," my father said. And then he swung the gun around and pointed it directly at Kieran. Panic welled in me, my heart trying to beat its way out of my chest. "But I'm definitely enough of an asshole to shoot my son's faggot boyfriend."

Without even thinking about it, I stepped between Kieran and the gun, as Kieran exclaimed, "No Christopher, stay back!"

In the next instant, Reggie Longotti was crumpling to the ground, his eyes rolled back in his head. As he fell he revealed Nana behind him, holding her big silver revolver by the muzzle, having just used it like a hammer to knock my father unconscious. "Faggot is such an ugly word," she said.

My knees started to buckle, but Kieran caught me and held me securely. "Oh God, Kier, I'm so sorry," I said.

"Why are you apologizing?"

"For putting you in the middle of that."

"It's not your fault, baby." He sat down and pulled me onto his lap as he said, "And by the way, I think we should take your father off our Christmas card list. He's kind of a douche." I smiled at him, and he kissed the tip of my nose.

"This is the best party ever," someone said, and we all glanced toward the buffet table. I'd forgotten Olaf was even there. He grinned at us happily, his mouth full, a tray of hors d'oeuvres in his hand.

While we'd been talking, Dante had snapped into action, disarming first Reggie and then his grandmother. As he took Reggie's pulse, Nana asked, "Is he dead?"

"No, but he'll most likely have a concussion, maybe even a fractured skull. We should get him to a hospital. I don't think an ambulance will make it up the street with all the congestion outside, so I'll take him in my car."

"I'll go with you," I said.

"No Christopher, stay and enjoy your party," Dante said. "I've got this."

"I'm not really in the partying mood after this."

"By the way, you had a bit of a situation downstairs," Mrs. Dombruso said. "A couple thick-necked thugs were leaning on Bobby the security guard, Dante. I took care of it."

"How?"

"I kicked one in the nuts while I hit the other one with my purse. In the nuts. I had a couple members of your security team with me, but I did all the work. They just detained 'em when I was done with 'em. I think the thugs were taken to that office at the back of the building."

Dante fought back a smile and said, "That was a dangerous situation, Nana. Next time, just let the security team handle it."

"Fuck that!"

Dante had been patting down my still-unconscious father, and so far had pulled two more guns from him. "Shouldn't Kieran be the one to do that?" I asked Dante.

"He has his hands full," Dante said with a grin. Both of Kieran's arms were firmly around me. "Besides, I've done plenty of pat-downs, I know what I'm doing." He pulled my father's wallet from his pocket and flipped it open with one hand, his other full of weapons. "Huh," he said as he read the ID, his eyebrows raised. Then he returned the wallet to its jacket pocket.

"What does it say? Who is this dirt bag?" Nana wanted to know.

"My father," I said.

"Reginald Andrews," Dante lied. He was obviously keeping the mob connection under wraps.

"What kind of father pulls a gun on their kid and his boyfriend? Was this a hate crime? Does he not accept you for being a gay homosexual? It's a damn shame," Nana said. "And he was kinda sexy, too. I would've slipped him my number, had I not known he was a total asshat."

"Man, and I thought my dad and I had issues, but he stopped short of ever actually pulling a gun on me. I mean, that is some epically bad parenting," Hunter said.

Several of Dante's male cousins came barreling up the stairs then. They all none-too-subtly had their hands inside the lapels of their jackets. Did the crowd downstairs really not know any of this was going on?

One of them, Louie maybe, said, "We got a situation downstairs. The security team apprehended a couple guys, turns out they're Reggie the Roach Longotti's men. We think he's somewhere in the building."

Dante looked up from my father's prone body and raised an eyebrow. "Ya think?"

"Oh," Louie said, relaxing his posture.

Nana exclaimed, "First a hate crime and now Reggie the Roach! What the fuck is with this night? Dante, give me my piece back, I gotta go help these boys look for the Roach."

"Over my dead body." My father stirred a little, and Dante asked, "Kieran, do you happen to have your handcuffs with you?"

"No, sorry, I'm off duty," Kieran replied.

"What difference does that make?" Hunter asked, pulling a pair of cuffs from the pocket of his black leather jacket and handing them to Dante. "I'm off duty too, but you never know when you might need to cuff somebody." He gave Kieran a flirty wink, and tossed me the keys.

After Dante cuffed my father, he stood up and hoisted him over his shoulder like he weighed nothing. But Kieran chimed in, "I can take him to the hospital, Dante. You have a lot going on here that needs your attention. I'll call for the car." We got up too, and he pulled his cell phone from his pocket and dialed a number, then plugged his opposite ear and spoke into the receiver.

When Kieran disconnected, Dante said, "Take him to Rosewood Hospital, I'll call ahead so they'll be expecting him." They threw a coat over my father, and transferred him to Kieran's shoulder in a fireman's carry.

"Please make sure Christopher gets home safely," Kieran said to Dante. And to me he said, "I'll call you from the hospital, baby."

"Oh no. I'm coming with you," I told him.

"You should stay and enjoy this. Don't let your father ruin your first art show," Kieran said.

"I want to go. And my show's far from ruined. Thanks to Dante, my paintings are reaching a huge audience, and I might find an agent after all of this exposure. Really, my being here doesn't add much."

"Still, you could just stay and have fun."

"Reggie's my problem. And if he comes to and starts giving you grief, I'm damn well going to be there," I said.

We said goodbye to our friends, and went down a rear staircase and out the back door. After cutting through an alley, we emerged onto a busy side street. A lot of people gave us strange looks, but Kieran just nodded at them and said, "Hell of a party."

Ed the driver was waiting right where he said he'd be, and when we arrived at the private hospital a few minutes later, a medical team met us in the parking lot and loaded my father onto a stretcher. He'd come to several minutes ago, but had done nothing besides moan and complain about his headache. I handed over the handcuff keys to a doctor, and she unhooked them from behind his back, then cuffed him to the railing of the stretcher. I wondered what Dante had told the hospital when he'd called them.

When they'd wheeled him into the building, Kieran asked, "Do you want to wait while they admit him?"

"I...don't know."

"Let's go home. You've had a rough night, and you were already tired to begin with."

I nodded and let him lead me back to the town car. We curled up in the back seat, Kieran's arms around me as Ed drove us back to the Sunset. After a while, Kieran asked, "Are you going to press charges?"

"I don't know. Are you?"

"It's really your call. Whatever you decide, I'll back you up."

"Believe it or not, that wasn't the first time he pointed a gun at me," I said quietly. "Not that you ever get used to something like that."

"No, you really don't. I've been drawn on a few times in the line of duty. It never gets easier." He tightened his grip around me and said, "What were you thinking, stepping between me and that gun, Christopher?"

"I needed to protect you."

He sighed and rested his cheek on the top of my head. "Baby, I'm a police officer. You didn't need to protect me, you just needed to keep yourself safe."

"I get that you're a big, tough cop, Kieran. But you're also the most precious thing in the world to me, and I'll always try to protect you."

"I'm the most precious thing in the world to you?"

"Of course."

He smiled at that, and said softly, "I'd say the same about you, you know." I kissed him gently, and he added, "That's why it's so hard to watch you putting yourself in harm's way."

"I get that."

After a couple minutes, he said, "So. Thirty-two million dollars, huh?"

"It's blood money. I would never have used it for myself."

"Havilland House is a great place, it fills a real need. I'm proud of you."

"Did Jamie not tell you about the trust fund?"

"Jamie knew?"

"Yeah. It came up in that conversation he and I had a couple weeks back."

"Sounds like a heck of a conversation. I'm sorry I missed it."

"I think you're all caught up now," I said, nestling into the space between his neck and shoulder.

*****

I ended up lying awake half the night, staring at the ceiling and thinking about the confrontation with my father. Kieran was asleep beside me, his warmth and his presence a comfort, and I caressed his back as he slept, reassuring myself that he was okay.

I'd been horrified when Reggie pointed the gun at Kieran – that had been vastly more troubling than having the gun pointed at me. I had known for a while now that I was falling in love with Kieran, and the full depth and breadth of my feelings for him were spelled out so clearly the moment he was threatened. Stepping between him and the weapon was automatic, instinctual: protect what you love. Protecting Kieran was as natural as breathing.

I'd had so many fears about entering into a relationship with someone. I had really thought I might be so broken that it wasn't even a possibility. But being with Kieran just felt so incredibly right on every level. Trusting him also came naturally. He was good and kind and decent, and would never hurt me. He'd protect me, the same way I protected him. I was sure of him.

I thought about my father too, as I lay awake. He'd flown across the country because I pissed him off. But instead of telling me off, what he'd actually tried to do when he got here, in his own misguided, incredibly fucked up way, was help me. The fact that I neither needed nor wanted help was obviously lost on him.

Our relationship had always been strained, as far back as I could remember. And maybe it never had a chance to be anything but. When my mother killed herself, she left both of us gutted to our core. My father and I were like two guilty survivors of a war, both blaming ourselves and each other for things that weren't our fault, shell-shocked and scarred, unable to ever fully recover. We'd turned on each other when there was no one else to blame. Neither had it in us to blame her.

When I'd run away from home, it wasn't just to get away from him, though that was part of it. I thought he hated me, I thought maybe he'd be glad I was gone. I knew I reminded him of her, I looked enough like my mother to make it tough for him to be around me. He'd purged the house of every picture of her, after all, every reminder she ever existed, except for one: me.

But after I left, he kept finding me, kept dragging me back home. He never came himself to get me, he sent an employee. In my mind that reinforced the idea that he was just bringing me back out of spite, not because he actually loved me or cared about me. But he kept doing it, again and again, up until three years ago, when I finally came of age and threatened him with kidnapping charges.

He'd called me a few times over the last three years, but I never picked up when I saw it was him. The last call was almost six months ago, and since then I'd figured he'd finally given up on me, that he no longer cared what I did or what happened to me. But now, all of a sudden, here he was, ostensibly because he was mad about my trust fund (and, okay, he probably really was furious about that).

Instead of just yelling at me and calling me an idiot, though, what did he do? He tried to make me come back home. His reasons for doing so and his method of choice were indisputably fucked up, in true my-father fashion. He was used to using threats, violence and intimidation to get what he wanted – it somehow never occurred to him that there might be something wrong with applying his usual thug mentality to his own child.

Yet if I could somehow look past all of that (yeah, *a lot* to look past, I know), in his own fucked up way, he actually was trying to help me. Not that I was justifying his actions. I was furious that he'd threatened Kieran, and none too thrilled that he'd threatened me. Still though, despite layer upon layer of fucked up and dysfunctional, I could see a father underneath all of that who still thought his son was worth saving.

*****

After much deliberation, I went to visit my father the next morning. I didn't really expect him to listen to anything I had to say, but I needed to say it anyway, for my own benefit.

Reggie didn't notice me for a moment, so I paused in the doorway to his hospital room and studied him. He was propped up in bed, looking pale, thin and tired, staring out the window. He usually didn't look his age, but he did right at that moment. The cuffs were gone, and I was actually kind of surprised he hadn't checked himself out of the hospital yet.

When he finally noticed me standing there, he sat up a bit straighter and raised his chin. "Come to gloat, Chris?"

I said quietly, "It's Christopher Robin. Not Chris. My mother gave me that name, and I want you to use it."

He rolled his eyes at that, then winced in pain. He obviously still had a headache. "It's a fruity name. I never liked it."

"Tough shit. Use it anyway."

"What are you doing here? You wanna kick me when I'm down? Is that it?"

"No. I wanted to talk."

"So go ahead," he said.

I wasn't quite sure what to say, so I fidgeted with the strap of my backpack for a while and finally just asked, "How do you feel?"

"Like I got hit on the head with a sledgehammer. Who clocked me, anyway?"

"An eighty-year-old woman."

"Bullshit."

I crossed the room and sat in the chair near his bed, setting my backpack on the floor beside me. I was still scrambling to figure out what I wanted to say to him, and ended up blurting, "You know, normal people don't pull guns on their children and their loved ones."

"Yeah? Well, you gave me no choice."

I knit my brows at that. "Really? You think that's a rational response to an adult son telling his father no?"

"It was for your own good. You need help, and you won't come home with me willingly."

"First of all, I don't need help. And secondly, Georgia isn't home anymore. This is."

"Of course you need help! You're skin and bones, you're obviously using. And now I find out you been working as a hooker to support yourself! If I'd known that, I would've come here sooner and forced you to come home. I would've checked you into one of them rehab clinics."

"Hooker rehab?" I said flatly.

"No, smartass. Drug rehab."

"I've never taken drugs in my life, Reggie. Do I seem like I'm on drugs?"

He considered that for a moment and finally conceded, "Well, no."

"And I don't know why the hell you're suddenly pretending to be the caring father, trying to clean up his son – who, by the way, doesn't need cleaning up. You're not that kind of parent. You're the kind who pulls a fucking *gun* on his kid."

"Of course I care about you. It don't even matter that you hate my fuckin' guts. I will always care about you, and if that occasionally means havin' to resort to desperate measures to try to get through to you, so be it."

"That's not even 'desperate measures,' it's your go-to! Something doesn't go your way? You immediately default to threats and violence."

He shrugged and said, "Yeah, well, that's who I am."

"It was bad enough you threatened me, and probably a sign of how deeply warped our relationship is that I'm even here talking to you after that," I said. "But I need to say something to you, and I need you to really listen. You are *never* to threaten Kieran again. That's crossing a line, and I *will not* tolerate it."

"Oh yeah? What're you gonna do to stop me?"

I stared him down, my voice low and rock solid as I said, "Whatever it takes."

He watched me for a long moment, then grinned a little and said, "That's the very first time you ever sounded like the son of Reggie the Roach." I sighed and leaned back in the chair, and my father asked, "Are you talking about that big guy in the grey suit?"

"Yeah. My boyfriend. The one you pointed a gun at."

"So is that the real reason you're here? To warn me away from your boyfriend?"

"In part. I also came to tell you that it all needs to stop. I thought you'd gotten over this need to control me. But then, there you were, showing up and trying to ruin the biggest night of my life."

"I wasn't trying to ruin anything."

"Did you even bother to look around you in that warehouse? Do you know what that was all about? That event you dismissed so flippantly as a circus was actually my debut art show. Hundreds of people came out to see my paintings. It meant the world to me, not only because it's going to launch my career, but because some friends of mine put that event together for me as a surprise. But you walked right through it with tunnel vision, concerned only with your own agenda." He looked away, and I asked, "Did you even glance at any of the paintings?"

He shrugged his shoulders and didn't say anything, so I reached for my backpack and pulled out a little square bundle wrapped up inside an old pillowcase. It was a ten-by-ten inch-square canvas, which I unwrapped and put on his lap. "This is what I can do. A lot of people who see my work think it's good, they think I have a gift." He didn't say anything, so I added, "I paint because I *have to*, because I'm driven to, and I work really hard at being the best I can be." He glanced at the painting and crossed his arms over his chest, turning his head away from me.

I sighed and picked up my backpack. "You can keep that portrait. It's part of a whole series I did of Mom, so I have a lot of others. I'm not sure I remembered her exactly right, I didn't have any pictures to go by." I got up from the chair and said, "I don't even know why it matters to me. It shouldn't. But I'd like it if you'd just try to understand this most fundamental thing about me, if you could somehow get that this is who I am." I turned and walked away from him.

I'd reached the doorway when he said quietly, "You got it right." I turned back to him. The expression on my father's face was unreadable, the painting held carefully in both his hands. "And you don't need pictures to go by," he said. "All you gotta do is look in the mirror. Christ, you're her spitting image. Looking at you, it's almost like a part of Isobel is still here."

After a moment he continued, "I know you blame me for her death. I know that's one of the main reasons you hate me so much. You know what? I blame myself too."

"I've always blamed myself every bit as much as I blamed you," I admitted quietly.

"What? You were a little boy when she took her own life! How could you possibly think it was in any way your fault?"

"I could have been a better son. I was bratty and prone to temper tantrums. I must have been such a pain to deal with."

"*No.* You were a great kid, and she loved you so fuckin' much."

"Just not enough to stick around."

"Chris, your mother was mentally ill. I didn't know what to call it at the time, but I figured out much later that she was bipolar. She'd have these huge mood swings, she'd go from being so happy and full of life to just being racked with despair. I didn't know what to make of it. I was ignorant, I didn't know there were medicines that could have helped her. And that's where I blame myself for her death. I didn't know enough to get her the help she needed."

I'd always known that on some level. But still, I had blamed my father and myself. Even knowing it was kind of irrational, part of me still clung to that. Maybe I just had to blame *someone.* All my hurt and anger had to go somewhere, and as I said before, I just couldn't let myself blame her.

Thinking about all of this now was like driving a knife into a wound that had never really healed. I could so clearly remember that day, the ambulance coming to the house, Mom in her bed, so pale. She just wouldn't wake up, I'd tried to wake her again and again and again....

"I have to go," I said, and turned away from my father.

"You know why I keep chasing you?" he asked. "Because you keep running away from me. If you stopped doing that, maybe I'd stop, too."

I looked at him over my shoulder. "You and I are really bad for each other, Reggie. Neither of us is ever going to be what the other one wants. You can't stop being a gangster, and I won't stop being gay, or an artist, or the million other things you hate about me. Maybe it's time you let go."

"No. I'm never, ever letting go of you, Chris. Don't you get that? I love you, kid. I mean, okay, maybe I have a really fucked up way of showing it. I've never really known how to be a father to you, that's probably pretty obvious. You came along when I was fifty-six, and then your mother, she went and left us both alone when you were just this tiny little guy. I thought I was doing good, just because my old man used to beat the shit out of me, and I figured as long as I wasn't doing that, I was doing alright by you. I know I made mistakes, but I always honestly believed I was doing the right thing."

I turned to face him, and we both just sort of watched each other for several long moments. Finally, I admitted quietly, "I'd never have imagined you'd be capable of that speech."

"Well, maybe if you'd ever stopped and listened instead of always running from me, I could've gotten it out years ago. Oh, and by the way, I retired from the business almost ten years ago. I'm not a gangster anymore."

"You pulled a gun on me *last night*. Like hell you're not a gangster."

"So, old habits die hard. But I showed a hell of a lot of restraint last night, too. You think I don't know who your friend was? It fuckin' killed me, seeing my own kid hanging out with Dante Dombruso. Every part of me wanted to put a bullet between his eyebrows. But did I do it? No."

I stared at him and said, "Congratulations. You managed to avoid committing homicide. I'll be sure to write that on your parent of the year application. Unfortunately, on the line above that, I'm going to have to include threatening your kid and the most important person in his life with a firearm, which just might make the application null and void."

"Most important person in your life? That's what that guy is to you?"

"Yeah. Kieran's the best thing that ever happened to me. And I meant what I said about you *never* threatening him again."

"You know, I wouldn't have had to threaten anybody if you'd just agreed to this – just to talk to me."

"Oh, do not make it my fault!"

"Okay! Christ, you're touchy."

"Touchy? How would you have felt if someone had pulled a gun on Mom?"

"It's not the same thing, you can't compare the two."

"It's *exactly* the same thing, Reggie. It's the same love, gay or straight. There's absolutely no difference."

He thought about that for a few moments, then asked, "You love that guy?"

"Yeah. I love him. I haven't gotten up the courage to say that to him yet, but I love him with all my heart."

After another pause while he mulled that over, he said, "What did you say his name was? Kevin?"

"Kieran."

"What is that, Irish?"

"Yeah. It's Irish."

He considered that too, then said, "I got no problems with the Irish. Back in the old neighborhood, me and Pat

O'Shea were thick as thieves. And believe me, it don't get any more Irish than a red-haired kid name of Patrick O'Shea."

I grinned a little. That was probably as close as my father could come to saying he was okay with the fact that I was dating a man in general and this man in particular. He'd been so mad when he found out I was gay, but gradually, over the years, it seemed like he was coming to grips with it. Apparently age was mellowing my father, in some pretty surprising ways.

I said, "I think I'm going to go. We're on an unprecedented roll here and should really quit while we're ahead. You know, before one of us starts screaming at the other and then firearms come into play."

"That reminds me. Someone confiscated all my guns, and I want 'em back."

"No."

He thought about that for a beat, then said, "Yeah, okay. I couldn't have taken 'em on the plane anyway."

"How'd you even get them here?"

"I bought 'em when I got to San Francisco, on the black market."

"And you're not a thug anymore."

"So sue me for having connections. I was coming into Dombruso territory, I damn well was going to be armed to the teeth. Finding them with you, by the way, that I hadn't counted on. I was trying to make it in and out of town without a confrontation."

I frowned at that, and after another pause asked, "What did the doctors say about your head injury, by the way?"

"She said I'll live. It's a mild concussion. Takes more than a bump on the head to bring the Roach down."

"Alright. Well, I'm going to go."

"Yeah, okay."

"Take care of yourself, Reggie."

"You too, Chris."

I sighed and said, "Is it really so hard to call me Christopher?"

"Tell you what. I'll start calling you Christopher when you start calling me Dad."

"Fair enough," I said, and turned to go.

"One last thing," he said, and I glanced over my shoulder at him again. "A bit of advice. Never wait to tell people you love 'em. If there's one thing I've learned, it's that life is unpredictable. If this Kieran kid is your happily ever after, for Christ's sake, what are you waiting for?"

"Really? You think you and I are at a place where you can give me fatherly advice?"

"It's damn good advice, no matter who gives it to you."

I considered what he said, then told him, "It is, actually. But we've only known each other a few weeks. I don't want to freak him out by saying it too soon."

"I knew your mother three days before I proposed marriage. And I knew within minutes of meeting her that she was the one for me. My point is, the right person's not gonna freak out at those three little words. You shouldn't hold back."

"You kind of have a point. Thanks, Reggie."

He grinned at me and leaned back against the pillows, looking very satisfied. "It's been good talking to ya, Chris. Don't be a stranger, okay?"

I nodded and left his hospital room, kind of in a daze. I'd just had a relatively normal conversation with my father, which had almost never happened before. Maybe we were *both* mellowing with age.

Chapter Eighteen

When I stepped out into the parking lot at Rosewood, I found Kieran in full police uniform, leaning against his patrol car. "Hey," I said, coming up to him. "What're you doing here?"

"Just making sure you're okay. I know you said you wanted to do this alone, but I don't trust your father. I wanted to be close at hand just in case the situation got out of control."

I smiled up at him. "Thank you, you're always looking out for me. I really appreciate that about you."

He grinned and said, "Really? I thought you'd be mad, because you wanted to handle this yourself."

"Nah. It's nice to know you've got my back. Just like I have yours."

His smile lit up his face. "Always."

"So, you know what?"

"What?"

"I love you."

Yeah, I just blurted it out, without build-up or fanfare. It wasn't some big, Hollywood moment. It didn't need to be. The words were enough.

He stared at me for a moment, his lips parted in surprise. And then he grabbed me in his arms and lifted me off the ground, and kissed me with such incredible, overwhelming passion that I just melted into him. I wrapped my arms around his shoulders and my legs around his waist, and when we finally broke apart a little I murmured, "Kier, you're in uniform. We shouldn't be making out in public, you could get in trouble."

"Don't care." He kissed me again, and then he said, "You know what?"

"What?"

"I love you too." He beamed at me and added, "I've been wanting to tell you that for a while now, but I figured it was too soon and I'd freak you out."

"Ditto."

"So, what made you finally take the plunge?"

"The first good piece of advice I ever got from my father. He reminded me that life is unpredictable, and telling you how I felt about you was far too important to put off."

"That *is* good advice." He kissed me again before saying, "I really didn't expect that from Reggie the Roach."

"Me neither."

I kissed him deeply once more, and when we came up for air he asked, "Can I come over tonight?"

"Hell yes. Do you even need to ask?"

"I don't want to be presumptuous," he said with a smile.

I kissed him yet again and finally untangled myself from him, straightening the collar of his shirt, and said, "Be careful out there, Kier. See you in a few hours."

"Can't wait." He winked at me and slid behind the wheel of the police car, then pulled out of the parking lot with a wave out the window. As usual, worry settled in the pit of my stomach. I doubted I'd ever learn to relax while he was out on patrol.

*****

A few minutes after I got home, Dante dropped by. He handed me the painting I'd asked him not to sell, which he'd had beautifully framed for last night's art show. It still amazed me how much he'd gotten done on short notice, right down to that little detail. "I wanted to deliver this personally," he said, "just to make sure nothing happened to it in transit."

I thanked him and invited him in (which again felt weird, because I thought of this as his and Charlie's apartment), and removed one of my paintings from the wall, hanging this one in its place. "Maybe I should have tried to sell it," I said. "Though I doubt anyone would want to buy it. It's such a personal piece, I can't imagine anyone else identifying with it."

"Since the overriding theme of this painting is loneliness, I think a hell of a lot of people can identify with it. Someone offered me fifteen thousand dollars for it last night, as a matter of fact," he said with a grin. "But that could also be because this is the painting that was featured in the paper and on the cover of that national magazine. It's highly sought-after."

I stared at him wide-eyed and murmured, "Oh." Then I said, "Is it too late to sell it? Kieran paid my tuition for next quarter. I'd be able to pay him back the majority of it if I sold this." I started to reach for the painting, but Dante stopped me with a gentle hand on my arm.

"Keep it," he said. "You don't need the money."

"Sure I do. I stopped turning tricks, and haven't had any income in days. And I really want to be able to pay Kieran back as soon as possible."

"You told me I could sell the rest of your paintings, remember? I'm going to be handing you a check in the next day or two once all the payments are in."

"Some of them sold?"

"*All* of them sold," he said with a grin. "All seventeen of them. I priced them based on what I've paid at galleries in the past for similar works. I hope you'll think I priced them fairly."

"I'm sure you did fine. What did you get, a couple hundred dollars apiece?"

His dark eyes shone with amusement as he said, "No."

"Oh. Well, that's alright. Even if it's less than that, I can still use the money."

"Christopher, I sold your paintings for five thousand dollars each." I sunk to my knees right on the spot, and Dante chuckled and crouched down beside me. "You okay?"

"But that's…I mean, there's no way. I'm a total unknown. No one would pay that kind of money for a student's paintings."

"You *were* a total unknown. Not anymore. Now a hell of a lot of people know the name C.R. Andrews."

"This is…I mean, seventeen paintings at five thousand dollars *each*?" Dante nodded, and I stammered, "My God, that's eighty-five thousand dollars."

"Before taxes. Don't forget that the IRS is going to want their share, and you don't mess with those guys."

I shook my head and dropped into a seated position. "I have to be dreaming. This whole day is just too good. Kieran told me he loved me today," I said.

Dante grinned and replied, "That's awesome." Then he too sat down on the floor, wrapping his arms around his knees, making himself comfortable.

"And my father and I actually carried on a conversation without screaming or gun play, which is unprecedented. And now this." I shook my head. "I'm trying to absorb it all, but I just can't."

"It's about time your luck turned around. Life has owed you a break for quite a while."

"That kind of money means I can pay Kieran back, and pay for at least a couple more quarters of school. And it means…God, it means I really don't have to go back to prostitution. I quit a couple weeks ago, but I thought it was just temporary. I thought sooner or later, I'd have to return to that life."

"You really don't."

"This is all because of you, Dante," I said. "If you hadn't thrown that gala art opening last night—"

"Then your big break would have happened some other way. This was inevitable."

"I don't know about that."

"So, you know," he said, "now that you've gotten some public exposure, you're going to start getting a lot of calls from agents and art dealers."

"Yeah, they've already started. I've been letting them go to voice mail, so I can sit down later and sort through them."

"Please remember that not all of those people are going to have your best interest at heart, Christopher. You're a rising star now, and a lot of people will try to ride your coattails to fame and fortune. As I was reminded with Ian, sometimes it's hard to tell the good guys from the bad guys. So with that in mind, I have a suggestion for you."

"Okay. Let's hear it."

"Don't sign with anyone. Go independent, open your own gallery. I own properties all over the city, and I can think of a couple spaces that would be perfect. You can show your own stuff as well as other artists you believe in, maybe fellow students from your school. That way, no one's taking a cut of the earnings, or trying to take advantage of you."

"You know I wouldn't let you give me a gallery space."

Dante grinned and said, "I knew you'd say that. So, lease it from me with an option to buy down the road. I will insist on making you a hell of a deal on your lease, however. I don't believe in profiting from my friends."

He added, "You know, now that I think about it, one of those spaces has a nice apartment above it. I don't know if you were planning to renew the lease on this place when it expires, but the unit I'm thinking of might be a good option. It's more than big enough for two." He smiled at me cheerfully.

"Kieran and I are still way off from the moving in discussion."

"I know. I'm just looking ahead," Dante said, as he pushed himself to his feet. "And I know this gallery idea is a lot to think about. So sleep on it, but you shouldn't put off the decision too long. You're white hot right now, and it'd be best to run with that momentum."

"I don't have the first clue how to run a business. Why do you think I'd be able to do this?" I asked as I walked him to the door.

"Because you know me, and I can help you out."

"I'm sure you have better things to do."

"Than assist a friend? No way. Plus, this is fun for me. I love building businesses from the ground up, and I think an art gallery would be an exciting project."

When we reached the door I said, "Thank you again, Dante, for everything. You really are a good friend."

"So are you, Christopher."

*****

A couple hours later, I went to meet Hunter in the studio at school. As I cut across the Sutherlin campus, the few students who were around on the weekend greeted me by name and congratulated me on my art show. "It was just a matter of time," Gwen, a pretty girl with blue hair, told me. "We all knew you'd go on to rule the art world."

I smiled at her as I felt the color rising in my cheeks. Her companion, a tall boy with a pierced lip that had been in my life painting class last quarter, slapped me on the back and said, "Way to go, C.R. Watching you succeed gives me hope, it shows that there's life beyond art school."

"We should hang out some time," Gwen added. "Go for coffee."

I nodded and said, "I'd like that. Well, I'm meeting my model in the studio. Talk to you later, okay?" They both called goodbye as we went off in different directions.

I'd been so shy, so unsure of myself when I began my freshman year here, and had felt like such an outsider. I had been out of school for a few years at that point, obtaining my G.E.D. in lieu of completing four years of high school. I'd also been working as a prostitute for quite a while, and living on the streets. All of those things made me feel like I was from a different planet, when compared to the privileged upper-middle-class kids that made up most of the private art school's population. I'd always feared that if people knew the truth about who and what I was, they'd shun me, so I'd kept quiet and kept to myself.

Despite my being so closed off, the students at Sutherlin had always been supportive. They'd praised and respected my work, and had always been nice to me. To this day though, I still kept to myself. I knew no one here could possibly understand my struggles. But I didn't feel like an outsider anymore, I knew I belonged here. The campus felt like a safe haven. It felt like home.

Hunter and I had finally gotten to the painting portion of my junior project, and we were doing a nude today. When I stepped through the studio door, I found he'd beat me here and was already buck naked, reclining casually on the big, draped sofa in the center of the sunny space, firing off a text. He was really quite comfortable in his own skin.

"Well hey there, Michelangelo," he said with a big grin, setting his phone aside. "How's your day going?"

"Extraordinarily well," I said, coming over to him and kissing his cheek.

"Awesome. I was concerned about you and your dad."

As I set up my paints and easel, I gave him a run-down of all the good things that had happened today, and he said, "I'm so happy for you, Christopher. It couldn't happen to a nicer guy."

I grinned at him and said, "Thanks." The painting we were about to begin garnered my attention, and I said, "Sit up a little, bend your right knee, and turn your shoulders toward me."

He did exactly as I asked him to, then joked, "Aw, so we're not doing a full frontal? You're leaving out some of my best features." His bent leg shielded his genitals from my view.

I grinned at that and said, "I'm still deciding how to arrange you. This is kind of a classic pose, I wanted to see how it looked. Why don't you shift around, find a comfortable position? I'll tell you when we've got it." He again followed my instructions.

After a minute I got up, went around to the back of the piece of furniture, and pulled up a wooden support, laying the futon flat. I bunched the sheet up a little as Hunter slid to the center of what was now a bed and stretched out on his back, one hand resting beside his head.

"Oh wow, that's perfect," I murmured as I hurried back to my easel. "Can you hold that position?"

"Uh, yeah. I'm just laying here. Sure you don't want me doing something more dynamic?"

"No, that's wonderful," I said, looking quickly around the room. I dragged a wooden table over so it was right beside the couch and climbed up on it, checking the angle. I then set up the easel and my paints on the tabletop, climbed up again and grabbed my palette. I squirted six dollops of oil paint onto the wooden surface, quickly mixing colors together with the bristles of my brush, smearing them onto the edge of the palette.

Hunter was so perfect, his pose so exactly right, that I began to paint hurriedly, compelled to capture the moment on canvas. I roughed in his shoulders, his torso, his head, and painted like a man possessed for a while, pausing only when I needed to mix more paint. The light was wonderful, filtering in through the huge bank of windows all along one wall, casting a golden glow over his luminous skin. "You look so beautiful," I murmured.

He smiled at that and whispered, "Thank you," as if trying not to interrupt me.

When the illumination in the room changed, I swore under my breath and muttered, "I just lost that perfect light. I don't know what happened."

"The Earth's rotation happened. You've been at it for over three hours," he said with a grin, his voice gentle.

My eyes went wide. "Oh shit, Hunter, I'm so sorry." I leapt off the table and held my hand out to him. "Here, let me help you up. You must be so uncomfortable."

He took my hand and stood up, then kept hold of it as he said, "I'm fine. And that was amazing. I've never seen anyone so enraptured in what they were doing. It made me wish I had something in my life that I was even half as passionate about."

I'd been massaging his arm and shoulder with my free hand, he had to be achy after holding still for so long. "I forgot to warn you that I zone out like that when I'm painting. I'm really sorry. You should have interrupted me."

He shook his head no, and then drew me into a hug. This probably should have seemed odd, since he was still completely naked. But his and my perception of "normal" was probably a bit skewed. "I really didn't want to interrupt." He kept holding on to me, his need for physical contact obviously really pronounced today, and I ran my hands up and down his back, massaging some of the stiffness away as he rested his head on my shoulder.

"Are you doing alright, Hunter?"

He nodded against my shoulder, his voice soft when he said, "I'm fine. This feels really good. Will you keep holding me for a while?"

"Sure. As long as you want," I told him.

I felt him chuckle at that. "Careful with that promise. I might never let go of you."

I kissed the side of his head and said, "Something's wrong, isn't it?"

"No, not really. I'm just being stupid."

"Talk to me, Hunter," I said gently. "Tell me what's on your mind."

"Just…don't forget me, okay?"

"What are you talking about?"

"You and Kieran are right on the brink of getting really serious." I'd told him what had happened in the parking lot of the hospital, and apparently he'd been mulling that over these last few hours. "I know you and I haven't known each other very long, but you mean a lot to me. You're so different than my other friends. Every single one of them would be fucking me right now instead of holding me naked in their arms. But not you. You're the only person who's ever seen me as more than a sex object."

"Your friends have sex with you?"

"*Everyone* has sex with me. My friends, my agent, my publicist, my directors, strangers that pick me up in bars, shops, restaurants – everyone but you."

"Hunter…why do you let them?"

He shrugged. "Maybe I know that's all I'm good for," he said quietly.

"You have to know that's not true. You're an amazing person. You're sweet and funny and kind, and so much more. And I say this as a friend…maybe you need to start setting some limits with people."

He sighed and said, "I'm making it sound like sex is all negative. It's obviously not. I like being touched. I like the feeling of someone inside me, and the feeling of a big body on top of mine. I *need* that." After a pause he said, "Anyway, I guess I'm just scared about losing you, maybe that's making me feel insecure."

"I get it, I felt the same way when my friend Charlie got married. But you're not going to lose me, Hunter. It's not like I only have room for one person in my life. Hate to break it to you, but I'm going to be kicking your ass at Madden for years to come."

Hunter laughed at that and pushed me away playfully. "Jackass. Let go of me, I have to go pee."

I chuckled and said, "There's a restroom through that door in the corner."

As he headed across the room he called, "Do you want to keep painting me this afternoon? I have an appointment, but I can push it back."

"No, I've monopolized enough of your day," I said. Then I grinned and called, "Is the appointment with the bacon lube people?"

"Not exactly. And I can meet you the same time tomorrow, if you want."

"Thanks Hunter, that'd be great." When he emerged from the restroom I said, "Come on, get dressed and I'll buy you some lunch, followed by one of those obscenely huge buckets of coffee you're so fond of."

"I'm sure as hell not going to say no to a bucket of coffee," he said, stepping into a skimpy pair of black briefs, followed by black jeans. "And um…my appointment this afternoon is with a police officer."

"What? Why?"

"Well, it's probably nothing. But you know that cyber stalker I mentioned a while back? He's stepped up his game a bit, the threats have gotten kind of scary. So I'm handing it over to the police, just like you and I talked about. I don't know if they can really do anything, but I think I'll feel better knowing they're looking into it."

"Hunter, I'm so sorry. I had no idea! And here I am, taking up all your time, and going on about what a good day I'm having—"

He silenced me by pressing two fingers to my lips. "Don't even. I'm glad you're having a good day, and I'm thrilled to have this distraction. Can I take a look at the painting?"

I kissed the fingers that were pressed to my mouth, and when he removed them I said, "Do you want to stay at my place until the police find this guy?"

"I don't think it's come to that, but thanks for the offer. Besides, security is actually pretty good in my building, I feel safe there."

"If you change your mind, let me know."

"I will. So how about showing me the painting?" He seemed determined not to talk about this anymore.

I reached out and tucked a strand of golden blond hair behind his ear and said, "I'm glad you told me what's happening." I hoisted the easel off the table carefully, then turned it to face him. On the large canvas was the start of a life-size image of Hunter from the hips up, his hair strewn around the bed, his eyes solemn as he looked up out of the canvas. It was a good start, I thought.

"Holy shit."

"Is that a yay-it's-awesome holy shit, or a God-I-hate-it holy shit?"

"It's a what-planet-are-you-from holy shit! I can't believe you just did that in a few hours. It's breathtaking."

I grinned at him and said thanks, and added, "I still have a ton of work to do on it, but you get the idea of where it's headed."

"This is probably going to sound incredibly vain, but could I buy this from you when you're done?"

"Uh, no. But you can have it for free, right after my teacher signs off on it for my term project."

"I don't feel right about that. Your paintings are valuable."

"So's your time, and you will have put as many hours into this as I have by the time it's completed. I was trying to think of what I could do to thank you for posing for me, and now I know."

"You're sure?"

"Positive."

"Thank you, Christopher. That's just above and beyond."

"Since we're doing three paintings in all, you may want to wait until they're done, then pick your favorite."

"I already know I want this one. I want it as a reminder."

"Of what?"

"Of our time together, for one thing. And also, I want it as a reminder that someone in the world sees me like this. Whenever I start to feel down, all I'll have to do is look at this painting and know that I matter to someone."

That statement broke my heart, and I pulled Hunter to me and kissed his cheek before hugging him again. He sank into it. And I said gently, "Of course you matter, Hunter. And if this painting reminds you of that, then it's the most important piece I've ever done."

He let go of me and tried to laugh it off by saying, "People are going to think I'm so damn stuck up when I hang it in my apartment. They won't get what it means to me, they're just going to think I like looking at myself."

I shrugged and said, "Who cares what people think?"

"Good point." He grabbed his t-shirt and pulled it on over his head. "Now come on, do whatever you need to do to clean up. Because if I don't get that bucket of coffee soon, you're going to have to add two Xs over the eyes on my masterpiece."

Chapter Nineteen

Kieran picked me up that night at six sharp, announcing plans for dinner and a show.

"You know I don't actually eat," I reminded him.

"We're going to work on that."

"Oh no," I exclaimed. "You're going to try to fix me, aren't you?"

He grinned and said, "You love me. You can indulge me a little."

I grinned at him, too, and got in the Mustang.

Kieran drove us up to Twin Peaks. Since it was a cold January evening, the scenic overlook was deserted. He spread a blanket out on the hood of his car, then hopped up onto it, picnic basket in tow, and leaned back against the windshield. He patted the space beside him, and I too climbed onto the Mustang. He pulled a second blanket over us, and began rummaging in the basket, eventually producing a pack of the crackers I ate, which he handed to me. I smiled at him and started to open them, but he said, "Hang on. Those come second. We're going to try a few other foods first."

"Kieran—"

"Baby, hear me out. I've been reading up on food phobias. And no, I don't now think I'm an expert on the subject. I also am not going to pretend I understand what you're going through," he said gently. "But because I love you, I want to help you. I want us to try a couple things. Are you okay with that?"

"I guess."

"Good."

He began pulling all kinds of groceries out of the basket, lining them up between us. "Please don't tell me you expect me to try to eat all of that," I said, dread settling heavily on me.

"Nope. Here, hold this," he said, and handed me an empty plastic bowl. "Actually, I don't expect you to eat any of it." He picked up an apple and a knife and peeled a small section, then cut out a thin little slice and popped it in his mouth. When he'd swallowed it, he said, "I'm going to give you little bites of different things, after first eating them myself. Don't try to swallow them, I know that's where you run into trouble. Just hold them on your tongue for a few seconds, and then split them out into that bowl. It may help you get comfortable with the idea of reintroducing different foods into your diet at some point in the future. Ready to try the apple?"

"Kieran, I know you mean well. But I'm afraid that if I try to fix this, it'll end up getting worse. What happens if I start to reject the crackers? What if I end up being unable to eat anything at all?"

"That's not going to happen."

"How do you know?"

"Because I believe in you. I believe you're strong enough to beat this thing. Little by little, you can overcome it. I absolutely know that for a fact." He held my gaze steadily.

And after a long moment, I said, "Give me the apple."

He cut a thin sliver, and I took it from him and put it on my tongue. I didn't even try to swallow it. I just enjoyed the freshness and sweetness of it for a few moments, before taking it out of my mouth with my fingertips and putting it in the bowl. I felt stupid, but Kieran looked absolutely delighted.

We tried this several more times with the different foods he'd brought. I was doubtful that this would actually lead to overcoming my phobia, but getting to taste things I'd missed for over a year was actually pretty wonderful. Finally he took the bowl from me and said with a smile, "You did great. I think that's plenty for one night."

"You're right."

We both leaned back against the windshield, and he ate the rest of the apple while I opened my crackers and ate them slowly. "Is this the show you promised me?" I asked with a smile, gesturing at the view. The city sparkled all around us, gaudy and beautiful.

"Yup. Best show you'll find anywhere," he said.

We leaned against each other and he peeled back the cover on a kids' pudding pack, the kind parents put in school lunches, and dove in with a plastic spoon.

"As long as I'm being a pain in the ass about your eating thing," he said, "can I ask if you ever called any of those clinics in the printout I left for you a few weeks ago?"

"No. Thank you for doing that, by the way, but I had already researched all those places. It's like I said before, I'm afraid of someone tinkering with it and getting it wrong."

"You let me tinker with it just now, and I couldn't be less qualified. Would you please consider giving one of those places a call?"

"Aren't you going to make me feel guilty about it by adding 'for me'?"

"Nope. You wouldn't be doing it for me. You'd be doing it for you. And you owe it to yourself to beat this thing. I know you're hungry all the time. I know you're often light-headed, but try to pretend you're fine. I know you live in fear of getting worse. And baby, you deserve *so much better* than that. You deserve to let yourself heal."

I mulled that over, absently running a fingertip over the rim of the chocolate pudding cup in his hand and sticking it in my mouth. "I guess…I guess a phone call wouldn't hurt," I finally conceded.

Kieran flashed me a huge smile. "Do you realize what you just did?"

"Agreed to make a phone call?"

"Yes. *And* you just put some pudding in your mouth and swallowed it."

My eyes went wide. "Oh my God. I didn't even realize I did that." After a moment, a smile spread across my face.

"There's hope, Christopher. There is absolutely, one hundred percent, no doubt about it *hope*." He looked so happy as he grabbed me in a hug.

"This was a ton of progress for just one night. Maybe I *am* ready to face this."

"I'll be with you every step of the way, baby," he said, then kissed my forehead as I snuggled against him.

We watched the lights of the city for a while, and eventually he said, "So, your twenty-first birthday's coming up in just a few days, and I had an idea for how we might celebrate it."

"We don't need to do anything special."

"Sure we do. Your birthday falls on a Saturday, and I thought it'd be nice if we went up to the cabin for the weekend. I already asked for the days off, I want to spend the whole weekend with you no matter what we do, but I'm hoping you'll say yes to Tahoe."

"That sounds perfect actually, I'd love to go back there. But please don't make a fuss. I don't need a present or anything."

"Try and stop me," he said, and when I shot him a look, he smiled and winked at me. Then he swung off the hood of the car and leaned in the driver's side door, turning on the radio. After spinning the dial for a few moments, big band music filled the air. He came around to my side of the car and held out his hand. "Dance with me, Christopher."

I grinned at that and slid off the hood. "I really don't know how to dance."

"Me neither. So we'll make it up as we go along." He gathered me into his arms, and I hugged him and rested my head against his chest as we swayed to the music, a gentle breeze stirring my hair.

After a while, he said quietly, "I love you so much, Christopher."

"I love you too."

"When you told me that today, it was the happiest moment of my entire life. I just want you to know that."

"Thanks for not running in terror." I grinned and stretched up to kiss his cheek.

"Nope, no running. I'm right where I want to be."

I held him a little tighter and said softly, "So am I."

Chapter Twenty

Tahoe had received a fresh blanket of snow the day before we arrived, the white hills and mountains a beautiful complement to the deep blue lake. It was my birthday weekend. We had just piled out of the Mustang, stretching after the long drive, and Kieran went around to the trunk and draped a backpack over one shoulder, then lifted out a huge, long, gift-wrapped box, grunting a little from the effort.

"Okay, whatever that is, it's way too much!" I exclaimed.

He grinned at me. "No it's not. Hey, can you grab my keys and get the door?"

I slid the keys off his index finger and said, "If you can barely lift it, you know I won't be able to budge it. Whatever it is."

"You won't have to."

I went ahead of Kieran and unlocked the cabin, then held the door open for him and flipped on a light switch, and he went inside and set the box on the low coffee table. I almost expected it to collapse under the weight. "That box is part two of your present," he told me as he went to a wall unit and turned on the heat in the cabin, then knelt down and got the fire going in the big stone fireplace.

"I hope part one was the trip to the cabin."

"Nope."

"Oh no. I hope you didn't spend more money on me."

He shot me a big smile as he stood up and pulled his blue sweater and t-shirt off over his head. "I didn't spend any money at all on phase one of your gifts."

"Well, that's good. And aren't you freezing? It's so cold in here."

He pulled off his shoes and socks, then reached for his belt, his eyes glinting mischievously. "It'll warm up really fast in here. Especially when I explain to you what phase one is." He dropped his pants and boxers, and came to stand right in front of me. Then he sank to his knees and looked up at me as he said, "I'm yours, Christopher. That's always true, actually. But this weekend, it means I'm giving myself to you as your own personal boy toy. Do whatever you want to me. I belong to you completely." He smiled at me as arousal washed through me.

I grinned at that. "Okay, the first thing I'm going to do with my boy toy is get him under the covers before he gets frostbite. Come to bed."

"Yes sir." He jumped up and preceded me into the bedroom, then quickly got a fire going in the second fireplace before heading to the bed.

I'd intended to just cuddle him, but as I pulled him to me and kissed him, running my hands up his broad back, my cock stirred to life. I cupped his butt and licked his earlobe, and he said, "By the way, I went to my doctor's office and had an STD test last week, and all the results came back negative. So, if you ever decided you wanted to be done with the condoms, I'd be more than willing."

"I got tested too actually, just a few days ago. But no way will we stop using condoms."

His brow instantly creased with concern. "Are you okay?"

"Yeah, I'm fine. Sorry, I didn't mean it that way. I get tested every three months because I'm kind of paranoid about it, and have always tested negative. But as recently as a few weeks ago I was a prostitute, so condoms are mandatory."

"Have you had unprotected sex?"

"No."

"I guess I'm confused. If we both tested negative for STDs and we're monogamous now, why would we still need protection?"

"Well, something could still show up, as far as six months down the road."

"I know the statistics though, and the chances of that happening are incredibly slim."

"Still though, I'm not about to take unnecessary chances with your health."

He knit his brows in concern as he looked at me closely. I didn't know what else he saw in my face, but he asked gently, "There's more than that going on here, isn't there?"

I didn't even know if I could explain it. I sat up, and after a pause murmured, "I feel...stained, somehow. Maybe I'll never stop feeling like I whore."

"Baby—"

"You shouldn't let a whore fuck you without a condom. Not now, not ever."

"You're not a whore."

"I am. And I'm not good enough for you, Kieran," I blurted.

He gathered me in his arms, resting his head on my shoulder. After a moment, I relaxed slightly and I reached up and began caressing his hair. "Please don't talk that way about the man I love," he said softly. "You're not a whore, and you're more than good enough. I wish you could see yourself the way I see you."

"I don't get how you could possibly love me," I admitted.

"What brought this on all of a sudden?"

"Just…God, the thought of having sex with you without protection. It made me feel like I should come with a warning label." He sighed quietly, his arms still around me, and I said, "I'm so sorry I lied to you. I should have told you what I was the day of Charlie's wedding, before you brought me here for the first time. It was really deceitful and selfish on my part. You had a right to know you were bringing a prostitute to your family's cabin."

"I wasn't bringing a prostitute. That's what your job was, but it's not *who you are*. I brought Christopher Robin Andrews to this cabin, a sweet, beautiful boy that I was drawn to from the moment I laid eyes on him."

"Even that was a lie, Andrews isn't even my real last name. Although I did file the paperwork to legally change it last week. But my point is, I wasn't honest with you, and I feel terrible about that."

"Well, don't."

A felt a little shiver go through him. He was completely naked, and the cabin hadn't warmed up yet. I grabbed the big comforter, then went over to the fireplace with it and said, "Come here, Kieran, it's a lot warmer over here." I knelt down on the rug and held the blanket open for him, and he crossed the room to me and snuggled in my arms.

"And you wonder why I fell in love with you," he murmured as he put his head on my shoulder and I wrapped him up, then kissed the top of his head and held him securely.

"I love you, Kieran. I just…I wish I had more to offer you. You're so sweet, and so good. God, you're perfect, and I—"

"You know, I'm really not. And actually, that reminds me that there's something I need to tell you. I went to my police captain and turned myself in, I told him that I'd let a suspect walk because he was a friend of mine."

"Me? The day I got caught in that police sting and taken to the station?"

"Yeah. Don't worry, I'm not naming names, you won't be brought back in."

"Oh God, Kieran."

"I know what I did was wrong, I violated the law. And I wouldn't change a thing. Given it to do over again, I would always choose to help you, no matter what. But as a police officer, I just…I couldn't break the law and not expect to face the consequences."

"What's going to happen?"

"I face disciplinary action next week. I have a hearing on Tuesday in front of an in-house committee."

"Could they arrest you for turning me loose?"

"They could, but that's pretty unlikely."

"Could you lose your job?"

"Yeah. But I still wouldn't change anything."

I asked, "Would it help if I turned myself in?"

"No. And really, if you did that, then this was all for nothing."

"Why are you willing to bend the law for me, but not for yourself?"

He looked up at me and said, "I'm not supposed to make judgment calls like this as a police officer, but honestly? I think the prostitution laws in the state of California are unjust, and I think that sting operation was one technicality away from entrapment. Thinking that makes me a lousy cop, and should show you there's nothing perfect about me."

"What are you going to do if they take your badge? You love being a cop."

"You know, given what I just said, maybe I don't deserve the badge. It's not my place to question, I'm just supposed to uphold the law. All of them, not just the ones I agree with."

"It breaks my heart that you could lose your badge because of me."

Kieran sat up and turned to face me. "No. Christopher, I could lose my badge because of *me*. I'm the one that chose to turn you loose, it was my decision and mine alone. Please don't blame yourself."

"But what are you going to do if you can't be a cop anymore?"

"I've been thinking about that. Maybe I'd go to law school, and afterwards try to get a job in the public defender's office. That wouldn't be a bad thing. As this incident has shown me, maybe I'm just not cut out to be a cop after all."

I shook my head. "You're exactly what the police department needs. You're compassionate and kind and understanding, and there need to be *more* cops like you on the force, not fewer."

He stretched out on the rug, putting his head in my lap. "Thanks for saying that. But it's out of my hands now. I'm glad I turned myself in, I just couldn't live with that hanging over me. And if I do get booted off the force, well, it's not the end of the world."

"But you'll be so disappointed. I know you will. And what will your family say?"

"They'll be disappointed in me, too, of course. But I'm a grown-up, I can deal with it."

I was quiet for a while, stroking his hair. Then I said, "Speaking of your family, you never told me how they reacted to the fact that you're dating a prostitute."

"Uncle Ray didn't tell anyone else, actually. Jamie didn't either. And you're not a prostitute anymore, baby."

"Yeah…but it's like I was saying before, I guess it's not something that you ever really leave behind. I still feel the same. I'm starting to think the stain is permanent."

"You're not stained. You just need more time to adjust, to really accept the fact that you never have to go back to that life and finally let it go. It really is in the past. And the past only has power over us if we let it."

"True…although letting go of the past is so much easier said than done. It has such a hold over me, not just the prostitution but a lot of other stuff, too. There are so many wounds that are still so raw, and I kind of wonder if they'll ever fully heal."

He rolled onto his back so he was looking up at me, his head still in my lap, and asked gently, "Do you want to talk about it?"

I looked into the fire for a while, then said, "There's one big thing in particular, something I never told you about. I've never talked about it with anyone, actually." I paused again before saying, "When I ran away from home at fifteen, part of that was to get away from my father. We had such a volatile relationship, it was really toxic. But he wasn't the real reason I ran."

"What else were you running from?"

"The memory of my first, and before you, only boyfriend. It had been so hard to let him get close to me. I carry the scar of my mom's suicide right at the surface, and it was even more raw back then. I feel like she abandoned me," I admitted. "And that feeling made it hard to trust people. But I was drawn to Jason, despite my fears. He made me believe he would take care of me, that he'd always be there for me."

Tears prickled at the back of my eyes, but I held them back. Kieran sat up and took both my hands in his, the blanket falling from his shoulders. He didn't ask, he didn't prompt. He just waited patiently. After a while, I said, "I was a freshman when he and I got together, first as friends. He was two years older, a jock, one of the popular kids – in the hierarchy of high school, he was a god and I was nonexistent.

"I was so flattered when he started paying attention to me, when he wanted us to hang out. It was shocking the first time he kissed me, but it made me so happy. Shortly after that, he said he wanted to have sex with me. I was so caught in his spell that I didn't question it. I thought I was in love with him, but at that age, I don't know if I even understood what that meant."

I was quiet for a few moments, then said softly, "I'd never slept with anyone before, and he'd never had anal sex. He took me without preparing me in any way, and with just a little spit for lubrication. He just didn't know better, I didn't either. I cried all the way through it, and bled for days afterward. But I let him fuck me again and again. I would have let him do anything he wanted to me."

"God, I'm sorry."

I smiled just a little and said, "This isn't actually the bad part of the story. This is just the wow-was-I-stupid part." I looked at our joined hands and said, "We kept our relationship a secret from everyone, because that's what he wanted. We snuck around for five months, and even though he didn't want anyone to know about us, he started to take chances. We hadn't been caught, so that made him feel overconfident. He started having me suck him at school – in the stall of the boy's bathroom, at the back of the library, in the equipment room in the gym.

"It was a completely one-sided relationship: I was the bottom, end of discussion. He never once sucked me, or even touched my cock. It was all about his pleasure. And I was so desperate for his love and attention that I didn't question it." I sighed and looked into the fire again.

"Finally, one day just a couple weeks after my fifteenth birthday, our luck ran out. It was after school, and we were at the very back of the locker room, thinking everyone had gone home. I was on my knees giving him a blow job, when a group of his friends came around the corner and caught us in the act. Jason quickly shoved his cock in his shorts. And then he did the very last thing I'd ever expected. He pushed me and said, 'Fucking faggot, get off of me.' To his friends he said, 'This goddamn queer just tried to suck my dick.' I was beyond stunned, all I could do was stare up at him in disbelief. And then one of his friends grabbed me by the hair and pulled me to my feet. They were all so much bigger than I was. They were a couple years older and all of them were athletes, on the baseball team together. I barely weighed eighty pounds, I was just this scrawny kid."

A shiver passed through me as I remembered that day. And I said quietly, "They started hitting me, calling me every name they could think of. I was completely terrified. One of them pinned my arms behind my back while another punched me in the face. And then…then one of them said, 'Come on, Jason. You're not going to let this homo get away with that, are you?' And…." I paused for a moment to steady myself, then said, "And Jason drew his fist back and punched me in the stomach. He joined them, he…." I had to pause for a few moments, wrapping my arms around myself. Finally I said quietly, "He was so afraid of being found out, of his friends discovering he was gay, that he started to beat me, just like they were doing.

The one holding my arms threw me on the cement floor after a while, and they all started kicking me. I remember looking up at Jason, tears streaming down my face as he towered over me, kicking me, calling me a faggot...."

"Oh God," Kieran whispered.

It was a while before I said, "If the P.E. teacher hadn't heard the commotion and broken up the fight, I think they could have killed me. I was in the hospital for two weeks. Both my arms were broken, and I had to have surgery because I was bleeding internally. I was stuck at home for almost two months after that while my injuries healed. I didn't know what had happened until I finally went back to school."

I fell silent again, for so long that Kieran finally whispered, "You okay?"

I nodded, then said, "My father didn't know that Jason was my boyfriend. He'd just decided telling me what happened would be upsetting to me, so he didn't say a word and kept me away from the news. And I was a loner, I really didn't have any friends, so no one else told me, either." After a pause, I said, "I walked into school that first day back, and all the kids were staring at me, whispering and pointing. They looked angry, and I didn't understand why. But then I saw the memorial, at the end of the hall." I closed my eyes and could see the shrine before me, every last detail – the photos, the letterman jacket, the trophies, the notes from all the students....

"Jason had killed himself, two days after he helped his friends beat me up. I guess the guilt was just too much for him. And the whole school somehow blamed *me* for his suicide. Maybe if the homo hadn't come on to him, he wouldn't have been forced to beat me up and then feel guilty about it...I mean, I guess that was the logic. In the note he left his parents, he'd written 'I feel terrible about what I did to Chris. He didn't deserve that.' He didn't out himself though, not even in death. He didn't tell them I was his boyfriend."

I sighed quietly. "Jason had been a star athlete, a golden boy, a local hero in a town that thrived on sports. I was nothing. Less than nothing, just a small, quiet kid who liked to draw. Oh, and gay, which everyone always suspected, but which was now confirmed. They needed a scapegoat for his death, and I was it."

I watched the fire for a while before I said, "You can see why I couldn't stay in that town. I left Georgia just days after going back to school and vowed never to return. And I never have willingly, though my father had someone bring me back a few times, as you know. He could never keep me there, though. First chance I got, I always fled. Wexley,

Georgia is my own personal hell. I don't know why my father could never see that."

When I finally looked up at Kieran, tears were streaming down his face. His voice was a rough whisper when he said, "I am so sorry that happened to you."

I gathered him in my arms and said gently, "It's alright, Kier. It was a long time ago."

"And now you're comforting me," he said with a sad little smile. After a pause, he said, "I hate that life has treated you so unfairly. I absolutely fucking hate it."

I stroked his hair absently for a while, and said, "Between my mom and Jason, maybe you can see why I never wanted to rely on anyone, and tended to assume people would let me down." Then I added, "Oh, I forgot part of the story. Jason had left a note in my locker. All it said was, 'I'm so sorry. I love you.' He didn't sign it, like maybe he didn't want to leave any evidence behind that I'd meant something to him. But I knew his handwriting as well as I knew my own." I sighed quietly and let go of Kieran, running a thumbnail along the edge of the area rug.

Kieran looked at me closely, his voice little more than a whisper when he said, "You blame yourself, too. You blame yourself for Jason's death."

I shrugged and stared at the rug. "I know that's irrational. I know I was the victim in all of that. But…yeah.

I guess a part of me always has felt it was my fault somehow. I always thought that about my mom's suicide, too. I know it doesn't really make any sense, but I still carry it around with me."

"Christopher—"

I looked up at him and stuck a smile on my face, cutting him off. "I really shouldn't have told you all of that now. We came up here to celebrate and be happy. Instead, I've just cast this grey cloud over everything."

"No you didn't. And I'm so glad you opened up to me," he said softly. "Given all that's happened to you, I'm honored and humbled that you've let your guard down and let me get close to you."

"You're the greatest gift I've ever given myself. I really didn't know if I'd be capable of this, of having a relationship, but I had to try because I wanted you so much." I took his face in my hands and kissed him before saying, "I'm sure of you, Kieran. I know you'll never hurt me, and I love you so much."

"I love you, too." He ran his hand down my arm and said, "You've carried so much for so long on your own. I hope you'll learn to let me help you. I can bear some of the weight, help you lighten the load."

"It's not like I'd want to burden you."

"You wouldn't be."

I climbed onto his lap, straddling him, and kissed him deeply, then said, "You're the best thing that's ever happened to me. I'll always love you, and I'll always take care of you."

"Right back at you, every word of it."

I kissed him again and his lips parted for me, my tongue caressing his. We kissed for a long time, his cock hardening between my legs along with mine, and I tilted him onto his back after a while. He parted his legs for me and I stroked his cock gently, then slicked my fingertip with his precum and pushed it inside him. He sighed with pleasure against my lips and spread his legs wider, giving himself to me. I took my time working his little hole, then got up and retrieved my backpack from beside the front door.

I squirted lube onto my palm, then went back to stroking his cock with one hand as I slipped two slicked fingers inside him and worked him open. When I unzipped my jeans and reached for a condom, he said, "Six months. I know you need time to get comfortable with the idea of unprotected sex. But in six months, when you're tested again and you know for an absolute fact you're not going to hurt me, I want us to stop using condoms."

I considered that, then said, "Okay. I think I can do that."

When I'd prepared myself, I pushed into his body and took him slowly, deeply. He looked so perfectly blissful underneath me. I grinned at him and said, going back to what he'd told me when we'd first arrived at the cabin, "My own personal boy toy, huh? That's a hell of a birthday present."

He grinned too. "I'm hoping you'll get a lot of use out of your present."

"I'm guessing I will."

We took our time, building slowly. I stroked his hard cock as I thrust into him, and said after a while, "The few times you've been inside me, it was all on my terms, me on top riding you. I was thinking you might want to fuck me a different way. Is that something that you'd like to try? Or are you really just more comfortable bottoming?"

"I love bottoming, but I want to try anything and everything else with you, too."

I smiled at that and kissed him. "Well, okay then." I eased out of him and discarded my condom, and handed him a new one. "I belong to you, Kier, just like you belong to me." I grinned at him and said, "Take control, baby."

He sat up and smiled at me. "If you insist," he said with a wink, and then he scooped me up in his arms and kissed me passionately. And take control he did. He stripped me completely and lubed me just like I always prepared him, rolled on a condom, then pulled me onto his lap and pushed himself into me.

I sighed with pleasure as I wrapped my arms and legs around him, my head on his shoulder. He grasped my butt and thrust up into me, and after a while he stood up, our bodies joined throughout, and fucked me by raising and lowering me onto his cock. I moaned and threw my head back, surrendering to him.

After a few minutes like this, he spun us around and pushed my back up against the wall, kissing me hungrily as he took me hard. Oh God, it was so good. I would have thought it impossible, after years as a hooker, for there to be any firsts left for me. But this *was* a first. I opened up to him, heart and soul, as he took me, holding no part of myself back, letting myself feel and enjoy all of this, all of him. I'd never felt so connected to someone, so in love, partners in every sense of the word.

My Kieran apparently had quite a few ideas about how to top me, and he next carried me across the room and laid me on my back on the dining room table. As he fucked me, he reached down and took my cock in his hand, stroking me. "God you're beautiful," he murmured as he thrust into me, and I smiled at him and ran my hands down his big arms, spreading my legs wide for him.

When we finally came it was incredibly intense, both of us yelling as our orgasms shook us, Kieran thrusting into me forcefully as my cum spattered across my body. And after he came, he continued to slide in and out of me, but slowly, gently, bringing both of us back down. A huge aftershock went through me, my body almost convulsing. His hand gently massaged my spent cock for a few moments, until finally he let go of it and scooped me up in his arms, lifting me to meet his kiss.

I was completely spent, my body shaking from the force of my orgasm, and he eased out of me carefully and discarded the condom, then carried me to the bedroom. He laid me down on the pillows, then cleaned me up gently, the expression on his handsome face so blissful. Finally he retrieved the big blanket from in front of the fireplace. It was nice and warm when he draped it over me, and he climbed in bed and gathered me into his arms. "I love you," I whispered, sleep closing fast, my head on his chest and my arms around him.

"I love you too, Christopher. Always."

*****

It was late when I awoke, the cabin lit by the soft glow of firelight. Kieran was already awake, and smiled at me and leaned in for a kiss when my eyes opened. I grinned at him happily, wrapping my arms around his shoulders, and returned the kiss deeply.

Despite having exhausted ourselves a few hours before, both of us were soon hard again, stroking each other's cocks as we kissed. Kieran grabbed one of the pillows and tossed it toward the foot of the bed, and I grinned when I saw what he was up to. We lay diagonally across the mattress and rolled onto our sides facing each other. He took my cock between his lips as I did the same to him, draping an arm over his hips.

We sixty-nined slowly, sensually, working each other back up, his cock swelling in my mouth as mine swelled in his. I savored the taste of him and took him deep, then slid all the way to his tip before sliding back down, my free hand caressing his balls. Kieran came right before I did, his load warm and rich and salty on my tongue. My yell was muffled around his big cock as he sucked me hard and I unloaded into his warm, wet, sweet mouth.

Finally, when we were both completely spent, I eased off him and collapsed onto my back. "God that felt good," I murmured.

He sat up quickly and stared at me wide-eyed. "What's wrong?" I asked.

Kieran let out a bark of laughter before covering his mouth with his hand and murmuring, "Oh my God."

I sat up too and raised an eyebrow at him. "This is a really weird form of afterglow," I told him with a grin.

He dropped his hand, an astonished expression on his face, and said, "You have no idea what just happened."

"Um…we sixty-nined. I know it was your first time doing that with a guy, but your reaction is kind of unusual." I was still grinning at him.

All of a sudden, he burst out laughing and grabbed me in a hug. "I love you so much," he exclaimed, burying his face in my hair.

"I love you too." My arms encircled his shoulders.

Finally, he pulled back a few inches and said, "Christopher, you just swallowed my cum."

"Yeah, I know. I—" All of a sudden, the full impact of that statement hit me right between the eyes, and I burst out laughing.

"So now," I said when I caught my breath, "I'm going to have to explain to the doctor at the phobia clinic that the only thing I've been able to swallow in almost a year and a half, besides water and crackers, is my boyfriend's semen. That's going to be embarrassing."

Kieran gathered me in his arms and settled us onto one of the pillows, a huge smile on his face. "It's awesome," he said.

"I didn't even think about it."

"You were too busy cumming."

"Yeah, I was."

He kissed the top of my head, and after a moment asked, "You're going to a clinic?"

"I have an appointment Thursday. It seemed like the place with the most straightforward approach, out of all the options in that printout you gave me. And they specialize in trauma-induced phobias."

"That's so great." He beamed at me, then glanced over the top of my head. "Oh hey, it's twelve-oh-five. Happy birthday, baby."

I stretched up and kissed him. "Thanks, Kier. And thank you for bringing me back to Tahoe. I love it here."

"You're welcome. This is the second of many, *many* weekends we'll be spending here, you know. You're going to get sick of this place after a while."

"So not possible."

Kieran sat up in bed and smiled at me. "I think you should unwrap your present. Your *other* present," he amended with a wink.

"Shouldn't we wait until morning?" I asked, but he was already out of bed and heading to the living room.

"Nope. Definitely not," he called.

He was back a minute later, the big box in his arms, each hand closed around something. He put the box on the bed beside me, then turned his back to me and quickly arranged whatever he was holding. When he turned back around, I saw that he'd predrilled a little hole in one of my crackers and planted a red-and-white swirled birthday candle in it, which he'd lit. He tossed a lighter onto the nightstand, then sat down beside me and said, "Happy twenty-first birthday, Christopher. I love you so much. Which is actually why I'm not singing to you right now." He grinned and added, "Make a wish."

I smiled at him and closed my eyes, then blew out the candle. "What did you wish for?" he asked.

"A thousand more nights exactly like this one. And I'm not worried about telling you and cancelling out the wish, because I already know it's going to come true."

He smiled at me and set the cracker on the nightstand. After I leaned in and kissed him, he exclaimed happily, "Open your present." He was so excited that he very nearly bounced up and down on the mattress.

I got up on my knees and very carefully unstuck the tape at one end of the big box, then unfolded the flap of paper. I repeated that with another piece of tape, and he asked, "What exactly is this thing you're doing?"

"The paper's really pretty," I said. "I'm trying not to mess it up."

"Oh my God," he said with a grin. "You're completely nuts. You know that, right?"

"I do know that." I smiled at him and carefully peeled back another piece of tape, and Kieran moaned and face-planted onto the bed. After a moment he resigned himself to what I was doing and sat up, tilting the big box onto its side for me so I could carefully remove the tape along the bottom seam.

"I have never in my life seen anyone do this," he pointed out, and I just grinned and peeled off yet another piece of tape. "Next time, I'm gluing it together. Then you'll have to tear it up."

"Last piece." I peeled back the strip of tape, then lifted off the bright, colorful paper. He set the box back on its base as I swung the paper and its stuck-on bow off the side of the bed, and then I murmured, "Oh wow." The picture on the box showed a beautiful midnight blue and black telescope, and I ran a hand over the glossy image.

He looked nervous. "Do you like it? I was thinking about how much you enjoyed that meteor shower, and I know a lot about astronomy, so I thought maybe I could show you some more stuff. But, I don't know, is this a really self-centered gift? Is it too much about me? If it is, tell me honestly, and I can take it back. I can—"

I silenced him with a kiss, then said, "It's the second-greatest present I've ever gotten." I grinned at him and added, "The first, of course, was you."

"Do you really like it? You promise?"

"It's absolutely wonderful."

He looked relieved, and smiled happily. "I was thinking you could keep it here at the cabin. The visibility's so much better in Tahoe than in the city. But, you know, only if you want to."

"Great idea."

"Want me to set it up for you?" He looked like a kid on Christmas, his face alight with happiness. And yet he was this excited about *giving* a gift, not receiving one. That was so like him.

"Yes please."

We sat cross-legged on the bed and unwrapped the big telescope together, then went to work assembling the fairly complex stand. "The moon's almost full," he said as he concentrated on deftly attaching two small pieces to one another. "Wait until you see it through a telescope, it's amazing. I think the sky's clear enough tonight, we should be able to get a good look at it."

Kieran launched into an account of all the great things he was dying to show me up in the heavens. He was animated and absolutely adorable, his enthusiasm infectious. I leaned back, propping myself up with my hands behind me, watching him and grinning happily.

He loved me. This gorgeous, amazing, wonderful man *loved me*. I was so incredibly lucky.

Chapter Twenty-One

It was kind of sad to see the apartment so empty.

Charlie obviously felt the same way. He scooped up my hand and looked around the vacant living room wistfully as he said, "There's so much history in this place. It's hard to say goodbye to it."

It was the end of March. It had been over two months since my art show, and I was moving out of the apartment I'd shared with Charlie and Dante because the lease had just run out. For two years before that, it had belonged to his then-boyfriend Jamie, so Charlie really did have a lot of history here. Far more than I did, and even I was having a hard time letting go of this place.

"But onward and upward to better things, right?" he said. I had leased a building from Dante in the Marina district, just two blocks from Charlie and Dante's home and new restaurant. The ground level was a light and airy gallery space, the second floor a pretty apartment that was about to become my new home.

The past couple months had been incredibly hectic. I divided my time between working on my school project with Hunter, and painting, and trying to get the gallery ready for business. And of course, Kieran. He and Charlie and Dante had been incredibly helpful with all the work that needed to be done to get the gallery up and running.

I'd also been attending twice-weekly counseling sessions at a clinic addressing trauma-based phobias. Progress had been slow. I still wasn't able to swallow anything besides water and crackers (and, um…the other thing), but I felt good about the fact that I was doing something about it. I held out a lot of hope that sooner or later, we'd have a breakthrough.

I also volunteered one afternoon a week with Jeffrey at Havilland House. I had been reminded of just how much the Havilland meant to me when I'd gone by there a couple months ago. It felt good to be giving back to the place that had helped me when I was at rock bottom.

Their new location was a former warehouse in the same neighborhood. It was actually even bigger than the old place. It was also up to earthquake and other safety codes, and its purchase had been funded in large part by my anonymous donation.

As for the thing that had brought me back to the Havilland in the first place, the case had gone cold again. I still carried flyers with me everywhere I went, and had put them up all over town, not just in the rough neighborhoods, but in the affluent ones as well. They had yet to produce any viable calls to the police tip line, even after I included a sizeable reward. But giving up wasn't in my nature. I was going to keep canvassing, keep asking questions. Someone had to know this person, even if he'd just come into the city briefly and left again, as I was beginning to suspect. It was just a matter of time.

"Come on, let's do one last lap," Charlie said. We circled the living room, then went through to the kitchen hand-in-hand.

"Remember that ridiculous livestock pen that Dante set up in here for Peaches?" I asked, and Charlie burst out laughing.

"Worst dog ever. I'm sure he and my father are very happy together," he said.

A lap through the bedroom made Charlie grin. "A lot of memories in this room."

I smiled and said, "Yeah, for Kieran and me, too."

We finally headed to the front door and paused for a long moment, taking one more look before pulling the door shut behind us. "Goodbye to the past," I said.

And Charlie added, "Hello to the future."

I stopped in the lobby on the way out and used my key in the mailbox. A big manila envelope was waiting for me, with a Georgia postmark. My father and I hadn't been in touch since our talk in the hospital. Maybe we were both worried about disrupting the delicate truce between us.

From what I heard, his visit a couple months ago had ended with Dante's cousins escorting him and his men to the airport and (hopefully politely) asking them to check in next time they decided to make an appearance in San Francisco. That was a lot better than running them out of town on a rail, which had seemed like another way that could have gone.

I opened the flap on the envelope, and glanced inside. It was full of photos, and I could tell at a glance they were pictures of my mother. I swallowed the instant lump in my throat and pulled out the single sheet of paper included with the pictures. It said:

Dear Christopher Robin (did you notice I used your full name?): I thought you might want some pictures of your mother, since you said you didn't have any. I'd packed these all away in a storage unit after she died, along with her paintings and the rest of her stuff. It was just too painful to look at. Anyway, I thought you might like them. If you want any of her other stuff, let me know and it's yours. Call me sometime. I don't want to have to trespass on enemy territory again just to get to visit with my own son. Love, your father.

If I looked at these photos now, I was going to start sobbing right here in the lobby of my now former apartment. I returned the letter to the envelope and folded down the flap as Charlie asked, "You okay, Christopher?"

"Yeah, fine."

"What's in the envelope?"

"My dad sent me pictures of my mom."

"Oh wow."

"I'm going to look at them later, when I can devote a big block of time to losing it."

He nodded at that, and gave me a hug before leading me by the hand out of the building.

Charlie dropped me off at my new apartment, and upstairs I found Kieran sitting cross-legged in the middle of the floor, a big set of instructions on his lap. I'd returned the furniture from the old apartment to Dante and Charlie, then gone to Ikea. My new stuff was cute and practical and affordable – and in about a million pieces. Kieran and I had been slowly working on putting it all together. He actually loved this kind of thing, he had a handyman streak a mile wide.

"Hey baby," he said when he saw me, his whole face lighting up.

"Hi, sweetness." I put the big envelope on a chair and bent down and kissed him before asking, "So what's this going to be?"

"A coffee table and two end tables. They're pretty straightforward. And guess what I just finished building?"

Given the way his eyes were sparkling, I went with, "The bedframe?"

"Bingo. Want to go test my construction?"

"Well, I think we really should. For safety's sake, we should probably subject it to rigorous earthquake testing, tons of shaking and rattling."

"Safety first," Kieran grinned.

"Exactly."

"Race ya," he said.

"It wouldn't be fair, you're in a seated position," I said.

He flashed me a huge smile, then rolled backwards and leapt to his feet before taking off at a run for the bedroom. I laughed and gave pursuit. Right before he got to the bed, Kieran circled back around, lifted me off my feet and carried me the last couple yards, and we both fell onto the mattress together. "It's a tie," he announced.

"That backwards roll was a pretty slick move. Did they teach you that in police training, Officer Nolan?" I asked with a grin, brushing his hair back from his forehead. And he still *was* Officer Nolan. He'd received a month's suspension and a formal reprimand for letting a suspect go. His punishment would have been much harsher, apparently, but his record to that point had been exemplary. That worked in his favor, as did several ringing endorsements from some of his fellow officers. He still had the idea of law school in the back of his mind though, and had begun researching programs, though he wasn't fully committed to the idea just yet.

"Nope. I actually think I learned it from watching the Karate Kid. Are you impressed?"

"Very."

He let go of me and bounced up and down on the bed a few times. "So far so good. But I'm thinking we should subject it to some rigorous stress testing, just to make sure. Although just to warn you, there's somewhere we need to be in about an hour, so this should be a stress-testing quickie."

I smiled at that and rolled over on top of him. "I can do that."

Just then, the bed crashed straight down onto the hardwood floor. We started laughing, and peered over the edge of the mattress. All four legs of the frame were sticking straight out at ninety degree angles. "Fail," he said, and we both burst out laughing again. "Okay, so, I had a few bolts left over when I finished this. I thought they were extras. Turns out, not so much."

"That's really unlike you. Usually this DIY stuff is a no-brainer."

He smiled at me. "I was a bit distracted today."

"Oh yeah? By what?"

"You'll find out later," he said cryptically, and swung out of bed. "Let me see what I did with those bolts."

I sat cross-legged on the area rug in the bedroom while he set the mattress aside and went to work on the frame. After a while, I ventured, "So, you know...I was thinking. You spend the night with me every single night. And you're doing so much work to fix up this new place, make it a home. Do you think...do you think maybe you'd like it to be your home, too? I mean, I know you have a lot of responsibilities with your brother, and with your house, but...I don't know. Maybe...maybe you might want to move in with me," I said quietly, studying the pattern in the rug.

He crawled over to me on his hands and knees and tilted my chin up, kissing me gently. And then he said, "I've been thinking about that a lot, too. I like my house, I grew up in it, after all. But it's such a negative environment these days, given Brian's moods. I can't see you and me ever making that our home, not as long as he chooses to live there."

He sat back and crossed his legs like I was, then added, "I do have a responsibility to Brian, but the fact is, he never actually lets me help him. He's so prideful, and so stubborn. The only thing he lets me do for him is grocery shopping, since he never leaves the house." Kieran was quiet for a moment before he said, "I keep trying to figure out how I can make Brian get help. He's in desperate need of counseling and physical therapy. Also, his doctor said he's a good candidate for prosthetics, and I wish I could get him to see what a positive thing that would be."

"Maybe he needs some tough love. Have you tried yelling at him?"

He grinned at that. "I have, as a matter of fact, but he just laughs it off."

"I could try. He hates me anyway."

"Oh no. I don't want to put you in a position where he can verbally abuse you." The couple times we'd gone by Kieran's house since we'd been together had been met with a lot of hostility. Brian hadn't accepted the fact that his brother was gay, and he sure as hell hadn't accepted the fact that I was a part of his life now. So we pretty much just avoided going over there.

"It's not right that he's verbally abusive to you, either."

"I know." Kieran thought about it for a few moments, then said, "Even if I moved out, I could still do the shopping and cleaning for Brian, and check on him regularly. And I'd continue to work on the house. It'd just become more of an investment property. I guess that's sort of what it is now, anyway. It hasn't felt like home in a long time."

"It hasn't?"

He looked up at me and gave me a beautiful smile, punctuated by his one dimple. "Nope. Home is wherever you are."

I grinned at that, then leaned forward and kissed him. "Only you could pull off a line so unapologetically sweet."

"Which is a nice way of saying I'm sappy."

"I never said that."

"Sweet, sappy, same thing." His smile made his eyes sparkle.

"So, if you're officially moving in, don't you think that big main wall in the living room would be perfect for your mom's art prints?"

"Yeah, it would, actually."

"That reminds me, I got a huge surprise in the mail today. My father sent me a bunch of photos of my mom, and a note saying he has the rest of her stuff, including her paintings. He says I can have them."

"Oh my God, Christopher, that's incredible! Where are the paintings?"

"In a storage unit in Georgia. I guess I'll have to go back there to get them at some point. That's going to suck. But I'll be so happy to see her paintings again."

"I'll go with you, of course. And we don't have to linger. We can get what you want from the storage unit and leave Georgia immediately."

"I should probably stop off and visit my dad, though," I said. "You know, now that we're entering this whole new era of not screaming at each other and pointing guns and so forth."

"We can do that." Kieran watched me for a moment, then asked, "Do you regret giving all his money away, now that you and your dad are kind of getting along?"

"No, not in the least. I did the right thing with it. Havilland House helped me, and I'm so glad that I was in a position to give back to them. Besides," I added, "every penny of that money came from illegal activities. Blood was shed for it, I have no doubt about that. For that reason, I really never would have used it for myself. But using it to help people…that kind of feels like restoring balance to the universe or something."

"You're one in a million, Christopher," Kieran said, smiling at me. He actually looked proud of me, and that felt so good. "Or should I say, one in thirty-two million."

Someone knocked on the door then, and I kissed him one more time before going to answer it. Hunter looked surprised to see me, but immediately covered it was a blinding smile. "Hey there," he said as I stepped back and let him in to the apartment. "I didn't think you'd already be finished cleaning your old apartment."

"I just got home about fifteen minutes ago. So, you came by to not see me?" I asked with a grin.

Kieran had appeared behind me, and said, "He came by to see me. He needed to borrow something. And here it is." He handed a sealed-up bulky brown paper bag to Hunter, and then shot him an are-you-kidding-me expression when he thought I wasn't looking.

Hunter tucked the bag under his arm, his smile still set to stun. "Yup. Just borrowing something."

I rolled my eyes and grinned at both of them. "Man, you two are transparent. What are you up to? Does this have something to do with whatever you have planned for this evening?"

"No." They both said it in unison, so quickly that I burst out laughing.

"Smooth." I turned to Kieran and said, "Last time you took me somewhere that was a surprise, it ended up being my gala debut art show with half of San Francisco in attendance. This isn't something like that, is it?"

"Nope," he said.

And Hunter blurted, "It's *so* much better."

Kieran gave him an oh-my-God-shut-up look and said, "Don't you need to be somewhere, Hunter?"

"I didn't say anything," Hunter reminded him. To me he said, "Christopher, it was lovely to see you. I look forward to seeing you again, next week when I'm meeting you on campus." For some reason, that made Kieran press his eyes shut and run a hand down his face.

"I'll walk you downstairs," I said.

And Kieran chimed in, "I'll go with you."

Hunter rolled his eyes dramatically and stage-whispered to Kieran, as if I couldn't hear him, "I'm not a total spaz. I won't blab about anything."

Kieran's latest in his looks-for-Hunter collection seemed to say oh-my-God-I-want-to-smack-you-right-now. But he managed to pull up a smile, and said, "See ya, Hunter."

"Bye Kier. See you whenever." That earned him a you-can't-be-serious look.

I chuckled and said, "Well, this has all been immensely entertaining. Come on Hunter, let's go before Kieran bursts a blood vessel." To my boyfriend I said, "See you in a minute, baby," and left the apartment with my friend.

When we got downstairs, I said, "Am I not allowed to know what's in that bag?"

"Shhhh. No questions."

"Fine. So, how are you, Hunter? What's new?"

"Good. Actually, a lot's happened since you saw me two days ago. My agent convinced me to hire a body guard." He actually looked pleased about that for some reason.

"Oh my God! Are you okay? Has the stalker done something?"

"A note was left at the Man-on-Man offices. It might not even be from the same guy. But it made my agent all paranoid, so he convinced me this is a good idea." He smiled when he said that.

"And…you're happy about this why?"

"Because I provided my agent with a very specific list of requirements for a body guard."

"Ah, now I get it. Let me see if I can guess: southern accent, six-two, eight pack…."

He winked at me and said, "You do get it."

I pulled him into a hug and said, "I'm so sorry this is happening to you. It really scares me."

"Don't worry, babe. I'm fine. This is just some delusional fucker that lives in his mother's basement and watches way the hell too much porn, he's probably really not a threat. And even if he is, I'm taking precautions, as you can see."

"Was the note hand-delivered?"

"Yeah."

"So then this guy's local. Do the police know about the note?"

"They do, I handed it over to the officer assigned to my case. Unfortunately, I didn't get the kind of cop you have. Mine's about sixty-two and bald." He looked so disappointed. "I didn't want to insult the guy and ask if I could be assigned someone hotter. Though that really would have been a lovely silver lining to this whole situation."

"What did the note say?"

"Oh, you know, the usual. If I can't have you, no one can, blah blah blah."

"Move into my spare bedroom, Hunter. That way, you'll have a police officer in the next room."

"That's going to be your art studio, I can't move in there."

"Sure you can. I don't need a home studio, I have the one on campus."

He leaned in and kissed my cheek. "I love you. You know that? I'm fine, though. Between the I-hope-to-God hot Texas Ranger that will soon be guarding my body twenty-four seven and the shooting lessons, I've got this more than covered."

"Shooting lessons?"

"Yup. I've been going to the range with Mrs. Dombruso. I think she's ready to adopt me, she told me last week to call her Nana. Oh, and she's right, by the way. A gun range is a really good place to meet men." He grinned at me happily.

"Oh God. Now I'm worried about Nana accidentally shooting you at the range."

"She's a hell of a shot, actually. You'd be surprised. Well, as long as she has her glasses on. She's blind as a bat, did you know that? But she refuses to wear her glasses all the time because she thinks they make her look old." He grinned and added, "Gotta love her."

"That you do."

"Okay, I'd better run. Take care, Christopher, I'll talk to you soon."

I still had a cloud of dread around me when I went back upstairs and repeated the stalker story to Kieran. "It'll be okay," he told me. "In ninety-nine percent of these cases, the stalker doesn't follow through on his threats. But if it makes you feel better, we can try again to get him to move in here temporarily so he's not alone." When I nodded, Kieran kissed the tip of my nose and said, "I'm going to get a shower and change. We should leave in about twenty minutes."

"Do I need to dress up?"

"Nope. You're perfect just the way you are, baby," he said with a big grin before heading to the bathroom.

I smiled and rolled my eyes at that, then dropped onto my new couch. I glanced at the envelope on the chair and tried to gauge just how much of a wreck I was going to be if I looked at that now. After a while, I decided to ration it out in small doses, rather than just overwhelming myself with it all at once, and reached for the envelope.

I stuck my hand in and retrieved a single photo, then returned the envelope to the chair. I'd grabbed a little wallet-size print, which was currently face down. I took a deep breath, and flipped it over.

"Oh God," I murmured.

It was a picture of my mom and me. I was just a little baby, all wispy blond hair and enormous blue eyes. And Isobel...God, I really did look like her. She'd been in her late twenties when she had me, but in the picture she looked like she was barely out of her teens. Her hair was a cascade of soft blonde curls reaching her elbows, her blue eyes round and luminous. She was laughing in this photo, a soft blush warming her pale cheeks. I wondered if my dad had taken this picture, and if he might remember what had made her laugh.

I stared at that photo for a long time. My reaction to it was different than I expected. I'd thought I would feel that heart-breaking sense of loss all over again, that these pictures would devastate me. But instead, the picture felt good, almost reassuring.

"Oh God. Baby, are you alright?" Kieran had come into the room and dropped to his knees beside me, looking at the object in my hand.

"Yeah." I smiled at him and said, "These are happy tears. Look at this." Tears were streaming down my face, and I made no effort to brush them away. I was cradling the photo carefully in both hands, and turned it toward him.

"She's beautiful," he said softly.

"Yeah, she was. That's one of the main things I remember about her."

After a moment, he whispered, "You sure you're okay?"

I nodded and said, "Seeing her after so long somehow gave a little piece of her back to me. It's an amazing gift."

I stood up and crossed the room to some still-empty built-in bookshelves, and stood the little photo up in the center, leaning it against the back of the shelf.

Kieran asked, "Do you want to look at the rest?"

I finally dragged my sleeve over my face and said, "I'm going to make them last and just look at a few a day. It'll give me something to look forward to."

He smiled and got to his feet. "Still feel like going out, Christopher?"

"Absolutely." I noticed then that he was wearing a big ski jacket, which was buttoned up to his chin. "Are we going somewhere cold?"

"Nope."

I grinned at that and said, "Okay. Lead the way."

He drove us to the Richmond and circled around looking for parking. We were in the neighborhood that housed Nolan's, and I asked, "Are we going to your cousin's bar? I know I'm twenty-one now, but technically, I still can't drink. Not yet, anyway." I smiled at him.

He grinned at me, but didn't say anything. A few moments later, he executed a slick three-point turn and snagged a parking space, then came around and opened my door for me and took my hand. His hand was trembling ever-so-slightly, and I realized he was trying really hard not to appear nervous about something. I knit my brow at that and studied his handsome profile as we walked down the busy sidewalk.

We stopped right in front of Jamie's bar. I was still watching him, and asked, "You okay, Kier?"

He looked at me and nodded, a little smile on his lips. He still didn't say anything, which was odd. Instead, he inclined his head toward the bar. A sheet of paper was taped to the door, announcing that the place was closed for a private party. It seemed like the party was a no-show, however. The bar looked dark, from what I could see.

"Do you want me to go in?" I asked.

Again he nodded, then swallowed hard.

"Okay," I said, taking his hand.

As I tugged the big door open, he put a hand over my eyes. I grinned at that and just went with it, and he guided us inside, the heavy door swinging shut behind us. "This is all very mysterious," I said.

He pulled his hand away, and I tried to figure out what I was looking at. All around the dark room were little red lights, blinking on and off. There must have been close to a hundred of them. "That's really pretty. And super odd," I said.

"Now," Kieran said softly, and all around the room, candles flared to life. Someone brought up the house lights too, just a little, and I realized the room was full of people, some of which I knew, many of which I didn't. I spotted Charlie and Dante, Hunter, Mrs. Dombruso, Jamie and Dmitri, and several members of the Dombruso family. And every one of them, every single person in this room, was wearing a reindeer sweater identical to the one Kieran had been wearing the night I met him. The red lights had been a hundred flashing Rudolph noses.

Following some cue that I didn't see, everyone in the room began softly singing Silent Night in unison, all of them holding big white candles. And as my eyes adjusted to the soft lighting, I realized that hundreds of bunches of mistletoe hung from the ceiling. "Oh wow," I murmured.

I turned to Kieran, and realized he's taken off his ski jacket. Underneath, he too was wearing a reindeer sweater. He was watching me closely, nervously.

The crowd stopped singing after the first two stanzas of Silent Night, and Kieran cleared his throat nervously.

And then he got down on one knee.

"Oh my God," I whispered.

"This past Christmas eve, I met a man that would change my life forever," he said.

"Louder!" Nana called, and laughter flowed through the crowd.

He smiled at her, then continued, more loudly, "My cousin Jamie was throwing a party, and I spotted this amazingly gorgeous guy across the bar. He had soft blond curls and big blue eyes that you could just drown in, and from that moment on, I couldn't think of anything but him. I wasn't out at that point, and the thought of going up to him scared the hell out of me. So I did what any normal human being would do. I proceeded to get utterly smashed."

The crowded laughed at that, and I reached out and stroked his soft light brown hair. He continued, "After a couple hours of me drinking and staring, my dream boy got up, obviously getting ready to leave. And I started to panic. It was now or never, the ten or so beers would have to suffice for liquid courage. He went into the back of the bar, and I followed him. I only sort of remember what I said, I'm sure it was all incredibly lame and pathetic. And just to make sure I seemed like a total lunatic, I was also wearing this sweater. You all look great in it, by the way," he said, looking over his shoulder and smiling at the crowd. They responded with hoots and whistles.

"Thankfully," he said, turning back to me, "my cousin Jamie had had the good sense to tack up a freakishly huge bunch of mistletoe back there, and in a moment of drunken desperation, I went in for a kiss, pretty sure that I was about to get kicked in the nuts."

The crowd broke into laughter, and I did too. Kieran said, "Oh man, I should have waited until the end to get down on one knee. Hang on." He shifted around, resting on his right knee now instead of his left, then asked, "Okay, so where was I?"

"About to get kicked in the nuts," Hunter called, and everyone laughed again.

"Oh, that's right. But you know what? It didn't happen. It was a Christmas miracle, that's the only explanation. I kissed this gorgeous, amazing boy, and he *actually kissed me back.*" The crowd cheered and applauded.

"And then I passed out drunk." More applause and laughter.

"But despite that inauspicious beginning, my Christmas miracle has been going strong ever since. I am totally, completely, head-over-heels in love with you, Christopher," he said. "I want to spend every day of the rest of my life with you, and I want to make you so happy, now and forever. Christopher Robin Andrews, will you please do me the extraordinary honor of being my husband?"

"Yes. Oh my God, yes," I stammered, my heart pounding in my chest, and the crowd erupted into a cacophony of cheers and hollers and applause.

I bent down and took his face between my hands and kissed him under the clouds of mistletoe, and when I finally let go of him, he exclaimed, "Oh, there's a ring!" He pulled a beautiful silver band out of the pocket of his jeans and held it up triumphantly before slipping it on my finger. "And there's a sweater." From inside his ski jacket he produced a reindeer sweater just like his and held it out to me.

I burst out laughing as I took the sweater, then fell to my knees in front of him and grabbed him in a huge hug. "I love you so much," I whispered in his ear.

"I love you too, baby. And you've just made me the happiest man alive."

I kissed him again, deeply, passionately, before we both got to our feet, grinning embarrassedly at the huge round of applause the kissing had garnered. As the crowd closed in to offer their congratulations, I leaned over to Kieran and whispered, "Who are all these people?"

"Your family and my family. I know you haven't met a lot of mine yet, so I decided to go with total Nolan immersion. They're almost easier to swallow as a whole."

The first person to push her way through the crowd, of course, was Nana. She most definitely was family. She kissed both of us on each cheek, then clapped her bony hands together delightedly. "Another wedding! I can hardly wait to get started. How about an Easter theme? Eggs, bunnies, daffodils...."

"Easter's in only two weeks, Nana," I said. "How about a summer wedding?"

Her expression got all dreamy, and she said, "The theme can be summer in the French Riviera. Or no, wait – nautical Cape Cod. No, no, Beach Blanket Bingo."

"For Christ's sake, Stana, the kids just got engaged. You wanna give 'em a chance to catch their breath before you have 'em pickin' out placemats?" That came from a little old man that had appeared by her side, a dapper gent of about eighty-five with thick white hair, sharp brown eyes, and of course, a reindeer sweater.

"Who's this gentleman, Nana?" I asked.

She replied, "Oh, that's no gentleman. That's my husband."

"Husband?" I echoed, suddenly concerned about bigamy laws in the state of California.

"Yeah. This is Donatello Dombruso. My husband. Dante's grandfather. You can call him Pop-Pop."

"Or Don," he interjected.

"Oh," Kieran exclaimed. "I thought he was—"

"Shacked up with a slut in Florida?" Nana asked. "He used to be. But then, I sent him a little email with a link to my online dating profile, and told him about all the hot men I was meeting. He was on the next plane to San Francisco." She grinned smugly.

"He suddenly realized what he'd been missing," I said.

"He got jealous," Nana corrected.

"It's true," he agreed.

I asked, "So...all is forgiven?"

"I was stupid, I got tempted by big boobs and a short skirt," he said. "But fortunately, my Stana chose to forgive me. She's a saint, and one hell of a gal. I'm never straying again."

"Because he knows if he does, I'm gonna shoot him in the nuts," Nana said. Kieran and I exchanged worried looks, but then she grinned at Don, kissed him on the cheek, and slapped his ass playfully.

"Oh!" Don exclaimed with a huge smile. "Like I said, a hell of a gal."

Just then my friends made it through the crowd, and first Hunter and then Charlie and Dante grabbed Kieran and me in huge hugs. "Congratulations to both of you," Charlie said. He was absolutely beaming. "I couldn't be more thrilled."

Someone put their arm around my shoulder and kissed my cheek, and I turned my head to look at Jamie. "Welcome to the family," he said, his smile genuine.

"Thanks, Jamie. And thanks for hosting this beautiful proposal."

Kieran grinned at that and slipped his arms around my waist. "You thought it was beautiful?"

"Absolutely. Thank you for doing all of this. I don't know how you pulled it off. I mean, where did you even find so many of these sweaters? That was adorable, by the way," I said, snuggling against him.

"Actually, Dante helped me," Kieran said. "It was kind of miraculous that he tracked them down."

"He's a man of many talents," Charlie said with a grin. He kissed his husband's cheek, which earned him a smile and two big arms around his shoulders.

"Congratulations, both of you," Hunter said with a smile. "I came by earlier to get a different sweater, by the way," he said. "My nose was broken." He tapped the red plastic ball on his current sweater, which was blinking on and off.

"Hold on to your hat, here come the Nolans," Kieran whispered. A woman with a cute short haircut led the way, pulling me right out of Kieran's arms as she grabbed me in a huge hug.

"Christopher," she exclaimed, crushing me to her. "I don't know if you remember me. I'm Kieran's cousin Erin, Jamie's sister. We met at Charlie's wedding. I'm the one that bought Kier the reindeer sweater!" she announced gleefully. "Who knew it would lead to this!"

"Quit hogging him," a young woman with long strawberry-blonde curls exclaimed. When Erin let go, I was crushed in another huge hug. "I'm Maureen, Kieran's cousin, also Jamie's sister. You can call me Mo, everyone does. Welcome to the family! We haven't met, I was on my honeymoon while all of this was going on!" she said, gesturing at the mistletoe with her big, white candle. I tried to duck out of the way of the flame, but she shook the candle upside-down and exclaimed, "Don't worry, it's electric. You know Kier always thinks of everything, he kept it all safe."

I grinned at that. "Of course he did."

She had a big purse draped over her arm, and a little black and brown head suddenly poked out of it. "Oh, and this is Tippy!"

"We've met." I ruffled the dog's fur, and was rewarded with a slobbery lick to the palm.

The moment she let me go, I was enveloped in a cloud of perfume and another bone-crushing hug. "I'm Carol," the pretty brunette said, "also Jamie's sister and Kier's cousin. You two are just adorable together, and I just know you're gonna make my cousin so happy."

"Thanks. I'm sure going to try."

As the next deluge of relatives cued up, I turned to Kieran and whispered, "How many cousins do you have?"

He shot me an apologetic smile. "Twenty-seven. But good news. Only twenty-four of them live locally and could make it here today."

*****

That night when we were back home, wrapped all around one another in our new (and still standing after some vigorous stress-testing) bed, I whispered in wonder, "You're going to marry me."

"I am. Because my dream boy said yes." He smiled happily.

"I love you more than anything, Kier. I hope you know that."

"I love you too, baby." Kieran's head was on my chest, and he looked up at me and said, "Did I totally freak you out with the whole proposal surprise party thing? It seemed like a fun idea when I first thought of it, but I'm kind of used to my family. I was afraid they were going to break you in half with all that hugging."

"One thing you can definitely say about Nolans, they're vigorous huggers," I said with a grin. "And the proposal was magical. Thank you again for doing all of that."

"Well, I knew I had to go big, since I was proposing to the guy who actually made it snow indoors at his best friend's wedding."

I smiled at that. "I didn't think you even noticed the snow."

"I didn't. Someone told me about it later. At the time, I only had one thing on my mind, and that was kissing you."

I rubbed my cheek against the top of his head and teased, "Followed immediately by an indecent proposal."

"That was lame of me, I'm sorry. I should have asked you out on a proper date. I guess I was so eager to get to dessert that I skipped the main course."

"Well, that and you didn't want to be in a relationship."

"I was dead wrong."

"You know," I said, "You're marrying the first guy you ever slept with. Aren't you going to feel, somewhere down the road, like you missed out? You never got to date different guys, or experience the whole San Francisco gay singles scene, or any of that."

"I hit the jackpot with my very first lottery ticket. Why on Earth would I wish I had bought a ton of other losing tickets first?"

I chuckled at that. "Good analogy."

"Thank you."

"But really, though."

Kieran propped himself up on his elbow and brushed the hair back from my eyes. "I missed nothing, and I know that for a fact because I have absolutely *everything*, right here. You astonish me, and fulfill me, and care for me, and make me feel so incredibly loved, and I'll spend every day of the rest of my life trying to make you as happy as you make me."

"You really love me," I said with a smile, a warm feeling of contentment settling inside me.

Kieran leaned down and kissed me before saying softly, "Now and forever, Christopher."

The End

****

Hunter's story continues,
Christopher and Kieran take a supporting role,
and questions are answered in Gathering Storm,
the fourth book in the Firsts and Forever Series.
Following is a look at Chapter One

Gathering Storm Sneak Peek

"Say my name, baby."

Crap, what was this guy's name again? I should probably know that, given the fact that I was riding him like I was racing to the finish line of the Kentucky Derby. Since I actually had no clue, I went with a diversion. "Your big cock feels *so good*," I purred, bouncing a little harder and faster. He reached up and twisted both my nipples like he was trying to tune in his favorite radio station, and I fought the urge to roll my eyes.

"Say my name, Hunter."

Gah! I stepped up my diversion tactics and moaned, "Oh God, I'm so close."

"Yeah babe, cum for me," he said as he thrust up into me. The fact that I wasn't even remotely hard seemed completely lost on this guy. I took hold of my cock and began to stroke it for all I was worth.

"Oh shit, oh *shit*," I gasped, closing my eyes and throwing my head back as I rode him feverishly. Who says men can't fake orgasms? It's totally doable, especially if your sex partner is too self-absorbed to realize you aren't actually jizzing on his six-pack.

"Oh fuck baby, yeah." He thrust wildly, then let out a long, loud, "MMMMNNNNNNFFFFGGGGGGGG" as he came. I almost asked him if he wanted to buy a vowel, but didn't think he'd get it.

When he finally stopped twitching like he'd just taken ten thousand volts to the nut sack, I reached underneath me and held the condom in place as I eased off of him. "That was fucking incredible," he said, once he'd caught his breath.

"Yes it was, sweetheart." I snuggled up beside him and slipped my arm around his waist. "You're welcome to spend the night if you want to."

But he untangled himself from me and swung out of bed, saying, "Thanks babe, but I gotta be up early in the morning." He sauntered into the bathroom and turned on the shower.

Brushing off my disappointment, I muttered under my breath, "Sure, use my shower. Make sure to use a ton of my Bulgari body wash while you're at it."

I got up and wandered into the living room, looking around for my underwear. I finally found it dangling from the top corner of the mirror in the entryway. That had been a nice shot. I probably couldn't have done that intentionally if I tried. Just to test it out, I flung the little black briefs at the corner of the mirror. Nope, missed. I retrieved the underwear again and pulled it on, then wandered around gathering up the rest of my clothes, which I carried to the walk-in closet.

When Mr. Tall-Dark-and-Whoever was dressed, I walked him to the door (he had used so much body wash that I could practically see a cloud of fragrance around him, like a cartoon). He turned toward me, and I thought I was going to get a goodnight kiss. But instead, he whipped out his iPhone and asked, "Mind if I get a picture? My friends are never going to believe I banged Hunter Storm." Before I could answer, he blinded me with the flash and said, "Awesome."

That right there sums up the glamorous life of a porn star. Jealous?

"Okay. Well, see ya," I said as I held the door open for him.

He paused right in front of me on his way out. "You don't have a clue what my name is, do you?"

"Nope."

He considered that for a beat, then said, "I don't care. You're smokin' hot," before disappearing down the hall.

I locked the door behind him, then went into the living room and sprawled out on my couch, still in just my underwear. According to the silver clock on the end table, it was only ten-thirty. Ugh. I considered getting dressed and going back out to the bars, but was feeling highly unmotivated at the moment.

So instead, I reached for my phone and shot a text to my friend Christopher. It said: *I have terrible taste in men. And also, I think you should come over so we can play Madden. Your winning streak must end, I fear it's going to your pretty blond head.*

I didn't really expect him to come over. He was engaged to a hot cop named Kieran with huge biceps that must tear through shirts like the Incredible Hulk. Why would he leave that to come play video games with his home-alone-at-ten-thirty-on-a-Friday loser of a friend?

He texted back: *You* do *have terrible taste in men, I keep trying to tell you that. It'll take me twenty minutes to get there, I'm going to walk over. See you soon.*

The hot cop must be working. I texted *Yay!* and reached for my game controller, so I could practice before he got here. After a few minutes, though, I glanced out the floor-to-ceiling windows comprising one wall of my living room and noticed it had started raining heavily. I dropped the controller and went to retrieve my friend, throwing on a black overcoat and stuffing my feet in a pair of boots before grabbing my keys and an umbrella.

Once outside, I started jogging toward Christopher's apartment, along his usual route. By the time he and I crossed paths, he was soaked, his cotton sweatshirt providing no protection from the rain. I threw my arm around his shoulders and held the umbrella over both of us, and he kissed my cheek as he slipped his arm around my waist. "Hi, Hunter. What are you doing out here?"

"It wasn't raining when you started walking over, so I figured you could use an umbrella."

"That was very sweet of you, but you probably shouldn't be out here by yourself."

I sighed at that. "I'm not going to let fear rule my life, Christopher." I had a stalker, another super fab perk of being a porn star. In the past few weeks, his threats had gone from harmless loser in his mom's basement to unholy spawn of Norman Bates and Hannibal Lecter. It was really special.

When we got back to my apartment, I dropped my umbrella in the entryway and flung my arms around Christopher, who held me for a good long time. He was a great hugger. "Thanks for coming over," I said.

He rubbed my back. "I'm glad you texted. I thought about calling you earlier, but figured you'd be out having fun on a Friday night."

When I finally let go of him, I asked, "Is Kieran working?"

"No. There was some kind of plumbing crisis at the house. His brother Brian called a couple hours ago and had a screaming fit over the phone."

"So naturally, Kieran dropped everything and ran right over." I took his hand and led him into the apartment.

"Well, the house does belong to both of them."

I towed Christopher into the master bathroom. My earlier 'guest' had left damp towels (three of them – really?) all over the floor. After I handed Christopher a clean towel from the cupboard to use on his damp curls, I scooped up the wet ones and deposited them in the laundry hamper that was *right there in the corner*. Then I unbuttoned my dripping overcoat and hung it on a hook as I used my foot to push off one of my boots.

"Wow, that's quite a look," he said with a little grin, rubbing his hair vigorously. "A trench coat, galoshes, and see-through underwear. And you went out in public like that."

I looked down at myself. I'd forgotten I was wearing nothing but the sheer black briefs. "The coat was completely buttoned up. And I was on a mercy mission," I said with a grin, pushing off the other boot. "I knew you'd be out there looking like a sad little half-drowned kitten, so I didn't have time to plan my wardrobe."

Christopher's blue eyes flickered down to the briefs one more time. He had zero interest in me sexually (trust me: *zero*. I couldn't believe it at first, either), so that extra glance was nothing more than incredulity at what I was wearing. I decided to tease him about it anyway, and wiggled my eyebrows at him. "You totally just checked out my package. Don't think I didn't notice."

He threw his towel at my head and grinned at me. "I did not. Get dressed, Hunter."

I pretended to be disappointed. "You're the only person that's immune to my porn star superpowers," I said, then turned and trudged from the bathroom.

Christopher followed me, peeling off his soaked sweatshirt. "The only one, huh?"

"Well, straight guys are immune, too. But they don't count."

I went through to my walk-in closet and pulled some things from the shelves as Christopher said, "Man, it's like Johnny Cash came by and hijacked your wardrobe. Why do you wear nothing but black?"

I handed him some clothes and said with mock seriousness, "It matches my soul."

"Uh huh."

"Actually, you wouldn't know this because, as I said, you're immune to my superpowers, but I happen to look

425

damn hot in black. That's not all I own, though. Look, there's a blue shirt right over there."

I pulled on a pair of old jeans and a t-shirt while Christopher changed into the sweats I'd given him. When he finished, I took his wet things and put them in the dryer, which was tucked away in a little closet off the kitchen. I grabbed two bottles of water from the fridge, and found a packet of weird peanut butter-filled crackers in the cabinet. Christopher ate those things almost exclusively, because he had an odd eating disorder. Well okay, technically, it was a, what did he call it? Trauma-based phobia involving food. He'd been getting help at some kind of specialized clinic and was able to eat a couple more things these days, but those gross little crackers were still the mainstay of his diet.

He was a couple pounds heavier now than when I'd met him four months ago, but still looked fragile as a little porcelain doll. His appearance was deceiving though, because Christopher was tough as nails. He'd survived things in his life that would have killed lesser men, and I admired the hell out of him for being so strong.

We went to the living room and settled in on the sofa, and after I handed him his game controller and the snack, I draped my legs over his lap. Here was another of the many great things about my best friend: he accepted my almost constant need for physical contact without judging. I'd

426

actually be sitting on his lap right now if I didn't outweigh him, and I really believed he'd let me do that without making me feel like a freak.

As the game loaded, I asked, "So, why didn't he just call a plumber?"

"What?"

"Kieran's brother, Brian. Why didn't he just get a plumber to come to the house, instead of calling up your honey and harassing him?"

"Because it's more fun to harass Kieran."

"Brian sounds like a total douchebag."

"Yeah, he kind of is. But I feel bad saying that."

"Why, because he's in a wheelchair? People in wheelchairs can be douches, too, you know. It's not just a term reserved for the ambulatory."

Christopher smiled at that. "I know. But I always feel like a jerk when I think badly of him."

"The guy calls his own brother a faggot, treats him like his personal buttmonkey, and trashes the house they grew up in faster than Kieran can repair it. Somebody seriously needs to tell him that losing his legs in Afghanistan didn't actually give him a get-out-of-nice-free card."

He grinned and said, "I believe you're misusing the term buttmonkey."

"Doesn't it mean, like, personal servant or something?"

"I'm pretty sure it means ass-kisser."

"Perhaps there are nuances to the term buttmonkey that you aren't taking into consideration."

"Well, I never claimed to be an expert."

I smiled as I clicked through the on-screen menu. "I'm glad you're here, Christopher."

"Me too." After a pause, he ventured, "So, who was Mr. Damp Towel?"

"How do you know I didn't leave wet towels all over the bathroom myself?"

"He missed the trash can when he threw out the condom."

"Ugh," I muttered. "I hadn't noticed that. And I literally don't know who he was. Right in the middle of sex, he was all—" I lowered my voice several octaves, "— say my name, baby." In my normal tone of voice I continued, "And I completely drew a blank."

"Oh man, that's awkward. So what did you do?"

"I faked an orgasm to distract him."

"You did not. Men can't fake orgasms."

"Sure we can." I shot Christopher a bright smile. "If you need evidence, I can pop in one of my films."

"Porn stars always finish on camera. The movie doesn't end until there's a money shot."

"Yeah, but the bottom's cum shot is usually spliced in at the end, after about twenty minutes of wanking that are edited way down." I glanced at my friend and asked, "Didn't you ever fake an orgasm when you worked as a prostitute?" He'd been a teenage runaway, supporting himself the only way he could for the last five years. A couple months ago, he'd finally been able to quit the business. He was now a rising star in the art world after a smash-hit debut show, and was about to open his own gallery. Christopher was a total success story, another reason why I admired him so much.

"I faked everything *but* that. People tend to notice if you don't ejaculate."

"The guy tonight didn't. And that sounded very professorly, by the way."

"What did?"

"*Ejaculate*. I usually just go with jizz, splooge, bust a nut, cream – I could go on, for about a day and a half. But you get the idea."

"I do," he said with a grin.

I rubbed my eye then and exclaimed, "Hang on, my contacts are killing me. I'll be right back," as I jumped off the couch and headed for the bathroom.

When I returned a couple minutes later, I said, "Okay, promise not to laugh."

"At what?"

"I needed to take my contacts out, and I'm completely blind without them. So I had to resort to these." I stuck a pair of thick, black-framed glasses on my face and said, "When I picked them out, I was shooting for a retro-hipster vibe. But I kind of ended up with mathlete."

Christopher shot me a brilliant smile. "You look so cute."

I rolled my eyes. "I look like I'm here to fix your computer." I dropped back onto the couch and draped my legs across his lap again, picking up my controller.

"I'm serious, you look adorable. I can't believe I haven't seen these before."

"I'm getting far too comfortable with you. The romance is dead. Next time you come over, my hair will be in curlers and I'll be sporting a green face mask and ratty housecoat."

He laughed and said, "I'm totally picturing that."

"Well, stop it." I was smiling too. I was never happier than when I was hanging out with Christopher. I would say he was like the brother I never had, but I actually had *three* brothers and they were all complete tools.

We played the football video game for a while, and every so often, Christopher snuck a look at me. Finally I said, "Out with it. What is it that you're thinking about saying to me?" Before answering, he executed a game-winning move that made me collapse against the couch and yell, "Holy crap, not again!"

Then he balanced his controller on the arm of the couch and said, obviously choosing his words carefully, "Hunter...do you really think it's the best idea to bring strange men back to your apartment? It just seems so risky. I mean, that stalker's somewhere out there. We even know he's local, since he hand-delivered a threat letter to your production company."

"My taste in men isn't *that* bad. I'm not going to pick out a total psychopath and bring him home with me."

"But Hunter, this guy's not going to be wearing a tag that says, 'hi, I'm psychotic.' In all likelihood, he's going to blend in with everyone else. Remember what I told you about the man that attacked me? He seemed completely harmless. I didn't have a clue what he really was until it was way too late."

A little over a year and a half ago, when my friend was still working as a prostitute, he'd been drugged, raped, and almost beaten to death by one of his customers. That incident was at the root of his food phobia, since the drugs had been hidden in a sandwich.

The assailant was still at large. When the police ran out of leads and let the case go cold, Christopher took matters into his own hands and began distributing sketches of his attacker all over the city. He learned that a couple boys had disappeared around the time of his assault, and were presumed dead. A pattern linked Christopher's attacker to those disappearances, which could mean that man was even more dangerous than anyone had imagined. But Christopher didn't worry about his personal safety, or about drawing the attention of a possible killer. He was more determined than ever to bring his attacker to justice, and was still out there every week with his sketches. He was incredibly brave.

I leaned in and gave him a hug as I told him, "I know you're concerned, and I appreciate that. I really do. But like I said, I'm not going to let fear dictate how I live my life. So far, it's just a bunch of letters. I really don't think there's much to worry about."

Christopher pulled back to look at me, a crease of concern between his eyebrows, and reached out and tucked a strand of my shoulder-length blond hair behind my ear. "It's more than that. You know that as well as I do, which is why you went to the police with those letters. It's just not safe bringing strangers home with you, or going home with them. Actually, that's risky with or without a stalker out there somewhere."

"I know. But what am I supposed to do, put myself under house arrest?"

"I think you're in denial, Hunter. Maybe that's why you haven't really changed your behavior since all of this began. I think this scares you so much that you're refusing to address it head-on." He was probably right, but I just looked away and shrugged noncommittally. My friend watched me for a long moment, then asked, "What happened to the idea of hiring a bodyguard? Are you still looking into that?"

"I interviewed a few applicants."

"And none of them were good enough?"

"None of them were *gay* enough," I said with a little grin. "That line of work tends to draw a lot of hetero alpha douchebags. If I'm going to be stuck with someone 24/7, I need to be able to stand them."

"Is that really the issue?"

"Well, no. Actually, I've been thinking about it, and I decided a bodyguard is overkill. I know those letters are pretty unnerving, but this person hasn't actually done anything."

"He's threatened your life, Hunter."

"But that's all it is, a threat. He probably won't ever act on anything in his letters."

Christopher looked like he had a lot more to say on the subject, but I was spared a lecture by his buzzing phone. He pulled it out of his pocket as I sat up a little, tucking my legs under me. The worry line between his brows got a little deeper as he read his screen. "What's wrong?" I asked as he got up.

"It's Kieran, he hurt his back trying to fix that plumbing problem. He asked me to take a cab over to the house, so I can drive him home in his car. It must be pretty serious if he thinks he can't drive."

I jumped up too. "I'll come with you," I said. "If it's that bad, you might need my help to get him to a hospital."

*****

Maybe fifteen minutes later, our cab pulled to the curb on a quiet street in Noe Valley. It was the first time I'd seen the compact Victorian that Kieran and his brother inherited a few months ago, after their dad died. Two people were on the little front porch, one in a wheelchair, the other flat on his back. After we paid the cab driver, Christopher ran up to the prone figure and I trailed after him, eyeing Brian suspiciously as I turned up my collar against the heavy rain.

Like his brother, Brian was a big guy with broad shoulders. He was dressed in a grubby t-shirt with a bandana tied around his head, arms crossed over his chest. A thick beard and long, brown hair kind of made him look like a Hell's Angels wanna-be. And he was a double amputee, both legs ending somewhere below the knee, but this was obscured by his baggy sweatpants. From everything I'd heard about this guy, he was a homophobic asshole, and most definitely on my shit list.

"Kier, are you okay?" Christopher asked as he dropped to his knees and rested a hand on his fiancé's forehead.

"I will be, baby," Kieran said with a little smile.

"What happened?"

"Well, turns out I'm not much of a plumber."

"Ya think?" Brian muttered.

I glared at him as I came up the stairs, and said, "Wow, way to instantly live up to your douchey reputation."

"Who the hell are you?" Brian asked, raising an eyebrow at me. "Because I don't remember calling anyone to fix my computer."

"Bite me, Duck Dynasty," I said with a sneer. Then I shot Christopher a look and tapped my thick black glasses with a fingertip. "Told you."

"What happened?" Christopher asked Kieran.

"I dropped the toilet I was trying to replace, and wrenched my back trying to catch it," he said.

Brian added, "Don't forget the part about it falling all the way through to the basement, and rupturing the main sewer line in the process."

"Turns out, the toilet had a slow leak, which rotted out the wood beneath the tiles," Kieran said. "It's surprising the floor didn't collapse sooner."

"Fucking awesome," Brian muttered.

"God, you're ungrateful," I told him, hands on my hips. "Your brother was trying to fix things for you."

"My brother just caused a crater in our only downstairs bathroom!" Brian exclaimed.

"He was still trying to help, and he doesn't deserve your shitty attitude."

"Screw you," Brian said.

"Wow, clever comeback."

"Who the hell are you?" he repeated.

"I'm your very favorite thing, yet another gay guy. You're totally outnumbered."

"Yeah, because I really needed you to tell me you're gay," he said.

I narrowed my eyes at him. "And I didn't need to be told you're a rude, homophobic dickhead."

Christopher interrupted us, asking his fiancé, "Why are you out on the porch?"

"Well," Kieran said, "turns out when you rupture a main sewer line, your entire house reeks of raw sewage. It's uninhabitable in there, and the plumber I called can't get replacement parts until tomorrow."

"Come on," Christopher said, sliding his arm behind Kieran's shoulders. "Let me help you up. I'll drive you to the emergency room."

Kieran sat up slowly, wincing with pain. "That might be an idea. I don't know what I did to my back, but it's definitely not good."

"What're you going to do with Grizzly Adams over there?" I asked, tilting my head toward Brian.

"They don't need to *do* anything with me," he snapped.

"Oh really?" I asked. "Because last I checked, it's pissing down rain and you're stuck on the tiny porch of a poop-scented house." That earned me a hard glare.

"Brian will need someplace to stay for the next few days, until I can get that bathroom floor rebuilt," Kieran said, standing very, very slowly.

My friend chewed his lip as he helped his fiancé to his feet, Kieran's face contorting with pain. "Well," Christopher said, "I'd suggest dropping him off at our apartment, but there's no elevator. The gallery downstairs is accessible, but other than four walls, it doesn't have much to offer." Kieran tried to straighten up a bit, but doubled over with a grunt, and Christopher tightened his grip on him and spoke to him soothingly.

"I'll make sure Cro-magnon Man gets situated somewhere," I said. "You just worry about Kieran, he's not looking so good." All the color had drained from his face and he'd broken out in a light sweat, breathing quickly and shallowly to try to manage the pain that standing up had caused.

"That seems like a really bad idea," my friend said, glancing from Brian to me.

"It'll be fine," I told him. "I'm not going to roll him off the Bay Bridge or anything, no matter how tempting that is. Now go on, get Kieran to the hospital and hooked up with some pain killers, stat."

Christopher weighed his options for a few moments, and came up empty. "Well, okay. I'll check in with you as soon as I can," he said, and focused on his injured partner. They started down the wheelchair ramp, moving at a snail's pace, and I tugged off my overcoat and draped it over Kieran's slumped form to keep the rain off him.

"Thanks," he murmured.

"You're welcome. Feel better, Kier," I called as I ducked back under the roof of the porch. When they reached Kieran's rusty old Ford Mustang, Christopher helped him into the passenger seat before jogging around to the driver's side. After he started it up, the car kind of lurched away from the curb. I'd never seen my friend drive before, and wondered if he actually had a license.

"What are you still doing here?" Brian wanted to know. "Aren't they expecting you back at Geek Squad headquarters?"

I pointed a finger at him. "Don't think I won't bitch slap you, Chewbacca. Now who do you want me to call to come get your sweatpants-wearing ass?"

"Just go away."

"Gladly. As soon as you tell me who to call." I pulled my phone from my pocket and waved it in the air.

"I can dial a damn phone, nerdboy. Leave."

"Is your phone on you?"

"No, it's inside." He rolled over to the door and tried the handle, then ran a hand over his face.

"Lock yourself out?" I asked, and he sighed and glared at me. "Here, use mine." I held the phone out to him, and he looked at it and then looked away.

"Don't tell me, let me guess. You've alienated all of your friends and family with this angry-at-the-world pity party you've had going on for God knows how long, and now there's no one to call. Am I right?"

"Eat me."

"I'm exactly right, aren't I?"

That pissed him off, and he yelled, "Just go to hell, you fucking f—"

I cut him off, getting right in his face and yelling back, "I swear to God, if you say faggot I will force feed you your nasty-ass ZZ Top beard!"

Surprisingly, he grinned, just a little. Then he said, "I was going to say fucker."

"You were going to call me a fucking fucker?"

"Yeah, I was." When I shot him a look, he added, "What? It's not like I rehearsed it." That tiny grin still lingered.

"Do I amuse you?" I asked, straightening up and putting my hands on my hips again.

"You just threatened to force feed me my beard. Was that not supposed to be amusing?"

"I'm colorful. So sue me." I waved the phone again and said, "Really? There's not a single person you want to call?"

"I was going to call a cab and have it take me to a motel, except that my wallet's locked inside, too."

"Okay. So, I'll take you to a hotel and check you in, and you can pay me back later."

He glanced up at me suspiciously, one eyebrow raised. "Why would you do that?"

"Because I promised Christopher I'd look after you, and he and Kieran have enough to worry about right now. I want to be able to report that you're safe and sound."

"I'm not a child. I don't need you *looking after me*."

"Like hell you don't."

"Fuck you."

"Wow, another damn fine comeback. And you know you need my help, Brian. That probably hurts your big, stupid, hetero ego, but I really don't give a shit."

"Stop acting like you know a damn thing about me."

"I know plenty," I said. "For example, I know that a while back, you didn't like what your brother made you for dinner, so you threw a plate through the living room window."

"That wasn't about dinner. I was having a bad day."

"Were you also having a bad day when you met my best friend for the first time and called your own brother a faggot?" I held my hand up and said, "Don't answer that. I don't care what kind of day you were having, because that was *not okay!* That's your kid brother, you jerk! And here you are, calling him names and acting like a schoolyard bully. How dare you treat Kieran like that? I mean, what the hell is wrong with you?"

"I'd assume that would be pretty fucking obvious!"

I stared at him incredulously. "Are you seriously trying to tell me it's okay to treat your brother like shit because you lost your legs and ended up in a wheelchair? Are you *kidding* me?"

"No, that's not at all what I'm saying! Shit!" Brian grabbed the metal rims on the wheels of his chair and propelled himself forward, gliding quickly down the ramp.

"Where are you going?" I called. He didn't respond, so I ran after him, the rain immediately soaking through my t-shirt. When we reached the sidewalk, I jumped in front of him and acted like a human brake, stopping his momentum with a palm on each armrest of his wheelchair.

"Move," he growled.

"No. I'm serious about not letting anything happen to you, for Christopher and Kieran's sake."

"God, you're a pain!"

"Look who's talking! Just let me get us a cab and get you checked in to a hotel, and then you never have to see me again."

He sighed and pushed a strand of wet hair out of his face, glaring up at me for several long moments. Like Christopher earlier, he too was obviously weighing his options and coming up empty. Finally he admitted defeat and muttered, "Fine."

I let go of his chair and watched him for a beat to make sure he didn't take off down the sidewalk. Then I ducked under a tree and dialed a cab company. When I disconnected, I called over to him, "They said ten minutes." Brian was giving me the silent treatment now, which was a plus, as far as I was concerned.

When the taxi finally arrived, he rolled up beside it and tugged the back door open, then positioned himself as close to the side of the cab as he could get. He hesitated for a long moment, then glanced up at me. For the first time, I saw a hint of vulnerability in his blue eyes. But then he pulled up his veneer of anger and said, "I don't really need a fucking audience for this."

I half-turned away from him and pulled out my phone, scrolling through a few texts. Out of the corner of my eye, I watched as Brian struggled out of his chair and into the taxi, awkwardly pulling himself onto the back seat. He then reached out the open door and flipped a couple levers on his chair, collapsing it flat, and tried to pull it into the cab with him. It was never going to fit. I went over to him and took the chair from his hands, called to the driver to pop the trunk, and deposited it in the back for him without discussion.

When I got in the taxi, I directed the driver to the nearest hotel I could think of. As we pulled away from the curb, Brian muttered, "I didn't need your help with that chair. I had it."

"No, you didn't. And I can't believe that anyone would be stubborn enough to refuse basic mobility training. I mean, what the hell, Brian? Not only that, but you're supposedly an excellent candidate for prostheses, but you refuse to go to the clinic and find out about your options! What are you trying to prove?"

He stared at me, his eyes blazing with anger as he growled, "I can't believe my brother's been blabbing to strangers about my personal business."

"He's not *blabbing to strangers*. He was talking to his fiancé about it once and I happened to be there, since your future brother-in-law is my best friend. My name's Hunter, by the way. Not that you asked."

"This is none of your damn business, *Hunter*."

"Of course it is, because I care about Christopher. He loves your brother, you make Kieran miserable, and in turn, that makes my best friend unhappy. Oh look! Now it's my business."

"You're a real piece of work. You know that?"

We bickered all the way to the hotel, and when the cab pulled up before the big glass doors of the Marriot, I patted my pockets and murmured, "Shit." My wallet must have been in my overcoat, which I'd lent to Kieran. I pulled a few crumpled bills from the pockets of my jeans and chewed a nail for a moment, thinking through my alternatives. Then I told the cab driver, "Change of plans," and recited my address.

As the taxi pulled out of the circular driveway, Brian asked, "What exactly are we doing?"

After I explained the whereabouts of my wallet, he muttered, "Fucking awesome. So where are you taking me now?"

"My apartment."

"Why?"

"Why do you think? No hotel is going to let you check in without a credit card, and neither of us has access to one at the moment," I told him. "This is the only alternative I can think of, unless you can give me another address to take you to. I know you have a huge family, surely all of them can't hate you."

"I have no idea if they hate me. All I know is, I don't want to see any of them."

"My apartment it is then, just for one night. In the morning, you're back to being Kieran's problem. Hopefully by then, he'll be hopped up on enough painkillers to make you tolerable."

He shot me a look, and after a moment said, "Why don't we go back to my house and break a window? Then you can climb in and get my wallet."

"Oh yeah, because I really want to experience the fascinating aroma of raw sewage. Plus, can't sewer gas blow up?"

"All the pilot lights were shut off, it's not going to ignite."

"Well, I still don't want to go in there."

"Wimp."

"Neanderthal."

"Bite me."

"You first."

After another pause, he suggested, "We could go to the hospital and retrieve your wallet from Kieran."

"Let's just leave your poor brother in peace tonight. This'll be fine. I have a big apartment, you and I will barely see each other. Plus," I admitted, "I'm not positive my wallet's in my coat. Now that I think about it, I might have left it at home."

He rolled his eyes and fell silent during the remainder of the ride to my place.

After I retrieved the wheelchair from the trunk and gave the cab driver all the cash I had on me, apologizing profusely for the measly tip, I unlocked the door to the lobby. Brian rolled ahead of me wordlessly to the elevator, and we rode to the top floor.

Once inside my apartment, I said, "I'll get you some bedding for the couch, it's pretty comfortable. I fall asleep on it all the time." I locked the door behind us, then muttered, "What's that smell?" Something sharp and chemically hung in the air.

Brian preceded me into the living room, glancing around. "It's paint," he said. "How do you not know that?"

"I just couldn't place it for a minute, and I don't see why it would smell like paint in here. I haven't been having any work done." But then I shrugged it off and said, "Maybe it's coming from one of my neighbors' apartments. I'll get you a blanket and pillows."

At the door to my bedroom, I stopped short. It took a moment to process exactly what I was seeing, fear trickling like ice water down my spine. Someone had spray-painted a single word in four-foot high red letters on the wall above my bed. It said: *Whore*.

*****

For more about Alexa Land and the series,
please visit:
alexalandwrites.blogspot.com

28886939R00253

Printed in Poland
by Amazon Fulfillment
Poland Sp. z o.o., Wrocław